I'd like to thank the following people
for sharing their expertise:

Lisa Chaplin, a writer friend who generously
used her Aboriginal background and studies
to help me with Dinny and her family.

Margaret Mendelawitz, who helped me
with some of the West Australian history
and local Aboriginal information.

PROLOGUE

JANUARY 1876: WESTERN AUSTRALIA

The man they called Fiery Dan took his time, slipping quietly through the West Australian bush, taking great care to avoid any cleared land or farms, always heading south. He was used to his own company and did not feel the need to hurry. This job must be done right because if he completed it successfully, he would have the thing he craved most, the only thing he craved now – enough money to return to England.

The damned Government had brought him out here when he was little more than a lad, had ill-treated him in almost every way known to man – yet he had survived, served his sentence, learning to live quietly beneath their yoke. Eventually they had set him free, certain he had been taught his lesson.

The shadow of a smile twitched at the corners of his mouth. Oh, yes, he'd been taught his lesson well and had not cared that some of his teachers had darker skins than his own, had only cared for what they could show him: the ways of this new land, especially the uses of fire. Fire had brought him out here, rick burning to be precise, and fire would get him home again to England. And in the meantime, fire had been his revenge – as two of his former tormentors had found out.

When he had been offered this job, he had sailed round the coast to Western Australia on the same ship as his employer. He had watched the family and seen the bitterness on Mrs Docherty's face. She had not wanted to come here to Perth, poor shrew. And though Mr Docherty spoke of revenge, Dan reckoned it was only habit, something to talk about. If he had really wanted to hurt his enemies, Docherty wouldn't have waited this long. Dan hadn't.

He turned off towards the small settlement they called Brookley, travelling openly and stopping at the inn there to order a glass of ale. Good ale, it was, too. He sipped it slowly, listening and watching, then ate appreciatively the hearty meal the inkeeper's wife brought him. She had been gentry once, he could tell. Wasn't gentry any more, though, for her hands were reddened and worn with work. It pleased him greatly to have a lady like her waiting on his needs. Serve the bitch right for coming to this godforsaken land! But he spoke to her pleasantly, drank only moderately, then went on his way armed with the knowledge he needed.

He waited three days in the whispering shadows of the forest before he acted. The homestead was built of wood, dry old wood that had stood in the sun for years, slowly turning silver-grey. If sparks started flying, it'd catch fire easily and burn beautifully, with the bright colours and fierce crackling noises Dan loved so much.

How comfortably they all lived there! Why should these folk have so much and he so little? Well, that was going to change. He didn't know what they had done to offend his employer, didn't really care. All Dan cared about was the money he was to be paid.

He woke before dawn, eager to finish his task. As the summer heat beat around him, teasing sweat from his scrawny body, he sipped sparingly from the lukewarm water left in his tin canteen, hoping the sea breeze would blow strongly enough today. Bloody breezes! Fickle as women, they were. All over you one minute and gone the next.

Mid-morning he sat up, nose raised to sniff like a questing hound. The air was stirring. Was that a hint of salt in it? Yes, yes! A feral grin stretched his features briefly then faded, leaving the sullen mask with which he habitually faced the world.

The breeze began to gust more strongly, bringing cooler air from the sea, making the gum leaves whisper and rustle. This breeze often blew on hot summer afternoons, bringing the relief of cooler air after the searing heat of the morning. It would be his tool today.

Purposefully he hurried towards the place he had chosen. There he set his first fire and lit it with one of his carefully protected safety matches.

The wind whipped the smoke inland and sun-dried grass just beyond the tiny pile of dried grass and twigs caught fire, then a small gum tree which turned within minutes into a flaming torch. From there the fire spread quickly to other trees.

And still the wind blew, so strongly that there was no need for him to light other fires. As the blaze grew fiercer, clumps of burning leaves broke off here and there, floating through the air as the wind, the beautiful wind, bore them eastwards.

He laughed aloud, the sound hidden by the crackling of the flames which were roaring their pleasure as they fed from the eucalyptus oil in the leaves. He could not have stopped the fire now if he had wanted. No one could. Let it burn! Let the whole damned country burn as far as he was concerned!

CHAPTER 1

JANUARY

Cathie stood in the shadow of a big gum tree near the lake and stared across at her mother and stepfather, on the long veranda of Lizabrook homestead. She felt a sharp pang of jealousy at how close they always seemed to be, how much they still loved one another. At eighteen, she was of an age to want a man of her own, but since she and her family lived in the depths of the Australian bush, she wasn't likely to find one. She wanted other things, too, and if she'd been a man would have found a way to become a doctor. She'd been patching up her brothers, sisters and all the family pets since she had first developed an interest in the working of the human body at the age of nine.

But women weren't allowed to become doctors. It sometimes seemed to her women weren't allowed to do anything but marry and have babies and do endless housework and washing.

Feeling even more restless than usual she walked a few paces further on, taking care to keep out of sight. She stared down at the grave of her real father. Would things have been different if Josiah

Ludlam had lived? She didn't really know because her mother rarely spoke of him, but Cathie doubted it.

Picking up some twigs and gum nuts, she began to vent her frustration by hurling them into the water. She had to find a way to escape from here or she would go mad with frustration. Even the lake wasn't a real lake, she thought scornfully, but only a band of shallow water lying beside a half-cleared swamp. It could look really pretty if her stepfather ever found the time to clear the rest of the swamp, but he was always too busy. All he cared about was that the partly finished lake gave them enough water to last through the long, hot summers. They weren't gentry to need fancy gardens for parading round in. Josiah Ludlam, her father, had been gentry, though, and her mother had once said the lake had been his idea.

'In another of your black moods?' a voice teased and she turned to smile at Brendan, her childhood playmate.

He smiled back, his teeth gleaming white against his dark skin. He was very like his mother's people, as if his body refused to acknowledge the part played in his creation by his Irish father, though his next brother's skin was much paler than his.

'Don't you ever get tired of living here at Lizabrook?' Cathie demanded.

Brendan's smile faded. 'You know I do. But at least I'm treated like a human being here. The minute I leave the homestead people treat me like an animal – and a worthless one at that – because of this.' He pointed to his skin.

She reached out to squeeze his arm. They were both misfits, but it was even harder for him. Maybe that was what drew them together. She was closer to him than to her half-brothers. Glancing over her shoulder to make sure they were out of sight of the homestead, she took off her shoes and rolled down her stockings. 'Let's have a paddle. It's so hot today.'

'Aren't you supposed to be helping your mother?'

Cathie shrugged. 'The housework will still be there when I get back.' It always was. Boring, dreary work, the same day after day.

Liza Caine stood on the veranda and leaned against her husband, enjoying both the feel of his arm around her shoulders and the sea breeze which had just begun to blow, bringing some welcome cooler air. Smoke was drifting across the big external kitchen where Dinny was baking bread and roasting meat, for everyone at the homestead took the main meal of the day together. If you listened carefully you could hear her friend singing one of the little Aboriginal songs that went with the various daily tasks. Dinny seemed to have a song for everything.

Liza and Benedict often stood here together for a few moments before the midday meal, chatting quietly of this and that. She and her third husband had been happy together for thirteen years now, but with five young folk about the place it was sometimes difficult for them to find time alone. Their two younger children, Josie and Harry, were still in the schoolroom with Frau Hebel. Finding the money for a governess was a strain, but they weren't close enough to a school for a daily attendance. Both of them wanted their children to be decently educated, so when a friend had told them about Ilse Hebel and said she wanted to find a position in the country, they had appointed her simply on Agnes's recommendation, and had not regretted it.

From the far side of the house came the sound of Dinny's husband, Fergal, whistling happily as he worked in the small furniture manufactory in which he and Benedict were partners and which supplemented their farming income. Sadly, this had not done as well as they'd hoped because there simply weren't enough people with spare money in the colony of Western Australia to sell to, even though the pieces were beautifully crafted and embellished with Benedict's skilled carving. And some people were such snobs they were certain colonial goods must be inferior and only wanted furniture which had been brought out from the mother country. The same people continued to talk about England as 'home', but Liza didn't feel like that. Western Australia was her home now.

Across the beige, sun-burned grass of the

paddock two figures came into view, arms waving as they paused to argue about something.

'That's where Cathie's got to, is it?' Liza muttered, frowning across at her elder daughter. 'I told her to give the parlour a good bottoming today. Just wait till she gets within reach of my tongue! And wasn't Brendan supposed to be working in the vegetable garden, Benedict?'

'He was indeed. He'll never make a farm worker, that one. But he's Fergal and Dinny's problem, not ours. I only pay him day rates now for the time he actually works.' Benedict glanced down at his wife's troubled face, thinking as he often did that she looked too young and pretty to have grown-up children. 'I'm getting worried about Cathie. Be honest, love. She's been causing you a lot of trouble lately, hasn't she?'

Liza sighed. On good days her daughter was energetic and lively, making everyone around her feel happy – but the good days were getting fewer and she had taken to slipping away instead of helping about the house, spending hours tramping through the woods like a truant child. If these outings had made Cathie happy, Liza would have been more tolerant of them, but lately nothing seemed to please her daughter. 'I don't know what to do with her, that's for sure,' she admitted.

'It's about time I had a word with that young madam.' Benedict silenced his wife's protest with a kiss. 'She claims she's a woman grown, but she certainly doesn't act like it.'

Liza hesitated for a moment then said quietly, 'She needs to meet people, see new things. I don't think she'll settle down otherwise. And a lass of her age needs to meet young men, too.'

Benedict made a soft exasperated sound. 'She's too young to be thinking of marriage.'

'I was carrying a child by the time I was her age,' Liza pointed out.

'Not by your own choice!' he snapped.

Liza closed her eyes as his words brought back the memories of just why she had come to Australia. Her father had wanted her to marry their neighbour, a widower of thirty-five, and when she had refused, Teddy Marshall had raped her, to make sure she would have to marry him. Only she hadn't. She'd run away to Australia instead, sailing with her former employers, the Pringles, as their maid.

On board ship she'd discovered she was pregnant and then Josiah Ludlam had married her, wanting the child more than he wanted her, for he'd never touched her as a wife. And that child had been Cathie. Was it any wonder that with a father like Teddy Marshall Cathie wasn't an easy girl to manage? And yet she was a warm, loving girl, the first to rush and help you in times of trouble.

Liza realized Benedict had asked her something. 'Sorry, my mind was wandering.'

'I was saying we can't afford to send Cathie back to England for a visit, let alone spare someone to go with her.'

'We could if we sold some of the jewellery.' She had inherited some pretty pieces from her first husband and they must be worth something.

'We can manage without touching that. I can't leave the farm and I don't want to lose my wife for a whole year, thank you very much, and the other children need you just as much as Cathie does, especially Josie.'

'We could send her back on her own.'

'And where would she stay when she got there? I've not heard from my brothers in England since my parents died.'

She knew that hurt him. Losing touch with your family was common out here, though. 'You've got a sister in Australia. You see her and her family sometimes.'

'Once a year, if I'm lucky.' Benedict stared blindly out across the lake.

After a moment's silence Liza resumed the discussion. 'Cathie keeps asking about the Ludlams lately. Do you think we should tell her the truth about who her real father is? She wants to know why Josiah's family never try to contact her and yesterday she threatened to write to them. Well, she knows I keep in touch with Sophia Ludlam, his mother.'

Her husband made an angry growling sound in his throat. 'Eh, that wouldn't do! Mrs Ludlam's no true connection of Cathie's, for all the lass bears their name. I think we're going to have to tell her the truth – Josiah married you to give your baby a name but played no part in fathering her. We can't go on like this, love.'

'Perhaps we should make up some tale – say it was a stranger who attacked me and left me pregnant? If she ever met her real father, it'd break her heart.' Liza shuddered. You never forgot it when a man raped you. And the older Cathie grew, the more she resembled the Marshalls, for she was a tall, sturdy girl with a strong temper and a stubborn determination to get what she wanted from life – though she could be kind, too, and had a way with children and sick people that was nothing short of miraculous. Her younger brothers and sisters adored her, as did Dinny and Fergal's children.

Fortunately, in Cathie the strong Marshall features had been softened and she had her mother's thick dark hair, not dull light brown. Liza had told her many a time that she would be pretty if she would only stop frowning at the world, but Cathie considered herself too tall and solidly built, complaining that no man would ever love a great lump like her.

'It was a lot easier when they were younger,' Benedict murmured. 'Now there's Lucas too saying he wants to see a bit of the world before he settles down, though at least he wants to see the rest of Australia, not go back to England.'

'It's easier for a young man to travel, and anyway, he's not so *angry* at the world as she is. Lucas is very sensible. His mother would have been very proud of him, I'm sure, if she'd lived.'

He looked down at Liza indulgently and could not resist planting a kiss on her rosy cheek. 'We have a confusion of children between us, don't we, my love? One of mine, by Grace, one of yours, by Marshall, and three of our own.'

'And another of mine whom I never see.' Her voice broke as she said that, for her eldest son Francis had been taken away from her by her second husband's family, the Rawleys, and had grown up in England. His loss was an abiding sadness to her.

Benedict gave her another hug and said bracingly, 'They're a fine healthy brood, thank God, except for Josie – and even she's better this year.'

Liza hesitated, wondering whether to tell him she might be expecting another child, but decided against it. It was too early yet to be sure and she'd had false alarms before. Besides, this had taken her by surprise, and she was not yet used to the idea of becoming a mother again.

Cathie and Brendan strolled by the edge of the lake for a while longer, both reluctant to return home and face a scolding.

Suddenly he sniffed the air. 'I can smell burning. The kitchen roof hasn't caught fire again, has it?'

They both swung round and saw blue-grey smoke rising behind the house.

'Hell, that's a bush fire – and the wind's blowing it in this direction!' Brendan was starting to run towards the house even as he spoke.

13

Cathie raced after him, her skirts flapping about her legs and her boots pounding the ground, the untied laces whipping from side to side.

Bush fires were the thing everyone feared most in summer. They could destroy your life in an hour.

At almost the same moment, Benedict also stopped talking in mid-sentence to sniff the air, rush round the veranda and stare at the bush behind the house. 'Oh, my God! Liza, that's a big one! Let's hope our firebreaks will keep it back.'

Even as he spoke, the sea breeze seemed to grow stronger and they heard the dreaded roaring and crackling sounds of a fire burning out of control.

He ran to the emergency bell that would summon everyone on the farm. Even before he had let go of the rope he saw Brendan and Cathie running towards him and other people coming out of the various outbuildings. They all knew what to do because Benedict made them practise at the start of every summer. So far the cleared land had protected them, but this fire had a strong sea breeze behind it and was gaining ground fast.

Under the governess's supervision Josie and Harry rushed to gather some treasured possessions and clothes, stuffing them into the sacks kept in their bedrooms for that purpose. Liza did the same for herself and Benedict, then left Ilse to shepherd her charges down to the lake. Benedict had deliberately left a small spit of land jutting out into the water when he dug out the original swamp, because like all settlers he knew the dangers of bush fires.

Dinny's two youngest children were already rushing along the edge of the lake to join them, carrying some of their own family's possessions.

Liza dumped the box containing the family's main valuables on the ground by the water's edge and cast a quick glance at the sky behind the house, horrified to see how quickly the fire was spreading. A dark haze of smoke blurred the skyline now and below it flames were shooting high, racing along the ground and leaping from treetop to treetop as well. If only the breeze would drop! She decided to bring out a few more things, just in case. 'Josie, you stay here and keep an eye on the little ones. You two boys go back to the houses and grab whatever clothes and blankets you can. Anything useful. But keep an eye on the fire.'

Josie nodded, her thin face even paler than usual. With her tendency to wheeze, it was no use her trying to do things in a hurry. Harry was already rushing back towards the house. At seven he was almost as big as she was though nearly three years younger.

A chain of people formed to swing buckets of water up from the lake while Benedict dumped their contents on the wooden shingles of the roof, for the rainwater barrels were empty at this time of year. Liza was torn between saving possessions from the house and joining the others. Benedict shouted, 'Get what you can – just in case. Ilse, you help her! Brendan, get the animals out and shepherd them towards the water.'

By the time Liza made her second journey, clutching the bulging blanket, the flames had jumped the firebreaks and were racing across the tinder-dry grass towards the farm. She heard those passing buckets utter a groan of disappointment, but they kept on working.

Within minutes one of the outbuildings had caught fire. Liza paused to stare at it with tears in her eyes, then followed Ilse, the governess determinedly back into the house.

When Fergal moved towards the blazing building, Benedict yelled, 'Leave it to burn! Brendan, go with your father and see what you can rescue from the workshop. But be careful!' There was glue inside, which would fuel the fire, and piles of sawn wood were set out nearby to season. He didn't feel optimistic about their chances of saving much of that if this wind kept blowing so strongly, but perhaps some of the finished pieces of furniture and tools might be carried to safety. He went to pass buckets, standing in line next to his son Seth, the son who also thought Josiah was his father but who had none of Cathie's intensity and always said cheerfully that Benedict was his 'real' father as far as he was concerned, since he couldn't remember Josiah.

They held the fire at bay for over an hour,

breaking line at Benedict's orders to beat out smaller blazes in the straw-like grass of summer. Fergal and his son managed to carry out the finished pieces of furniture and expensive tools from the workshop, stacking them on the little spit of land where the children were installed with a jumble of possessions. Even there they were keeping watch with buckets of water, standing ready to tip over anything which caught light from the sparks whirling everywhere.

By now smoke had turned the sunny day into a false twilight and people were choking and coughing as they toiled frantically.

When the far end of the workshop suddenly burst into flames, Benedict groaned aloud and Liza sobbed. She knew how hard he had worked to develop the small furniture-making business so that they would not be totally at the mercy of the weather and the farm yield.

The whole workshop was soon burning fiercely, adding black and acrid smoke to the grey woodsmoke. Cathie ripped up a sheet, soaking the pieces in the lake and bringing them to people to tie across their mouths, for hot air burned harshly in the throat. Faces lost their identity as they became smoke-blackened. All they could think of were the buckets, heavy with water, tugging at their shoulders one after another.

As the fire approached the homestead itself, Liza went to join the line of those passing buckets. She found herself working side by side with her daughter and marvelled at Cathie's strength, for her own arms were aching and heavy. When she dropped a whole bucketful, she moved out of the line, panting, knowing she had to take a break for a moment or two.

Dinny and Fergal's house was closer to the fire. It seemed to catch light all of a sudden and be engulfed in flames within minutes. Liza saw Dinny stand still for a moment, rigid with pain, then move back into line with her lips pressed tightly together. Her heart ached for her friend, ached for them all.

Before Liza could move into the bucket line again, Benedict came and tugged her arm, saying hoarsely, 'It's no use, love. Our house has caught fire at the other side. We'll move out what furniture we can from this end, then we must retreat to the lake and leave it to burn.'

Liza stared at him blankly for a moment before the meaning of his words sank in. She saw the anguish in his eyes and knew it was mirrored in her own, then he turned to Cathie and said, 'Take your mother to safety, love. She's exhausted.' Even before he had finished speaking, he had turned to check that everyone else was all right, counting heads with a sooty finger, then leading the way towards the house.

Liza shook her head at her daughter, who was pulling her towards the water, and drove back the tears and momentary weakness with anger. 'I'm all right. I'm going to help carry things out.'

She moved towards the house before anyone could try to stop her, following her son Seth inside.

People staggered past, carrying whatever came to hand from the smoke-filled interior, dumping their burdens near the water and then running back inside.

But after only a few journeys, the heat from the blazing end of the house was so intense, and the smoke inside so thick, that Benedict shouted to them to stop and take refuge near the water. He counted heads again and nodded in relief to find all accounted for. Neither he nor Liza would ever forget that her first husband, Josiah Ludlam, had been killed by a falling beam in another house fire – killed saving Cathie's life.

Liza wept openly as she stood there watching everything they had worked so hard for being devoured by the flames, which seemed to dance through the blackness of the smoke as if mocking the watchers with their searing power. As Cathie put an arm round her, Liza noticed paler stripes down her daughter's smoke-blackened face. It took her a moment to realise they were tear marks. She felt exhausted now, so leaned on the strong young arm, standing in the middle of a silent group of people.

Moving like an old man, Benedict came to join them. He nodded to Cathie. 'You've done well, lass.' Then he bent his head to kiss Liza's dirty cheek. 'I'll build you a new home, love. I promise.'

She forced back the tears. 'We'll build it together.'

Then they could only hold on to each other and watch their home burn to the ground. Ilse stood beside Josie, shocked to the core by what had happened, for she too had lost many of her possessions.

By sheer chance the fire only went round the southern part of the lake. To the north the cleared farmland interrupted its mad race until – too late to help the Caines – the sea breeze dropped. The swampy ground to the south had also slowed the flames' advance, but by then all the buildings that had made up Lizabrook homestead were reduced to ashes.

Lucas was the only member of the family missing and they were worried he might have got caught by the fire on his way home from Mandurah. There was no way to tell, no way to move through the burnt land till the layers of ash had cooled down.

'Lucas is a sensible chap. He'll be all right,' Benedict said, as much to reassure himself as Liza.

As night fell people slept on what they could, staying near the lake for safety. Benedict and Fergal took it in turns to keep watch, just in case a stray spark set the northern side of the lake afire.

The following morning Dinny and Brendan went to check the land which she and her son knew better than anyone. She might not have been born here, she might have Irish as well as Aboriginal blood, but she had put strong roots down and considered this her place now – and was equally sure it had accepted her, as had the Aboriginal tribe whose land it was.

They found that the main fire had burned out, though the ground was still hot in patches and the occasional tree trunk still smouldering. Everyone at Lizabrook homestead gathered to work out what to do and they were a solemn group, conscious of how very much they had lost. There was a grimness to Benedict's face that had not been there before.

Liza felt numb and disoriented. Once she looked at the governess and saw Ilse staring into the distance, tears welling in her eyes. 'It's a harsh land,' Liza said softly.

'I hadn't realised how quickly it could happen,' Ilse admitted.

'How much did you manage to save?'

'Most of my clothes and my books. Also the photographs of my family.'

'That's something, then.'

Benedict announced, 'We can start rebuilding almost immediately if we can get some sawn timber from Mandurah. We'll make mud bricks this time for the walls. They don't burn as easily. The new house will have to be smaller at first, I'm afraid.' He looked at the governess. 'I hope you'll still stay with us, Ilse?'

'Of course I will. And help in any way I can as we rebuild.'

Liza hugged her, then she and the governess set to work moving the pieces of furniture that had been saved to the shade of the few trees left standing in irregular groups near the water, covering the better pieces with what blankets and sacking remained.

'We'd just stocked up the provision shed with sacks of flour,' Liza mourned later as she worked with Dinny to take stock of the food that had been saved. 'Now it's all wasted.'

'Do you not have fire insurance?' Ilse asked.

Liza shook her head blindly. 'No. They don't insure places like this. You just look after yourselves.' Then she went back to work.

Benedict's oldest son, Lucas, appeared mid-morning from the direction of Mandurah, followed a short time later by some of their neighbours from Brookley. Liza burst into tears of sheer relief that he was still alive, for he was as dear to her as her own children.

Cathie, who had been watching her mother and worrying about how strained she looked, made her sit down on one of the chairs they'd saved.

'I'm sorry,' Liza gulped. 'It's just – I'm having another child and I always get t-tearful—'

Benedict overheard her and came striding across to kneel beside her and cradle her in his arms. 'What a way to tell us!' He turned to gaze at the blackened ruin of the home he had built with his own hands, adding quietly, 'And anyway, who does not want to weep today?'

★　　★　　★

22

Fifty miles away in Perth, Christina Docherty paced up and down the veranda of the house they had rented, waiting for her husband to return from a meeting in town. Her sons started shouting at one another nearby and she stood still for a moment to frown in their direction, then shrugged and left the governess to settle the fight.

When she saw Dermott striding back up the street, she jumped off the veranda and rushed to greet him, careless of her dignity. 'You've been gone for ages!' she complained, linking her arm in his. 'Did that man turn up?'

'Yes.' He grinned slyly. 'And I'm sorry to tell you my sister Liza's farm was burnt out by a bush fire.'

'Good. Now we can sort out our own lives. I'm fed up of living in this hovel.' She had never understood this stupid obsession of her husband's with getting revenge on his sister. To her mind, what had happened had been an accident and Niall Docherty a lout who deserved all he got. She had only met him once, when he came to her mother's inn, but that had been enough to take his measure. Dermott had always followed his brother's lead. The two of them had come to Australia, hoping to get money out of their sister's rich husband, and Niall had been about to rape Dinny when Liza shot him, as far as Christina could make out. Serve him right. She'd shoot someone who tried to rape her, too. But of course she didn't say that to her husband, who still idolised his brother's memory.

Dermott put his arm round her. 'Well, we'll be moving soon, though not back to England. I thought we'd spend some time at that farm I bought cheaply. It's closer than I'd realised to my dear sister's homestead.' He frowned. What if he'd burned his own property along with hers?

She looked at him in horror. 'Dermott Docherty, have you run mad? I thought you were just going to sell that place and make a nice little profit! You don't know the first thing about farming and I certainly don't want to live in the country, least of all here in Western Australia. I married you to *escape* all that!' She had been horrified when her father forced the Pringle family to emigrate to Australia. Her mother had made the best of it, but then Dorothy Pringle had always made the best of things throughout her unhappy marriage. Christina despised her for that. As for her father, he had lost all their money with his stupid schemes. No wonder she'd run away with Dermott.

'Well, I hadn't realised it was just down the road from Lizabrook. I swore when Niall died that I'd make my sister pay and—'

'She has paid! She's lost her home. Surely that's enough?' Even though Kitty had hated Liza, who had made all the eligible men fall for her, she didn't wish her any more ill.

He scowled at her. 'Might be enough. Might

24

not. Anyway it won't hurt for me an' Matthieu to live fairly quietly for a year or two, and I fancy trying the life of a country gentleman. I can always sell the place later.'

She moved away from him, close to tears. When he set his mind on something he was bull-headed about it and she'd learned to fear his sudden whims. 'We're living quietly enough here in Perth, Dermott. I can't believe how small this place is and how backward compared to Melbourne. I don't call this a capital city! And the Australian countryside isn't like England, you know.'

'We'll do things my way, Christina!'

'I don't see why we have to stick with Matthieu Correntin, either. We don't need him any more. We've enough money now to live like gentry in England.'

There was an edge of steel in his voice as Dermott answered, 'A bit more never hurts. I want to be really rich when we eventually go back to England and Matthieu's both clever and useful.' In fact, if Dermott had heeded his business partner's advice he'd never have had to leave Melbourne, something he regretted as much as his wife after spending a few weeks in a backwater like Perth – though he wasn't going to give her the satisfaction of telling her so.

Realising they were standing in the middle of the street arguing and that a neighbour was approaching, he muttered, 'Say hello to Mrs Fenton.

She may be short of money, but she's still got some useful connections.'

Christina took a deep breath and turned to smile at their neighbour, who was taking the air dressed in her widow's black. 'And how are you today, Mrs Fenton?'

'I'm well, thank you.' Agnes started to move on.

Dermott said quickly, 'Perhaps you'd like to join us for a cup of tea to hear our news, Mrs F.? We've just bought ourselves a farm.'

'Another time, perhaps, Mr Docherty. It's a year since my husband died and I'm off to town to buy something a little lighter than unrelieved black. In fact,' Agnes looked down and grimaced, 'I don't think I'm even going into half-mourning. I've had enough of dark colours.' With a nod of her head, she walked briskly on.

As she passed a shop window, Agnes glanced at her own reflection with approval. She might be approaching fifty, but she had retained her figure and her health was still good.

Catching sight of a friend in the distance she hurried along the street, eager to chat. She was so bored with living alone! And with being a widow. What she needed was a man, both to support her and to share her bed. She had debated going back to England, but did not fancy living on her son-in-law's charity or even that of her son in Sydney. Besides, she'd have more chance of finding another husband here in Australia than in England because women were still in short supply – though this time she'd be a bit more careful. Her late husband had been a spendthrift and latterly a drunkard as well.

She needed to find someone else before what was left of her money ran out.

In Lancashire Magnus Hamilton went to see the doctor after tea on Friday evening to talk about his mother, whose behaviour was growing increasingly strange and who had recently taken to wandering the house at night, disturbing everyone's sleep.

Clifford Barnes, an earnest man in his late-forties with a reputation for caring about all his patients, rich or poor, showed Magnus into his consulting room, looked at the younger man sympathetically and gestured to him to sit down. He eased himself into his big comfortable chair behind the ornate mahogany desk, hesitated for a moment then said what he had to say bluntly because he knew of no way to soften this type of bad news. 'I'm afraid your mother is suffering from softening of the brain, which has led to a degeneration of the mental faculties. It – um – happens to some older folk.' He sighed and added, 'Regrettably, there is nothing medical science can do to help.'

Magnus stared down at the dark red carpet with its pattern of squares and lozenges, struggling to come to terms with this, his thoughts fragmenting and twisting away from the dreadful news. He had often wished he could afford a carpet as soft as this for his mother's swollen, aching feet to tread on. He had wished to do all sorts of things for her, because Janey Hamilton had been a good mother to them all, but although he earned an adequate living as foreman in the workshop of Ludlam's cotton mill, he had little put by. Since his father's death when he was eighteen years old, he had had to support his three brothers, sister and mother, so there had never been enough coming in for luxuries like fancy carpets.

He'd been foolish to indulge in such dreams! Should have grown out of that by now. He'd grown out of just about everything else – his own plans for finding a wife and having children, his desire to better himself, his love of learning. He had enough on his plate just surviving at the moment.

He looked down at his long legs, remembering the way he had grown out of his clothes so quickly in the years of his youth, until he reached his present height of six foot four inches. That had given them extra expense, for it cost more to find clothing that would cover his tall, spare frame decently. You couldn't buy suitable things from the second-hand clothes shop, but had to have them made specially. His mother had gone without new clothes for years in order that he be decently clad for work. He'd known that and been unable to do anything about it, for it was his wages that kept them all.

When Dr Barnes cleared his throat, Magnus

realised he'd been lost in his own thoughts and squared his shoulders to ask, 'What's going to happen to her, then? I mean – what can we expect?'

'I'm sorry to have to tell you that she'll grow more and more vague and will gradually lose the ability to care for herself. She'll have to be looked after like a helpless baby in the end. And that may happen quite quickly or slowly. One can never predict.'

'Oh, God!' For a few moments, Magnus buried his face in his hands and fought against his emotions.

'I can arrange for her to be taken into the Benevolent Home. They treat the poor creatures in their care pretty decently, I promise you, not like the old days. We're more enlightened about such things nowadays.' And the Ben was no longer dependent on the Ludlam family's grudging charity. The days of men, even millowners, acting as if they owned a town and its inhabitants, body and soul, were past.

'I'd never put her in there!' Magnus didn't even pause to consider it. His mother hated the Ben and had always tried to avoid even walking past it. The poor inmates who were not violent sat outside in the sun on fine days, their faces usually blank, and from inside there was always the sound of the ones who were really bad, moaning and screaming, especially when the moon was full. He would not confine his mother to a place like that for her final days, however sad her mental state. 'We'll continue to care for her at home, thank you, doctor. We'll manage somehow.'

Dr Barnes nodded. A decent fellow, Magnus Hamilton. Scottish originally, but the family had lived here in Pendleworth for many years. He'd always had a fancy that Magnus must have Viking blood in his ancestry, such a giant of a man he was with that bright red-gold hair. A woman would make the most of such hair, but Magnus cropped it as short as was decent and shaved his face too, as if he didn't want to be bothered with his appearance, though most men were wearing at least a moustache these days if not a full beard. The doctor let silence hang between them for a few seconds longer, then said simply, 'As you choose, Magnus. But the offer will always be open. People with your mother's affliction can be very difficult to care for towards the end.'

Magnus walked slowly home feeling sick to his soul. He hadn't needed a doctor to tell him something was dreadfully wrong. They'd been hiding his mother's vagaries for a year or two now and his sister Mairi had had to give up her job at the Emporium to care for her, though she had loved serving the customers and seeing half the town pass through the big haberdashery and fabrics shop. It was she who had insisted on calling in the doctor, saying she'd never forgive herself if they didn't try everything they could.

When he got home Magnus could hardly bear

to look at his mother, who was sitting rocking quietly in front of the fire while his sister set the table, her expression grim.

'She's been bad again, today,' Mairi said abruptly. Her mother had pulled the tablecloth off, though luckily there had not been much on it, and then cast it aside to begin moving her hand backwards and forwards over the wood as if she were sandpapering it. When Mairi had tried to stop her, knowing that she would rub until her hand was raw, Janey had thrown a temper tantrum that had left them both exhausted. Sometimes Mairi felt she could not bear another day like this.

'Where's Hamish?' Magnus did not want to tell his news twice.

'Out at the Working Men's Institute.' Mairi hesitated, then added, 'Someone's giving a talk about Australia.'

The words burst out before Magnus could stop them. 'Not him as well!'

She shrugged. Not for her to fight her younger brother's battles. If Hamish was determined to emigrate, nothing she said would make any difference. It hadn't when their other brothers set their minds on Canada. 'What did the doctor say about Mum?'

Magnus glanced towards the rocking figure. 'I'll tell you later.'

'She doesn't understand what we're talking about now, you know.'

'She does sometimes so I'd rather wait. I don't want to upset her.'

'Then I'll tell you my news instead.' Mairi took a deep breath. 'Magnus, Elwyn Bebb at chapel has – well, he's asked me to walk out with him.'

'And you want to?'

She nodded vigorously. 'Aye, I do.'

'Then I'm glad for you.' But he could not prevent himself from feeling envious, though he tried not to show it. After all, Mairi was twenty-six, some might have said a confirmed spinster by now, and she was needed at home – desperately. If she married, how would he look after his mother? Well, time to worry about that when it happened. Mairi deserved some happiness. It had been hard for her these past two years. 'I *am* glad for you.' He went over and gave her a cracking great hug.

Afterwards she held him at arm's length and studied his face. 'Why don't you find yourself a lassie, Magnus?'

He shook his head, eyes going to his mother. 'What have I to offer anyone now but hard work? It's getting *you* down and she's your mother. How could we ask a stranger to live like this?'

Mairi leaned against him for a moment. 'You're a wonderful brother, Magnus, and a caring son. You'd make a good father.' She glanced up, seeing that grim expression return to his face. He seemed to have forgotten how to smile lately. She could remember him a few years ago, before their mother had started to grow vague and forgetful. How lively he had been then, in spite of the hard work! Always the one to lead a sing-song with his clear baritone voice. Going down to the Institute to hear a lecture on anything and everything, so eager was he for knowledge. And now? Now he spent his time mainly at home in the evenings. Oh, he still borrowed books from the library and still tramped across the moors occasionally on fine Sundays, something that he had always loved doing, but he was a quieter, sadder man.

First their brother Athol, always the adventurous one, had left the country and gone across the sea to Canada, then his twin, Dougal, had followed him, unable to live without his brother, though the two of them had parted in anger.

With each departure Magnus had grown a little quieter. Now, Hamish was talking of Australia and she – she had fallen in love with a plump little man with a heart of gold, whose kindness shone out of his face, and was hoping desperately that he loved her, too. Elwyn had asked her out walking, talked of going to the lantern show at church the following week, smiled at her warmly whenever they met and lingered to chat to her. Surely . . .

She shook away those thoughts. 'I'll make you a cup of tea, shall I?' Raising her voice, she added more loudly, 'Mum? Would you like a cup of tea as well?'

Once their mother would have jumped up and

insisted on making it herself, now she just stared at them blankly as if she didn't understand the question. It was heartrending to see the changes in her.

Mairi looked at Magnus, her eyes brimming with tears, and saw that his eyes were over-bright, too.

CHAPTER 2

JANUARY

Fiery Dan returned to Brookley a week later with Mr Docherty, who insisted on covertly checking that the job had been done properly before he paid. Dan was delighted to see that the Caines' house had burnt to the ground, as had all the outbuildings. He glanced sideways at his employer, standing next to him behind the sturdy trunk of a huge gum tree. A man might expect a compliment or a thank you for a job well done, but he received no praise of any sort. Typical of rich folk. Never appreciated anything, they didn't.

'I burnt it down for you, then,' he prompted.

Dermott didn't even hear him. As he scowled at the busy scene before him, he was annoyed to see how many of their possessions his sister's family had managed to save and how quickly they were rebuilding the farm. Pieces of furniture stood under trees, covered in strips of bark or layers of branches to keep the sun off them. Beside the lake two men were busy making mud bricks, with many rows of them already standing in the sun to harden. 'Will nothing stop that damned Benedict Caine?' he muttered.

Dan sniggered. 'He thinks brick houses are safe, don't he? Well, they burn too, because they've got wooden floors and roof timbers. Just need a bit more help to get started.' As he had proved more than once.

Dermott ignored his remark. 'See that big pile of furniture over there, under the rough shelter?'

As he pointed one meaty finger, Dan nodded.

'Can you set it alight?'

'Easy.'

'Good. Do it then, as soon as it gets a bit darker. The big fire could have been an accident. I want this one to look deliberate so they'll start worrying about who's after them.' He poked Dan in the ribs. 'I'll go and look at that farm I bought hereabouts another time. Once that stuff's blazing we'll head back to Perth. You've earned your money. I've got a berth booked for you in five days' time under the name of John Roberts. I'll see you to the ship myself. And make sure you keep your mouth shut about all this. If I hear you've been talking to anyone . . .'

A week after the bush fire the biggest of the temporary shelters went up in flames just after nightfall. Benedict had been strolling by the water with his eldest son, Lucas, and quickly reached it, yelling for help. They both began dragging out the things stored there. Benedict let out a startled exclamation as a burning piece of the bark they'd used to make a temporary roof fell across his head but Lucas knocked it away quickly.

People came running with buckets of water and the flames were soon doused. Not much had been damaged.

'Now how the hell did that start?' Fergal wondered.

'There's only one way,' Benedict said grimly. 'It's nowhere near our cooking fire so someone must have set light to it deliberately.'

There was a gasp behind him and Liza came to clutch his arm, gripping him so tightly he could feel her fingernails digging in. 'Surely not?' Her voice had a pleading tone to it. 'Oh, Benedict, surely not?'

'I'm afraid so, love.' He raised his voice. 'We'll keep watch tonight. Everyone is to stay away from this shed. I want to examine the ground round it once it's daylight.'

Cathie was furious when her father refused to let any of the women help keep watch. After a short, sharp argument, she flung off to her makeshift bed in the rough shelter where all the family slept at night.

She lay down beside her little sister. It was always like that, she thought. She was bigger and stronger than many men but they wouldn't let her do anything interesting.

Josie reached over to cuddle her. 'Don't be mad, Cathie. You're always mad at something lately.'

She returned the cuddle. 'Not at you, chicken, never at you.'

'I know you want to go away.'

'Do you, indeed?'

'Yes, but I don't want you to.'

'Ah, Josie lovie, I'll go mad if I have to spend my whole life here in the bush. I want to meet people, see different things. I *need* to!'

She cuddled her little sister till Josie fell asleep and tried yet again to work out how to get away. It was England that called to her, the land her parents seemed happy to have left. She wanted to see the lively bustling Lancashire towns they had described, live close to other people, have something to see besides trees.

One day she'd find a way to get what she wanted. She was quite determined on that, whatever her mother said.

In the morning Dinny spent a long time checking the ground near the hut with her son Brendan. Like his mother and her people, he was at home with the ways of nature – unlike his younger brother, who was more concerned with furniture-making and seemed happy with a quiet life at the homestead.

'Someone with worn boots stood here.' Dinny pointed to marks in the dry sandy soil. She moved around the perimeter of the hut, pointing out this and that. Her mother had taught her enough about her people's ways to help her understand the messages the earth carried. 'Then he went off that way.' She pointed.

'Can you follow him?' Benedict asked.

'We can try, but it's probably too dry and if he's careful how he goes, we'll soon lose him. I'm not an experienced tracker.'

She was right. But before they lost the trail, they did find a place where horses had recently been tethered and where two people had stood, one of them a heavy man, one the man with worn boots who had set the first fire. They followed the horse tracks till they came to the main road to Perth, then lost them in the churned-up ground left by an ox wagon.

When they got back Benedict went to sit beside his wife on one of the rough benches he'd cobbled together after the fire, clasping her hand in his.

'Do you really think this fire was deliberately set?' she asked, sharing the thoughts that had kept her awake half the night.

'Undoubtedly.'

She shook her head in bewilderment. 'I can't imagine anyone who would hate us so much.' Then she remembered her brother Dermott's vow of revenge. No, surely even he would not do this to her?

'Neither can I. But I'm going to teach all the children to shoot from now on, even Josie. We've only got ourselves to rely on out here.' His lips twisted a little as he added, 'I hope that will cheer Cathie up a bit.'

But nothing seemed able to cheer her up now that the immediate crisis of the fire was over.

As the weather was still quite warm they were living in rough bush shelters till the new house was built – and it would be a much smaller house than before. Cathie would have to share a bedroom with Josie, which meant she wouldn't be able to read in bed or even sit with the lamp on mending her clothes, enjoying her own company, because Josie wasn't strong and needed her sleep. And to add to Cathie's woes, most of their books had been burned. Though there had been nothing she hadn't read a dozen times before, still she missed them.

She confronted her stepfather about the situation as the new house took shape. 'Are we going to build a proper house again, or will this be it?' She waved a scornful hand towards the foundations of the new building.

'We can't do much else for a year or two. We lost quite a bit in the fire and it'll take us some time to recover from that.' He'd had to go up to Perth to sell one of Liza's pieces of jewellery even to do this, something he hated. They had considered letting Ilse go, but decided the children's education was more important than a bigger house – for the time being, anyway. But he intended to be careful with every penny and to see that his family were equally frugal.

Cathie scowled at the ground. 'I thought life here at Lizabrook couldn't get much worse, but it has.'

He looked at her sternly. 'You're behaving like a spoiled brat.'

'Maybe that's because you always treat me like a child,' she snapped back. 'Or a servant. I'm fit for nothing but housework, it seems. The boys have the furniture-making or the farm, while I have nothing to do but wash the same clothes week in, week out, or cook and clear up. I sometimes think I'll go mad stuck out here.' People did go mad from loneliness in the bush. Cabin fever, they called it. You read of it in the newspapers, which arrived at irregular intervals from Perth, passed round the small settlement by their old friend Dorothy Bennett at the inn, who had once been Dorothy Pringle, her mother's employer.

'We just have to make the best of things, Cathie,' he said quietly but with an edge to his voice.

'It's *your* best we're working for. This sort of life is not what I want for myself.'

'I'm your father and I'll decide what's best for you.'

'You're not even my real father. And you can't keep me prisoner here for ever! I won't *let* you. I'll find a way to escape – you'll see.'

He had promised Liza not to lose his temper again with their troublesome daughter, so he bit back the hasty words and strode away.

Cathie watched him go, already ashamed of her taunt for he had always treated her just like his own children. But she was too upset to apologise now. Her life was being wasted, absolutely wasted. How would she ever find a husband stuck out here?

41

It wasn't that she didn't love her family. She did. But she'd seen spinsters who'd sacrificed themselves for their families, toiling until they died with nothing that was really their own. There was such a one living in Brookley, a pleasant, faded woman at the beck and call of her ageing parents, helping with her brother's children when they were ill, never seeming to do anything for herself, never looking happy and fulfilled as Cathie's mother had looked before the fire.

'I won't let that happen to me,' she vowed. 'I won't.'

A week later, in her desperation and loneliness, Cathie tried once more to persuade her mother to send her to England to visit her father's family. 'Don't you have any money left from selling that brooch? I'll go steerage. I won't mind the hardship. Anything would be better than this life. Surely Mrs Ludlam would let me stay with her for a little while? Next time you write you could ask her, just till I'd found a job in service or work in a shop – I'd do *anything*.'

'No! The Ludlams wouldn't even consider having you.'

Cathie stared, surprised at how sharp her mother's voice was. 'You always say that, but you never say why not. Yet when you read Mrs Ludlam's letters to us, she's always hoping you'll go and visit her one day.'

'She isn't the one with the power in that family.

Josiah's brother is, and he's just like his father.' As her daughter stared at her in puzzlement, Liza added, 'When your father quarrelled with his family, they cast him off completely and made it plain they didn't want to see him again – ever. I took you back to England with me after I married Nicholas Rawley and Saul Ludlam behaved very badly towards us. You can never trust the Ludlam men and I don't want you going near them. They're still rich and powerful.'

Though she hoped things had improved since the time Josiah's father had found out that Cathie and Seth were not his son's children, and that Liza wanted to take them back to Australia. He had threatened to have her shut away in a mental asylum to prevent people from finding out. She had never forgotten that terrifying night when Saul had locked her in the stables and Benedict had rescued her. Even then they would not have got the children away if Sophia Ludlam hadn't stood up to her husband on their behalf. But since Liza had never told Cathie that Josiah wasn't her father, she could not tell her about all that now. She was sure it would upset her daughter to find out that her real father was a man called Teddy Marshall and that she was the result of a rape.

Cathie realised suddenly that her mother was avoiding her eyes and smoothing her apron over and over again. 'You're not telling me the truth,' she accused. 'There's something else. What is it? What's the real reason you're keeping me here?

If you can't find the money, I'll sell my gold locket to pay for the fare.' She seized her mother's arm and shook it slightly, trying to make her understand. 'Please, I *have to* get away from here.'

Liza chose her words with care. 'I'm not telling you everything I will admit, love, but I'm telling you as much as I can. There are other people's feelings to consider as well as your own.' Cathie's arrival in Pendleworth might still trigger a scandal. Liza's first husband had not been like other men and had been her husband in name only, but he had given her and her bastard child respectability – and then died saving Cathie's life. Let him and his secrets rest in peace.

When her daughter continued to stare at her pleadingly, Liza said crisply, 'Please don't go on about it. You know we're going to be short of money for some time. Besides, you can't go halfway round the world on your own and I certainly couldn't go with you at the moment, even if I wanted to, which I don't.' She glanced down at her stomach which was beginning to show her condition.

'I could perfectly well go on my own,' Cathie pleaded. 'I'm eighteen not twelve, and I'm not exactly a helpless little flower.' She looked down at herself disparagingly, wishing yet again that she were not so strongly built. 'Besides, you've told me how carefully single women are supervised on the ships, so I'd be quite safe once I was on board. And after I'd arrived I could catch a train to

Pendleworth.' She had never even seen a train but she had read of them. Everyone travelled round England on them, it seemed, so it couldn't be all that difficult to use them.

When her mother didn't answer Cathie let go of her arm and took a step backwards. 'You're just making excuses.' She laughed harshly. 'It's not only the convicts who got transported to Australia, you know. You've done it to me as well. But I'm *not* going to stay here for ever and I'm *not* marrying a farmer. I'll find a way to escape, you see if I don't.'

'When you love someone you don't mind where you live as long as you're with him,' Liza said softly. 'And I definitely don't want you to marry anyone you don't love. That's not,' she shuddered, 'at all comfortable.'

Cathie stared at her in shock. 'Didn't you love my father?'

'No!' It was out before Liza could stop herself.

'Why not?'

'I can't tell you.' Her voice softened. 'Please, Cathie darling, try to be satisfied with what you've got – you know we all love you.'

Why would they never tell her anything? Cathie's eyes strayed to her mother's swelling belly, to the hands that were cradling it unconsciously. 'You don't care where you live because you're besotted with your husband. Well, I think it's disgusting, a woman your age having more children. Haven't you got enough between you by now? If you had

45

fewer children, you'd have more money to spare and—'

'*How dare you speak to your mother like that?*' a voice roared behind her.

Cathie turned round, stiffening, and fell silent.

'Apologise at once!' Benedict demanded.

'Sorry, Mother.' But she said it in an indifferent tone which left them in no doubt that she didn't mean it. Then she looked from one to the other, putting one hand to her mouth to hold back the sobs, and ran out of the tiny new house into the bush where no one would see her weeping.

Liza tried not to let her own tears show because she knew that would upset Benedict, but she cried easily when she was carrying a child and they spilled over anyway.

He came over to put his arms round her, making soothing sounds and kissing her forehead. 'I'm going to have a long talk with that young woman. And *you*, madam wife, are going to stop working so hard and rest more. You've been looking very drawn and weary lately.'

'I am a bit tired,' she admitted. 'I think we all are, Cathie as well. It's been a difficult few months. And she works very hard, for all her defiant talk. I don't know what I'd do without her.' Even Benedict had changed since the fire, grown grumpy and was always working too hard. Liza was worried about him as well as their daughter. When he drew her over to the shade of a tree and made her sit down on a stool there, she let him because it made him sit down, too.

'I blame myself.' He clasped her hand in his, patting it absent-mindedly. 'We'd not be in this position if I'd cleared bigger firebreaks. Before next summer I'm going to clear enough ground to make certain we're quite safe from fires.'

She leaned against him. 'Oh, Benedict, love, we've been over all that. You'd taken better precautions than anyone else in the district. It was just hard luck that there was a fire on such a windy day.'

'After the second fire we both know there's a good chance the first one was lit deliberately and one day I'll find out why. We won't be burnt out again. I'll make damned sure of that.'

She sighed. He had already cleared everything for a full two hundred yards beyond the new house and makeshift workshop, and was talking of clearing more. She missed having the bush nearby, for she loved to wander among the rustling, whispering gum trees when she had a few minutes free from her daily chores. But she hadn't told him that.

At bedtime Liza heard voices and paused outside the girls' tiny makeshift bedroom. Through the doorway, which had only a sacking curtain for a door, she could see Josie curled up against Cathie, with the older girl telling her little sister a story. She stayed watching her daughters for a moment, listening to the strong young voice spinning its story of magic and fairies, and the soft exclamations and questions with which Josie punctuated the story. With a smile Liza crept away again.

'I don't understand that girl,' she whispered to Benedict later as they lay in bed in the next room to the girls. 'If there's an emergency she's a tower of strength. Josie's not been feeling well lately – she always gets these breathless attacks when it's dusty like this – and suddenly Cathie's marvellous with her. And did you see her when Brendan cut his foot?' She burrowed against her husband for a moment, enjoying the feel of Benedict's hand stroking her hair, his big strong body against hers. 'Maybe we're wrong to keep Cathie here. Maybe we should help her get away for a while, even if it's only to Perth. Do you think Agnes would have her for a few days?'

'Does she deserve it? Even a short visit would cost money we can ill afford.'

'We can't afford to grow estranged from our daughter, either,' said Liza sadly. 'It's tearing me apart to see her so unhappy, Benedict love. Please, let's see if we can arrange something. It need not cost too much and there's a bit left from the brooch.'

Because he loved her and could deny her nothing he let her write to Agnes Fenton, who had travelled out to Australia on the same ship and had remained their friend.

When Agnes wrote back saying she'd be

delighted to have Cathie for a visit, Benedict agreed to take the girl and her luggage up to Perth in the cart.

Liza put the letter away and called Cathie over. 'Come for a walk by the lake, love. I've got some good news for you.'

Cathie shrugged and fell into step beside her, not at all convinced that her mother's idea of good news would be the same as hers.

'How would you like to spend a few weeks in Perth with Agnes while your father is finishing building the house?'

Cathie stopped dead, staring at her in disbelief, then swallowed hard. 'Oh, Mum! Do you really mean that?'

'Of course I do.'

Cathie threw her arms round her much smaller mother, weeping and laughing at the same time, then swept her round in a clumsy dance across the sandy ground near the lake.

'It was the right thing to do,' Liza told Benedict that night in bed.

'She was certainly sunny-tempered at dinner.'

'We've been wrong keeping her here. Farming is our life, not hers. If only . . .' She sighed.

'If only what?'

'If only there was someone in England she could go to.'

'I wouldn't let her.'

'Benedict, you can't mean that!'

'Oh, can't I? Look, love, she'd only stir up old

trouble if she went to England. And do you really want to risk her meeting her real father?'

His voice had risen without his realising it and Cathie stiffened as the words echoed clearly in the stillness of the night. *Real father!* Did that mean Josiah Ludlam wasn't her father – and that her real father was still alive? How was that possible?

She lay straining her ears, for the thin walls of the temporary shelter were made only of hessian, and heard her mother say, 'No. Never that.'

Benedict's deep voice rumbled on, 'Then let's hope she'll be content with the trip to Perth, because it's all she's getting.'

Their voices fell to whispers again. Cathie lay awake for a long time, trying to take in what she had overheard. She felt like demanding to know who her real father was, but her step-father's voice had had that stubborn edge to it as he spoke that all his children recognised. That tone meant he would not be moved from what he had decided was best for her – and he took his fatherly duties very seriously.

So how, Cathie wondered, could she find out about her real father? Excitement hummed through her. Surely he would want to see her? And she certainly wanted to meet him. What harm could there be in that? Did he know about her or had her mother kept her existence a secret? She frowned as that thought brought another question. Why had Josiah Ludlam married her mother if she was already carrying someone else's child? Had he known Cathie wasn't his? Was that why they refused even to consider asking Sophia Ludlam to let her stay?

Who else could she ask about this? Mrs Bennett? Cathie considered their neighbour and sighed. No, Dorothy was her mother's friend, for all she was so much older, and would not go against Liza's wishes. She was another person who seemed content to live quietly, keeping the small inn and shop in nearby Brookley. Though she always looked sad when she spoke of her runaway daughter. She didn't even know whether Kitty was alive or dead, but clung to the hope that she'd see her again one day. Her second husband was a quiet man who was a cobbler and jack of many trades. He made and mended shoes, though some of the women got their fancier shoes from Perth. He grew vegetables for the inn, brewed the beer and helped his wife, seeming to have no ambitions beyond reading voraciously anything that came his way. He ran a small lending library, too, charging a penny to borrow a book for a month – or swapping book loans for other goods or services needed at the inn, because ready cash was always in short supply among the struggling settlers.

No, Cathie decided reluctantly as dawn brightened the sky, there was no one here to help her find out about her real father. But this meant she had even more of a reason to go to England. Surely he would want to meet her, even if she was – she faced the fact squarely – a bastard?

★　★　★

Mairi Hamilton waited till everyone had finished eating, then cleared her throat to gain her two brothers' attention. 'I would like to invite Elwyn to tea on Sunday. And – he wants to speak to you, Magnus.'

He smiled at her. 'Like that, is it?'

She flushed. 'Yes. Yes, it is.'

He was glad to find something happy to dwell on, for their mother was growing stranger by the month. They had had to make the tiny bedroom over the stairs into a sort of – well, there was no word for it but 'prison cell' and the doctor had given them some medicine to make her drowsy at night. They needed their sleep even if their mother didn't.

He realised his brother was chuckling and looked up, banishing the sad thoughts.

'I don't know what you see in that little man, our Mairi,' Hamish teased. Unlike the other two, the youngest Hamilton's voice had no Scottish lilt in it at all, for he had been born here in Lancashire.

Mairi fired up at once. 'Elwyn's kind, that's what I see in him, and I love being with him, and—' She broke off, realising she was being teased. 'Oh, you two!' She flapped one hand at them. 'Just make sure you behave yourselves on Sunday, that's all.'

'Yes, Mairi.' Magnus hesitated, then looked sideways at their mother, who was making patterns in the crumbs on her plate with half the sandwich lying uneaten. 'What have you said to him about – our situation here?'

'Elwyn had an auntie who was the same. He understands and will be kind to Mum.' Well, he was kind to everyone, her Elwyn was.

On the Sunday, both Hamilton men put on their chapel clothes and Mairi set the table with the best china and tablecloth.

Their mother had been having one of her better days and had tried to help, carrying plates to and fro like a docile child, but setting them down wrongly and then drifting off in the middle of one journey to stand gazing into space, a plate cradled against her breast. She had even hugged Magnus, something she rarely did nowadays, which had made him remember with a pang how affectionate she used to be.

When the door knocker went, Magnus and Hamish ranged themselves in front of the fire and waited. They had met Elwyn Bebb, as they'd met most of the men at church, but they'd never had much to do with him. He was a little older than Hamish, a little younger than Magnus, and lived on his own in lodgings.

When he came in, Elwyn was carrying an oval box of Cadbury's chocolate dragees, with a picture of a little girl on the top. As he was introduced to Mrs Hamilton, he offered it to her.

She snatched it from him without a word of thanks and stared at it, running one finger across the top and muttering to herself, ignoring everyone. After staring at the picture for a moment she tried to open the box, but failed and began weeping in frustration.

Elwyn stepped forward and with gentle gestures showed her how it opened. Picking up a chocolate dragee, he offered it to her, but she only stared at his outstretched hand.

'Eat it, mum,' Mairi coaxed. 'It's nice.'

But Janey had turned stubborn and refused to open her mouth. When Magnus tried to take the box from her for safe keeping, she shouted, 'Mine! Mine!' and clutched it to her, so he slid the lid on quickly and left her to her rapt contemplation of the little girl's face.

'I'm sorry,' he said to Elwyn, hating to have his mother's weakness displayed like that to a stranger.

'She can't help it, poor thing,' said their visitor softly, his expression understanding. 'My auntie was just the same.'

'Let's have tea, shall we?' said Mairi, and they all took their places round the kitchen table, leaving their mother by the fire to continue crooning over the chocolate box, which seemed to have taken her fancy.

After the meal Elwyn turned to Magnus. 'May I have a word with you in private?'

'Aye. Come away into the front.'

Mairi closed her eyes in relief then began to clear the table. She had been terrified her mother's behaviour would put Elwyn off. There were younger and prettier women at chapel who didn't have her disadvantages.

'I like your Elwyn,' Hamish said, grinning at her and helping her carry the crockery into the scullery.

She paused for a moment. 'Do you really?'

'Yes. He may be shorter than you are but he'll do.' He glanced towards the closed door, hesitated, then said softly, 'I'm still thinking of going to Australia. It sounds so wonderful. Sunshine and parrots flying around. No snow. No chilblains.'

'Nothing's perfect,' she said flatly. 'And don't you think Magnus has lost enough of his brothers now?'

'I'm a man grown, Mairi. I have to make my own life – as you're doing.'

'I'll still be here to help with Mother. Will you?'

He didn't answer, just pushed past her with a closed expression on his face. 'You don't need me now. I'm off to change and get a breath of fresh air.'

She stood motionless as she heard him leave the house, wondering what exactly he was planning. He was definitely up to something. She had always been able to tell.

CHAPTER 3

JANUARY–FEBRUARY

In Melbourne, Matthieu Correntin strolled round to his current mistress's rooms. He intended to take his final leave of Alice tonight and give her a generous present, then he'd conclude his last remaining business deal and sail west to join Dermott in Perth. He preferred land travel, but there were as yet no roads from east to west of this huge country, let alone railways, so you had to travel round it by ship.

A grim expression sat briefly on his face at the thought of his partner. When he'd first started to work with Dermott he had not realised quite how reckless and unprincipled the man was. But they had made good money together, doing anything that came to hand – buying and selling, importing, running two or three eating houses, a pawnshop – even a brothel.

It was Dermott who had got them into this latter business without even asking Matthieu, who did not relish the thought of being a whoremaster. And it was this venture which had landed Dermott in trouble with Pat Blaney, who ran the district's other brothels and objected strongly to anyone

56

encroaching on his territory. Blaney had made it clear that it would be dangerous for them to stay in Melbourne by burning down both their new brothel and one of their eating houses. Furious, but knowing when he was outclassed, Dermott had prudently left the state first and Matthieu had let it be known that he was winding up their business affairs before following his partner. He did not think Blaney would come after him with quite the same vengeful fury.

Christina had protested vigorously about the move, but she didn't know half the things her husband was up to; sometimes Matthieu suspected that *he* didn't know, either. The business they had conducted together was quasi-legal, a bit sharp at times, but Matthieu drew the line at some of the shadier deals which Dermott had suggested. He had no intention of landing himself in gaol, nor did he have his friend's confidence in the stupidity of the police. But he couldn't help enjoying Dermott's company. The man was a likeable rogue.

Although Matthieu wrote to his family from time to time, he doubted he would be able to go back and fit in again in France. Here the sky was wide and you were free to make money if you could without entrenched custom breathing down your neck – well, you were unless you tried to open a brothel in the wrong place and fell foul of a master criminal!

When Alice opened the door she looked flustered.

A quick glance beyond her showed a man's trousers on a chair.

'It seems you are busy tonight, *chérie*,' Matthieu said mildly, but he was annoyed. He had been paying the rent on this room, more fool he! Then he saw who the other man was and gasped in shock.

Pat Blaney got out of bed and walked towards the open door, wrapped in a sheet, a nasty smile on his plump face. He put one hand on Alice's shoulder possessively. 'You should look after your property better, Correntin.'

Matthieu was so surprised he could not speak for a minute. Alice's eyes flew to something behind him and terror showed clearly on her face. He turned quickly, just in time to dodge the cudgel of the man who had crept up on him. Another fellow stood beside his assailant, grinning evilly and hefting a knife as if it were an extension of his hand.

Matthieu surprised them by rushing forward into the room, using his foot to shove the door shut in their faces and thanking providence for the quick reactions which had saved him from trouble before. He pushed Alice towards Pat, knocking him over easily enough because the over-confident fool was hampered by the sheet.

As Matthieu wrenched the french windows wider, he thanked God for hot nights. He leaped over the wooden rails of the veranda and made off swiftly through the back garden. From the crashing noises and curses behind him, he knew his way rather better than his pursuers.

He had no trouble losing them, but took a lot of care before re-entering his new, temporary lodgings. Did Blaney know where he lived? Probably. With a curse Matthieu sent his landlady's son out with an urgent message, then began to hurl the rest of his possessions into his half-packed trunk.

When the two men who had attacked him at Alice's rooms arrived at his lodgings, they found their prey guarded by two men of similar ilk whom Matthieu had paid well for their services.

'You'd better get out of Melbourne if you know what's good for you, Correntin!' one of the Blaney men tossed across the few feet between them.

'I'm leaving, *mon ami*. Tell your master not to worry.'

'Don't mind if we tag along with you to the ship, do you? Just to be sure you get away safely. And don't try to come back to Melbourne again, either.'

'You can follow me if you want, but come any closer than that and you'll regret it.'

One of Matthieu's own bodyguards took a step forward at his words, fists bunched, and the two pursuers shrugged and stayed where they were.

Matthieu had to bribe the steward to let him board the ship early. He scribbled a hasty note to another friend, then handed it to the two body-guards, who were waiting patiently on the docks

59

and would do so until the ship sailed. More money exchanged hands for this extra favour, but Matthieu made sure of the note's safe delivery by promising them a further payment from Bob Sharpe once the letter was in his hands.

Then, having done all he could, Matthieu leaned on the rail and stared out across the moonlit water. He could only hope Bob was friend enough to tidy up his remaining business affairs – though he knew that favour would come at a price. He'd not been able to withdraw the rest of his funds from the bank before he left, either, something he had planned to do this morning before boarding, so he was not feeling at all happy about the situation. However, those funds would be safe enough and he could get them sent after him once he arrived in Perth.

But it would take weeks for his money to come through so he'd have to be a bit careful. Unlike Dermott, he did not have a huge fortune stashed away.

By the time the ship weighed anchor the following afternoon, Matthieu was able to laugh at himself – or at least to smile wryly. He had always found humour a saving grace because life had a way of tweaking your tail however hard you tried to arrange things to your liking.

A feeling of excitement followed the amusement. It was always like this when he set off for some-where new. There was a sense of promise, a sense that this time he might find what he was looking for – or there again, he might not.

He tossed the stub of his cigar into the water and watched it swirl away. Why had he been cursed with this restless streak? Why could he never settle down as other men did?

Within the hour he had set his worries aside and was chatting to his fellow passengers. Western Australia, everyone told him gloomily, was the Cinderella Colony. If you didn't have a very good reason for going there you'd never bother to visit it. Two of the men on board were government officials and these Matthieu cultivated carefully, because even minor functionaries could be of use.

He made his way down to his tiny cabin that night somewhat the worse for wear since the ladies had retired early and the men had shared a bottle or two. He lay smiling into the darkness. He was alive, wasn't he? Still in possession of his faculties and looks – which made it easy to gain the ladies' attention. He twirled his moustache, then laughed at himself for doing so, and wondered whether to shave it off for a change.

He probably wouldn't stay in Western Australia for long, he decided, just until he got his money through from Melbourne and finalised his financial arrangements with Dermott. He did not want to make a habit of narrow escapes. Where should he go next? India, perhaps? Or America? There was a lot of the world still to see.

And why he couldn't think of a place he really wanted to visit this time he could not understand.

61

Oh, he'd been too busy to think about it, that was all. It would come to him. It always did.

As the Caines' cart approached Perth, Cathie sighed in pleasure. 'Isn't it wonderful, Dad? So many people living here! So much to see and do! Heavens, how the city has changed since we were last here! Look at all those buildings.'

'I'd rather see fields and trees than city streets,' Benedict said flatly. 'I can't see why anyone would want to spend their whole life in towns.' He pointed into the distance at a clock tower. 'And what good does building fancy town halls do ordinary folk like us? Those who grow food do more good than those who build fancy monuments, and don't you forget it.'

She suppressed a sigh. Since the bush fire he had been so touchy. She knew he was working far too hard – but he had always worked hard and never been like this before. And her mother was clearly worried about him.

But even though Cathie felt sorry for them both in their great loss, the thought that they had been lying to her about her father still galled her. She was not sure she could ever forgive them for that.

'Perth may be the capital of our colony,' Benedict went on, jabbing one finger towards the huddle of central buildings, 'and we who live here may call it a city, but it's still only a small town by English standards. I was reading somewhere that there are ten times as many people living in

Manchester as in the whole of Western Australia. Just think of that.'

She sighed. He was always coming out with such information, culled from the newspapers he loved to read. What did she care?

'. . . and you'd be lost over there in the old country after growing up here, Cathie! Lost! Why, you'd never even seen a train till we crossed the timber line to Rockingham on this trip, yet over there even ordinary folk use them every day to get to and fro.'

They drew to a halt outside Agnes's house just then and Cathie sighed in relief. How she had kept her mouth shut on the slow, two-day journey up to Perth she didn't know.

When her things had been unloaded and carried inside to the small bedroom at the rear, her father drove off to find a livery stable for the horse and cart while the two women went back inside.

'I'm grateful to you for having me, Mrs Fenton!' Cathie felt shy all of a sudden, because she had never been on her own with her mother's friend before. Her hostess looked so elegant that the girl felt even bigger and clumsier next to her, with her limp, crumpled skirts hanging anyhow and not even the smallest of bustles at the back. She eyed Agnes Fenton's elegantly draped skirts surreptitiously, thinking how strange bustles looked – though no stranger than the crinolines her mother had once worn to please her first husband. Cathie had played at dressing up in them when she was a child, but the hoops, big spreading skirts and tightly fitted bodices had been lost along with many other possessions in the fire.

'It's my pleasure to have you. And do call me Agnes! "Mrs Fenton" makes me feel old. I was feeling a bit down, I must admit, till I got your mother's letter. It was such a bore being in mourning!' She spread her arms and twirled round. 'How do you like my new dress?'

'It's lovely.' Cathie looked down at herself ruefully. 'Mum's given me some money to buy material for a new dress or two, because all mine seem to be either torn or stained. And I've grown again, so these are a bit short for me, as well. Sometimes it seems as if I'll never stop growing till I hit the ceiling. I hate being so tall!'

'Goodness, and I'd sell my soul for some extra inches! How nice it would be to look gentlemen in the eye for a change, or even to look down my nose at one!'

They both laughed and Cathie began to relax. It had never occurred to her before that being short might have its problems as well, though she would still have preferred it. When her mother was dressed up for church, she might not be fashionably clad, but she looked so dainty and pretty that Cathie could not help feeling jealous sometimes.

'That must be her, because that's definitely Benedict Caine,' Christina Docherty said, peering out of the parlour window.

64

'She's a big strapping lass. How did my tiny sister have a child who looks like that? The daughter must take after Da's side of the family, like I do.' Dermott put the opera glasses to his eyes again. 'You know, this lass reminds me of someone else. Who the hell is it?'

'Let me have a look now.'

'In a minute. I want to . . .' His voice trailed away, then as Cathie scowled and made a vigorous gesture, he sucked in his breath suddenly. 'It can't be!'

'What? It can't be what?' His wife tried to snatch the opera glasses and he pushed her aside impatiently with any angry, *'Leave it!'*

While the three people across the road remained standing in the garden, he continued to study the girl. Could he be imagining things? Only as Caine drove away and the two women turned to go inside did he pass the opera glasses absent-mindedly to his wife.

'You might have let me see her face,' Christina grumbled when all she got was a brief glimpse of Cathie's back.

'Ach, you'll be meeting her in the next few days. We'll make sure of that. You can invite them both over to take tea and stare at her face for as long as you like then.'

Christina gave an exaggerated sigh. 'I'm sure I'll hate her as much as I hated Liza.'

'You'll do no such thing!' he corrected sharply. 'You're to become good friends and play the fond auntie. And you won't say anything, not a single word, to let her know how we really feel about her bloody mother. We'll be an aunt and uncle who're sad that we've never been welcome to keep in touch with my sister and her family, absolutely delighted to have a chance to get to know our niece. Don't let me down in this, now.'

Christina pulled a face. 'Oh, very well. But surely the fire has paid Liza back for what she did to your brother?'

'Mebbe. Mebbe not.' His sister had claimed it was an accident all those years ago, that she'd not meant to kill Niall only frighten him away. But she should have known better than to fire at him at point-blank range. As well as ruining Liza and her family, Dermott still wanted to find out where they'd buried Niall and see his brother's remains placed in a proper grave, with a headstone.

Christina, whose mother had always called her Kitty, frowned at him. Why did he go on about his stupid sister? When they were both young it had been Liza who'd attracted all the eligible men, leaving none for Christina. She had had to be satisfied with Liza's brother, who was not a gentleman and hadn't even married her till he'd got her with child. Even then, he'd forced her to convert to Catholicism first, a religion she still secretly despised. He'd been furious when she'd lost that first child and it had been years till she'd had the others. For a man who had been a thief and opportunist for most of his life, Dermott

Docherty held singularly rigid views about his own family's respectability.

She remembered his other remark. 'Who is it the girl reminds you of?'

'One of our old neighbours in Pendleworth.'

His voice was abstracted and she could get no further information from him. He was the most frustrating man on earth, but at least he provided for them all generously. Which was more than her own father had done, gentleman though he had been. All he'd done was waste the family's money on silly schemes, then drag them out to Australia almost penniless.

She stared round the little rented house. Oh, why had they left Melbourne? Life had been so much better there. But you couldn't talk sense into Dermott once he'd fixed his mind on something and she hated it when he did things impulsively, like buying this stupid farm. She could think of nothing worse than living in the country here in Australia, but would he listen to her? No, he rarely did these days. Tears welled in her eyes. She hated it in Western Australia, absolutely hated it.

The following day Cathie returned young James Docherty's ball when it sailed over the fence into the street near Agnes's house, then got talking to his governess.

'Go and join them!' hissed Dermott, poking his wife in the back. 'It's a heaven-sent opportunity to meet her.'

So Christina strolled out, smiling graciously and sending governess and children away with one sharp glance. 'I'm so pleased to meet you. I knew dear Mrs Fenton was expecting her young friend Cathie Ludlam to stay with her.' They had been astonished to hear that name and delighted that chance had given them an opportunity to meet Liza's daughter. She was amazed at how tall the girl was and how ill-dressed, looking more like a servant and a poor one at that, especially as Liza was a short woman who never had any style. Comparing that to her own affluence and modish clothes gave Christina deep satisfaction.

Cathie stood wondering why their neighbour had not introduced herself by name. 'It's very kind of Mrs Fenton to invite me to stay. She's taking me shopping later.' She looked down ruefully at her skirts, carefully ironed that morning but still limp and faded. 'I need some new clothes, something more stylish.' She gazed enviously at the other woman. 'Yours are beautiful.'

'Why, thank you.' Christina twirled to show off her elegant gown with its fashionable apron-front, the folds knotted up into a bustle at the back and the skirt flowing into a small train beneath it. 'That means you'll want something with a bustle and train, though to tell you the truth trains are very inconvenient in winter.'

'I don't know how you manage them at all. Don't they get dirty?'

Christina caught up the hem to show the

brush-like braid beneath it, speaking as one woman to another. 'See – this is to protect the underneath of the hem. And in wet weather one loops the train up, of course. We women are slaves to fashion, are we not?'

'I've never had the chance. But your dress is such a pretty colour. I love the deep rose with the paler pink. Is it real silk?'

'Yes. Mind you,' Christina leaned forward confidentially, as if treating the girl as an equal, inwardly amused at how the silly fool was drinking in her words as if she was the fount of all wisdom, 'one has to wear very tight lacing to get this straight appearance down the front.' With one hand she gestured to her own slender body. 'When we were living in Melbourne I used to get my clothes from England or France. We prided ourselves there on being only three months behind European fashions. But here in Perth,' she fluttered the hand scornfully, 'I don't know how I'm going to manage.'

'Perth seems wonderful to me. My family has a farm and I've not visited the city very often.'

'Then I mustn't spoil it for you. We can rest assured Perth will be more exciting than life in the country! May I hope that you and dear Mrs Fenton will come and take tea with me one day, perhaps tomorrow? I haven't had much chance to meet people here yet and, I must say, I'm missing my old friends.'

'Why did you leave Melbourne?' Cathie flushed

then clapped one hand over her mouth. 'Oh, I'm sorry! That was rude of me.'

'No, just honest.' Stupid girl, thought Christina. She has no more style than a cart horse. 'We left for the usual reason – my husband's business interests. Ah, there is your kind hostess.' As Agnes came across the sandy unpaved street to join them, she cooed, 'My dear Mrs Fenton, I was just making the acquaintance of your young visitor and hoping the two of you would take tea with me tomorrow. Now do say you will!'

'We shall be delighted. But I must take Cathie away from you now. We have some shopping to do.'

As they re-entered the house Agnes murmured, 'She's a dreadful woman! What a pity you got talking to her. Now we shall have to pay a visit and listen to her going on forever about how wonderful Melbourne is and how behind the times we are in Perth.'

'She's very finely dressed,' Cathie said wistfully.

'For a woman at home in the morning, she's *over*dressed,' corrected Agnes. 'And she wears too many bright colours for a woman of her age. It makes her skin look faded. You'd think she'd see that in her mirror. And did you see the amount of trimming on that dress? It was ridiculous!' She still privately wondered if these Dochertys were any connection of the girl's mother, who'd been plain Liza Docherty, lady's maid when they'd first met aboard ship – and who had horrified the cabin class passengers by contracting a shipboard marriage to Josiah Ludlam scandalously soon after his frail first wife Catherine died and was buried at sea. Dermott Docherty did not resemble Agnes's old friend in the slightest, but she would ask them about it the next day, though.

Cathie didn't know what to think about their neighbours. After the simple clothes she had worn all her life, the gorgeous colours of the neighbour's clothes had made her long for something more cheerful, and she'd have given anything for just a couple of those fringed frills on her own skirts. What were bustles made of? she wondered. Were they like little cushions, or where they small wire frames like crinolines? She would have to ask Mrs Fenton.

When Cathie and Agnes went round to take tea with their neighbour the following afternoon, they found Dermott sitting with his wife.

'I hope you don't mind if my husband joins us?' Christina asked, indicating seats on a plush-covered sofa.

Agnes inclined her head. 'Of course not, Mr Docherty.' She was a bit surprised to see him, however, since gentlemen did not usually participate in such tea parties.

Cathie stared at her host and hostess. 'Docherty? Why, that was my mother's maiden name!'

Dermott smiled at her. 'I know that, my dear. I hope you'll excuse this abrupt introduction but I'm your mother's brother.'

She could not think what to say, for her mother would not even speak the name of her eldest living brother and seemed to hate all mention of him. Cathie looked to Agnes for guidance.

'Does Liza know you're here?' her friend asked, startled.

'No. My sister and I – well, let's face it, Liza and I never got on. And I must confess it was mainly my fault. I was a rather, um, wild young man. Didn't treat my sister as well as I might have. I regret that now and am hoping for a reconciliation.'

Agnes was still frowning. 'Until you have seen Liza, I don't think Cathie should —'

Christina burst in, 'Oh, please don't deny us this chance to get to know our niece, Mrs Fenton! I have no close relatives and my husband doesn't know where the rest of his family is, so there's only Liza and her family left now.'

'This places me in a very difficult position,' Agnes protested, wondering why they hadn't said anything about the relationship when she'd told them about Cathie's proposed visit.

'Give us a few weeks, though, before you tell my sister. At least let us get to know our niece.' Dermott smiled across at Cathie. 'If you'd like that, of course, lass?'

Cathie studied her uncle, feeling unsure of herself. He had a commanding air to him that said he was used to having his own way, but at the same time his eyes twinkled with amusement and she had a strong desire to smile back at him.

It wasn't until she was lying in bed that night, thinking through this amazing day, that it suddenly occurred to her that her uncle might know who her real father was. That settled things. She would get to know him better and ask him.

After some thought, Agnes decided to write and tell Liza about the situation straight away. She didn't say anything to Cathie or the Dochertys. For all their show of friendliness to their niece, she still didn't quite trust her neighbours, though she couldn't say exactly why.

When she had put the letter in the post Agnes felt better. And until she got a reply, she would keep the girl busy, make sure Cathie didn't see too much of her relatives.

CHAPTER 4

FEBRUARY

Dinny saw Liza sigh as she contemplated the pile of washing. Her friend looked weary even before she started work. It was time to intervene. 'Let me do that today.'

'I can't ask you to—'

'You didn't ask. And you need more help now you haven't got Cathie,' Dinny went on, steering her away from the copper full of hot water.

As Liza leaned against her for a moment, the two women smiled at one another. They had been close friends ever since the day Liza had rescued Dinny from the two white men who had been keeping her prisoner and using her body.

Dinny had lived with Fergal O'Riordan, an ex-convict, for seventeen years now and been married to him for ten of those years, since his Irish wife's death, though the minister had been doubtful as to whether he should marry a native to a white man and would have refused to do it but for Benedict's intervention.

Life was good for the O'Riordans at Lizabrook, where no one cared about Dinny's colour, but if she went into Mandurah or Pinjarra she was at risk of being insulted in a variety of ways for being Aboriginal. And yet, ironically, her own mother had had to flee from New South Wales because she had met with equal hostility from her own people for going to live with a white man instead of the husband her father had chosen from their tribe. She had always been afraid of her people finding her, even though she had travelled right around Australia on a big ship to escape from them. Aboriginal fathers had the main say about marrying their daughters off, and about punishing any daughter who disobeyed them.

Unlike her son Brendan, whom she called by another name in her heart, Dinny was content with her small world. She might not have been born in this area, but she felt an affinity with the land and was sure it had accepted her. And the local tribe had accepted her as well, giving her a skin name and adopting her as one of them because she helped them when they were ill, especially the women. 'You're not carrying this baby as easily as you did the others,' Dinny observed to her friend, frowning.

'Well, I'm a lot older than I was when I had the last one,' Liza admitted, pulling away from her and rubbing her aching forehead.

'You shouldn't have any more children after this one. I'll give you something to stop them.'

'If you say so.' Liza trusted her friend's healing skills. 'Cathie said it was disgusting at my age to have another baby, but I've enjoyed all my children.'

'If you want to keep this child, from now on till it's born you must get help with the heavy work.'

'How can I? I can't ask Ilse to do the washing, except for her own. Governesses don't do things like that. And servants are scarce even in Perth, let alone here in the bush.'

Dinny hesitated. 'Would you try the girl I've taken on to live with me for a while? Willerin doesn't have many skills yet, but she's strong and learns quickly.'

Liza considered this for a minute, head on one side. 'I'd be happy to meet her and see if we like one another.'

Dinny smiled at her friend. 'Only you would say that.'

'Say what?'

'Only you would say, "see if we like one another". As if her feelings matter.'

'Well, of course they matter.'

'Not to most white people.'

So Willerin came to work, a shy young girl of fifteen, still somewhat overwhelmed by this close contact with white people.

A few days later as Liza took the mail from the man who brought it out to the homestead once a week the world seemed to waver around her then darkness swallowed her up.

Willerin saw her collapse and shouted for help.

Josie ran out from the schoolroom, sobbing, and tried to throw herself on her mother's still body. Ilse followed and pulled her away, before helping

Willerin carry Liza into her bedroom. Noticing the letters blowing around she called to Josie to pick them up and the child did this hastily, still sobbing, not noticing one which had blown under a bush. From there it drifted towards the lake where it slowly sank.

Hearing the cries, Dinny came running across. When it came to child-bearing, with no doctors nearby even the white people of Brookley had learned to ignore the colour of her skin and trust her skills because the women she had attended did not fall ill as often after the birth and you could not fault her cleanliness.

'You'll have to stay in bed from now on if you want to keep this baby,' Dinny warned Liza, who was lying there looking boneless, her face chalky-white and the skin around her eyes shadowed.

With her head swimming and still feeling very distant, Liza said faintly, 'I don't think I *could* get up yet.'

Dinny went out to talk to Benedict, who was waiting anxiously nearby. She took the opportunity to warn him strictly not to have any more children after this one.

'It's Liza who matters, not the baby. Of course I'll be careful from now on. Is she going to be all right?'

'If she rests. She's a bit over-tired now.' Liza had carried her other children easily, but Dinny was worried that there might be something wrong this time.

Benedict ran one hand through his hair. 'How are we going to manage to slow her down?'

Ilse came up to join them and when he explained the problem, immediately said, 'If you don't mind my neglecting my teaching duties for a while, Mr Caine, I'd be happy to help out.'

He stared at her in surprise. She was usually so quiet and self-effacing. 'I can't ask you to do that!'

She smiled ruefully. 'You're not *asking* me, I'm volunteering.'

'I must admit I'd be grateful for any help you could give us. I think I'd better send for Cathie, though. We're going to need her.'

Dinny touched his arm. 'Don't do that yet, Benedict. Your daughter's not been gone long and she needed to get away as much as you need to stay here.'

He hesitated, chewing the corner of his lip. 'Well – we'll try it for a few days, see how we go on, but I'm not having Cathie idling around in Perth if Liza needs her help.'

So Ilse found herself doing the household tasks she had once done for the husband she had come out to Australia to marry. How long ago that seemed now! Johannes had been far older than her, a widower in need of a young wife to care for him. He had been very set in his ways and had insisted on being absolute master in his own house. She had soon regretted letting her family persuade her to come to Adelaide to marry him, but by then it was too late.

She was well and truly trapped in a loveless marriage.

Then Johannes had been killed in an accident and although she had been mildly sorry, she had also seen it as a way to find freedom at last – until she found he had left everything to his eldest son by his first marriage, with instructions for the heir to look after her. Andreas's charity was grudging and when he began to talk of finding her another husband, Ilse had refused point-blank to marry again. He had been very angry but she had stood her ground.

When he brought in the Minister and his wife to try to persuade her, and then locked her in her bedroom to 'think things over', she had realised that the only way to gain her freedom was to run away. She had pretended docility and made her plans carefully, guessing she would only get one chance. She had sailed to Western Australia because there was no ship due to leave for Sydney and had stayed in the west because she did not want to spend her precious savings on another sea voyage.

She had a facility for languages, speaking good French as well as her native German, and her English was by then almost perfect so she hoped to find a job as a governess but was prepared to do anything honest to earn a living. In the meantime she had found lodgings with another widow, Agnes Fenton, while she searched for employment. It had been harder to find a position than she had expected because of her nationality, so when Agnes had introduced her to the Caines, who were looking for a governess, she had been greatly relieved.

Her relief had not lasted. The Caines were very pleasant people, but like their daughter Cathie, Ilse found life in the country too quiet. In a year or so she intended to move back to Perth and try to find another husband, one more to her taste this time. Everyone said they were short of women out here and she knew she was not unpleasant to look at. Surely it should be possible?

With Liza spending her days on the sofa, Ilse took over running the house, enjoying the change from teaching. In the evenings after her work was done, she watched wistfully as the whole family cosseted Liza and conspired to keep her as happy and contented as possible. It must be wonderful to have such a family – children, a loving husband, your own home.

What worried Ilse was how, when she went back to live in Perth, she would meet suitable gentlemen and intimate to them that she was interested in marriage. She had not yet worked that out. But she would. She was very determined.

In Perth Dermott arranged to take Cathie out for a walk without Agnes keeping an eye on them. His niece was an energetic young woman and he liked to keep himself in good fighting fettle. He didn't invite Christina to go with them for she now considered it unladylike to go faster than a dawdle.

'So you're not ashamed to be seen out walking with your old uncle?' he teased as they strode off towards the city.

'Of course not.' As they walked along Cathie nerved herself to ask the question that had been hovering on the tip of her tongue ever since their first meeting. It came out in a rush. 'Uncle Dermott, I found out recently that Josiah Ludlam wasn't my real father.' She hesitated, not knowing how to continue.

'Now how did you discover that?' A sideways glance showed him an angry young face.

She avoided looking at him. 'I overheard Mum and Dad talking. Since the bush fire destroyed our home we've had to live in temporary accommodation while the new house is built and – and they don't realise how their voices carry at night.'

'What exactly did they say?'

'Just that they didn't want me going back to Lancashire, in case I met my *real father.*'

Dermott's voice was soft, coaxing more confidences from her. 'And did you ask them what that meant?'

She shook her head. 'I didn't even try, because I knew they wouldn't tell me. My mother once said it'd hurt other people if she told me everything about myself.' She stopped walking to plant herself squarely in front of him and look him in

81

the eyes. 'Do *you* know who my real father is, Uncle Dermott?'

'Yes. Well, at least, I'm pretty certain I do.'

She stood very still, hands clasped tightly at her breast. 'Will you tell me?'

He pursed his lips, pretending reluctance. 'Maybe I shouldn't, since your mother obviously doesn't want you to know.'

She grabbed his arm. 'Oh, please, Uncle! There's only you I can ask and I *have* to know.'

'Why?'

'Because one day I'm going to find a way to go back to England.' She stared into the distance, her expression determined. 'And if I have a father still living there, I want to meet him. What's he like?'

Dermott chose his words carefully. 'A strong man. He would have married your mother, you know, but she ran off to Australia. I suppose she didn't know then that she was carrying you.' To his relief Cathie didn't ask him how her mother had got pregnant in the first place to a man she didn't like enough to marry.

'What's my father's name?'

'Teddy Marshall. He's a clogger. Used to live across Underby Street from us. A bit rough, but earns an honest living and looks after his family. You have some half-brothers, too, you know.' But to his surprise, that information made her frown.

'Not more of them!' Her voice was bitter. 'I've got plenty of half-brothers already, thank you very much, including one in England whom I've never met.' She fell silent, frowning. 'What I don't understand is why a man like Josiah Ludlam married my mother? She was his wife's maid, after all, and he was a gentleman. We have some of his furniture and it's lovely, though some got burned. I used to touch pieces and be glad they'd belonged to my father, that I still had something of his. Though I didn't, did I? It was all lies.'

A sob escaped her so she started walking again, sniffing away the tears that threatened. 'Now – well, I don't know who I *am*.'

And then Dermott realised what he could do with this situation that had been handed to him on a silver platter. It would be yet another way of getting back at Liza. 'If you want – well, I would be happy to pay your fare back to England. I've plenty of money, after all, and you're the only niece I've got.'

She went so white he took hold of her arm. 'Are you all right, lass?' And he found to his surprise that he didn't really want to hurt his niece.

Cathie's voice was a mere whisper. 'I can't believe you mean it.'

'Ah, it's nothing. I've done well for myself and if you can't use it to help your own kin, what's the point of having money?' He continued to watch her more carefully than she realised.

She had her head bent now and was walking along slowly, pretending to concentrate on where she was putting her feet. 'I don't think my parents would let you do that – even though *they* can't afford to send me back for a visit at the moment. There's some other reason they don't want me to go back, I think, apart from my real father. But I'm going one day, whatever they say. Surely I can find a way to earn a living over there? I'm no fine lady, afraid to dirty my hands. I know my father quarrelled with his older brother but I do have a half-brother there. His family took him away from my mother. Do you know *them*? They're called Rawley.'

'Of Rawley Hall? *Our Liza married a Rawley?*' This was news to Dermott. When Cathie nodded, he let out a long, low whistle. 'Imagine that, she only married into the two richest families in Pendleworth, my little sister did.' And must have done something to offend them both if she'd come back to Australia as a poor farmer's wife. How stupid could you get? They'd have kept her in luxury for the rest of her days if she'd buttered them up properly.

'I don't think she got on very well with the Rawleys. They took Francis away from her and won't let her contact him – though she won't say why. She pays for a report every year from a lawyer in Pendleworth about how my brother is and it always upsets her. So do Mrs Ludlam's letters sometimes. But that's nothing to do with me and whatever she and Dad say or do, I'm definitely going back there one day.' Cathie scowled into the distance.

'Then let me buy you the passage, lass.'

'I'll think about it.' And she did. In fact, she thought of little else during the next few days.

Once they'd finished their evening meal, Mairi looked at Magnus across the table. 'I need to talk to you so I'll get Mum to bed early.'

Not without some difficulty she persuaded her mother to go out and use the privy at the end of the back yard and then took her upstairs, getting her undressed, giving her the medicine that helped her sleep and putting her into bed in the small bedroom with the new lock on the door. When her mother sighed and lay back with a faint smile, she looked almost her old self, which made a lump come into Mairi's throat. But after a moment the blank expression returned and Mairi left the room quietly, bracing herself to talk to her eldest brother and break her news to him as gently as she could.

He was sitting staring into the fire, his expression so sad she almost changed her mind, then she summoned up her courage. Best get this over with. She'd been dreading telling him all day. Sitting down opposite him she said baldly, 'Magnus, there's a problem.'

He looked at her in surprise. 'What?'

'Elwyn and I want to get married.'

He smiled at her. 'Well, we know that. I don't see it as a problem.' His smile faded. 'Oh, you mean we'll need to get a bigger house once you're married. Yes, of course. I'm quite happy to move.'

Mairi swallowed hard. 'It's not that. I'd have done

85

that and looked after Mother as we'd agreed only – well, things have changed. They want Elwyn to move to Bury, you see, as Assistant Manager of the shop there. When the present Manager retires, he's to take over. It's the chance he's been waiting for, his big chance. How can I ask him to give that up?' She saw Magnus swallow hard and bent her head to avoid his eyes as she answered her own question. 'I can't. I won't. And – and I won't give Elwyn up, either. I'm nearly twenty-seven and this may be my last chance of a normal family life.'

His words were so faint she could barely hear them.

'No. Why should you give up your life, lassie?'

'You shouldn't give yours up, either, Magnus. You've done enough, more than enough, for her. For all of us. We owe you so much. And the Benevolent Home isn't a bad place, you know. She'd be looked after there, kept clean and – made as comfortable as possible. You could visit her every week and—'

'No.' His voice was flat, determined. 'She'll not end her days in the Ben. I promised her that once.'

'But how will you look after her without me?'

'I don't know. I'll find a way, though.' Maybe he should look for a wife himself? No, who would take him on with a burden like his mother? 'How long can you give me to work things out – three months? Six would be better and—'

Mairi shook her head and interrupted before he

could make any more plans, 'Barely four weeks, I'm afraid, love. Elwyn has to start in Bury next month. We hope to be married by then so that I can go with him.'

Magnus let a sigh sift out slowly. 'Aye. It makes sense for you.'

Her eyes filled with tears and she stretched out one hand to him, knowing how generous this was of him. His Scottish accent had grown stronger, which it only did when he was upset or particularly happy. She loved the soft musical sound of his voice normally, but today the thicker burr that slowed his words made her feel guilty. 'Oh, Magnus, I'm so sorry to do this to you.'

He leaned forward to take her hand between his big ones, patting it gently. 'It isna your fault.'

'It isn't yours, either, and yet you've had the burden of us for all these years since Father died. You're thirty now. Don't you think it's time you had a life of your own?'

'I've never regretted doing my duty. Family is the most important thing there is.'

Mairi closed her eyes and did not even try to answer that. If their mother could understand what was happening, it'd be different, but more and more Janey Hamilton was withdrawing from them to live in a world of her own – if you could call that blank stare living. Last year their mother had been anxious, restless, aggressive at times, and it had been a struggle to care for her. This year she was increasingly apathetic, forgetting how to do the most simple daily tasks, soiling herself sometimes, even.

Why had God let this happen to her?

Two weeks after she'd left home, Cathie received a letter from her stepfather. As usual with Benedict Caine's communications, it was curt and to the point:

You're needed at home again, Cathie. Your mother is not well, and Ilse is having to neglect the children's education to help out. I'll be coming up to Perth next Tuesday and will bring you home with me then.

She stared at the piece of paper in horror. Go and live at home again! Already she could not bear the thought of it. To have no one new to talk to, nothing to see but trees and animals, day in, day out! No, never!

But her mother was ill! And Cathie loved her mother. She frowned at the letter. How ill? And what was wrong? Her step-father didn't say. Was he just using it as an excuse to make her go back? It seemed likely. He hadn't wanted her to come to Perth in the first place, that was certain.

For an hour, her thoughts see-sawed to and fro. Her mother was never ill. She was probably just tired because of the baby. And that was *his* fault for getting a woman of her mother's age in the family way again. It was typical that he now expected his stepdaughter to give her own life up to deal with that. Men got the best of everything. They wouldn't have asked a son to do this.

Cathie shook her head, silently rejecting the demand. She was sorry for her mother, very sorry, but she wasn't going back.

She looked round the elegant little sitting room. Agnes was out taking tea with one of her friends but Cathie could guess what her hostess would say. *They must need you. You'll have to go, I'm afraid.* So she wasn't even going to tell Agnes about the letter.

With that thought she put down her sewing and marched across the street.

Her uncle was just going out, but one look at her face and he stopped. 'What's wrong?'

'I've had a letter from my stepfather *ordering* me to go home. My mother isn't well – she's expecting a baby – and they need another slave to work in the house. *And I'm not going to do it!*' She burst into tears.

He drew her into the house, winking at Christina behind her back. 'Come into the parlour, love, and let's talk about it.'

When they had her sitting down they offered soothing words, then her uncle said, 'My offer of a passage to England still stands, you know.'

Cathie looked at him, swallowed hard and asked, 'But is there a ship sailing? If I have to wait a month or two he'll . . .' She didn't need to finish her sentence. Benedict could be a very determined man when he wanted something and she wasn't yet twenty-one.

'I believe there is a ship going shortly. I have to keep track of them because of my business dealings.' Which was a lie. Dermott had found out about sailings in case he could persuade her to go. 'I can easily get you a berth. Are you sure about this, though?'

'I am. But I insist on going steerage.'

He hadn't intended to offer her the luxury of cabin class, but made a token protest. 'No need for that, love.'

She wrapped her arms across her chest and stared at him. 'I mean it. I don't want to borrow more money from you than I have to – and one day I'll find a way to pay it all back, I promise.'

'Eh, lass, I don't need it back. It means nothing to me, that small sum.' But he was touched by her offer.

Cathie raised her chin. 'Well, it means a lot to me. I've not been raised to get into debt. It's only because you're my uncle and . . .'

He held up his hands in a gesture of surrender. 'All right, all right. I'll go and book you a passage right away – steerage.' He pretended to hesitate then said, 'You'd better not mention this to Mrs Fenton, though. She'll only try to stop you going.'

Cathie looked stricken. 'I don't like to deceive her. She's been so good to me.'

'Sometimes we have to think of ourselves. I haven't

gone from poor to rich without some effort and, yes, some selfishness too.'

'I suppose so.' Cathie took a deep breath. 'All right, then. I'll say nothing. Mrs Fenton doesn't know about the letter anyway.'

It was going to be hard to keep the secret, but as well as her desire to visit England, Cathie's longing to know who her father was ran deep and had been eating away at her ever since she had found out he was still alive. What if he died before she could meet him? How would she bear that? He couldn't be a young man if he was older than her mother.

No, there was no way out but to accept her uncle's offer. She was never going to work or live on a farm again as long as she lived.

Early the next morning a man turned up at the Dochertys' house, followed by a lad pushing a handcart with a pile of luggage on it. Cathie, who had been staring out of the front room window as she waited for Agnes to get up, saw the man arrive and lingered to watch, thinking how elegant and European he looked. He was not as old as her parents, but was older than she was, though still rather attractive in spite of being barely medium height. He was staring around him with a scornful twist to his lips, as if he didn't like what he saw.

When the two Docherty children saw him, they stopped playing in the garden to screech, '*Tonton*

Matthieu! *Tonton* Matthieu!' and hurl themselves at him.

He swung them up in his arms, one after the other, laughing and teasing them about growing too big for this, then set them down and gave them a little push towards their governess who was smiling and blushing in a foolish way that made Cathie sniff in disgust. The front door of the house opened to show a beaming Christina and the stranger went to kiss her cheek before disappearing inside with his arm round her shoulders.

Cathie sighed. The newcomer must be her uncle's partner from Melbourne. They'd spoken of him a few times. But she was more concerned with how her uncle would go on today. Would he manage to book her passage? Did she really dare run away to England on her own?

She had nearly blurted out her news to Agnes several times and was feeling more weighed down by guilt with every hour that passed. Leaving like that would hurt her mother so much – and her stepfather, too.

Perhaps she shouldn't do it. No, she couldn't bear to go back to the farm and she absolutely *had to* meet her real father! She brushed away a tear impatiently. Her uncle was right. Sometimes you had to act selfishly and do what was right for yourself – but why did that have to hurt others?

'Well, you old devil,' Dermott greeted his business partner.

Matthieu Correntin grinned at him. 'What sort of greeting is that?'

'Would a glass of rum please you more?'

'I'd prefer a cognac.'

'You'll have rum and like it.' Dermott led the way into the parlour. 'I didn't expect you here yet.'

'No. I had to leave Melbourne rather suddenly. Our friends are still annoyed and wanted to take it out on me. Bob Sharpe is going to tie up the loose ends of the business for us.'

Dermott scowled as he passed Matthieu a glass. 'He'll take a percentage for that.'

'*Bien sûr*. But I didn't have much choice. It was get out or risk being killed. And Bob's more or less honest. I offered to work with him if he had any stuff to sell over here. We'll see what comes of that.' Matthieu rotated his shoulders, let out a soft relaxed sound and looked round. 'You seem quite cosy here. Is there a bedroom for me?'

'I'm afraid not. You can't get a decent house for love nor money here in Perth. You can sleep on the sofa tonight, but you'll not want to do that for long.' Dermott eyed the piece of furniture with disfavour. 'It's a damned uncomfortable thing, but this was the only furnished house available to rent – well, the only half-decent one.' He grinned. 'And even so, you should have heard Christina going on about how small it was when she first saw it!'

She sniffed. 'Well, after what we had in Melbourne, can you blame me?'

'The sofa will do me for a few days,' Matthieu said easily. 'Or even a mattress on the back veranda. It's warm enough still to sleep out. We have quite a few matters to discuss.'

'We do indeed.' Dermott drained his glass and stood up. 'But first I have a piece of business to deal with, so I'll have to leave you to enjoy my wife's company. I've discovered a niece, would you believe, and she's staying right across the road. The poor lass is in trouble, so I'm sending her back to England.'

'Your sister's girl? Who's the baby's father?'

Dermott chuckled. 'Not that sort of trouble. No, Miss Cathie wants to run away from home and I'm helping by buying her a passage to England.'

'Which is more than you'll do for me!' Christina said in a voice grown suddenly hard and bitter.

He didn't even look in her direction. It was an old quarrel, though Christina had grown more pressing about it lately. He'd never seen her so upset about anything as she was about moving to the country and she was making all their lives uncomfortable.

Matthieu intervened. 'Why, Dermott? You're not usually a philanthropist.'

'Because it'll upset my dear sister, of course.'

His partner looked disapproving. 'Can you not let this matter of revenge drop, *mon ami*?'

'I'm getting there. We burned their farm down a few weeks ago.'

Matthieu whistled in amazement.

Christina gave a scornful sniff. 'It's gone to his head. Has he told you yet he's now planning to live on a farm he bought because it's near his sister's?'

'Is this true?'

'Aye.' Dermott nodded.

'Another of your wild impulses?'

'I have a fancy to become landed gentry. They tell me it's a good piece of land, with a decent house on it – though madam here will be sure to find fault with it. She's never satisfied, are you, my pet? Wants to go back to England, or Melbourne.'

'I doubt it'll ever be safe for us to return there,' Matthieu said thoughtfully. 'I'm not risking it, anyway. They tried to kill me after you'd left.'

'Ah, we'll see about that. There'll be plenty of room for you at the farm, if you want to stay for a while.'

Matthieu shrugged.

'It looks out on to a small lake, apparently.' Then Dermott glanced at the clock on the mantelpiece and clicked his tongue in annoyance. 'I haven't time to chat now. I've got to sort out my niece's passage.'

Christina put out a hand to prevent him from leaving. 'Why don't you let me travel to England with Cathie? My Aunt Nora keeps writing begging me to visit her. If we want her to leave me her money, I'd better go back before it's too late. We don't want her leaving it to some stray cousin.'

Dermott's expression was implacable. 'When you go back it'll be with me.' He didn't trust her to return to Australia if that aunt of hers really did have as much money as she said. Christina might not be the most comfortable wife in the world, but she was his and she was the mother of his sons. He wasn't letting her go anywhere without him.

CHAPTER 5

FEBRUARY

Late that afternoon Dermott came back from Fremantle looking smug, but as usual the horse he had hired looked jaded and weary. Matthieu watched him ride up the street and thought yet again that his partner must be one of the worst riders he'd ever seen. Dermott sat on his horse like a heavy sack of potatoes, wrenching at the reins whenever he wanted the poor creature to do anything. He took little care of the animals he rode, not even bothering to rest or water them properly on short journeys. When taxed with this, he said their health was the owner's concern.

Suddenly Matthieu could not stand to see it. He erupted out of the house and grabbed the horse's reins. 'What the hell have you been doing to this poor creature?'

Dermott shrugged. 'Riding it. That's what I hired it for.'

Matthieu saw James peering over the fence. 'Fetch me a clean bucket of fresh water – at once, lad!'

Dermott strolled into the house, leaving the

horse's care to anyone stupid enough to wait on a dumb animal.

The boy returned with the bucket and watched as Matthieu tended the poor animal's needs, not allowing it to drink too much too quickly. 'Why *do* you bother doing all that? Da says it's for the livery stable to look after their horses and they're coming to pick it up later, so they can see to it then.'

Matthieu knew better than to tell Docherty's son that it was simply the right thing to do. 'I look after my mounts because you never know when you'll need to get the best out of an animal – same with a man. It makes more sense to treat them well.'

James traced a pattern in the loose sand of the street with one toe as he considered this. 'Da says it's everyone for himself in this world and only folk who let themselves get trodden on deserve it. He says animals don't count.'

'Your da grew up in a harder world than yours, lad. Times are changing. Besides, people notice if you ill-treat your animals and then they don't respect you. It's the same with dogs. That pup of yours would do anything for you if you were a bit kinder to it.'

'It's only a dog.'

'*Oui.* It is only a dog if you treat it like that. But it's a loyal watchdog and even a friend if you treat it well, the sort that'll die protecting you. You can't buy that sort of loyalty with money, only with kindness.'

He watched James slouch off and wondered why he bothered to offer these concealed lessons. But he knew really – because he hated to see children set such a poor example by a mother who alternately neglected or spoiled them and a father who hadn't the slightest idea how to bring out the best in them. The lads always hung about Matthieu when he was visiting, calling him '*Tonton*', the French word for 'uncle', and he felt he had softened their attitude to life a little. It made him smile sometimes to think of himself playing a father's role, for he had got on badly with his own father – though he had at least had a grandfather to care for him and teach him about life, and had not left France until old Hervé Correntin died.

That evening Dermott strolled across the road to thump heavily on Agnes's door. 'Could I have a word with my niece, please, Mrs Fenton?'

Agnes was beginning to wonder what was going on, because Cathie had been very edgy all day and had rushed towards the door the minute she heard her uncle's voice. She turned to look at the girl standing right behind her. 'Come in, Mr Docherty. Is something wrong?'

'No, nothing at all. Only it's such a lovely evening, I thought Cathie might like a stroll into town with her old uncle.'

So Agnes could do nothing but agree, even though it was obvious that this was merely a ploy for them to talk privately. Why hadn't she heard from Liza about the Dochertys? After fidgeting

99

around for a while she wrote another letter to her friend, explaining the situation once again just in case the other note hadn't got through – though the post was pretty reliable these days. Then she went outside and paid a neighbour's lad to take it to the post office.

And why she should remain so uneasy about what Cathie and Mr Docherty were doing she could not think.

Once they were out of sight of Agnes, Cathie stopped walking and turned to face her uncle. 'Well?'

'There's a ship sailing next week from Albany.'

She looked at him in puzzlement. 'My mother's ship came to Fremantle.'

'They did sometimes in the early days and a lot of them got wrecked, too, they tell me – but Albany's the mail port and that's where most passenger ships sail from now.'

'Oh.'

'Don't look so upset. You've time to take the coaster and sail down to Albany in comfort. It leaves tomorrow. If you still want to go to England and meet your father, that is? I'll perfectly under-stand if you don't and—'

She didn't wait for him to finish. 'I *do* still want to go, of course I do!'

'How are we going to arrange it, then? I doubt Mrs Fenton will let you go openly.'

Cathie picked some leaves from a nearby bush

and began to shred them. 'I'll have to find a way to leave without telling her.'

'Matthieu can drive us both to Fremantle tomorrow and I'll put you on the coaster myself. He's a dab hand with horses, that one.' Dermott chuckled but there was no real humour in the sound. 'We'll have to leave very early tomorrow morning, though. Can you slip out of the house at dawn, do you think? And what about your things?' He frowned, thinking it through. 'I've got a trunk I can let you have. Toss your things out of your bedroom window on to the back veranda and after Mrs Fenton's gone to bed, I'll nip round and get them, then your aunt can pack everything for you.'

'I haven't enough things with me to fill a trunk.'

'Oh, I dare say Christina can find you a few bits and pieces of clothing. She never wears anything out.'

'She's much smaller than I am.'

Dermott waved one hand dismissively. 'Well, you can alter them, can't you? It'll give you something to do on the ship.' He remembered his own journey to Australia and that was another reason why he'd delayed going back to England. He'd been seasick a lot of the time and had hated every minute of the voyage. Rotten food. No privacy at all in steerage. Half the time stinking hot, the rest freezing cold. He didn't envy his niece her coming experience.

Cathie considered her escape as they continued

their walk and at one stage suggested they pop into a drapery so that she could buy a few things.

With an indulgent smile Dermott insisted on buying them for her.

As they walked on, Cathie said abruptly, 'Agnes never wakes till late because she stays up till midnight. She says only maidservants needed to rise at dawn. The woman who comes in daily to do the rough housework doesn't arrive till eight o'clock. She won't notice whether I'm in my room or not.' She swallowed hard. It all seemed to be happening too quickly.

Dermott saw her hesitation and said in a jollying tone, 'You're an adventurous lass – a bit like your old uncle, eh? It's natural to want to see something of the world.'

They walked on in silence for a while, then she asked, 'Will you give my mother a letter for me, Uncle Dermott?'

'Aye, of course I will. I'll be travelling down that way in a week or two on business and I'm going to see our Liza to try once more for a reconciliation.'

'I hope you manage to persuade her, but Mum is – well, she can be a bit stubborn and Dad's even worse. I'll give you the letter in the morning.' She would have to write to Agnes as well, Cathie decided. Another pang speared through her. This was not as easy to do as she'd expected.

*　　*　　*

Over the evening meal Dermott boasted to his partner about what he had arranged and Christina crowed with glee.

Matthieu scowled at him. 'You're a nasty devil, Dermott Docherty. What has that poor girl ever done to you?'

'Ah, she *wants* to go to England. She's just found out who her real father is and wants to meet him. I didn't put the idea of going into her head. I'm just – helping her do it.'

Matthieu knew his partner well enough to ask, 'What's the father really like? Is he worth meeting?'

Dermott shrugged. 'He's a bully. He raped my sister, which is how Cathie was born, no doubt. He was a nasty sod in those days and I don't suppose he's improved much with keeping. If he's still alive.' Actually, now he came to think of it, Niall had been paid to drag Liza across the street and hand her over to Teddy Marshall – who had wanted to make certain she'd be forced to marry him. She'd have been about as old then as Cathie was now. For the first time it occurred to Dermott that Niall hadn't been fair to their sister. If he himself had a daughter, he'd kill anyone who raped her. He blinked in surprise. Why was he thinking things like that? He'd never before questioned his brother's behaviour.

'Don't you even know whether this man is alive or not?' Matthieu demanded, horrified.

'How could I? I've never been back.'

'But you're sending that girl halfway round the world to meet him!'

Dermott shrugged. 'What I'm doing is sending her *away* from her mother and father. It doesn't matter a fart to me where she ends up. And Teddy Marshall probably is still alive. He was a tough old bugger. But I'd be grateful if you'd do the driving tomorrow. I don't want anything preventing us from getting her to Fremantle in time.' Those sodding horses sometimes turned stubborn on you.

Matthieu was tempted to go across the street and suggest very strongly to this Cathie that she think again about what she was doing. 'Everything will be very strange to her over there,' he said to Dermott. 'Are you sure—?'

'Oh, Teddy had several sons, so Cathie won't be without relatives even if someone has murdered the old sod.'

'She might not even tell this Marshall fellow who she is if she doesn't like the look of him,' Matthieu suggested.

'Mmm, you're right. I think I'd better send old Teddy a letter telling him about his little girl and suggesting he watch out for her in Pendleworth. It can go over on the same ship as she does!' Dermott laughed heartily.

The frown lines on Matthieu's forehead deepened.

When Dermott went into their bedroom, he found Christina weeping again and she turned her back on him in bed, something that rarely happened.

★   ★   ★

104

In the morning Cathie's departure went smoothly. There was no sound from Agnes's room as her guest crept out along the back veranda in the grey light of early dawn. Cathie paused a minute to mouth a silent and guilt-laden farewell then moved quietly round the side of the small house.

Her uncle had come for her things during the night. She'd heard him as she lay sleepless in bed. Now she found him and Mr Correntin waiting for her at their gate with a trunk on a handcart. 'Your aunt put in a few of her old things as well,' Dermott said as he took the bag holding the rest of her possessions from her and put it on top of the trunk. 'Look sharp now, lass!'

He set off at a brisk pace and she followed, casting one glance back over her shoulder then looking only ahead.

When they arrived in Fremantle, Cathie shivered. 'I hate that jail. It seems to loom over the town, doesn't it? I'd go mad if I was locked up in there.'

'Serve 'em right for getting caught,' Dermott said. 'They're the stupid ones.'

Cathie thought of Dinny's husband Fergal and decided she didn't agree with him, but it was not worth arguing.

Matthieu changed the subject firmly. 'We'll need to get you a ship's kit before you go on board, Cathie.'

'I don't want to cost my uncle any more.' She had no idea what a ship's kit would contain, but was determined not to be extravagant in any way.

'He's right. Come on, lass,' Dermott said, amazed that he hadn't thought of that himself. 'There's a ship's chandler's just down the street. They'll have what we need.'

'We'll get her one of the better kits,' Matthieu said firmly. 'And if you don't want to pay for it, I will.'

'I can bloody well afford it! She's my niece, so you keep your nose out of this.'

Cathie's face was scarlet with humiliation. 'Oh, please don't quarrel over me. I'm sure I can manage without one.'

'*Chérie*, you need the right equipment for a long journey like this,' Matthieu said quietly. 'I've travelled a great deal and I know what a difference it makes.' He tied up the horse and signalled to a lad to come and watch it, then offered his right arm to her with such an imperative gesture that she could not refuse to take it, though she looked back apologetically at her uncle.

Sodding Frenchies always had to be gallant with women, Dermott thought grumpily as he followed them. If he treated Christina that way, she'd soon be ordering him around in the home he paid for.

However, when they got to the chandler's he made sure his niece got the best kit they had, containing bedding, toilet articles, a water bottle, wash basin, jug, plate and pint drinking mug, not to mention three pounds of marine soap.

Matthieu wandered off as Dermott was paying and came back with two smaller packs. One contained writing paper and ink, as well as a diary; the other contained some embroidery silks and a tablecloth. 'You will need something to pass the time during the journey.'

Cathie was overwhelmed by all this and pressed her hands against her hot cheeks. 'I never realised I'd be costing everyone so much! I'll pay you both back one day, I promise.' She had had so little money in her life that it seemed amazing how much these two men were spending on her.

Matthieu laughed. 'You can try, *chérie*, but I shall not let you.'

'Heavens, what a fuss!' growled Dermott. 'All for a few bits and pieces to keep you comfortable.'

They drove down to the quay and found the coaster. Cathie stood at the bottom of the gangway and hesitated as she looked at her uncle. England was so very far away. How would she ever find the money to return to Australia?

For the first time it occurred to her that she might not return, might never see her family again. And that was a truly shocking thought because, whatever their differences, she loved them all dearly. She tried desperately to hold the tears back, but they welled in her eyes and rolled down her cheeks.

'Don't go if you're at all doubtful, *chérie*.' Matthieu ignored the scowl his partner gave him and put one arm round her shoulders. 'You can always catch a later ship, after all.'

But the thought of returning to the farm in

disgrace stiffened Cathie's spine and she shook her head emphatically. 'No, I must do this, Mr Correntin. It's just – it's a big thing to leave your family behind. I shall miss them so.'

Her uncle stared at her as if she'd said something stupid, but Matthieu said quietly, 'I know. I did the same thing myself.'

'And do you regret it?' she asked, feeling torn in a thousand different directions.

He shook his head, not even needing to think about it. 'No. I am not the sort to settle down quietly and follow in my father's footsteps.'

She looked at him for a moment, then nodded. 'I don't think I am, either.'

'*Bien.* What matters most is that this is the right thing for you. It is not, after all, your family who are going to England.'

As she turned towards the ship again, Dermott surprised himself by thrusting a few sovereigns into her hand. 'Here. Take these, lass. You won't want to be without money when you arrive.'

A young woman who had stopped to watch them smiled at Cathie then walked past them.

Matthieu, who had already slipped some money secretly into the parcels he'd given Cathie, stared at his colleague in amazement. Dermott Docherty was normally the last man to perform acts of generosity.

Cathie had no such reservations. She flung her arms round her uncle and gave him a hug such as he had never experienced in his life before, pressing her smooth young cheek against his and saying huskily, 'Thank you, Uncle Dermott! For everything. You've been so kind to me. I'm sorry we haven't been able to spend more time together. Maybe if – when – I come back to Australia, we can get to know one another better.'

He gave her an awkward hug back. 'Ah, y're a good lass,' he muttered.

She walked a few steps, then turned and rushed back, fumbling in her handbag. 'I nearly forgot! This is the letter to my mother.' She thrust a crumpled, sealed envelope into his hand, tried to smile at the two men but failed signally, then hurried on to the ship, without looking back.

As she vanished from sight, Matthieu threw a dirty look at Dermott. 'You shouldn't have done this. It's cruel sending her so far away. *She* hasn't done you any harm.'

Already ashamed of his brief display of weakness, Dermott made a rude noise. 'Ah, she'll be all right. She's got her head screwed on properly, that one has.'

'Sensible or not, she's a naïve young girl who's been brought up in the bush. She'll be prey for anyone and everyone.'

'She's a Docherty. She'll come through. Besides, I gave her some money, didn't I?'

Matthieu frowned. 'Yes, you did. What got into you?'

Dermott gave his rather hoarse chuckle. 'I'm wondering that myself. Must be getting soft in my old age. Come on, let's find ourselves a drink of ale. I've a hell of a thirst on me.'

Several drinks later, he said thoughtfully, 'You know, if I'd ever had a daughter I'd have wanted one like that – only I'd have taught her a few things, not left her so green and ready to be plucked.'

Matthieu had done his best for the girl and was now thinking about his own future. 'When do we go down to look at this land you've bought?'

Dermott grinned. 'When the ship's sailed from Albany. When a sailor I've got keeping an eye out for that lass sends me word she's definitely left with it.'

'I feel like a change. Shall I go down to the farm and look at it for you?'

'Why not? I'll sell it to you cheaply if you like it.' Dermott roared with laughter at his own joke, then looked at Matthieu in surprise. 'You're not joking, are you? I didn't have you figured for a country lover.'

'I enjoy a bit of peace from time to time.'

'Be my guest. There's plenty of peace in the bush.'

Cathie spent most of the daylight hours of the trip down to Albany on deck, not wanting to miss a thing. She could only vaguely remember the trip out from England to Australia when she was five and had heard her mother talk about shipboard life. Now she would experience it all herself. There were only two female passengers travelling alone,

110

the other being the woman who had boarded just before her, so they were sharing a cabin. Bessie Downham was a rather coarse young woman three years older than Cathie and much battered by life.

'When my husband died I decided to go home to England,' she confided the first day. 'Can't stand it out here. Too quiet by half.'

'Do you have family there?'

'If they're still alive. A brother, Nat, in Liverpool. He'll help me settle in again. I'll get myself a job – I used to work in a pub. Nice lively work, that is. It'll seem like heaven after living in the stinking bush.'

That remark alone was enough to win her Cathie's friendship and sympathy.

Bessie didn't mention that working behind a bar had been only part of her duties. The rest had been to accommodate the sailors passing through the port – and steal their money if they were drunk enough. She'd been foolish enough to fall for one of them who was looking for a wife, and had believed his tales about a fine new life in the colonies. Well, that hadn't worked out and he'd been a lying sod about how easy it was to get rich in Australia! Once she'd decided to return to England, she'd written to her brother, who'd pimped for her before, to tell him she was coming back and which ship she'd be on.

She was sure Nat would come and meet her in Liverpool. She'd brought him in some good money before and he'd treated her better than her rat of a husband had. She smiled. They'd not find John's body, not in that godforsaken spot. She hadn't really meant to kill him, had just swung out at him when he forbade her to go back, forgetting she was holding the carving knife and catching him in the throat. A good thing, really, because it had solved the problem of how to get away.

She eyed her companion shrewdly. She had seen the uncle press some money into Cathie's hand and hoped to get hold of some of it before they parted.

When they arrived at Albany Bessie took charge, telling the Matron on the ship that they were travelling together and arranging for them to get bunks in the same cabin. This was a modern ship and had small cabins opening off the main sitting area. Though they were more like cupboards than rooms, Bessie thought sourly, looking round theirs, and the rocking of the boat was already making her feel queasy.

She was so short-tempered that Cathie stared at her in surprise. 'Is something wrong, Bessie?'

'No. I'm just – not a good sailor.' She pressed one hand against her mouth.

By the time the Matron in charge of the single women came past to check that all was well, Bessie was vomiting into a bucket and her friend was helping her, looking very competent. Mrs Jebbings, who had made the journey several times since her husband had died and found acting as Matron an agreeable way of earning a living, made a mental note to keep an eye on Miss Caine. If the weather grew rough, they might need extra help from someone who was good at looking after people.

It turned out that all the single women of fourteen and over shared cramped quarters aft, which Cathie still thought of as the back of the ship. They were four to each tiny cabin, and already Matron had laid down rules about how they were to behave. In the middle of the ship were the married couples and their children, while the single men occupied the foremost compartment towards the bow, which was the name for the front end.

Cathie went up on deck, unperturbed by the way the ship was wallowing, to watch Albany disappear behind them. Bessie was still feeling poorly and had declined to leave the cabin.

Although Cathie was surrounded by other young women, some of whom smiled at her, it struck her all over again how far away she was going. As she stood by the rail she felt more alone than she ever had before in her life. They were mostly travelling with their families but she had no one, really, because you couldn't count Bessie. She had been with her mother and stepfather on her last voyage, with Seth as well, though he'd been only two. It was frightening to be on your own.

As she stared at the faint smudge that was all she could now see of Albany she could not hold back the tears. She wasn't the only one weeping, either.

At that moment, if she had been able to change her mind and go home, she would have done so.

Only she couldn't change things. She was on her way to England now and that was that. She would just have to make the best of it.

By the time she went below again she had calmed down. But she wept into her pillow that night and for several nights.

Benedict arrived in Perth several days after Cathie had left for Albany. Agnes watched him get down from the cart and stride down her garden path, looking grimly determined.

'Where's Cathie?' he demanded as he followed Agnes inside.

'I'm so sorry . . .' Her voice failed her for a moment or two, then she raised her head and forced herself to look him in the eye. 'I'm afraid she's run away – she's on her way to England.'

'What?'

'Benedict, please sit down and let me make you something to eat and drink, then I'll explain.'

He remained standing. 'Explain first.'

So she did, growing increasingly anxious as she saw the grim look on his face. 'I'm sorry,' she finished. 'I've failed you.'

'You have that! I thought we could trust you to look after her. Where's this damned uncle of hers?'

'I saw Mr Docherty go out earlier. I don't think he's back yet.'

'How am I to tell Liza?' he muttered. 'She'll be sick with worry. And how am I to find help for her now? Ilse is having to neglect the children to run the house.'

'Is Liza really ill?'

'Aye. She's gone so thin, except for the baby, that I fear for her life.' He buried his face in his hands and groaned. 'What the hell am I going to do?'

Agnes was weeping openly now but after a while she pulled herself together and went over to take his arm. She had to shake it quite hard to make him pay attention to her. 'I'll come and look after the house and Liza, Benedict.'

'You?'

She nodded. 'I'm not completely helpless, you know. Living in Australia has taught me to look after myself. You'd be surprised what a good housewife I've become.' Though like many other ladies in her position she pretended that the housework got itself done.

'Nay, I can't expect you to do that. You have your own life here.'

She sighed. 'Not much of a life for a widow – and not much money, either, to tell you the truth. Gerard was always a poor manager and he got worse as he grew older. All I own now is this house, and I've been wondering whether to take in lodgers again.' She brightened. 'Look, why don't

115

I come and stay with you till after the baby is born? I can rent this place out for six months and that'll help me financially.'

'Do you really mean that?'

'Of course I do.'

'Then I accept and gladly.'

Agnes looked at him. 'Cathie will be all right, I'm sure.'

He tried to smile and failed. 'She's so young – inexperienced. And we love her very much.'

He agreed to stay the night and allowed Agnes to feed him, but picked at his food and every time someone came along the street he went to the window and asked, 'Is that him?'

When a man of medium height, very neatly dressed, appeared from the direction of the town centre, Agnes hurried out to the gate. 'Good afternoon, Monsieur Correntin.'

He swept off his hat and inclined his head. 'Madame.'

She gestured to Benedict. 'This is Mr Caine, Cathie's father. He wants to speak to Mr Docherty.'

Matthieu studied Benedict, whose expression was grim. 'Dermott is away on business. He may not be back for days.'

'I don't believe you,' Benedict snapped.

Anger crackled between the two men then Matthieu gave a very French shrug, murmured, 'If you will excuse me?' and turned to leave. Inside the house he found Christina peering out of the window at the two people standing talking on Agnes's veranda.

'Benedict Caine's going grey now,' she said in some satisfaction. 'He's really showing his age.'

'You know him?'

'Oh, yes. I came out on the same ship as them. He had eyes only for Liza, even though he was married to someone else at the time, it turned out. And she fancied him, too – but since he wasn't free, she married Josiah Ludlam to give her baby a name – and of course that baby was Cathie. You'd better go and warn Dermott that Caine is here and he should stay away.'

Matthieu sighed. 'I suppose so. I'll slip out the back way.'

The following morning Benedict went across the street and banged on the door of the Dochertys' house. Christina fled to her bedroom with a muffled shriek, so Matthieu opened it.

'Is Docherty back?'

'*Non.*'

Benedict breathed deeply. 'He'll not avoid me for ever.'

'He'll be back in a day or two.'

'I've got to return to Lizabrook. My wife's ill. Tell him he's not heard the last of this, though.' He swung round and went back to help Agnes pack.

They worked until past midnight so that she could leave the place in her lawyer's hands to rent furnished for six months. Luckily, they would be able to carry all her more personal things back with them in the cart.

Even when he did get to bed Benedict lay fretting because it'd taken them two days to get home. He hated the thought of Liza being on her own – even though Dinny was there to help. Never again, he decided. My Liza's definitely not having any more children. She matters more to me than anything else. Or anyone. He could not imagine life without her now.

And he had failed her, failed to look after her daughter properly.

CHAPTER 6

MARCH–APRIL

In Pendleworth Mairi Hamilton stood near the window of the front room, not bothering to light the gas, just gazing out at the moonlit street and enjoying the peace. Her mother was now dozing in front of the kitchen fire, but had had a bad day. There was no doubt in Mairi's mind that she was rapidly getting worse.

Magnus was sitting with her now, ostensibly reading but doing more gazing into the flames. Mairi knew he was worrying about what would happen after she got married the following Saturday. It was so hard to find someone to care for their mother as they would have wished. A few slatternly women who didn't even look clean themselves had applied for the job, but neither Mairi nor Magnus had taken to them, so with great reluctance she had postponed her wedding once.

But she wasn't postponing it again. The Benevolent Home was not all that bad and Magnus would simply have to put their mother in. If Mum had been able to recognise where she was it would be different, but she couldn't even recognise her own children now. All she did was wander round the house, pacing to and fro, often getting very agitated for no reason that anyone could understand.

Mairi knew that even if she were not getting married she could not go on like this. Some women made martyrs of themselves, caring for relatives for years. Much as she loved her mother, she wasn't one of them. She had had several very difficult years and had come to the end of her patience now. She had a life of her own to lead, a man she loved waiting to marry her.

Since Elwyn had moved to Bury they had written to one another almost daily and she missed him dreadfully, but he was coming across to Pendleworth on Friday, ready for their simple wedding ceremony on Saturday. Her heart sang at the thought of moving away from here, of being with him, and of leaving this dreadful, tedious life behind – even though at the same time she was riven with guilt for deserting Magnus. But at least her brother would have Hamish's company and help in the evenings, and they had now found a woman who seemed suitable and was prepared to come in six days a week.

She looked up, smiling as she heard a faint whistling from the far end of the street. That would be Hamish. He always whistled when he was in a particularly good mood. Going back into the kitchen, she smiled at Magnus and moved the kettle over to the hottest part of the range top ready to make their evening cup of cocoa.

The front door banged open and Hamish called out a greeting from the hall.

'Can he not do anything quietly?' Magnus muttered, putting his newspaper down.

'You know he can't. He's young and full of life. I like to see it.'

Hamish breezed in beaming at them both, then grabbed Mairi and waltzed her round the room, humming 'The Blue Danube' in his tuneful baritone.

'Let me go, you daft loon!'

He did, but with another of his great roaring laughs.

'What's got into you the night?' As he flung himself down by the table, she went to brew the cocoa.

Hamish beamed at her. 'The talk at the Institute has got into me, that's what. It sounds wonderful, Australia does.'

Magnus stiffened visibly. 'Aye, well, I'm happy with my own country, thank you very much.' He remembered how sad leaving Scotland had made him and could not imagine wanting to leave Lancashire and everything he had grown to love here.

Hamish stared down at the steaming cup Mairi had just placed in front of him, then blurted out, 'Well, I'm not happy here.'

There was dead silence until Magnus asked with a harsh edge to his voice, 'What does that mean?'

'It means there's no future for a man like me

121

in Pendleworth. It's all right for you. You're foreman in Ludlam's workshop and the apple of Mr Reuben's eye, so you're set for life.' Hamish began to stir his cocoa round and round, slopping it into his saucer. 'I hate working in the mill, but in Australia – why, there's no limit to what a fellow can do out there.'

'Oh, aye? Paradise, is it?' Magnus snapped. 'Canada was the same, but don't you think that Dougal or Athol would have written by now if they'd done well for themselves? Or perhaps they just don't want to share the fortunes they've made with us.' His brothers had borrowed the fare money from him and promised faithfully to repay it, and the fact that they hadn't even written to say they couldn't manage that upset him greatly. Unless they were dead – and the idea of that was even worse.

'Oh, you always look on the black side.' Hamish set his spoon down in the saucer, avoiding Magnus's eyes and adjusting its position carefully, as if it mattered very much that he get it just so.

'Tell us what you've heard the night,' Mairi prompted quietly.

He started to tell them not only about what he had heard, but the sights he had seen on the lantern show. 'The sky's so blue out there. It never snows, you know – well, not in most places. And they're crying out for men on the land.'

'What the hell do you know about farming?' Magnus snapped.

'Nothing. But it's bred in me, isn't it?'

Magnus thumped the table. 'Bred in you! What are you talking about, man? You were born here in Pendleworth. All that's bred in you is a mill town.'

Hamish ignored that comment. 'And while we're at it, there's another thing we need to talk about. Our mother. Once Mairi's left—'

'We'll have Mrs Midner.'

'And if *she* leaves?'

'Then we'll find someone else.'

Hamish groaned. 'Magnus lad, are you out of your mind? We *can't* manage without Mairi. What do we know about looking after a house? And what happens after Mrs Midner goes home at night? I'd die of shame if I had to tend my mother's naked body. I tell you flat I won't do it – and she wouldn't want me to. Besides—'

Her sister closed her eyes and prayed for him to stop but he didn't. He went right ahead and said the things she'd been afraid to hear, for she too had studied the posters outside the Institute and knew what they were offering.

'— I won't be here to help you.' Hamish stared at them both challengingly, his jaw jutting out and his head jerking as he looked from one to the other, then back again.

Mairi spoke before Magnus could. 'You can wait a year to go, surely? Australia will still be there next year. You can give Magnus that much after all he's done for you.'

Hamish gave a quick, tight shake of the head. 'There are people offering to pay your fare out if you'll work for them for two years after you arrive – *and* they'll pay you wages during those two years, as well as your keep. It's a great chance for a man like me to save a bit of money.' He paused then blurted out, 'So I signed the papers tonight. I leave for Australia in about two months.'

With an inarticulate mutter Magnus got up and strode out of the house, leaving the front door swinging open behind him and cold damp air swirling in.

'Did you have to tell us now?' Mairi demanded, getting up to close the door, then coming back to stand next to Hamish, hands on hips. 'Just as I'm about to get married! Couldn't you even let me have a happy wedding day?' Her voice broke and she bent her head, fighting the tears.

Hamish's voice was truculent. 'I've waited long enough. *You're* escaping. Why shouldn't I?' He stared across the room at their mother who was sitting gazing blankly into the fire, humming under her breath. 'She doesn't know what's going on. She's not our mother any more!'

'Magnus won't put her in the Ben. He never breaks a promise.'

'He'll have to now.'

It was two hours before Magnus came home again. They were all in bed, but Mairi was still awake, lying worrying. She heard her brother climb the stairs slowly, as if he were old and weary, and go into the big front bedroom he and Hamish shared, but she didn't call out to him. She knew she was being a coward but she could not face his distress again that night because she did not want to risk giving in to her guilty conscience and saying she'd wait to join her husband in Bury.

In the morning Hamish looked at his oldest brother across the breakfast table. 'Mother would be well looked after at the Ben, you know.'

So Magnus said it all over again, flatly and emphatically, for he had thought it through as he walked the dark streets. 'She's *not* going in there and it's no use telling me she wouldn't know, because it's not true. She still gets distressed if we so much as walk past it. And if none of you will help me to look after her at home, then I will just have to – to manage somehow.' He looked at his sister, eyes softening for a moment, then back at his brother with a stern expression. 'Our Mairi's done her share, more than. Surely you could wait a wee while and do yours now, Hamish?' It was as near as he could come to pleading.

'I'll not. It's not a job for a man. I'd die of embarrassment if I had to wash her and . . . other things.'

'Then you're no brother of mine!' Magnus thumped his fist down on the table.

'Magnus!' Mairi said sharply. 'Don't say something you'll regret for the rest of your life.'

'But he—'

'— has made his mind up to leave. As have I.'

Her voice softened. 'And, laddie, you're wrong about the Ben.'

'I shallna break my word: not for you, nor for anyone!'

But he did not attack his brother again and when Hamish would have spoken, Mairi put a finger to her lips and shook her head at him. Least said soonest mended – if there was any mending possible.

Dermott laughed when Matthieu sent word that Benedict Caine had gone home to his farm and taken Agnes Fenton with him. 'Good riddance to them. I'll see them when I'm ready and not before.'

'I'm going to visit the farm in a day or two,' Matthieu said mildly. 'I may call on the Caines and tell them Cathie was all right, and well equipped for the voyage. They must be worried about her. Have you posted the letter to her mother?'

'I lost it.'

Matthieu stared at him in disgust. 'There was no need for that.'

'I'll judge the need where my sister is concerned. And you might want to stay here for a bit longer, because I've found a bit of business as'll bring us both in a few extra pence.'

The business was profitable, but Matthieu's conscience kept pricking him, so in the end he sat down and wrote a brief letter to the Caines, saying that when Cathie had sailed to England she had been in good health and very excited about her trip. After some hesitation, he signed his name to it. He found out from the tenants who Mrs Fenton's lawyer was and visited his office to find out her present address.

Then there were not only the things Dermott had purchased to dispose of, but the first load of goods from Bob Sharpe in Melbourne, so Matthieu was soon too busy making sure they got the best returns on their investment to visit the farm.

'Bob's done well by us,' he said, once they'd found a suitable warehouse and inventoried the load.

Dermott looked round at the neat stacks of household goods. 'And we've done well by him, too. He's a fool. Could have forced us to give him a higher percentage. He won't even be able to check the prices we get.'

'He wants reliable contacts over here – and besides, he knows I shall not cheat him.' Matthieu gave his partner a very straight look.

'But we could—'

'We'll deal honestly with him – and with everyone else here in Perth. You keep saying you want to be known as a respectable member of the community once you've made your fortune. Well, here's your chance to make a new start.'

Dermott chewed the corner of his lip thoughtfully.

'And don't think you can cheat me, either,' Matthieu added. 'I'll find out if you do, one way or the other, and that'll be the end of our partnership.'

There was a pregnant pause, then Dermott chuckled. 'I expect you're right, lad! I'll get Christina to come and help us. She's better than either of us at dealing with women's stuff.' She'd been in low spirits since Cathie's departure, weeping quite often, which was not like her. Having something to do would take her out of herself.

Matthieu nodded and let the matter drop, but promised himself to keep a very careful eye on what Dermott was doing. And since the Dochertys were not the most comfortable of companions, he found himself some lodgings a few streets away. A man needed a bit of peace sometimes. He was looking forward to getting away for a while to the quiet of the countryside.

Matthieu's letter arrived at the Caines' farm on a warm day in early April just as autumn was beginning to cool the land. Benedict read it through, then passed it on to his wife, saying in a voice choked with emotion, 'Cathie's definitely gone to England.'

Liza read the letter, tears rolling down her cheeks. 'It was kind of Mr Correntin to write.'

'It'd have been kinder still to stop her leaving.'

'How could he if both she and Dermott were set on it?'

With a snort of anger Benedict went out to tend the horses, while she went to tell the rest of the family what the letter had said.

Agnes watched her friend trying to maintain a cheerful front, for the sake of her younger children. *She* did not feel at all cheerful and was regretting that she'd volunteered to come and help here until after the baby was born. There was a sameness to days in this place that was beginning to wear her down. No wonder Cathie had been so desperate to escape.

After some thought, Agnes wrote to tell her lawyer not to allow the tenants to renew the lease on her house as she would be returning to Perth then. When she had finished her letter she went out to sit on the veranda, her favourite place.

Ilse joined her. 'When you go back to Perth' – she hesitated, looked over her shoulder and lowered her voice – 'I wonder if you'd consider taking a lodger again?'

'You?'

'Yes. Benedict and Liza have been good to me, but one does not meet many people living here. I'm not getting any younger and there's a shortage of respectable women there, they say, so—' She broke off, not daring to put her modest dreams into words and dreading the other woman's scorn.

Agnes finished for her '– you'd like to find yourself another husband before it's too late. And this time, one whom you can respect and like, perhaps?'

'*Ja*. Do you think I'm being foolish? Only I'm not ugly or malformed, so I thought . . .'

'I'd be happy to take you as a lodger again and I'm sure you'll have no difficulty whatsoever in finding yourself a husband in Perth.' Agnes smiled encouragingly. 'I even have hopes in that direction for myself. We'll go hunting together.'

That night Liza was wakened by cramping pains in her stomach and a stickiness between her legs. Her groans disturbed Benedict and he lit the lamp. By that time she was doubled up, rolling around in agony. 'Fetch Dinny!' she gasped.

When he had gone, the new bedroom seemed full of shadows and pain. Though she tried to muffle her cries in the pillow, the cramping was growing stronger. She didn't need anyone to tell her she was losing the child and when Dinny came hurrying through the door, started weeping helplessly.

By that time the rest of the household was awake. Agnes lit their lamp and looked at Ilse with whom she was sharing a room. 'Will you go and light a fire while I see if I can help? We'll need plenty of hot water.'

Ilse dragged on some clothes and went out to the small separate laundry at the rear to light a fire under the copper. She had been dreaming of a husband, children, a home. This was the reality for women: both pleasure and pain from marriage. She had failed to find happiness once. Did she dare risk trying again? A memory of the loving glances Benedict and Liza often shared made her nod. Yes, she would risk it.

In the bedroom Liza was alternately sobbing and groaning. Dinny tried to send Benedict away, but he would not leave and, after Liza had lost the baby, he held her in his arms and wept with her.

Relieved that this was taking place in the new house Benedict and Fergal had recently finished and which had proper doors to keep the noise down, Ilse went to sit with Josie. The child was terrified by the thought of her mother being ill, and within a few minutes an equally frightened Harry had crept in to join them. Ilse talked softly to them, telling them one of the fairy stories she had heard in her own childhood, pausing some-times to fumble for the right English word. It seemed a very long time until Benedict came to see them.

The children threw themselves at their father and he hugged them close as he said gently, 'Your mother's lost the baby.'

Josie burst into tears and he spent a few minutes patting her shoulder and assuring her that although this was an unhappy thing, her mother would get better. Harry sat huddled in a heap, so Ilse pulled him into her arms and began to murmur meaningless endearments. As she looked down at the sturdy little body, she knew she wanted children of her own.

When Benedict left them he went to tell Lucas

and Seth, then returned to his own bedroom. He found Dinny holding Liza in her arms, rocking her and letting her cry. She looked up at the sight of him, then said quietly, 'I have something to tell you both. Liza, listen to me.' When she had their attention, she said, 'The baby wasn't growing properly. It couldn't have lived, even if you'd managed to carry it for the whole nine months.'

There was silence then Liza pressed back against the pillows, her arm shielding her eyes. Dinny got up and gestured to Benedict to take her place before leaving the room quietly.

When Liza eventually fell asleep, he left Agnes sitting with her and went to find Dinny. 'Show me the baby!'

So she took him to see the poor deformed infant, with its twisted limbs and over-large head.

He stood there in silence looking down upon what would have been his son. 'Shall I bury him?'

'Not yet. Liza will need to see him, too.'

Two hours later, just as dawn was breaking, Liza awoke and demanded to see her child before they buried it. Dinny brought the baby in to her, washed and dressed in a little gown, its skin almost translucent in its whiteness. But nothing could hide its deformities.

'I want to give him a name!' Liza said suddenly. 'Ambrose.'

Dinny said nothing. Her people had different views on what happened after death but she usually kept these to herself.

Liza lay back and closed her eyes, beyond tears now, so deeply sad she could not think about anything but getting through each minute.

Benedict accepted Fergal's offer to dig the grave because he felt a great weariness as well as a sense of loss, but he made the baby's coffin himself in the new workshop, which had a roof of sorts, but no walls yet.

When evening came he carried his wife outside. Liza sat on a chair in the small cemetery by the lake and watched as he put the tiny coffin in the ground. Around them their other children stood silently and it was a comfort to see them, to know that they had not lost several to the various childhood ailments as so many of the settlers did. Afterwards they all prayed for Ambrose's soul.

When the short ceremony ended Ilse and Agnes shepherded the two younger children back to the house, relieved when they fell asleep, exhausted by their broken night and traumatic day.

Benedict and Liza stayed by the little grave and after a moment or two he sat on the ground at her feet, leaning against her knees, taking comfort from the hand that stroked his hair from time to time. He didn't say anything, nor did she. What could they say at a time like this? They were together and that was the important thing.

When Ilse went into the living room she found Agnes sitting with a glass of port in front of her and accepted a glass herself.

'I don't usually indulge but Benedict offered and it seems appropriate today,' Agnes said quietly.

The two women sat sipping the rich, sweet wine, not saying much but warmed by each other's company. Benedict joined them once Liza had gone to bed and he was sure she was asleep. Agnes poured him a glass too. He shook his head but she insisted. 'Drink it!'

Not until he had taken a few sips and had slumped back in the chair did she ask, 'Is Liza all right?'

He nodded. 'I think so. The funeral ceremony helped a little, I think, but we're both upset.' He stayed for a while then put his empty glass down, almost missing the edge of the table. When he got to bed, he expected to lie awake but fell deeply asleep from utter exhaustion.

Beside him Liza intermittently dozed and stared at the darkness outside the window. She wanted to weep but could not. She wanted to scream out a protest against the fate that had taken her child away from her so abruptly, but everyone else was asleep and this pain was hers more than theirs anyway. Her body felt strange and she missed the comfort of the baby moving gently in her stomach. But he was lost to her now. What would he have been like if he had lived?

As the slow hours passed, her thoughts turned inevitably to her other lost child. Where was Cathie? Was she all right? Then it occurred to her that she had two lost children. There was her son

Francis as well, who had been taken from her when he was a baby. Anguish hit her again in a great black wave. Her second husband had left the guardianship of their son to his uncle, and when Nicholas had been killed that uncle, Alexander Stephenson, had sent her to live with the Ludlams. At first they had let her see her son every day or two – which was no substitute for seeing him every day, caring for him, being able to cuddle him.

When had she tried to take her children and go back to Australia, Saul Ludlam had refused to allow it, so had she told him they were not Josiah's children. He had been so furious about her deception that he had threatened to put her in an asylum so that the secret would never be revealed. When Benedict had rescued her, Cathie and Seth from the Ludlams they had had to leave Pendleworth quickly or face a rich man's wrath. She had not even been able to say goodbye to Francis.

Since then she had paid a lawyer in Pendleworth, a kind man called Bernard Lorrimer, to send her a report on Francis every year, so that she at least knew he was all right. She had saved the reports from the fire among her other treasured possessions. But she had not seen her son for nearly fourteen years, and that was an abiding sadness for her. She tried not to let it show, but she knew Benedict understood when she had one of her sad days.

By the time light streaked the sky and birds

began crooning in the bush, she had taken a resolve and in it she found her greatest comfort for the loss of the baby. She was going to find her other two lost children. She had to, could not rest until she had done it.

As soon as she found out where Cathie was, she would travel to England and make sure her daughter was all right, even if she could not persuade her to come home. Then she was going to find Francis. He was nearly fifteen now. Both Mr Lorrimer, her Pendleworth lawyer, and Sophia Ludlam, Josiah's mother, said he was a fine-looking youngster, tall for his age and very like his father. But Mr Lorrimer also said that his great-uncle allowed him to associate with no one but the Ludlams and the lads from his boarding school, so Francis didn't have any real friends in the neighbourhood.

She could imagine that only too well. Alexander Stephenson, Francis's guardian and great-uncle, was an arrogant man. The boy must be lonely. Well, Liza had been without him for all these years, had wept for him in the darkness of many a night, and now she knew that she would not be healed from this fresh loss until she had seen Francis and made sure he was all right.

Perhaps he needed to see her, too? What had they told him about her? Not the truth, she was sure, which was that Alexander Stephenson and Saul Ludlam had forced her to leave him behind and forbidden her ever to contact him.

★   ★   ★

136

During the voyage to England Cathie had a lot of time to think and all too often found her thoughts turning to her mother and family. She didn't really like having no direction to her life. Oh, there were activities organised on board ship, reading and sewing circles, choirs and concerts, and she joined in many of them, but they weren't enough to use up her abundant physical energy. And although she tried to write a diary, as many passengers did, she kept forgetting and putting it off, so that she had only a few entries.

At the sewing circle she managed to finish her second dress, with the help of a motherly passenger. Cathie intended to save it to wear after her arrival, however, contenting herself with her old worn clothes on board ship.

She had only vaguely remembered the journey from England to Australia when she was five. Her stepfather had travelled to England when his first wife died to ask Liza to marry him and had brought them all back. Now, memories of that voyage began to return. The way you could stand at the ship's rail and gaze out across the water which seemed to stretch for ever. Of standing there on one rough day with her stepfather holding her, the two of them laughing as the ship rose and fell. The way storms howled around the ship. The movements and sounds, because even if the passengers slept, the ship never did. It creaked and groaned and whispered around you.

Bessie hated it and said only desperation had

driven her to come on a ship again, but Cathie enjoyed everything about it, relishing every new experience, thoroughly enjoying talking to anyone and everyone, playing with the children, helping Matron when a lot of people were seasick.

Inevitably she spent a lot of time with Bessie, who wasn't a very nice person but who made her laugh, at least. Having a friend of her own age to talk to was another new thing for Cathie, though some of the things Bessie said shocked her to the core. She had an uneasy feeling that her parents would not approve of her new friend but pushed that thought to the back of her mind and told herself it was because Bessie had been married that she spoke so freely.

The ship stopped to refuel and take on fresh food in Cape Town but the steerage passengers were not allowed ashore, although the Captain arranged for letters to be posted. Cathie sent one to her parents. When she tried to write it she wept so copiously that in the end she could only manage one page. But she was sure they'd be relieved to know she was still all right, and after all her uncle would have passed on her other, longer letter.

Crossing the Equator provided a little light relief, with mock ceremonies in which the First Mate took a leading role.

By now it felt as if Cathie had been travelling for ever and she could not help thinking how terrible it must have been on the longer journey in a sailing ship without auxiliary engines which her mother had experienced when going out to Australia the first time.

As they sailed further north the weather became much cooler, even though it was late spring in England now. Bessie lent Cathie a shawl because she hadn't taken her winter clothes to Perth and the shawls her Aunt Christina had packed for her were light things. She would have to buy herself some warmer clothing once they arrived, and if this was a sample of spring weather, how would she ever cope with an English winter? She had never seen snow, because it simply didn't get cold enough for that at home. Bessie told her snow gave you chilblains and had nothing good to say of it, but in the pictures Cathie had seen in books snow looked beautiful.

'What are you going to do when you get off the ship?' Bessie asked one day.

'I don't know. Get a train to Pendleworth, I suppose, and see if I can find my father.'

'You can stay with me and my brother for a day or two first, if you like,' Bessie offered.

Cathie could not help giving her a hug. 'Oh, how kind you are to me!' She was surprised to see tears in her friend's eyes. 'What's wrong?'

'You an' your soppy words,' Bessie sniffed.

'But you *are* being kind to me.'

Bessie began to sob in earnest and ran off to their cabin.

Cathie gave up trying to understand her friend, whose mood could change three times in as many minutes, and went back to gazing out across the grey-brown northern waters. The closer the ship got to England the more apprehensive she became. Not only were there the problems of where she would live and if she could find employment, but how did you approach a stranger and tell him he was your father? What if her uncle had not been right about this Teddy Marshall anyway? How could anyone be really sure who her father was except her mother?

And, oh, she did wish she had not left Australia this way! What had got into her to make her do it?

When the letter arrived from Cape Town Benedict recognised Cathie's handwriting and wondered whether this would make things better or worse. He went into the living room where Liza was dusting the furniture, working listlessly without any of her old vigour. They were all worried about her. Pulling her down beside him on the sofa, he took her hand, trying in vain to find a gentle way to break the news. In the end he said simply, 'There's a letter from Cathie.'

Liza sat bolt upright, one hand flying up to cover her mouth. It was a moment before she could speak. 'What does she say?'

He held it out to her. 'I thought you'd like to open it yourself.'

She took it from him with a hand that trembled, staring at the handwriting they both knew so well. As the words of the address suddenly blurred and ran together, Liza held it out to him. 'You open it and read it to me. Quickly, please.'

He tore open the envelope and unfolded the single sheet of paper.

Dear Mum and Dad
By now you'll have received my other letter and you'll know that I'm on my way to England. I explained all my reasons in that letter, so I won't go into them again. I just hope you've forgiven me.

He stopped reading to stare in puzzlement at Liza. 'What does she mean? We haven't received any other letter from her – only the one from Correntin.'

Liza could only shake her head and beg, 'Go on! Please.'

The voyage seems very long. I'm not used to being shut up like this and I'll be glad when it's over.

I've made a friend called Bessie. She's a bit older than me and widowed, going back to her family in England. She's invited me to stay with them but I'd rather go straight to Pendleworth. I'll call and see your lawyer and Mrs Ludlam once I'm settled.

I'll write to you again after I arrive. And don't worry about me. I'm fine, truly I am – but so ashamed and sorry that I ran away like

that, because I know it must have hurt you. I
do love you.
*   Cathie*

Liza stared at her husband and picked up the
envelope as if expecting to find another sheet of
paper inside it. 'Is that *all*?'

'She says she sent us another letter. I can't
understand – oh, my darling, don't!' For Liza was
weeping, great sobs racking her too-thin body.
He took her in his arms and when Agnes came
to the door and looked at him with an unspoken
question in her eyes, said simply, 'We got a letter
from Cathie.'

'At last! Is she all right?'

Liza tried to pull herself together, brushing
ineffectually at the tears. 'She's on a ship – going
to England. Only she says she sent us a letter when
she left.'

'Maybe it's time I went and hunted out your
brother,' Benedict said grimly. 'She probably gave
it to him to post.'

'*No!*' Liza clutched his arm. 'You promised not
to. I don't want you going after him. I don't want
to see Dermott again as long as I live.' She had
been having nightmares about him – something
which hadn't happened for years – reliving that
dreadful day when she had inadvertently killed
Niall.

'I didn't like him all that much myself,' Agnes
said, 'though he has a certain rough charm. His wife

is an absolute shrew. You should hear her shriek at the children and she treats that governess of theirs like a slave.'

'I sometimes think we treat *you* like a slave,' Liza said ruefully. 'You've worked so hard since you came here.'

'I've quite enjoyed myself, though I wouldn't like to live here all the time,' Agnes said diplomatically.

'We're so grateful to you,' Liza said. 'I've never in my life felt like this. Always tired.'

'Well, make the most of it!' Benedict teased. 'We're going to have you slaving away for us again as soon as you've recovered fully.' Though he was beginning to wonder if she ever would. It had been weeks now since she'd lost the child and she still didn't look herself, still wept at night when she thought he was asleep.

'That girl's gone off again today, though,' Agnes said. 'She's not very reliable, is she?'

Benedict frowned. 'Brendan's gone off as well. I hope he and Willerin . . .' He broke off, not voicing his concerns. Liza had enough to worry about. But he'd ask Dinny to have a word with Brendan – again.

Later, when they were alone, Liza told Benedict of her determination to return to England and find her daughter.

He stared at her in consternation. 'But we can't leave the farm!'

She avoided his eyes. 'I know *you* can't, but if we ask Agnes and Ilse to help – maybe I can.'

'No! I'm not having you going so far on your own.'

She looked up then. 'I think I need to be on my own for a while, love, need a change of scenery, too. I can't seem to pull out of this – this Slough of Despond.'

He took her in his arms. 'You're the light of my life, Liza. I can't bear to think of you going away.'

'I love you, too, but I need to see Cathie – and Francis. Something tells me he needs me, don't ask me why. I'm not usually fanciful like that. But I shan't be on my own. I thought I'd take Josie with me. I think it'd do her good. I wondered about taking Harry as well, but I decided he'd be better off staying here with you and the other lads. You know how he follows Seth and Lucas around.'

Benedict stared at her in shock. 'You've decided to go, whatever I say, haven't you?'

She looked at him sadly. 'Yes. I must, love. We'll sell another piece of jewellery to pay the fares.'

He struggled to find arguments which would change her mind. 'But we don't know Cathie's address. How will you find her? Hadn't you better wait a while, think it over more carefully?'

'Cathie said she was going to Pendleworth and would contact Mr Lorrimer and Sophia. They'll help me find her, I'm sure. It's only a small town.'

'But the danger? No, I can't let you risk it!'

'Saul Ludlam is dead and I'm sure Alexander Stephenson won't try to put me into a lunatic asylum – especially with Mr Lorrimer to look after my interests.' Liza laid one hand over his. 'Benedict, darling Benedict – I *have* to go. I can't get better, won't feel right, until I've seen them – both of them.'

He pulled her against him, burying his face in her hair, and they sat there together for a long time, not saying anything, just offering unspoken comfort and love. She knew he would let her go. Just as she knew how much they would miss one another.

But that didn't change her mind.

Benedict didn't need to ask Dinny to speak to her son. She was waiting for Brendan and Willerin when they came home from wandering through the woods.

'Go and help Mrs Fenton, Willerin. You should have been with her today.'

The girl shot a worried look sideways at Brendan but left quietly, as always.

'Don't do that again, Brendan!' Dinny said with an edge to her voice that all her children recognised and usually obeyed.

But today he was in no mood to do as he was told. 'Why not? You should be glad I'm spending time with your people.'

'Your people, too.'

'Well, it doesn't feel like it!' He glared down at his arm. 'Whatever colour my skin is.'

She sighed. 'Brendan, Willerin's father left her in my care so that I could teach her about bringing

145

children into the world, as my mother taught me and as Willerin's mother would have taught her if she'd lived. He trusts me to look after her as if she were my own daughter – and you know she's already promised in marriage.'

'To a man she's afraid of, a much older man!'

'That's the custom. You can't change it.'

'If you ask me, customs like marrying young girls off to older men are meant to be broken.'

Dinny kept herself calm only with an effort. 'If you do anything, touch her in any way, they'll kill her as well as you.'

He stopped short and stared at her. 'They wouldn't.'

'They would feel it necessary, believe me.'

He avoided her eyes as he muttered, 'Not if I take her away first.'

'How will you do that? You never manage to save any money. You can't live on dust and air.'

'I'll find a way. If those convicts can manage to escape from Western Australia, surely I can, too?' Only the previous day his father had told him with great relish about the escape from the American whaling barge *Catalpa* of six transported Fenians, political prisoners like Fergal himself had once been, men whose sole crime was to want freedom for their country. He and Brendan had laughed together to think of Irishmen confounding the British authorities like that.

'Those Fenians were white men,' Dinny said firmly, 'and they had help from people in America.

146

You're not white and if you try to leave with Willerin, her family will follow you, hunt you down and kill you both. And they'll be angry with me, too, perhaps punish me as well. When you throw a stone into a pond, son, it makes many ripples.' After a pause, she said firmly, 'I want your word that you'll not touch her, Beedit.'

He stiffened. When she used that special name she had for him, it lent more force to her words somehow. 'Mum, please—'

'And if you don't give me your word not to touch her, and not to go wandering through the woods with her again, then I'll send her back to her father tomorrow. To save her life. And yours. That I swear.'

'Can't she and I even be friends?' he pleaded.

'No. I've seen the way you look at her. She's younger than you, not sure of herself yet, easy to persuade. It's up to you to prevent things going further. Your word, Beedit!'

Fergal had come up behind her but said nothing, leaving this to her. Where their two cultures clashed, as they sometimes did, he left it to Dinny to mark the boundaries.

'All right, I promise!' Brendan flung at them, then turned and strode off into the bush.

Fergal and Dinny exchanged glances and sighed. Their son would not be back for a day or two, they knew. He did this sometimes, simply walked away when he needed time on his own.

'If only I had someone to send him to back

home,' Fergal murmured, taking Dinny into his arms, leaning against her soft warmth. 'A change of scene would be the best thing for him.'

'He'll go away from here one day,' she said sadly, 'and not return. That's why I've perhaps been a bit more lenient with Brendan than he deserves sometimes.'

Fergal held her at arm's length. 'One of your presentiments?'

She nodded, too full of emotion to speak for a moment or two.

'Oh, no!' he exclaimed, for Dinny's visions of the future usually did come true. He hugged her close. They both loved their children dearly, whether they were troublesome or not.

She pulled herself together and went to help Agnes serve the evening meal, which everyone on the homestead took together as long as the weather was fine, sitting at benches along a huge table made from wood felled on the property, under the rough shelter they had built after the bush fire. It would soon be winter, too cold and rainy to do so, and most of them would miss this sociable evening hour. They were like one big family, really, on the homestead, though Dinny knew Ilse and Agnes did not accept her as wholeheartedly as Liza did.

She noticed that her friend was looking in low spirits and didn't need to ask why, having heard about the letter and Liza's decision to go to England. They were both suffering from the rebelliousness of their children.

The two of them went for a stroll afterwards and as they wandered beneath the trees, Dinny sang one of her mother's songs to give them both a little comfort.

Trees, trees, your voices are soft
I can hear the song you sing
When you sing of the moon and stars.
Trees, trees, your voices are soft.

CHAPTER 7

MAY

As Cathie's ship docked in Liverpool, she stared in delight at the buildings. Such huge places some of them, and the city itself seemed to go on for ever to a young woman brought up in the isolation of the Australian bush.

'Ugly old place, ain't it?' Bessie pushed her way through the people at the rail to stand next to her friend.

'Not to me. I think it's beautiful! So many people.' Cathie sighed in delight. 'I can't wait to see more of it.'

'I thought you were going straight to this Pendleworth place?'

'I am. I'll definitely go there first and try to find my father, but I want to see other parts of England as well.' She spread her arms wide. 'London, Bath . . . they all sound so interesting.'

'Well, Liverpool will do me from now on. I was a fool ever to leave it.' As the ship moved gently into its berth beside the dock Bessie squealed loudly. 'There he is! Look, there's our Nat!'

Cathie smiled as Bessie jigged up and down in excitement, shrieking and waving, making as much noise as a whole flock of black cockatoos. The man her friend had pointed out was tall and plump, with rather a cruel face. If you didn't know he was Bessie's brother, you might pass such a man as quickly as you could on the other side of the street. Strange, that.

'Now remember,' Bessie said, linking her arm through Cathie's, 'me an' Nat will see you to the train. We don't want you getting lost on your first day in England, do we?'

Cathie suppressed a sigh. She wasn't a child to need looking after. 'I've got a tongue, haven't I? I can always ask directions.'

'Yes, but there are folk watching out for newcomers to rob them. You stick with us when we get off the ship.'

It was hours before they were allowed to disembark, then they had to wait for their luggage to be unloaded and find a porter to carry it for them.

The minute they stepped out of the big echoing customs shed, Nat appeared beside them, pushing a small handcart. His eyes flickered over Cathie then back to his sister. 'How are you, Bessie love? Had enough of travellin', then?'

'More than bloody enough. I'm never leavin' Liverpool again as long as I live.'

He turned to eye Cathie once more. 'This a friend of yours? Ain't you going to introduce me?'

To Cathie's surprise Bessie seemed nervous. In fact, she'd never seen her friend look so subdued. 'This is Cathie.'

He nodded and this time his gaze raked Cathie's body in a way that made her feel very un-comfortable. 'Pleased to meet you.'

She shook his hand reluctantly and let go of it as quickly as she could.

Bessie clung to her brother's arm for a minute. 'I said we'd see her to the railway station, Nat. She hasn't been on a train before. They don't have them in Perth yet. Talk about backward, that Australia! You've never seen such a nasty place.'

Cathie bit back the urge to defend her home. Everything about Australia wasn't bad, just living in the bush.

'Tell us about it later,' Nat said. 'Let's get your things loaded on my cart. We need to get a move on. I've got a busy evening ahead of me.' He made short work of piling up their trunks and bags.

'I don't like taking you from your work,' Cathie protested, seeking an excuse not to go with them because Nat made her feel uneasy. Even if he was Bessie's brother she couldn't like him, not at all. 'I can manage perfectly well by myself.'

'No, you come with us.' Bessie moved to link her arm in Cathie's and tug her until she started walking.

The girl suppressed a sigh. 'Well, if you're sure . . .'

Nat set off at a cracking pace. 'Keep up, you two. We'll go the back way. It's quicker.'

Bessie flung him a glance full of appeal but when he scowled at her began walking more quickly, still holding tight to her friend's arm.

Cathie was puzzled by this exchange but went along with them. It seemed strange that everyone else was going in a different direction and she began to feel uneasy. As they came to a deserted alley between two buildings she stopped. 'This can't be the right way, Bessie.'

'Oh, it is. It's a short cut. Most folk wouldn't know it, but Nat's worked around the docks quite a lot, haven't you, love?'

'Aye. You two go ahead of me.' He bumped the back of Cathie's skirt with his handcart, so she moved on.

At the end of the alley, Bessie turned right into another one, just as narrow. Here they were completely out of sight of other people. Feeling even more uneasy, Cathie stopped. 'I don't want to go this way.'

Before she could do or say anything else, Nat dropped the handles of the cart and stepped round it towards her.

She backed away, suddenly afraid. 'Bessie?' She could hear how uncertain and wobbly her own voice was.

Bessie began to cry and beg, 'Don't hurt her, Nat.'

He didn't reply, just shoved his sister aside and grabbed Cathie. When she pulled away and began to struggle, he gave her a backhander across the face and she cried out in both shock and pain. After that she began to struggle in earnest, screaming at the top of her voice and calling on Bessie to help her.

But her friend did not move.

Nat cursed as Cathie's fist connected with his face and was followed by a kick which if it had landed on the intended spot would have seriously incapacitated him. As she struggled with him, Cathie continued to scream at the top of her voice.

'Shut her up, Bessie, if you don't want to get caught,' Nat roared, 'then go through her trunk.'

She hung back. 'Please, Nat.'

'Do as you're – ouch! – bloody well told.'

As Cathie screamed again something hit the back of her head and everything seemed to explode around her.

In Pendleworth Hamish looked round the room where he'd slept for so many years, then picked up his last bag and walked downstairs. Magnus and Mairi were waiting for him, both looking sad. 'Well, that's it, I think,' he said, trying to sound calm but not feeling it.

Mairi burst into tears and flung herself into his arms, hugging him convulsively. 'You will write, won't you? Promise me you'll write.'

'Of course I will.' Hamish was struggling to hold back his own tears. He hadn't expected it to hurt quite so much to leave them.

She sobbed against his chest. 'Athol promised to write. So did Dougal. But they didn't keep their promise.'

'Well, I definitely will.' He put his hands on her shoulders and moved gently back from her embrace.

Drawing in a deep, ragged breath, he turned to the brother who had been more like a father to him. The two of them exchanged long glances which said more than either could have put into words, then Hamish squared his shoulders and said gruffly. 'I'm ready now.'

Magnus nodded. 'Aye, then. So am I. You'll want to kiss our mother goodbye, will ye not?'

With a sigh Hamish moved across to the figure rocking gently near the fire. 'Goodbye, Mother.'

She didn't turn, didn't even show she'd heard him. More to appease Magnus than anything else, Hamish gave her a quick hug. But his touch made her whimper and pull away, so he moved quickly backwards again. As far as he was concerned he'd said goodbye to his mother several months previously when she'd stopped recognising him. The warm, loving person who had once inhabited this body was no longer alive, and even being in the same room as her made him feel uncomfortable now. It would have been kinder if God had taken her cleanly rather than letting her linger like this, a mindless doll-thing. He was glad he'd not have to watch her any more and glad, too, that Mairi had got away. Surely it wouldn't take Magnus long to discover that he could not manage on his own?

As he left the kitchen and walked down the narrow hallway, Hamish resolved that he would remember only the old mother, who had been lively and full of fun.

Magnus turned at the kitchen door to ask,

'You're sure you'll be all right today, Mairi? I can still stay behind if you . . .'

'Of course I'll be all right. I don't have to leave till this evening and if you're late Mrs Midner has promised to come in. You should have plenty of time to get there and back, even with the Sunday train services. And you know full well you want to go with Hamish to Liverpool and see him safely on the ship.' Elwyn understood that she was glad to look after their mother occasionally, that it assuaged her guilt about leaving Magnus with the burden of daily care.

Such a wonderful man, her big brother – though he grew embarrassed if you tried to tell him so. She wished he could meet a woman, get married and have the normal family life he deserved. Why was he so determined to waste his life caring for a woman who no longer even recognised her own children? However, since nothing would change his mind about that, Mairi intended to continue coming over to Pendleworth now and then to give him some respite, even if only for a few hours. She knew better than anyone how wearing their mother could be, day in, day out.

Blinking her eyes in a vain attempt to rid them of tears she looked round and decided to give the place a good clean-through while she was here. That would mean tying her mother to the rocking chair, because you couldn't take your eyes off her for a minute nowadays or she did things which harmed herself as well as others.

This time tying her up meant a struggle for Mairi, who ended up sobbing in the other chair with a bruise and scratches on her face, while her mother moaned and tugged against the soft bonds that held her.

After a while, Mairi dried her tears and got started on the cleaning. But she felt sad all day. Her mother seemed to be worse each time she visited Pendleworth.

The two brothers were silent as they walked to the station carrying the big tin trunk between them, with canvas travelling bags in their other hands.

'Are you sure you should be coming with me?' Hamish asked yet again. 'You'll be exhausted tomorrow.'

'I want to come. Don't you want me with you?'

'Of course I do. I just – was worried about you.'

'Aye, well, and I'm going to be worried about you for a while now.'

There was silence, then, as the train pulled out of the station and passed the big mass of Ludlam's mill, Hamish laughed. 'I shan't miss that place.'

'I enjoy working there now that Mr Reuben is in charge of the workshop. He's much more reasonable than his father,' Magnus said mildly. Things had changed greatly since old Mr Ludlam's sudden death from a seizure ten years previously, and mostly for the better. Saul Ludlam's widow was still alive, though, living in a small house of her own out at Ashleigh and appearing happier than she'd ever done while her husband was alive. Everybody said so. Magnus passed her house sometimes when he went out walking and always received a nod and a greeting if he met her. She knew a lot of the men who worked at Ludlam's by sight and still helped their families if they were in trouble.

In Liverpool they made their way to the docks. Magnus had been here before to see off his other brothers and it brought back sad memories that made him close his eyes briefly. Like Hamish, they had been full of hope and suppressed excitement, looking round them as if they were children out for a treat.

And they hadn't written once! Would Hamish?

At the customs shed the two brothers hugged, then Magnus stepped back and let Hamish follow the porter inside. When his brother turned at the door to wave to him, Magnus called 'Good luck!' but wasn't sure his words had been loud enough to be heard above the noise and bustle. He raised his own hand, trying to force a smile on to his face, but couldn't manage it, so waved a couple of times, then swung round and strode away.

His eyes blinded by a sudden rush of tears, he looked for some private corner where he could get his emotions under control once more. A man did not weep in public.

When he found a narrow alley, he turned into it with relief, feeling almost overwhelmed by the

158

pain of losing his third brother and the thought of going back to live alone with his poor demented mother.

Gulping back the unmanly sobs he moved a little way down the alley, so lost in his own grief that it took him a minute or two to realise that somewhere nearby a woman was screaming for help. He glanced quickly round. At one end of the alley people were hurrying past, not seeming to hear the screams.

He ran quickly to the blank wall at the other end and saw a young woman fighting off a man who seemed to be attacking her. Another young woman was hovering nearby. Even as Magnus watched she picked up a half brick and used it to clout the struggling female on the back of the head. As the woman collapsed, the one who had hit her tugged a big trunk off the cart, stepping hastily backwards as it thumped down near her feet, then pounding at its padlock with the brick. She didn't even turn to look at her victim, whose skirts the man was now lifting.

'Hey!' Magnus roared, realising the thief was intending to rape as well as rob her. He began to run towards them. Fury filled him, for he loathed violence and thievery – but there was also a savage delight at the prospect of venting his emotions. He had not fought very often because other men were afraid of his size, but just occasionally it had been necessary and he had always given a good account of himself.

The man and woman looked up in shock then the man picked up the handles of the cart and shoved it past the unconscious victim, while his accomplice tried to pull a handbag off the victim's arm. But as Magnus continued to run towards them she pulled something out of it instead and fled after her accomplice.

Magnus ran a little way after them.

The young woman looked over her shoulder and shrieked that they were being followed. The man stopped, snatched a piece of luggage from the top of the cart and threw it at Magnus with such force that it sent him stumbling backwards, flailing to keep his balance. The two attackers took off running again, disappearing round a corner with the handcart rattling and squeaking.

Deciding it would be wiser to remain with the unconscious woman to protect her from further attacks, he picked up the piece of hand luggage and went back to where she was lying, worried that she had not moved at all.

He knelt by her side. Had they killed her? Her face was badly bruised and there was blood matting the hair at the back of her head. He bent closer to check if she was still breathing and heaved a sigh of relief when he saw her chest rising and falling. Her cheeks were bone white and the bruises shockingly blue against the soft, fair skin. She would be quite pretty normally, he guessed, and was neatly dressed in the sort of clothes his sister wore. Respectable, the sort who had to earn her bread. For some reason, that touched him more than if she had been a fashionably dressed lady. Why had they been attacking her? Surely they did not think she was worth robbing?

'Miss! Miss!' Still kneeling beside her, he shook her shoulder slightly.

She didn't stir.

He looked around but there was no one in sight. Indeed, if the attackers came back with any companions, he could still be in trouble. He dragged the trunk across, positioned it carefully, then picked the young woman up and sat her on it with the smaller bag on her lap. He let her limp upper body fall back against him and then, grunting with the effort, began to drag the trunk and its burden slowly along the ground. It was hard work and a lesser man might not have managed it but he was grimly determined. All the time he kept glancing along the alley, afraid her attackers might return with reinforcements.

It was a relief to turn the corner and see people passing by. As he got to the street end of the alley he glanced back over his shoulder and saw the man who had robbed the girl step out from the corner and stand there, hands on his hips and a furious expression on his face. There were two other men behind him. When they saw Magnus staring at them, the newcomers dodged back out of sight and the attacker shook his fist before following them.

Magnus looked down, wondering what to do next.

People were hurrying past them. Some glanced at the unconscious woman but none stopped to offer help. He propped the stranger against the wall and when he saw some ship's officers approaching moved to intercept them.

'Excuse me, gentlemen, but this young woman has been attacked and robbed and I need to find a policeman. Can you help me?'

One grimaced and said resignedly, 'I'll go and report it to the dock police. You stay here with her till they come.'

When Magnus turned back the girl was stirring.

A woman passing by said to her companions, 'Disgusting, I call it, to be drunk like that.'

'Madam! She's not drunk – she's been attacked,' Magnus protested.

The woman gasped and scurried away as if she might be assaulted herself.

'You'd think someone would stop and help!' he muttered. As he knelt beside the young woman, her eyelids fluttered open but she could not focus properly.

'Bide still, lassie,' he said gently. 'You've been hit on the head. Let yourself recover slowly.'

She let out a long trailing sigh and asked, 'Who – are you?'

Her voice was low and to his ear pleasing. He did not like shrill women. 'My name is Magnus Hamilton. I was passing and saw you being attacked, so came to your aid. I'm afraid they got some of your luggage.'

She made a mewing sound in her throat then tried again to focus on him. 'I can't see properly. Are there – two of you?'

'No, there's only me. You've had a thump on the head and it'll take a while for you to recover. What's your name?'

She blinked at him. 'It's—' Panic suddenly filled her face. 'I – can't remember!'

He patted her hand. She was a sturdy young woman with strong, capable hands. He liked her looks – well, he would have liked them normally, when she was not pale and dishevelled. 'That's all right, lassie. Just give yourself time to recover.'

She closed her eyes for a moment, then opened them to ask, 'Magnus, did you say you were called?'

'Aye.'

'You're Scottish.'

'Aye. And you?'

But again she shook her head and looked at him with haunted eyes. 'I can't remember *anything*.'

'It'll come back to you bit by bit. I was hit on the head once and it took a few days for me to remember why I'd been fighting.' He smiled reminiscently. 'When I did remember I went after the one who'd hit me from behind and made him very sorry.' He hesitated. 'There were a man and a young woman attacking you and she hit you on the head with a brick.'

She put one hand to the back of her head and winced. 'It hurts.'

He took the hand and clasped it in his own, finding it cold and clammy. 'We should be getting you warm. Where is that damned policeman?'

She seemed to lapse into semi-consciousness again and he could only crouch there and worry about her. It seemed a long time until a policeman came into sight, scanning the crowd until he saw them then hurrying forward.

As Magnus was explaining what had happened, she regained consciousness again and muttered, 'My head hurts.'

'We'd better get her back to the station,' the policeman decided.

'We're going to need help, then,' Magnus muttered. 'If we leave her luggage here, it'll be taken.'

A ragged fellow who had been watching agreed to help the policeman with the trunk and the bag, while Magnus pulled the young woman to her feet, drew one of her arms round his neck and helped her to stagger along. If he hadn't been there, she'd have fallen. As it was, he was more than half-carrying her.

At the police station they were taken into a small room, where they tried to question her. Even though she had not lapsed into unconsciousness again and had even regained a little colour in her cheeks, she still could not remember anything at all about the attack – or even her own name.

After gesturing to Magnus to join him outside, the policeman asked in a low voice, 'Do you know the young woman, sir?'

'No, I just happened to come along in time to save her.' He explained how the man who'd attacked her had returned with two other fellows.

'She's very lucky you intervened, and I congratulate you on doing your civic duty, sir. I'll write a report on the incident, but I don't know what we're going to do with her till she recovers. There's nothing in her handbag to say who she is. I think we'll have to put her into the poor house till she regains her senses – if she ever does. You can never tell with blows to the head. She might be damaged for life.'

Magnus had a sudden image of the Ben and this lassie stuck in a similar place among the drooling idiots. It was none of his business and he could never afterwards explain what made him do it but he found himself saying, 'Not that!'

The policeman shrugged. 'If there's no one to take care of her, what choice do we have, sir? She can't be turned loose on her own, and let alone she doesn't know who she is, they've taken all her money. We'll break the padlock on that trunk tomorrow and see if there are any more clues, but there's only me here on a Sunday and I have other things to see to.'

Magnus thought of the young woman with her poor battered face. She was younger than his sister, and at the moment, alone and defenceless. He smiled in relief as the solution came to him. 'I'll take her home to my sister. Mairi will know what to do.'

It was not quite as easy as that. First he had to give details of himself and prove who he was. Then he had to sign some papers. Finally the constable said that all the information would be passed on to Pendleworth Police Station and as soon as the young woman remembered what had happened, she was to report to them.

It was only then that Magnus looked at the clock and realised how late it was. He hated the extra expense but there was no way to avoid it. 'Is there anywhere I can find a cab? I've a train to catch. I'm going to be late home as it is and my sister is expecting me.'

'The ladies do worry if we're late, don't they, sir?' the Sergeant said sympathetically. 'But I'm sure your sister will forgive you when she sees this poor young woman and hears what happened.'

But the cab was slowed by a tangle of vehicles and didn't arrive at the station until some minutes after Magnus's train had left. The driver helped him find a porter and unload the young woman's trunk, then they had to wake her and persuade her to get out of the cab.

It being Sunday, it was an hour and a half until the next train. They sat on an iron bench and the young woman fell asleep with her head on Magnus's shoulder. He sat beside her, his annoyance at the delay subsiding and a wry smile taking its place as he listened to her breathing as softly as a baby. Her lashes were very long and as dark as her hair, which was in a sad tangle.

Two ladies walking past frowned at them in disapproval. Already he was regretting his impetuousness, but it was too late now to do anything but take the lass home with him. Well, he still couldn't bear the thought of them putting her in the poor house. Once you were inside those places you had trouble getting out again.

After sleeping uneasily for half an hour she woke with a start, staring at him fearfully and then looked round in bewilderment.

'It's all right, lassie,' he said gently, not attempting to stop her from drawing away from him. 'You've been attacked and you're not feeling well, but I'm taking you home to my sister. Mairi will help you better than I can.'

She gazed at him doubtfully then her face cleared and she managed a small, uncertain smile. 'You're very kind – Magnus. You did say you were called Magnus?'

'Well, you've remembered my name at least,' he said softly. 'I dare say after a good night's sleep you'll remember your own, too.'

'It all feels strange, as if nothing is real.' She sighed and snuggled against him so that he had to put his arm round her again. 'Perhaps this is just a dream,' she murmured. 'But you're nice.'

He smiled down at her. What must it be like to regain consciousness and remember nothing? Perhaps they could find out who she was from her trunk? He realised suddenly what that probably meant. A trunk and her down at the docks . . .

she was either just leaving the country or just arriving. Which one was it? He found himself hoping she was arriving, which was a silly thing to hope for when it was no business of his, but if so, why had no one met her?

Once she had remembered who she was, she'd go on to wherever she had been heading and he would probably never see her again. And if she didn't remember? a faint voice asked inside his head. What would happen to her if she didn't remember who she was? Well, he'd deal with that when it happened. For the moment he needed to get home as quickly as he could because he couldn't remember what time the last train went for Bury.

He had to wake the lassie to get her on the train and tip a porter for helping him get her trunk into the luggage van.

When they arrived at Pendleworth it was getting dark but at least she had recovered enough to stand up on her own while another porter helped him unload the trunk and find a cab to take them home. Another expense. If he went on at this rate, he'd have no money left.

There was a light on in his house and he sighed in relief at the thought of turning his charge over to his sister. After paying off the cab he dragged the trunk to the front door, surprised that Mairi hadn't come out to help him. She was usually watching out for him. As he reached for the handle the door opened. 'Mairi, I—' He looked up and saw Mrs Midner.

She stared at the stranger standing beside him, then looked back at him with disapproval writ large on her face. 'Your sister had to go home, Mr Hamilton. She thought you might have missed the train and paid me to come in to mind your mother. It's not what I like, working on the Lord's Day, and your mother's been in one of her funny moods. Did you meet a friend?' Her eyes went back to the stranger.

'This lassie has been hit on the head and doesn't remember who she is. I was going to ask Mairi to help her. Could you perhaps—'

A sour expression came over Mrs Midner's face and she folded her arms. '*I* can't do anything more today. I have to be getting home. My husband doesn't like me working on a Sunday and I only did it as a special favour because your Mairi was going to miss her last train if I hadn't come in. And I don't know what *you* think you're doing bringing strange young women home, Magnus Hamilton, I really don't. You must have taken leave of your senses as well as your brother today.'

'But she's—'

The woman pushed past him and hurried away, leaving him standing there with the stranger. He looked up and down the street, wondering about getting some other woman to help him. But there was no one outside at this time of day and most of the houses were dark. In the end he helped the lassie inside, installed her in his own armchair opposite his mother and went back to bring her things in. Well, he assumed they were hers. She didn't even know that.

When he returned to the kitchen the lassie had drifted off to sleep again and his mother was stirring the fire mindlessly, letting coals fall on to the rag rug which was smouldering and smelling of scorched wool. He rushed to snatch the poker from his mother's hand and she screamed at him, a mindless sound, then began to beat at him.

The stranger woke with a start and jerked upright, gaping at them in shock.

'What's wrong with her?' she asked once he'd got his mother a bit calmer again.

'Old age. Softening of the brain, the doctor calls it. She doesn't mean to do foolish things. She can't help it.'

The young woman came to stand beside them. 'There, there. It's all right,' she said soothingly.

Janey blinked at her and stretched out one hand to paw at the stranger's face and touch the dark hair, which seemed to please her. She then allowed herself to be seated in the chair and began to rock to and fro, crooning to herself.

'I'm sorry,' the stranger said with a blush, 'but I need to use the – the necessary.'

'It's down the back of the yard. Take a candle with you.' He gestured to the end of the mantel-piece. 'I'd come and show you the way, but I daren't leave my mother.' He sat down for a moment, feeling weary beyond measure and worrying about what to do with his unexpected guest.

After a few minutes the back door banged shut and she came in, rubbing her forehead as if it hurt. 'I'm sorry. My head aches so badly I can't think properly.'

'You need to rest. You can stay in my sister's old room, if you like. I have to lock my mother in the small bedroom or else she wanders the house. She doesn't seem able to tell night from day now. And she may call out, but just ignore it if she does.' He was going to ask the doctor if there was a stronger medicine to give her at night.

The young woman was staring at him owl-eyed. 'I don't feel I know you.'

'You don't. But you had nowhere else to go and I thought my sister would be here to help you. Only she'd already left. The trouble is, it's too late to find you somewhere else to go and I really can't leave my mother alone. Are you hungry?'

She was swaying on her feet. 'No. I'd like a drink of water, but what I really need is sleep.'

He glanced at his mother who was leaning back staring at the ceiling, then led the way upstairs. 'This is my sister's old bedroom. My mother sleeps in this one and the other is mine. I'll bring your trunk up once I've got Mum off to sleep.'

When he got downstairs he found that his mother had picked up the poker again and was staring at the fire as if it fascinated her. He took the poker out of her hand and drew her into the

171

hall, murmuring soothingly as he left her standing there. Keeping an eye on her, he began to heave the trunk up the stairs. After shoving it into the stranger's bedroom, he nodded and ran back down to his mother.

She was pacing up and down the hall now, in a strange mood, beating one hand against her thigh as she walked. She no longer talked any sense at all, just uttered disjointed phrases. This upset him, remembering how she had loved to chat in the evenings.

He was feeling ravenous, so he made some porridge, then fed his mother and himself alternate spoonfuls from the pan. He had to put the food into her mouth, for she just sat and looked at the spoon in her hand as if she didn't know what to do with it. His own food tasted like bitter ashes in his mouth and he'd have pushed it aside but he needed to keep up his strength.

Then, just as they were finishing, his mother looked at him, really looked at him, and for a few moments her face was her own again. She raised one hand and stroked his cheek, a gesture she had often made when she was herself. Though the light faded from her eyes soon after, the incident heartened him. It was such moments which kept him going, made him sure he was doing the right thing in not locking her away.

After he'd cleared away the dishes he got his mother ready for bed. He hated having to deal with her so intimately and always felt embarrassed, but it was no use getting upset. It simply had to be done.

By the time he had given her the sleeping medicine and got her to bed, he was bone weary. He paused outside the visitor's room, listening, but there was no sound coming from it. He hoped she was all right, but did not like to go inside to check in case he frightened her.

What had he got himself into? he wondered as he got undressed. Wasn't his life difficult enough without taking on a stranger's problems? The tears he had been fighting all day welled in his eyes again and he brushed them away impatiently with the back of one hand. But a sudden memory of Hamish as a little lad – such an eager, energetic little fellow – brought a lump to his throat and he had to brush away another tear. He was going to miss Hamish; well, he missed all his brothers. And what he would do with himself after his mother died, he didn't know.

Would he try to find a woman then and marry? Maybe. But he was shy with women and had never been able to joke with them and tease them as other young men did. He knew he was too serious for most folk's liking. And being so tall was a problem, too. You grew tired of looking down at people.

The stranger was quite tall for a woman.

He clicked his tongue in exasperation at himself. What was he doing thinking about her again? She'd probably remember who she was within a

day or two and be off to join her family. Or someone would report her missing and the police would
direct them to Pendleworth.

A great yawn overtook him and he got into bed.
Time enough to worry about this bizarre situation
in the morning. For once he was too exhausted to
lie there and worry, but fell instantly into a heavy
sleep.

CHAPTER 8

MAY

In the end, several weeks passed and Matthieu's longing for some peace and quiet grew even stronger. 'I've nothing pressing to do here,' he declared one day, 'so I'll go down to the farm on my own, if you don't mind?'

Dermott shrugged. 'Whatever I decide to do with the place it needs keeping an eye on, so that suits me. We don't want squatters walking in and thinking they can just settle there.'

'*Bien*. I shall set off as soon as I find myself a spare horse.' The idea of living quietly in the countryside for a while was surprisingly appealing.

Matthieu rode south one chilly winter morning in June, riding a neat bay mare with a comfortable gait and leading a sturdy pack horse. He intended to take his time about the trip. The plants of the bush fascinated him, they were so different from those in France, and here they were different even from those in the east of Australia.

He camped out on the first night, humming as he cooked a piece of steak, glad of the crackling warmth of the fire and enjoying his own company.

Lying warmly wrapped in blankets looking up

at the brilliant stars overhead, different from those he had seen in the northern hemisphere, he let out a long breath and wondered why he still could not decide where to go next. Wondered, too, how he had got himself so closely involved with Dermott Docherty, who had plenty of easy charm when he chose to use it, but who was undoubtedly a rascal.

Morning dawned crisp but fine and as he set off Matthieu found himself singing a song of his youth, '*Auprès de Ma Blonde*'. He had always been attracted to blonde women for some reason.

He turned left at a signpost to Brookley, surprised when he got there to find it consisted of half a dozen houses only, widely spaced, each surrounded by gardens and work areas of various types. Why had Dermott not checked more carefully before buying a house in a place like this? He stared up and down the sandy street before going inside a neat little inn where he was served a tasty stew with large chunks of beef in it that reminded him of the *boeuf en daube* his grandmother had sometimes made in his youth.

The inn had a tiny shop at one side of the main room, hardly more than a large cupboard with shelves of basic provisions: barrels of flour, sugar, currants, salt and a cask of rum. Staple provisions for settlers, these. He smiled as he studied the contents of the shelves. No one, it seemed, earned their money in only one way in this country.

After the meal he bought some fresh foodstuffs

to supplement his flour and the kangaroo meat he would kill for himself, and asked directions to the house.

'Oh, the old Bailey place.' The rather genteel landlady came outside with him and pointed along a narrow track opposite the inn. She looked hopeful. 'You and your family are coming to live here?'

He shrugged. 'Who knows? It was my partner who bought it, but he and his wife are too busy to move down here yet, so I've come to check that everything is all right.'

She smiled faintly. 'It should be. We don't get many people passing through Brookley.'

He rode off along the track, looking up at the sky, which was clouding over now, and wondering what the hell he was doing in such a lonely place after the pleasures of Melbourne. The horse stumbled suddenly, throwing him, and next thing he knew he was sprawled on the ground feeling shaken, which served him right for not paying attention.

From the distance a voice called, 'Are you all right?' and when he looked up he saw a woman and girl running along the track towards him.

He tried to pull himself together, but did not feel like sitting up yet. *Merde!* his head hurt. He must have bumped it on something.

'Don't try to move.' The woman knelt beside him, holding his shoulder with a slim, elegant hand and staring earnestly into his eyes. 'Does your head hurt?'

He stared back at her, enjoying her touch. It had been some time since he'd been near a lady. Unlike women of pleasure, this one radiated an air of cleanliness and smelled of soap and lavender, a strangely heady combination in the middle of the Australian bush. And she had the softest blonde hair he'd ever seen, so light in colour it was almost silver. She wore it simply in a chignon, without the frizzed fringes so popular with many women, which he detested. 'I will be all right in a minute or two.' He closed his eyes for a minute trying to gather his senses.

The child hovered nearby, jigging about from one foot to the other. 'Who is he, Frau Hebel?' she whispered. 'Why does he speak like that?'

'He's French, I think.'

So this woman wasn't the child's mother, Matthieu thought, and she was German which explained her slight accent. Not wanting to appear helpless, he managed to sit up and smile at the child. She was a scrawny little thing, pale and freckled with reddish-brown hair, but her eyes were very pretty and she had an alert, intelligent look to her. 'I'm Matthieu Correntin. And I am indeed French.' He inclined his head then winced as it throbbed.

'I think you should sit still, Monsieur Correntin,' Ilse said, worried by how pale he was. 'Josie, go and catch the gentleman's horses before they wander off.'

'One of them's limping, poor thing.' The child

went and caught hold of the reins of Matthieu's mount, whispering to it and rubbing its nose, then leading the two animals slowly back.

He decided he could not appear at his best sitting on the ground and tried to stand up, but his head spun and he would have fallen had she not knelt to support him. He summoned up his small store of German to apologise. '*Entschuldigen Sie, bitte, gnädige Frau.* I shall have to rest a moment longer before I move.'

'*Ça ne fait rien,*' she said, speaking his language far more easily than he had spoken hers. 'Perhaps I should send Josie home to fetch help?'

How long had it been since a woman had looked at him with such concern, not simply assessing the state of his wallet but caring about him as a human being? Matthieu leaned against her shamelessly, breathing in that crisp linen-and-lavender smell with deep appreciation. '*Mais non!* I shall be all right soon, I'm sure.'

Her face was very close to his as she reached out and with firm, slim fingers turned his head slightly better to study his face. '*Il faut se reposer un peu, Monsieur.*'

Her accent was flawless. '*Vous parlez bien français, Madame.*'

'*Un peu seulement.* There isn't much chance to use it here.'

He smiled. What luck! He had been hungry for the sound of his own language lately. 'Your accent is good.'

179

She smiled back at him. 'I have some facility with languages, monsieur. It helps me gain employment as a governess.' Not that she used them much. Liza said frankly she preferred Josie and Harry to concentrate on getting their own language right before they learned any others, though Josie had insisted on learning a few French and German words for the fun of it.

'You are a governess? I thought you were – married.' He couldn't keep the surprise from his voice. She didn't look like a governess. They were, in his experience, dowdy women while this one was elegant in dress and graceful in even the slightest movement.

'Widowed,' she said curtly, hating even to think of Johannes now. 'I work for the Caines and—' She broke off. 'What's the matter?'

'I – um – moved my head suddenly.' Damnation! Why did she have to work for that family of all others? He gave a sniff of wry amusement. Fate was like that, giving with one hand, taking away with the other.

'Dad's coming!' Josie called and ran back along the track to grab her father's hand. 'This gentleman's had an accident and he's hurt his head.'

Matthieu got to his feet, helped unobtrusively by Frau Hebel and wondering what her first name was. He liked the fact that she was almost the same height as him, liked the clean lines of her face with its straight nose and pale skin, and relished the air of respectability that was stamped all over her. He had had enough of whores. Quickly, before Caine got close enough to hear, he whispered, 'Frau Hebel, this is not the way I would have wished to make your acquaintance. But be sure that we'll meet again under happier circumstances, I shall make certain of that.' He noted with satisfaction the delicate colour that tinged her cheeks then he turned. 'Monsieur Caine, we meet again.'

'Mr Correntin.' Benedict stared at him, wondering what the hell the fellow was doing here. Noticing the bruise on his forehead and the slightly glazed look in his eyes, he felt obliged to ask, 'Are you all right?'

'A little battered and rather embarrassed, monsieur. I was not paying attention and when my horse stumbled, I was thrown.'

Automatically Benedict offered, 'You're welcome to come back and spend the night with us.' In the bush you did not turn people away. However, he was somewhat suspicious at finding a man who was involved with Liza's brother so close to their farm. Perhaps she was right. Perhaps Dermott Docherty did still intend to do her harm?

Matthieu made a negative movement with his hand, not daring to shake his head again. '*Merci*, but no. I've come from Brookley and am looking for the farm which used to belong to the Baileys.'

'There's no one living there now.'

'Yes, I know.' He didn't volunteer the information

that Dermott owned it because he hoped the Caines would assume he was just looking the place over with a view to buying it. He did not want them to prevent him from furthering his acquaintance with their governess.

Benedict's voice was crisp, businesslike. 'You took the wrong turn. Go back round the bend and turn right. The track is a bit overgrown at the moment but it's clearly marked.' He ran his hand down the riding horse's foreleg. 'Your mare will be all right, I think. It's not far to the Baileys' place. Could you walk her for a bit? Let her recover as well?'

'I shall have to, shall I not?'

'Are you sure you'll be all right on your own, Monsieur Correntin?' the governess asked.

Matthieu turned to smile at her. '*Oui*. But I thank you for your concern, Frau Hebel.'

Ilse inclined her head and turned to Josie. 'Come along, dear. I promised to help Mrs Fenton with tea. *Au 'voir, Monsieur.*'

Matthieu managed to engage her eyes for a moment and smiled – pleased to receive a smile in return.

Benedict took a step backward. 'If you're sure you'll be all right, then, Mr Correntin . . . ?'

'I shall be fine, but I shall take more care how I ride in future.' Matthieu watched the three of them walk away, the child skipping and talking in her rather breathless voice. As they turned a bend in the track, the governess glanced back at him

182

briefly, then bent her head again to listen to her charge.

Under other circumstances Matthieu might have liked Benedict Caine, who had a very direct manner. Under other circumstances he could have accepted the offer of hospitality and got to know Frau Hebel . . . *Bon dieu*, why had he not asked her first name? But as things were it seemed better not to get too close to the family.

As he walked away, however, Matthieu cast prudence aside with one wave of his hand. Prudence be damned! He wanted very much to get to know the governess. She was not pretty exactly, but she had style which had always appealed to him much more than mere looks. And she spoke good French, too. How rare that was in Australia!

He remained thoughtful as he strolled back along the track, letting his mare pick her own pace. After the bend he turned right and found himself on an overgrown track just wide enough for a wagon. It might be almost winter but most of the trees were in full leaf. You never got the bare brown branches of his own country's winter. Something about these rustling woodlands appealed to him, he decided, as he continued to stroll along with the horses' hooves sounding muffled behind him on the sandy soil. There were pretty vistas with occasional huge trees and at this time of the year the dry, sunburned land of summer was turning green again with the occasional rain. It was not the same green as his home and this part of the country was very flat, too, but still it had its own beauty.

One twist in the path revealed a view of a small lake which reminded him abruptly of a certain part of the woods near his home and sent an unexpected pang of homesickness through him. He had spent many hours wandering those woods as a lad, and getting into trouble when he returned home for neglecting his studies and escaping from his tutor. His father, ambitious for his children to rise in the world, had wanted his third son to become a lawyer. Matthieu had hated the dusty books and convoluted phraseology, the hours of sitting on a high stool poring over precedents. He had been born for action and loved being outdoors. And so, when Grand-père died and his father proved intractable, he had left. At eighteen one did foolish things – and lived to regret them.

Baileys' Farm, when he came to it, turned out to be a neat building, a simple oblong in shape with a veranda along the back and front. When he went inside it smelled musty, so he left the front door open. There was furniture, plain but adequate, and a good stone fireplace. He turned slowly round, liking what he saw.

He went out on to the back veranda and found a tumbledown cooking area a few paces away, with a pile of sawn firewood nearby under a rough bark shelter. To his surprise he felt instantly at home.

I had better be careful, he told himself with a wry smile. I do not want to turn into a settler.

He frowned and paused to stare around him. What did he want to do with the rest of his life, though? He was sure of nothing except that he was reluctant to change countries again. He must be getting old, though at thirty-five he did not feel it.

He banished his worries with one snap of his fingers and concentrated on unsaddling the two horses and turning them out into a small enclosure whose fence was still strong enough to keep them in. After that he lit a fire, cooked some food and made up his bed.

But his last thoughts as he drifted towards sleep in the quietness of a still night were of the governess. He must definitely see her again. That would cure him of this – this foolishness. She was bound to have faults which would lessen her attraction. All women did.

At Lizabrook the talk was all of Mr Correntin for the first part of the meal. There was much speculation as to whether he would buy the old Bailey place and why a Frenchman would even think of settling in the Brookley district.

Liza was more worried that he was her brother's partner. If he bought the farm, Dermott might come to visit him. She was leaving shortly for England, but she had never forgotten her brother's threat of vengeance. If Dermott found her gone, would he take out his anger on her family? As if she did not bitterly regret killing Niall! She saw Benedict's eyes on her, the worry in them, and tried to smile at him but failed miserably.

On the other side of the table Ilse was asked for her opinion of the stranger, but what she really wanted to do was go away and think about the encounter. 'This is not the way I would have wished to make your acquaintance,' Monsieur Correntin had murmured just before Benedict joined them. What had he meant by that?

The Frenchman was very handsome – no, not handsome exactly, but certainly attractive. 'Be sure we'll meet again,' he had whispered. Would they? What did he mean by that? Men did not usually show an interest in her. Well, not men like him. And did she even want him to? She had already decided that she wanted both kindness and solid worth in a husband, not mere physical attraction.

'Well, I thought Mr Correntin had a nice smile,' Josie said for the third time. 'Didn't he, Frau Hebel?'

'Er – yes. And he seemed very polite.' Ilse saw Agnes Fenton watching her from across the room. Her friend was rather too perceptive sometimes. 'I'll go and – um – clean my shoes.'

She fled to the back veranda and stood there with her hands pressed to her hot cheeks. She was being foolish. Very foolish. She would probably never see him again. Or if she did, he'd have forgotten her name.

★　★　★

When Cathie woke the morning after the attack, she was astonished to find herself in a strange room. It was just starting to get light so she slipped out of bed and went to stare through the window. The sound of her door opening made her whirl round to see a giant of a man with tousled red-blond hair standing in the doorway. She tensed, ready to defend herself. Who was he? How had she got here? His face seemed vaguely familiar so she searched through the muddles of her throbbing head for his name. Magnus, that was it.

He spoke in a deep rumbling bass voice. 'So you're awake, lassie. How are you feeling now?'

As he gave her a tentative smile she lost her fear of him. There was a gentleness to his gaze and he had made no attempt to come into the room. Looking down, she realised in surprise and relief that she had been sleeping in her clothes.

'Do you remember your name?' he asked.

'Cathie . . .' She frowned, then fear fluttered in her chest. 'I – can't remember the rest of it.'

'Last night you couldn't remember even your first name, so you must be starting to get better. I thought you would. You look like a strong lass to me.'

She looked up in puzzlement at the sound of someone yelling incoherently from the next room.

'That's my mother. She canna think or speak properly now. Do you remember how yesterday she nearly set the place on fire? I have to lock her in her room at night now, or she wanders.'

Cathie blinked as a vague memory of burning coals falling on to a rug came back to her.

He took a step backwards on to the landing. 'I have to go to work soon, so I'll just away and finish dressing. When you come downstairs I'll show you where everything is.'

Cathie tried to straighten her crumpled clothes. There was a trunk standing at the foot of the narrow little bed and it seemed familiar. In a tentative exploration of the back of her head she found a painful lump. How had that happened? And why had a complete stranger brought her back to his home?

Downstairs a fire was smouldering in the kitchen range so she found the damper and opened it up, watching the glowing centre of the ashes grow brighter. There were pieces of coal in a box by the side of the fire, so she picked one up and put it on. She'd never seen coal before, only heard of it, but she treated it like wood, using small pieces first, and by the time she heard his footsteps on the stairs, flames were beginning to show.

Her host came in, looking more tidy now. He frowned at the clock ticking away comfortably on the mantelpiece. 'The neighbour who looks after my mother is usually here by now. I'd better go and see what's keeping her. She only lives in the next street. Will you be all right for a moment or two?'

'Yes, of course.'

He was back within minutes, his face flushed

188

and his movements tight with suppressed anger. 'She's not coming. Says she's not condoning our immorality.'

'Immorality?' Cathie gaped at him. 'But we haven't . . .' Surely she'd have remembered if he'd tried to – to— But she did remember a man's hands, only when she looked at Magnus's she knew they weren't the ones. The others had been dirty, with black-rimmed fingernails, while his were well-scrubbed. She spoke her thoughts out loud. 'I remember a man attacking me – a burly man, not very clean.' She could summon up a memory of a brutal face, too, though she could not put a name to it.

'Aye. And there was a young woman helping him steal your things. If I hadna come along, he'd have . . .' Magnus broke off and finished lamely, '. . . attacked your virtue. She hit you on the head with a brick and when they saw me they made off. They had your trunk which they were trying to open and a bag that he threw at me, so maybe you haven't lost everything. I think they got your purse, though. It wasn't in your handbag. I'm sorry for looking in it, but the policeman and I were trying to find out who you were.'

Cathie stood stock-still, trying to fit her own fragments of memory to this tale. She did vaguely remember a young woman, but the face was still misty and she could not put a name to it.

Magnus glanced at the clock. 'Look, do you think you could possibly look after my mother for me today? I have to go to work, you see.' He broke off to yawn loudly. 'I'm tired already. It was a long day yesterday, seeing my brother off on the ship to Australia and—'

'*Australia!*' She stared at him. 'I think – it sounds like – home.'

He nodded, not seeming surprised. 'I thought you might be newly arrived in Liverpool.'

He pronounced it 'thocht'. She liked the soft Scottish accent. 'Yes, I did come from Australia.' She was suddenly quite certain of that and relieved to have another piece of the puzzle revealed. Only why had she come to England? And why had no one met her at the docks? 'I can remember – a house burning down!' She clutched her head. 'Oh, why can't I remember things properly?'

His voice was gentle. 'Because you've been hurt. But at least you're starting to remember. And Cathie's a pretty name, though I prefer our Scottish version – Caitlin.' He stepped forward to lay one hand on her shoulder, a comforting, not a threatening gesture. 'It'll all come back to you, lassie, if you give it time.' Another glance at the clock brought the harried expression back to his face. He asked again, 'Could you – I know you're not well – but could you possibly look after my mother for me today? I'm the foreman at a local mill and I like to get there early to show a good example to the men.' He tried very hard not to let his mother's needs interfere with his work.

'Yes, of course. What do I need to do for her?'

'Whatever you can. Treat her like a baby, and a naughty baby at that, for it's what she is now, poor thing. And whatever you do, don't leave her alone with the fire.' He fumbled in his pocket and tossed some coins on to the table. 'There's a baker's shop at the end of the street. If you buy a loaf and mebbe some cheese from the grocer's shop next door, you'll have something to eat. You'll have to cut hers up for her in small pieces and put it in her mouth. She can't seem to remember how to feed herself.' His face was ravaged with sorrow as he added, 'She was a good mother to us. It's hard to see her like this.'

Cathie's heart went out to him. 'I'll do my best with her. Won't she be frightened of a stranger?'

'We're all strangers to her now. She likely won't notice you half the time. Tie her to the rocking chair if she gets troublesome. I have to do that sometimes or I'd get no work done about the house.' He flicked some strips of material hanging from the bars of the chairback and added sadly, 'I hate doing it, though.' At the door he paused to say, 'Her name's Janey and our surname's Hamilton, in case you don't remember. She doesn't answer to her name any more but it seems only fair to use it.'

And then he was gone.

Cathie stood there in the cramped little room, hearing other footsteps passing by outside. They made a lot of noise. What sort of shoes were the people wearing? No, they must be clogs.

She remembered someone telling her once how practical they were for bad weather if they were made properly. Who had done that? The harder she tried to remember, the fuzzier her brain felt. With a sigh she abandoned the attempt and tiptoed into the front room to peer through the window. People were still clattering past, so many people. But within a minute or two the rush stopped. She jumped in shock as there was a loud noise like a ship's siren from somewhere close by. A man hurrying along the street set off running the minute he heard it.

And then it was silent, with not a soul to be seen on the street.

Standing in the middle of the room she turned slowly in a circle as she studied it. The furniture shone as if someone had polished it recently. Would that be the sister? Where did she live? Why could she not look after the mother?

There was a noise upstairs and she went up to unlock the other bedroom. The old woman was sitting up in bed with a blank expression on her face. There was a strong smell of urine and, when Cathie moved forward, the woman cowered back as if expecting to be hit.

Trying to sound soothing, Cathie coaxed her from the bed and stood her against the wall, then stripped the wet sheets, hoping the wetness had not spread to the feather mattress below. It had, and there were other similar stains that said it wasn't the first time this had happened.

It took her a while to coax the poor woman into coming downstairs. She picked up a bundle of clothing and took it with her, deciding to dress her charge in front of the fire so that she could wash her first. Pouring some hot water into a bowl from the big black kettle that stood at the side of the hob, she mixed it carefully with cold water and sponged Magnus Hamilton's mother down like a small child, continuing to make soothing noises as she did it because when she stopped speaking the poor creature started making sounds of distress.

Afterwards Janey Hamilton stood patiently as she was dressed. She spoke occasionally, but only disjointed phrases that had no relevance to what was being done to her.

Feeling hungry now, Cathie investigated the kitchen for food. There was oatmeal in a bin and not much else, so she made watery porridge, struggling to heat it on the small range. It was a messy business feeding the old lady and she decided she would not wash her until after break-fast the following day. That made her freeze for a moment. The following day? Was she intending to stay here with these strangers? Then she shrugged. What else could she do if her money had been stolen?

On that thought she raced up the stairs. Magnus had said something about a handbag and her purse being stolen.

She brought the bag back down to investigate

its contents. A crumpled handkerchief, a small sewing kit, an unfinished letter. A sound made her turn round and she saw Mrs Hamilton approaching the fire with one hand outstretched. With a sigh Cathie tied the poor woman to the rocking chair, hating to do that because the whimpering started again, but desperate to see what she could learn about herself.

Sitting down at the table she picked up the letter again.

Dear Mother and Father
The voyage has continued well and now we're nearly there. I haven't been seasick once, not even in the stormy weather, but others have, so I've been helping Matron look after them. For that she gave me half a crown. It's not a large sum, but it's the first money I've ever earned. I didn't want to put it with the rest of my coins, so it's in my trunk with the money Mr Correntin slipped into my bag when he kindly bought me the embroidery materials I told you about.

Cathie paused. Who was Mr Correntin? She could conjure up no face to go with that name.

We'll be arriving in Liverpool tomorrow and Bessie Downharn, the girl I've made friends with, is going to see me to the train. She seems to think I can't manage on my own, but I have a tongue in my head and I'm not stupid. Still, an offer of friendship is not to be spurned, is it?

With a cry, Cathie clutched her head, which seemed to be full of booming sound. Pain throbbed through her as images came tumbling in: Bessie's brother, the narrow alley, being attacked. She could not remember, though, how Magnus Hamilton had saved her, but if he said he had, well, she believed him. He had a sternly honest face – nice, though. And his hair was a lovely colour. She remembered with a wry smile how he had towered over her, something few other men had ever done. Goodness, what a giant he was! But he was also gaunt, with an unhappy look on his face.

She leaned her head on one hand and as the tide of pain ebbed her thoughts strayed back to Magnus. If she was in trouble so was he, trying to look after a mother in this state, with his sister obviously living elsewhere. Yet he had still found time to help a stranger. That said a lot about the kind of man he was. What would have happened to her if he hadn't brought her home?

She tried to remember her own family but could not bring their faces to mind clearly, only that they lived in Australia. What was she doing here in England, then? Oh, it was so frustrating not to remember!

She realised that Mrs Hamilton was wriggling

about uncomfortably, so removed the bonds and led her out to the privy, relieved when that worked. Afterwards she cleared up their breakfast things, talking to the woman as she did so. Though she received no answers the sound of her voice seemed to keep the poor thing quiet. She could see no sign that Magnus had had any breakfast and wondered if he'd simply dashed out to work.

It seemed obvious that the next thing to do was to go through her trunk and see what she had been left with. She took Mrs Hamilton upstairs with her and the old lady began to walk up and down the room, crooning tunelessly to herself. When Cathie investigated, she found the trunk filled mostly with dirty clothes but there was a small embroidered purse at the bottom containing several sovereigns and other coins. She bowed her head at the sight of that, feeling quite shaky with relief at not being penniless and muttering, 'Oh, thank goodness! Thank goodness!'

Before going downstairs again she looked into Magnus's bedroom, though she felt guilty about prying. She found it a spartan chamber, with a double bed which seemed longer than usual and of rather rough workmanship. Perhaps he'd made it himself to accommodate his long limbs. There was a chest of drawers and a small pile of dirty linen on the bare wooden floor in the corner. Like the rest of the house, the room was clean and the furniture free of dust.

Leading her charge downstairs again she kept

hold of Janey's hand while she studied the front room in more detail. It was by far the grandest in the house, but had a totally unused feel to it. There was a table at one side covered by a plush cloth in a rich red colour with a Bible standing squarely in the middle, a sofa and a few chairs, a highly polished sideboard and a few ornaments on the mantelpiece. There was also a shelf of books. She examined the titles. No novels. Serious subjects like *The History of Scotland*, *Birds of the Lancashire Moors*, *Domestic Economy of Great Britain* – which said something about the owner of the house, she supposed.

She went back into the kitchen. She would do some washing today, she decided, starting with herself. So she heated water then tied Mrs Hamilton to the chair again. The clothes she donned afterwards seemed to be the only clean ones she possessed, but there were plenty of dirty ones so perhaps, as Magnus said, he had prevented Bessie and her brother from taking her things. Which meant that all they'd taken had been the money in her purse. She couldn't even remember how much that had been.

It felt wonderful to be clean again. She rinsed out some underclothes and Mrs Hamilton's soiled nightdress in the bowl of water she had washed in and hung them to dry on a line in the back yard, then put the soiled sheets to soak and found others for the bed. She'd ask Magnus if she could do a big wash the following day – and would offer to wash his clothes as well.

When the clock on the mantelpiece chimed she realised it was midday. She found a shawl and bonnet hanging in the hall, and dressed Mrs Hamilton in them, then set out for the corner shops Magnus had mentioned. Feeling ravenously hungry she bought not only a loaf, but some cheese, jam, potatoes, onions and a cabbage, spending some of her own money as well as his. She'd find a butcher's shop later and get some meat to make a stew for tea. She asked the shop-keeper what time the mill workers finished and, although the woman seemed very disapproving, received a curt answer.

'Is something wrong?' Cathie asked in exasperation. 'You don't know me, yet you seem angry at me. What have I done?'

The woman gaped at her in shock at this blunt question, then pursed her lips and said with a sniff, 'You'll be the young woman who spent the night with Magnus Hamilton, I take it?'

Cathie suddenly realised where this was leading. 'I spent the night in his sister's old bedroom, actually, and I'm looking after his mother today because Mrs Midner didn't come to work this morning.'

'Martha Midner is a member of our chapel Ladies' Circle. She'd not share a house with an unmarried young woman like yourself – *given the circumstances*.'

Cathie leaned forward and said very clearly, 'Then you'd better tell her that I'm not sharing

Magnus Hamilton's bed, nor shall I be doing that. I, too, was brought up to be respectable – but also taught not to judge others without first seeking the truth.' She paused and added bitterly, 'Which is that I was attacked at the docks when I arrived in England, though luckily for me, my' – inspiration suddenly struck and she changed what she had been intending to say to – 'Cousin Magnus arrived in time to drive off the attackers. I was still very dizzy last night and couldn't think properly. I slept,' she slapped her hand down on the counter for emphasis, '*in his sister's bed*. And so you can tell Mrs Midner and anyone else who asks.'

Two women who were waiting to be served gasped aloud at her frankness.

The shopkeeper looked at her suspiciously. 'He's your cousin? He never said anything about a cousin, only about taking his brother to the ship.'

'I'm his second cousin, actually, but he promised my parents he and Mairi would help me when I arrived in England. And so he'd have told Mrs Midner if she'd given him time to explain. Which she didn't.' Cathie had no compunction about lying to these women. Why should they sit in judgement on her and blindly approve of this Mrs Midner who had left poor Magnus in the lurch today? She only hoped he had not told Mrs Midner last night that she was a stranger. She managed to summon up a vague memory of an older woman looking at her disapprovingly.

'You're very blunt,' the shopkeeper said.

'We speak our minds in Australia.' Cathie picked up her purchases, stuffed them anyhow into the string shopping bag she had found in the kitchen and took hold of Mrs Hamilton's hand. 'Come on, Auntie Janey. Let's get you home again.'

She heard someone say, 'Well!' as she left the shop, but didn't turn her head.

Janey smiled as they walked back, holding her face up to the sun. The smile faded as Cathie opened the front door of their house and the old woman pulled back, whimpering in her throat.

Cathie studied her. 'Do you like going for walks? Well, so do I. We'll go out again after we've eaten, shall we?' They'd find a butcher's shop and when they came back she'd cook a hearty stew for the man who had saved her – before confessing to him that she'd claimed him as a cousin.

She smiled briefly. Would he mind? Would he agree to keep up the pretence? Well, if he didn't she'd just leave him to deal with the gossip however he thought best and find somewhere else to live.

But somehow she didn't think he would mind because he needed her to look after his mother for a while. She had noticed bruises on Mrs Hamilton's body which could have been caused by blows and indignation filled her at the mere thought, both on her own and Magnus Hamilton's behalf. How could anyone hurt a poor helpless creature like Janey Hamilton? If this was how Mrs Midner had looked after her, she should be ashamed of herself.

'I can certainly do better than that,' muttered Cathie.

CHAPTER 9

MAY

When a letter arrived at the clogger's shop in Underby Street, Teddy Marshall stared at it in distrust. Who the hell was writing letters to him? He nearly tossed it in the fire then changed his mind and set it on the back of his work bench to wait till his eldest son came back. Those squiggly little lines meant nowt to him, but Bob could read and would tell him what was in the damned thing.

When his son returned, face ruddy, carrying a load of clog irons in a sack, Teddy scowled at him. He hated to see how strong his sons were, for they all took after him and were big men while he was fast losing what was left of his strength and his eyes weren't too good lately, either. Sodding old age! You worked hard all your life and this was your reward, a body that let you down. He couldn't even drink as much ale nowadays because it made him feel sick. Well, at least he had fathered five fine sons, and raised them to stand up for them-selves, too. No one could take that away from him.

He picked up the letter and thrust it at his son. 'This arrived.'

Bob took it out of his hand and stared at the envelope. 'It's addressed to you.'

'Fat lot of good that is. I can't read the bloody thing, nor I don't want to. Throw it in the fire if you aren't going to read it to me.'

'It's come all the way from Australia.'

Teddy gaped. 'Australia? I don't know anyone in Australia. Who sent it? What do they want?'

'Only one way to find out.' Bob ripped open the envelope and pulled out a single sheet of paper, reading it carefully, then hissing in shock and reading it all over again.

'What does it say? Read it out to me.'

Dear Mr Marshall

I'm writing to tell you that you have a daughter and that she's coming to England on the same ship as this letter. Her name is Cathie Ludlam, or she may be calling herself Cathie Caine now because her mother married again. Remember her mother? Liza Docherty, my sister, who used to live opposite you in Underby Street?

Liza ran off to Australia and did pretty well for herself. Married Josiah Ludlam no less, then Nicholas Rawley, but is now married to a farmer, Benedict Caine, who also comes from Pendleworth.

If you keep an eye open, you might meet your daughter around the town and introduce yourself. The girl certainly looks like a

*Marshall, tall and sturdy. A daughter to be
proud of.*
      Dermott Docherty

Bob grinned at his father. 'You lusty old bugger!
How come you didn't know about this?'

Teddy didn't smile back at him. 'It ain't true.
Someone's playing a trick on us.'

'Didn't you know this Liza Docherty, then?'

There was silence, then Teddy glanced over his
shoulder to check that his wife wasn't within
earshot and muttered, 'Might have.'

'Well, this Liza's brother says the daughter looks
like us. Wonder why he bothered to write, though?'
Bob waited as his father turned away from him,
shoulders hunched, kicking absent-mindedly at
the end of the wooden work bench with one
clogged foot. Thud. Thud.

'Dad?' When he got no answer, Bob grinned and
decided it must be true. The old devil! 'Are you
all right? Not going to faint from shock, are you?'

Teddy didn't answer. He was remembering the
time he'd forced himself on Liza. Pretty little thing
she'd been. He'd felt a bit guilty afterwards
because he'd hurt her. Suddenly he remembered
her face the next morning, chalk white, her eyes
dark-rimmed and her slender body bruised. He'd
wanted to marry her right and proper, though.
She'd been refusing to wed him, so he'd thought
it best to make sure of her. Only it hadn't solved
anything because she'd run off, the jade, and never

204

been heard of again till she turned up in Pendleworth years later married to Squire Rawley's only son. Had she really been married to a Ludlam as well? Teddy scowled. Buggered if he could figure it all out. Buggered if he wanted to try.

'You don't want to go getting mixed up with that lot,' he muttered as his son kept staring at him.

'What lot?'

'Them Ludlams. Or the Rawleys.' Teddy explained what had happened, enjoying the feeling of superiority that came from knowing more than his son for once. 'I saw her a few years ago when she come back to England with her husband – Mr Nicholas Rawley, no less. Well, she were a pretty piece, you have to give her that. I kept well away from her an' you should do the same with the daughter now. That old sod Stephenson is still alive and he's the meanest devil as ever rode in a carriage, that one is. You don't offend them nobs if you know what's good for you.'

A further minute or two of rumination and he added, 'That young Rawley is Liza's son, you know – what's his name again?'

'The heir?' Bob asked sharply.

'Aye, the son and heir.' Teddy spat a gob of phlegm triumphantly on to the floor as he remembered. 'Francis he's called.' He flicked the letter with one grimy fingertip. 'He must be the half-brother of this lass in the letter.' He didn't really want owt to do with it, just wanted to live what was left of his life quietly without any trouble. Anyway, by the time he'd seen Liza again he'd married Sal Pocklington, more fool him. He sighed, mentally comparing Sal to Liza. Not a looker, Sal, though she'd enjoyed a bit of bed play when she was younger an' given him two sons, though what use were they to a man when they'd gone off on the tramp and never been heard of again? But what a mistake his second marriage had been! Sal might be scrawny, but she had ways of making you pay if you upset her. A man couldn't call his life his own with her around. 'Don't tell Sal about this,' he said automatically.

'Don't tell Sal what?' asked a sharp voice from behind him. 'What've you done now, Teddy Marshall?'

He cursed under his breath.

'Well?' she demanded, hands on scrawny hips and *that* look on her face. 'What don't you want Bob to tell me?'

'I just didn't want to upset you, love,' he offered placatingly.

Bob laughed and tossed the letter across to his stepmother. 'Read that. It seems I've got a half-sister I didn't know about.' Out of pity for his father he added, 'Before your time, Ma.'

Sal scanned the letter, mouthing the words as she slowly spelled her way through it. 'You old sod!' she said affectionately, clouting Teddy round the ears. Then she frowned. 'Why would this

Dermott fellow bother to write to you? Was he a friend of yours?'

'That's what worries me. He weren't a friend of anyone, that one weren't. Used to hang out with his brother. Thick as thieves because they *was* thieves, them two. One of the nastiest sods I've ever met, Niall Docherty was. Born to be hung. Dermott weren't as bad, but bad enough.'

Bob chewed one side of his lip then said thoughtfully, 'He says the lass's family has a bit of money. Wonder if there's any chance of us getting our hands on some?' For he had a wife and three children at home and his wife was always asking for money for new clothes for them. Good thing he'd taken over his father's shop two years ago. The old fool had let it run down and had refused to change things till Bob had threatened to set up for himself as a clogger on the opposite side of the street.

He looked at his father sourly and picked up a piece of wood from the bench, inspecting the shaping. Poor quality of work, as usual nowadays. 'Where are those spectacles I got you, Dad? You haven't gone and lost this pair as well, have you?'

'I keep 'em safe for him,' Sal said. 'I'll go an' fetch 'em.'

'Well, go on keeping 'em safe, because I'm not forking out for another pair.' He turned to his father and raised his voice. 'Why aren't you wearing them? You know bloody well you can't see for close work without.'

Teddy muttered something and scowled at him.

Bob picked the letter up. 'I'll keep this, Ma. It wants thinking about.'

'Well, this lass, whoever she may be, isn't getting anything out of us,' Sal cautioned. 'I don't scrub my hands raw to help *his* bastards.'

'No, you do it to pay for your gin.'

As Bob had hoped this jibe distracted her and she forgot about the letter in cursing him and arguing about a woman's right to a sip or two of comfort of an evening to ease the ache in her bones.

He called in on his next brother on the way home. Jim had just come in after a day at the mill and was grumbling about Magnus bloody Hamilton, the foreman, who'd been driving them all mad today fussing about nowt. What did it matter if they missed oiling a machine part once in a while? It'd get done the next time round, wouldn't it? Fussy buggers like Hamilton should be taken out and shot, and Jim would volunteer to do that any day, by hell he would.

When he had calmed down a bit, Bob explained about the girl who was supposed to have arrived in England on the same boat as this letter, and the two of them speculated as to whether they really did have a half-sister.

'If we have, it'll be you an' me as'll have to deal with it,' Jim said angrily. 'Pat's too soft.'

Later they called in at their youngest brother's, after a stop at the Railway Arms. Much mellowed by a couple of pints of beer, they showed Pat the letter.

'You mean, we've got a sister?' He beamed at them. 'I wonder what she's like. Cathie's a nice name. I allus wanted a sister.'

'She's only a half-sister and don't talk so bloody soft. Who cares what she's like? It's whether her family's got any money as is more to the point.' Bob didn't reckon much to sisters. His wife had three of 'em, always turning up and expecting a cup of tea and who knew what else?

But he couldn't get it through the daft bugger's head that this might be an opportunity for them and Pat's wife, Tess, was just as stupid. The pair of them deserved one another, they did that! Soft ha'porths! Allus helping other folk instead of helping themselves.

Well, Pat would fall into line eventually. You only had to say things like 'Family first' and 'Family need to stick together', and the silly sod would do anything for you.

When Magnus got home, he stood in the hall sniffing the aroma drifting out of the kitchen. Someone was cooking and it smelled wonderful. 'I'm back!' he called before he moved into the house, not wanting to frighten the lass.

He stopped again at the door of the kitchen, his breath catching in his throat at the sight of her, wrapped in one of his mother's pinafores, stirring something on the cooking range and humming to herself. She looked clean today – and so did his mother. He'd forgotten how rosy newly washed skin could look and that made him realise how sloppily Mrs Midner had cared for his mother, even if she hadn't been cruel to her.

Cathie smiled at him. 'I hope you like stew?'

'I love it. Especially when it smells like that.' He frowned. 'Did I leave you enough money to buy meat?'

'I found some of my own in my trunk. There's no reason you should be paying for my meals.'

They stared at one another across the room and the thought suddenly came to him that this was what it must be like to return home to a wife. Longing speared through him followed swiftly by scorn at his own weakness. 'I'll wash, then.' He clumped past her into the scullery, closing the door on the surprised expression on her face. He wanted to sit with her and tell her about his day, as he used to tell his mother. Jim Marshall had been causing trouble again. Give that fellow an inch and he slid out of any work he could. Lazy devil he was and infected others with that same laziness. Though he could do good work when pushed and was definitely not stupid.

When he went back into the kitchen, Magnus found Cathie trying to persuade his mother to move to the table for her meal. Forgetting his earlier embarrassment, he hurried across to help her.

Cathie took a step back and watched, surprised

at how much more easily he did this than she had. It was as if his mother recognised his touch, even in her clouded state. 'I'll serve the food, then, shall I?'

'Please.' He watched her bustling to and from the kitchen range, getting dishes out and ladling the stew into them, then cutting big hunks of bread to go with it. 'How did you know what time to have it ready? I forgot to tell you when I finished.'

'I asked the woman in the corner shop.'

He saw a frown wrinkle her forehead as she said that. Well, he didn't like Mrs Naylor, either. The corner shop was convenient for a man with too few hours in the day and that was the best you could say of it. 'That old besom?'

She laughed. 'Besom! What a lovely word.'

'It's Scottish. Mum used to use it.' He looked sadly at his mother then smiled across the table. 'You've washed her. Thank you for that. She'd be grateful. She always liked to keep clean.'

Cathie hesitated. 'Didn't Mrs Midner do that – wash her, I mean?'

'Not very well. My mother looks different today – rosy and well cared for. I'm grateful to you for that.' He took a deep breath. 'I – um – asked around at work, but no one knows of a woman who can come and look after her, even temporarily.'

'I can do it for a while, if you like? In return for somewhere to live.'

He had been hoping she would say this – and

yet afraid of hearing it, too. What would it do to her reputation if they lived together? But how could he refuse her offer when his mother so badly needed help? 'Do you really mean that? You don't mind?'

She nodded, putting another spoonful of stew into Janey's mouth, then one into her own.

He followed their example for a moment or two, chewing slowly and with relish. 'This is a fine meal. You must tell me how much I owe you for the meat, though.'

'Nothing.'

'But I canna let you—'

She changed the subject. 'I have something to confess.'

His heart lurched. What? What had she remembered?

'I told the woman in the shop that you were my cousin – well, second cousin.'

'Why?' He watched her wriggle uncomfortably and when she didn't speak, prompted, 'Why did you do that, lassie?'

'Well, she was suggesting – things. About us. You and me.'

He saw her face flame and felt anger surge through him. Not only because the things were untrue, but because he wished they could be true. 'Did she believe you?'

Cathie looked up and a smile twisted her mouth briefly. 'I don't know, but when I told her straight out that we were not sharing a bed, she got angry and' – she hesitated then continued in a rush of words – 'I don't think she believes I'm your cousin, but if I'm to stay and look after your mother, it'll sound better to say I am.'

He stared at her. 'Have you remembered much more about yourself? Won't someone be waiting for you, expecting you?'

Her smile faded. 'I haven't remembered much more. It's all very patchy. I remember scenes, faces . . . There's a child, a little girl called Josie – and I remember being attacked. But I can't fit things together properly. It's very frustrating.'

He was sorry he'd caused her smile to fade. It was such a lovely smile, fresh and open. She was a sonsy lass, looking strong and healthy, a woman very much to his taste. 'It'll all come back to you eventually.'

She shook her head, her hands twisting together in her lap. 'Will it?'

He stretched out to take one of them and hold it still in his. 'Aye, lassie. I'm sure it will.'

For a moment their hands lay together on the table, both large and capable, hers reddened from the washing and his rough from his daily work. He didn't want to let go but he did, slowly, his eyes meeting hers and—

His mother began to choke and they had to pound her back and settle her down again. By then the moment had passed – and probably a good thing too, Magnus decided. He picked up his spoon and continued his meal, murmuring, 'You're a good cook, Caitlin.'

She didn't correct him. She liked his version of her name better than Cathie – well, when he said it with that soft Scottish lilt, anyway.

'All right,' he said as the meal ended. 'We'll say you're a second cousin from Australia – on my mother's side. They're Rutherfords, come from near Roxburgh. I don't usually approve of telling lies, but if it'll make things easier for you to stay, cause you less embarrassment . . .' He let the words trail away.

'Caitlin Rutherford,' she said slowly. 'All right.' But she could not help wondering what her real surname was.

It was only later when he was sitting reading in front of the fire that he remembered Mairi. 'I'd better write and let my sister know we've got a new cousin.' And then he had to explain about his sister, which somehow led on to his brothers and how they'd all gone away over the sea.

'And left you with the burden of your mother?' Cathie said softly, her feet tucked up on the rung of the chair, her arms clasped around her knees. 'That must be hard.'

'I'm the eldest. Head of the family. She's my responsibility.'

'You're a good man, Magnus Hamilton.'

He could feel himself flushing. He wasn't used to compliments. He got out the writing paper. It all sounded very far-fetched when he set it down and he was tempted to tear the letter up, but Mairi and Elwyn might come across on Sunday so they must be warned. Abandoning any thought of trying to make it sound better he scrawled across the bottom, 'I'll explain properly next time I see you, but Caitlin looks after Mum as well as you would, and far better than Mrs Midner did, so I think it's all happened for the best.'

He wasn't really sure of that, for seeing Caitlin like this with the firelight reflecting on her face and shining hair made him realise that his heart was already touched by her. The more fool he.

As they got his mother ready for bed, working together to persuade Janey to change into a nightgown, he smiled at Caitlin – he simply could not think of her as Cathie – and said softly, 'So you'll be staying for a while, eh, lass?'

'I'll be staying, but not for too long,' she warned. 'Just for a few weeks, maybe, till I get a bit more used to this England of yours. So it might be as well for you to keep your eyes open for someone else. I won't go until you've found other help, though.'

'I thank you for your help, Caitlin – Cathie, I mean.'

'Caitlin sounds more Scottish, so it's better to call me that if I'm to pretend I'm your cousin.'

Somehow he forgot his book as they settled downstairs, chatting like old friends in front of the fire.

He went to bed feeling better about life than he had for a long time. And dreamed of Caitlin. When he woke he didn't know whether to be upset about that or not.

★　★　★

In Australia Matthieu lingered at Baileys' Farm, considering his future. He took long walks, trying to work out where this property ended. The Caines' homestead marked one boundary very clearly, not only because there was a rough pole fence but also because the land beyond it had that indefinable air of being cared for. Fields had crops standing in them, because in this strange country, winter and spring were the main growing seasons. Even the patches of bushland on Caine land had well-used little paths curling around them without signs of new growth as if someone walked the perimeters regularly.

Had Caine's wife really killed her eldest brother, as Dermott claimed? Matthieu wondered. What was she like, then? He had met females who were whores and thieves but never, to his knowledge, one who was a murderess.

On one of his trips he met a young man and stopped to exchange greetings, surprised to be met by a scowl.

'Are you the new owner of Baileys'?' the young man demanded.

'No, I'm just keeping an eye on things for him.'

'Then I'll not trespass again.'

As he turned to leave Matthieu held out his hand. 'I'm Matthieu Correntin.' When his companion stared at the hand as if he had not expected that, Matthieu looked down at it in puzzlement. 'Is there something wrong with my hand?'

'No, with mine. I'm part-native,' the lad said, scowling and eyeing him challengingly. 'You won't want to shake hands with such as me.'

Matthieu grinned. 'I'm French. Are *you* sure you want to touch me? After all, my people used to be enemies of Britain.' He did not drop his hand and when the young fellow took it hesitantly, gave his a hearty shake. 'We French are not so worried about the colour of a man's skin,' he said. 'We care more about what's inside his mind. Look, there are some things I'd like to ask you about this place. Would you share a pot of coffee with me? It's not good coffee, but it's all I have to offer.'

Still Brendan hesitated. He was not used to being treated like this and could not help doubting the man's sincerity. Did the French really not care as much about the colour of a man's skin? If so, what was their country like?

'I'm trying to find out where this farm ends and other people's land begins but it's not very clear, except along Caine's boundaries.'

Bemused, Brendan began to walk with him, intrigued by his companion's accent and his trim appearance, so different somehow from the other men round Brookley. When they got to the house Brendan was even more bemused by the ritual for making coffee, which meant grinding some black seeds and making a dark brown brew out of them.

'I've never seen people do that before,' he said abruptly.

Matthieu shrugged. 'It is my weakness, coffee.

The English drink tea, but we French prefer coffee, so I bring the beans with me and make a small pleasure of preparing a drink. Though I would have preferred a good china cup to these clumsy things. The last owners have left most of their household goods. What happened to them? Did they die?'

'Mrs Bailey died. Mr Bailey was getting old. One day he loaded some things on his cart and drove away. We didn't see him again, but we heard that he'd gone over to Melbourne to join his son.'

'Do you live near here?'

Brendan shrugged. 'If you call it living, stuck in the middle of nowhere. My father is Irish. My mother is half-Irish, half-Aboriginal. They work for the Caines. I don't like it here – but I don't fit in anywhere else, either. People look at your skin and treat you as if you're stupid. And I'm *not* stupid.' And why he'd confided in a stranger like this he could not work out, for he usually avoided the company of white men. He raised the clumsy cup and sipped, frowning down at the dark liquid and rolling it round his mouth.

'You don't like it?' Matthieu asked.

'I'm not used to it. It seems very strong.'

'I shall add more hot water, then perhaps you will find it more palatable.' Matthieu did so and watched his young companion's valiant efforts to pretend he was enjoying it. He chuckled suddenly. 'I shall not be offended if you don't wish to finish it.'

And Brendan found himself smiling back. 'I'll finish it. After all, it's a new experience for me and I don't enjoy many of those. We only drink tea at home.' After a pause he said gruffly, 'I can show you the boundaries of the farm, if you want.'

'I would be grateful. Do you not have work to do, *mon ami?*'

Again that defensive shrug. 'I'm supposed to work for Mr Caine, but sometimes I get fed up and just walk away for a time. I'm on day rates. He only keeps me on because of my parents and because there are few others to hire round here.'

'You don't like working on a farm?'

'No. But if I leave, I'll be treated as an ignorant native and that would be no better. When Cathie was here, it wasn't so bad, but since she's gone . . .' He shrugged and let the words trail away.

'She too hated living here in the country,' Matthieu agreed tranquilly.

Brendan looked at him in surprise. 'You've met her?'

'Yes. Her uncle is my partner.' He explained what had happened to her and saw the distress on the young man's face. 'She will be all right, *j'en suis sûr.*'

'She was my only friend and now I may never see her again.'

'It is hard indeed to lose a friend,' Matthieu agreed. 'But she'll be back one day, with tales to tell, no doubt. And I have no friends here, either, so perhaps you and I can find time for one another.'

The only response was a cynical stare.

'I mean that.' Matthieu waited for a comment. When none came, he looked at the sky. 'It's too late to survey the boundaries today and I'm sure your mother will be expecting you back, but if you would come again tomorrow, I too will pay you a suitable daily rate.'

'I'm not going home tonight.'

'You have quarrelled with your family?'

Brendan shook his head. 'No. But sometimes I need to be away from everyone, so I camp out in the bush.'

'If you wish to stay here tonight, there are other bedrooms and I shall be happy to share a meal. I shot a kangaroo this morning.'

And so began an unlikely friendship. Which was, Matthieu thought, going to cause complications once Dermott arrived, for his partner despised natives. He grinned into the darkness of his bedroom, then thought of the governess and made a soft sound of exasperation. He kept thinking of her, wanting to see her again. She intrigued him. He was sure there was fire behind that cool exterior.

But at least he had found out her given name from Brendan: Ilse. A beautiful name. It suited her.

Matthieu spent two days walking the boundaries with Brendan, learning a great deal about the local wildlife and also about the way Brendan's mother and her people thought of the land. In return he spoke of France, suddenly sure he would never return there again. Which might or might not be a step towards finding out where he did want to go next.

He found the young man intelligent and interested in the world, and sincerely pitied him. To his mind, the English placed too much importance on the whiteness of a person's skin.

A mile away Liza was equally wakeful. How could she leave when her brother's business partner had come to Brookley? Was there some plan to harm her family again?

And then there was Benedict. He was working too hard, looking grim and determined, and he had become very short-tempered, even with the children. Poor Josie and Harry could not understand why their father had changed so much. He, Seth and Lucas were working every minute of the day. And during the evenings he would not stop, but sit on the veranda with an oil lamp, carving pieces of wood to embellish the furniture he hoped to make again one day.

She knew he was still deeply upset about Cathie's departure. What with the bush fire and their daughter running away, he felt he had failed his family, and to Benedict family was the most important thing in his life. He was a good husband and Liza loved him dearly, but she wished she could persuade him to take life more easily. She did not need riches or luxuries to make her happy, just him and her children, but he seemed determined to wrest a fortune out of this harsh land. It was as if he still felt he had to prove to everyone that he had made a success of his life here.

He had not tried to prevent her from going to England, and she and Josie would be leaving very soon, but she knew he would worry about them and miss her desperately – as she would miss him. Before she went she was going to insist he sold some more pieces of jewellery so that he'd have money to finish the new house and build a proper furniture manufactory.

But whatever pain she caused him, she was still going. She would not feel right until she'd done this. It wasn't just for her own sake now. She had a presentiment that both Francis and Cathie were going to need her.

Her own mother had sometimes talked about 'the sight' but Liza had not really believed in it until now.

CHAPTER 10

MAY

As Matthieu was riding back to the farm he saw Ilse Hebel and the little girl strolling along in the distance and urged his horse to a faster trot, catching up with them well before they turned off towards Lizabrook. He reined the horse in and slid off it because he wanted to stand close to her.

'*Bonjour*, Frau Hebel, Mademoiselle Caine.' He bowed to the little girl as if she were a grown-up and as he'd expected she giggled. In other circumstances he would have enjoyed teasing her, because little girls of that age could be charming. The governess was very calm today, but a pulse was beating rapidly in her throat and he had seen for himself how her colour had risen slightly when she saw him.

'Monsieur Correntin.' She inclined her head. 'How are you feeling? Have you recovered from your fall?'

'*Mais oui*. I've been into Brookley to buy fresh vegetables from the inn.' He gestured around them. 'A pleasant day to take the air. I enjoy the Australian winters.'

'I enjoy the summers as well.'

There was a short silence. The child hopped up and down playing some complicated skipping game as she waited for the adults to finish their chat, mouthing rhymes under her breath to match her steps.

'It is unexpected to find a lady like yourself here in the middle of the bush, and one who speaks French moreover. I must confess, I've greatly missed the sound of my native tongue.'

Ilse opened her mouth as if to speak, then closed it again and looked at him warily.

'I wonder – would you and the child have time to come and visit the farm? I would really welcome a woman's opinion of the house.'

She swallowed hard, then glanced down at a little fob watch pinned to her bodice.

Before she could say anything Josie skipped forward to urge, 'Do say yes, Frau Hebel. I haven't been out there for ages. They used to have some apple trees at the back.' She stared at Matthieu calculatingly. 'Our trees got burned in a bush fire, but it missed the Baileys' farm. I used to enjoy picking apples and eating them straight away. They taste best of all that way.'

Ilse clicked her tongue at this blatant hint. 'Josie!'

Matthieu smiled warmly at the child. 'You must come and show me the orchard, if you please, Mademoiselle Josie. I have not seen it yet. If there are any ripe apples, you can try one straight from the tree and see if they still taste as good.'

He offered his hand and she took it without hesitation, so he set off walking before the governess could say anything, leading the horse. After a moment's hesitation Ilse turned and followed them. He slowed down to let her catch up, giving her a warm smile that was not feigned.

As they walked they spoke of music and books. He found her French excellent. 'How did you learn my language so well?' he asked.

'I was well educated and our home was so close to France we all spoke both French and German. And I've always had a particular gift for languages.'

He kept her engaged in unthreatening conversation until she grew more comfortable with him. He could tell the moment that happened because the constrained expression vanished. He was surprised to see how warm her smile could be. It transformed her so much that he guessed her emotions were normally kept under very firm control.

When they arrived at the farm he unsaddled the horse and turned it loose, then let the child show them the orchard. Some of the trees were early producers and were loaded with fruit, so he begged Josie to try one and pick as much as she wanted for her family, finding an old sack for her to put them in. Then he took the governess to inspect the house, ignoring her wary look when he offered her his arm.

'What a waste!' Ilse mourned as they walked back through the windfalls lying on the ground.

'You could make apple pies or dried fruit from those.'

'I shall gather some of them and leave them at your gates – in return for a pie or two, perhaps?'

'That seems fair.'

He led the way into the house. 'Would a woman like this place, do you think?' he asked as they stopped just inside the front door. Instead of the usual central breezeway with rooms to either side there was a huge room, which was entrance hall, kitchen and dining area all in one. At the moment it was filled with golden light from the sun shining through the dusty windows.

He strolled to the other side of the room, watching her covertly from there, seeing the way her hand fluttered up to her throat then down again as she struggled to maintain her composure. She was, he thought, quite unversed in flirtation and although she was widowed, there was something almost virginal about her, as if she had never been truly roused. He found that thought piquant. He would like to be the one to show her what love could be like. Then he looked at her again and knew it would not be fair to seduce her, for he was not a marrying man and she was most definitely a respectable woman.

She took a few paces forward, filling the silence with a rush of words. 'I've always liked this room and I know Mrs Bailey loved the place. Poor Mr Bailey never got over her death.' She walked slowly up and down, running a hand along the dresser as she passed then stopping to ask quietly, 'Have you bought the farm, monsieur?'

'*Non. Pas encore.* But I am considering it now that I've seen the other attractions the neighbourhood has to offer.' He looked at her in a way which emphasised his hidden meaning. He might not wish to hurt her, but a gentle flirtation could be fun.

Instead of replying in kind she walked away from him, going back up the room with her hands clasped so tightly together in front of her that the knuckles were white. At the far end she turned to ask, 'And your partner? Will Mr Docherty be coming down here to visit?'

'I believe so. Mrs Caine is his sister, is she not?'

'Yes. But they don't get on.'

'She is upset at the thought of him coming?'

'Yes, very. They've had enough trouble lately with the fire and then her losing the baby she was carrying. She's not worried for herself – she and Josie are leaving for England in a couple of days – but she's afraid Mr Docherty will cause trouble for her family. Couldn't you tell him she's gone, suggest it's a waste of time his coming here?'

As she looked at him with her clear, blue eyes, something twisted inside Matthieu but he pushed it aside. 'I doubt Dermott ever lets anyone tell him what to do. He is not that sort of a man. And I'm afraid since he owns this place, I cannot forbid him to come here.' After an awkward silence, he changed the subject. 'How are you all managing at Lizabrook since the fire?'

'Mr Caine has worked very hard to rebuild the place, though we're still living in rather restricted conditions.'

'That must be difficult for you. Could you not find yourself another employer? In Perth perhaps? You're a long way from civilisation here.'

'I get on well with the Caines. They've been good to me. Though I have been thinking . . .' She broke off abruptly, as if regretting this confidence, and said hastily, 'But I shouldn't like to leave them at present. Nor should I like to see anything else hurt them.'

Here was another person who thought well of the Caines. It did not match with what Dermott had said about his sister. 'I have suggested to him that it is time to forget the past.'

'And did he agree?'

'He is considering the matter. I can do no more.'

After consulting the pretty gold watch pinned to her bodice Ilse moved towards the door. 'We must leave now. We have Josie's packing still to finish. It's a lovely house, though. I'm sure any woman would be happy to live here.' She didn't wait for him but hurried outside.

Josie had filled the sack with apples and was munching one with relish.

Matthieu went over to tie the top corners of the sack together. 'You've worked quickly, young lady. Let's saddle the pack horse. Ginger can carry that sack for us and another filled with windfalls, if you like. If we work quickly we can soon fill one.'

At the farm he lifted the sacks down and propped them by the back door, then turned to hold out his hand to the governess. '*Auf wiedersehen, Ilse.*'

She did not refuse to take his hand nor did she chide him for using her first name, so he clasped her hand for a moment longer than he should have done and murmured, 'It's a beautiful name. It suits you.' Only then did he let go and hold out his hand to the child. '*Au 'voir* to you as well, Joséphine. And *bon voyage!*'

'*Merci beaucoup, Monsieur.*' She giggled at her own temerity in using the French words Frau Hebel had practised with her the previous day.

He smiled as he watched them enter the house. The woman did not look back, but the child stopped at the door and waved vigorously.

He led the pack horse slowly back, thinking about her, this cool German woman with her silvery blonde hair and pale blue eyes. Did he really wish to pursue her? He shouldn't. The wisest thing to do would be to leave Brookley now.

Only he had never been wise where women were concerned. And Ilse was very different from others he had known, intriguingly different.

The following morning Cathie got up as soon as she heard the knocker-up coming along the street in the pre-dawn hush. He was rapping on bedroom windows with his long pole and calling out the time.

Determined to earn her keep, she flung her clothes on anyhow and hurried downstairs to get the fire going and water boiling for Magnus's shave and cup of tea.

When he came downstairs he stared at her as if he didn't believe what he saw, then muttered a greeting before going out to the privy. By the time he returned she had toasted some pieces of bread on the fire, buttered them and put them on the edge of the hob to keep warm. She busied herself making some cheese sandwiches for his mid-day meal.

'I don't expect you to wait on me,' he said as he took his place at the table. 'You could have stayed in bed a little longer.'

'I always wake early, and anyway I wanted to talk to you – to ask if I could take your mother for a walk? She seemed to enjoy being outside yesterday and kept turning up her face to the sun. When we came back, she didn't want to come inside.'

'She used to love going for walks. You could try it, see how she goes. Mrs Midner rarely took her out.' He gave directions for a pleasant walk towards the outskirts of the town.

'And the other thing is, what do you want for tea tonight?'

'Eh, lassie, anything is fine. Lately I've not been used to . . .' his voice came out choked, '. . . being cared for like this.'

'All right.' She tended to the fire, thinking what a bleak time he must have been having.

His voice made her jump. 'I usually get my mother up before I go.'

'I can do that. You take your time today.'

A long silence, then, 'Thank you. It's a rare treat not to be rushing around.'

She turned and looked him in the eyes. 'I could be dead if you hadn't helped me. I owe you a great deal, Magnus Hamilton, and I shan't forget that.' And even if the work was more of the domestic drudgery she'd hated, she was surrounded by people, not trees, which made life much more interesting.

He loved the sound of his name on her lips. 'I'm very glad you're not dead, Caitlin,' he said before he could help himself, then picked up another piece of toast and concentrated on his food.

She said teasingly, 'Will you be coming home at the same time today, *Cousin* Magnus?'

That made him look up and smile. 'Aye. I will, *Cousin* Caitlin.'

When the front door closed behind him, she ran into the front parlour to watch him stride down the street, arms swinging, head held high, one of the first to leave for work. His bright hair caught the sunlight and his height and proud bearing made the other people seem like drab and dwarfish creatures. He was, she decided, the most attractive man she had ever met and she could not help wondering what he thought of her.

Then a noise from upstairs recalled her to her duties.

Later that morning Cathie took her 'Auntie Janey' out for a walk, noting again how willingly the older woman went outside. They took the route Magnus had recommended, heading west and avoiding the town centre. Since Janey did not seem to be tiring, Cathie followed the road as far as some large houses which stood quite a distance apart from one another, surrounded by luxuriant gardens. She had never seen anything like them and slowed down to gaze at the massed flower displays, entranced by their vivid colour and beauty, not to mention the soft green of the neatly trimmed lawns.

A vision of a sun-baked field of beige grass surrounded by dull green foliage flashed before her eyes. Australia. That was followed by another image, even more vivid: a small woman with dark hair, hands on hips, scolding, but in a fond voice. 'Mother,' Cathie whispered. A dark-haired man walked into the scene in her head. Her father – no, her stepfather. Then his name: Benedict Caine. Was her surname Caine, then? It didn't seem right. Had he not given her his name? She felt – no, she *knew* – she loved him, but she was equally sure that Caine wasn't her real surname.

Tears trickled down her cheeks. From the half-finished letter in her handbag she guessed that she had run away and that must have hurt them. As soon as she remembered their address she'd write to them again and assure them she was all right.

But why had she run away from people she loved?

232

Then Janey whimpered and tugged her onwards. So Cathie banished her memories and simply enjoyed the walk, getting to know the English countryside as she had once known the Australian bush.

Meanwhile in Rawley Manor – the largest of the houses Cathie had walked past – Alexander Stephenson was berating his great-nephew in a low, furious voice, for Francis had been sent home from school due to a lingering illness. A Rawley should be well educated, able to hold his own in any company, as Alexander prided himself on doing. But the latest report from the expensive boarding school for the sons of gentlemen was worse than the previous one and said bluntly that Francis was more interested in painting than in study, showing no aptitude for sport, either.

The boy was such a disappointment! For all the careful upbringing Alexander had bestowed on him, he had not been able to mould his nephew into a satisfactory future owner of a great estate. The lad was a poor rider and the county gentry regarded him scornfully because of this. To make matters worse he also refused point blank to join the hunt or go out shooting, and no threats or bribes would change his mind about that. When he could, he slid away from confrontations of any sort; when he could not avoid trouble, he accepted punishment sullenly, but it seemed to make little difference to his behaviour.

It must be his mother's Irish blood which had done this and it sickened Alexander that *her* son would inherit this great estate. Why his nephew had married such a common creature he had never understood. Liza might have been pretty, but so were dozens of other young women.

Well, Nicholas had come to regret his hasty match and at least he'd left his son to the guardian-ship of people of breeding, not to *her*. Alexander had swiftly made sure she left the country so that she could not interfere.

But would his efforts make a difference? They said what was bred in the bone would come out in the flesh. If Francis grew up feckless and let the estate run to rack and ruin, Alexander would not be there to prevent it. He was over eighty now, and felt his age sometimes. The previous year he had had a small seizure, though he had hidden that from everyone except his valet. It had left one leg a bit numb and made him forgetful for a time, but that had passed. But it was a warning that he must do something about the boy. If he died before Francis was twenty-one, there were only lawyers to act as guardians because there were no other close family members left – well, none that he would trust. This idle great-nephew of his was the last descendant of a once-proud name, the only one left to continue the line!

Alexander realised that he had been muttering to himself, a habit that had crept up on him since his sister's death, and that Francis was staring at him. He forced back the anger. Anger was dangerous for a man of his age. He *had* to live long enough to find Francis a suitable wife, one from a good family, who would put some backbone into the next generation.

'Go to your room!' he snapped, suddenly weary of scolding someone who wasn't really listening. 'And you're not to leave it until dinner time.'

He waited until the library door had closed then sank into a chair, wiping his forehead with his handkerchief and willing his thudding heart to slow down. This happened occasionally. It meant nothing. Neither did the occasional forgetfulness. Just signs of old age.

Francis was glad to leave the library for his uncle's rages had become worse lately. He climbed slowly up the stairs to his bedroom, sighing in frustration as he looked through the landing window. He would have loved to stroll through the sun-dappled woods. Instead he had to sit in his stuffy room, treated like a child – again. He flung open the window and leaned out.

Life hadn't been so bad until his grandmother died because she'd always been there to cheer him up and intercede for him with her brother. He'd missed her greatly in the two years since her death. His uncle did nothing but scold. What did it matter whether a fellow did well at his studies or not? Francis wouldn't have to earn a living because the estate would take care of all that. He looked round him frowning. He had always loved his home, but lately it had begun to seem more like a prison. Dull, beige wallpaper with a small pattern in brown, dark furniture, faded green brocade curtains and a square of brown carpet. Dreary, faded colours to match a dreary place. How many unhappy hours had he spent here?

As soon as he reached his majority he would send his great-uncle packing. He wanted life at Rawley Manor to be happy and that wasn't possible with the old man in charge. He'd hated his uncle for as long as he could remember, just as he hated the mother who had abandoned him and never tried to visit him or even find out how he was doing. The thought that she was probably still alive somewhere in Australia with her other children always hurt. She hadn't abandoned *them*, just Francis.

But there were more than six years to get through until he reached his majority. He gave a low groan and beat out his frustration with one clenched fist against the wooden frame of the great bay window that overlooked the front gardens.

Once this had all been countryside dominated by the manor house, but in the past decade the town had reached out to swallow up the farmland and, to his uncle's annoyance, his father had sold some of their land, believing the days of great estates were past and money in the bank was what counted now. There were several large new houses close by, modern places with immaculate gardens, inhabited by people his uncle referred to scathingly as 'nouveaux riches'.

The new neighbours were not invited to visit the Manor, nor did Alexander Stephenson call on them. Some of them had youngsters whom Francis watched occasionally from the shelter of the woods. He'd have loved to join in their croquet matches or ride a bicycle along the lanes with the other young fellows, but not only was he not allowed to associate with them, he was not even allowed to possess a bicycle, which his uncle considered only suitable for mechanics and other common persons.

Francis slouched across the room to stare at himself in the mirror over the mantelpiece. He was still a bit pale after the influenza. All he really wanted was a peaceful, happy life and a few friends of his own age. Was it so much to ask? Apparently so. He had a couple of good friends at school, but dared not ask to invite them back because his uncle would sneer about their families, then write to the headmaster asking that the lads be kept apart. He had done that once when Francis was younger and had made an 'unsuitable' friend.

The lad leaned forward to examine his own features, something he had done many times before. Did he look like *her*, the mother who had abandoned him in return for money? His uncle denied any likeness, pointing out that not only did he have blond hair, like many of the Rawleys, but greatly resembled his father also. Francis's grandmother had more than once said that he had his mother's eyes, though.

He went back to sprawl on the window seat again, wishing he could go sketching in the woods. But his uncle had taken away his sketching equipment after reading the report from school and told him he'd only get his things back when he showed signs of buckling down to scholastic work. Crossing his arms behind his head Francis stared up at the ceiling, losing himself in dreams of better times.

When the bell rang for dinner it took him by surprise and he jumped up with a yelp of dismay. He hadn't changed his clothes and was so late that he rushed downstairs as he was, for his uncle detested unpunctuality.

Alexander took one look at him and breathed in deeply. 'You have not changed.'

'I forgot about the time. I thought you'd prefer me not to be late.'

'I'd prefer you to be both punctual *and* properly clad. You may return to your room and we'll see if hunger will teach you to behave like a gentleman in future.'

Francis walked out without another word. At nearly fifteen he bitterly resented being treated like this, though at least the punishment got him out of another boring formal dinner with the two of them sitting opposite one another at the long, gleaming table. Anyway, Cook would find a way to slip him something to eat. She always did.

He was very fond of Mrs Denham, who had arrived here when he was four and whose pet he had always been. Fortunately, her cooking exactly suited his uncle's troublesome digestion, so that the old man did not treat her as harshly as he did the other servants.

Ten minutes later Francis was working his way through a plate of sandwiches and an apple, knowing his uncle would not come upstairs until he had slowly picked his way through the four-course meal. The maid who had brought the food up to his room had begged him in a whisper to hide the plate under his bed afterwards or she'd be for it. While he ate, Francis bent his mind to how he was going to pass the time during the coming summer holidays and – most important of all – how to avoid his uncle as much as possible. It would be best to find some excuse for getting out of the house.

After a few minutes it came to him. Walking. He'd take up walking, claim it had been recommended to get him fitter for his return to school in the autumn. Would his uncle allow that? Well, he might if Francis pretended reluctance to take extra exercise.

The following morning his uncle asked curtly, 'Have you been set any tasks by your schoolmasters? I do not wish you to waste your time while you're recovering.'

'I'm supposed to read and do a lot of walking to get myself fitter.' Enjoying this venture into deceit, Francis put on a sulky expression.

'I think exercise an excellent idea. You will go out for long walks on fine days and we'll find you some suitable indoor occupations for the wet ones. And I myself will select your reading material.'

Francis heaved a loud, aggrieved sigh.

His uncle breathed deeply and slowly.

When Francis got to the woods, he could hold back his amusement no longer. He threw back his head and roared with laughter, stamping to and fro gleefully and wishing he had someone to share the joke with.

When Janey Hamilton heard the laughter she suddenly broke away from Cathie to run towards the sound. It took a minute or two for Cathie, who had been lost in thought, to realise what had happened and chase after her.

She found her charge in a clearing, standing very close to a young man with her face thrust out, rocking from one foot to the other.

He was gazing at her in pop-eyed astonishment and looked up in patent relief as Cathie came to a halt and put one arm around Janey.

'I'm so sorry. She got away from me.' As he smiled, something about his appearance seemed familiar and Cathie frowned at him as she tried to work out what it was. If only she had all her memories back. 'Have I met you before?'

'No. Never.'

Janey began to walk round them, so Cathie let her.

'I say, is she—?' He tapped his forehead.

'Yes. It's very sad, but she's not dangerous. She's my auntie and I'm looking after her.'

He was staring at Janey as if fascinated. 'That can't be much fun for you.'

'I needed a job, so it suits me for a time.' Cathie tried to take hold of Janey's hand, intending to leave him, but Janey had her own ideas and let out a scream of defiance, reaching out towards the young man instead.

He patted the older woman's shoulder as he would have done a pet, and when she resumed her walking round them, he thrust out one hand to Cathie. 'I'm Francis Rawley.'

The name seemed faintly familiar and she still felt as if she knew his face. There was something about the eyes. 'I'm Caitlin Rutherford.'

Janey stopped beside him again.

'I'm sorry,' Cathie said, tugging in vain at her arm. 'She seems to have taken a fancy to you.'

'Look, I'll walk with you to the road, if that makes her move on. *I* don't mind you being here, but my uncle hates people trespassing in the woods.'

'He should put up stronger fences, then.' They began walking, but as they reached a gap in the trees the house came into view, a huge stone place, and Cathie stopped to gaze at it. 'Is that your uncle's?'

'Um – no. Actually it's mine.' He shrugged his shoulders, trying to act as if it didn't matter. 'Or it will be when I'm twenty-one. My uncle's in charge till then.' His face grew bitter.

'What happened to your parents?' she asked, then realised how tactless this question was. 'Sorry, none of my business.'

He thrust his hands into his pockets and began to kick at some loose earth where a small animal had been digging. 'My father's dead and my mother left me to my uncle's tender mercies when I was quite little.'

She could hear the bitterness in his voice and laid one hand on his shoulder without thinking, squeezing it slightly as she would have done with one of her brothers. 'Have you never seen her again?'

'I've never seen her at all! I don't,' his voice broke on the words, 'even remember her face, though my grandmother used to say I had her eyes.'

'She must have been pretty, then.'

He glared at her. 'Are you saying I'm pretty? Like a girl? Thank you very much!'

He was so like her brother Seth, hiding his emotions behind a truculent attitude that she said without thinking, 'Oh, for heaven's sake, don't be so touchy.'

He jerked away from her, still scowling. 'The woods end there. You'd better get back on the road.' Then he walked off, shoulders hunched.

Janey tried to follow him, pulling at Cathie's arm, and did not calm down until he was out of sight.

242

That boy was very unhappy, Cathie decided as she turned her charge towards the town again. And very bitter towards his mother. Rightly so. How could any mother leave a child for others to bring up? Her own wouldn't have done such a thing – she paused on that thought. Strange how sure she felt of that. Again she saw the woman's face, dark-haired and laughing this time, and knew she'd been loved. Her mother's name was Liza! Liza Caine. Suddenly Cathie's own surname popped into her mind: Ludlam. Now how could that be? Ludlam's was the name of the mill where Magnus worked. She couldn't be related to them, could she? Her head began to throb and she realised Janey was growing restless, doing that mindless rocking movement again.

Taking a firmer hold of the older woman's hand, Cathie started walking briskly towards the town. Time to go back. And on the way she'd buy some food for the evening meal. But for some reason she couldn't stop thinking about poor Francis Rawley, who might be rich but wasn't happy and who was so bitter about his mother.

When they got back Janey fell asleep in the rocking chair and Cathie sat opposite her for a while, having no success in willing the phantom memories to return. Cathie Ludlam. Could she be related to the owners of the mill or was it a common name in Pendleworth?

Oh, it was so frustrating not to know things! But at least she was starting to get her memory back.

And in the meantime she had somewhere to live and was earning her keep, even if the job was not very interesting. That would have to do for the time being.

CHAPTER 11

MAY–JUNE

Josie burst into the house full of the tale of their visit to Baileys' Farm. Benedict listened with a scowl, but agreed that the apples would be most welcome. There was no sense in wasting good food, wherever it came from.

Liza asked, 'Is my brother intending to come and visit his friend?'

After a moment's hesitation, Ilse said, 'It's worse than that, I'm afraid.'

'What do you mean?'

'Your brother owns the farm.'

There was silence, then Liza covered her face with one shaking hand, making a faint, distressed sound.

'Is he so bad, your brother?' Ilse asked.

'He used to be dreadful, probably still is. I must warn Dinny. She might be in danger from him as well. Maybe I shouldn't go to England.' Liza saw the puzzlement in Ilse's eyes and realised that Agnes had stopped sewing to watch her. 'Dermott swore once to get his revenge on me.'

'What for?' Agnes asked quietly. 'May we know? It's better to be forewarned.'

Liza hesitated, then decided to tell them. Better they heard it from her than from Dermott. She glanced round, but Josie had gone off to her room to continue sorting out her toys for the journey and Harry was helping Dinny sort through the apples. 'My oldest brother, Niall – he attacked Dinny. This was years ago, before I married Nicholas. So I got the shotgun and threatened Niall with it, told him to leave us alone. Only he kept coming towards me, laughing. There was no one to call to for help, just me and Dinny, so I fired.' She drew in a ragged breath and went on shakily, 'He was very close to me by then and it – killed him.'

Horror flooded through her in a black wave as it still did every time she remembered that dreadful night, but she was determined to tell them the rest of the story so that they would understand. 'I told Dermott to leave. I still had the gun with the other barrel loaded, so he did. But he said,' she gulped, 'he'd come back one day and make me sorry. I knew he would, I've always known that.'

'Oh, Liza!' Agnes got up and went to hug her. 'How brave you were!'

'I wasn't brave, just desperate, but I didn't mean to kill Niall. *I didn't!* Benedict helped me bury him next to my first husband, down by the lake. I go there sometimes to pray for his soul.' And for her own.

Agnes said thoughtfully, 'I don't like Mr Docherty

myself, but surely he wouldn't attack you after all these years? You are still his sister, after all, and this is 1876, not the Dark Ages.'

'My being his sister doesn't mean anything to him. He was only ever close to Niall – and to Mum. Benedict believes the bush fires were set deliberately – and who else but Dermott would have done that? What if he does something else while I'm away, something worse?' Liza bowed her head for a moment. Thoughts like these were the demons that came to torment her in the night. 'What's his wife like?'

Agnes cocked her head on one side, thinking what to say. 'Bred a lady, I'd guess, but a shrew. Her name's Christina. She dresses in the height of fashion whether the occasion warrants it or not. I can't see her living down here in the bush for long. They have two sons, who are alternately spoilt and scolded from what I can see – which doesn't form very pleasing characters. Though Mr Correntin is very good with them, I will say.'

'He was good with Josie, too,' Ilse admitted. 'Treated her like a grown lady and she loved it. But if he's Mr Docherty's partner . . .' She let the words trail away. He was probably just using her to get information. His flirting didn't mean a thing.

She found it hard to settle to sleep that night because she kept going back over their conversation. They had not said anything personal, but she could not help being aware of him as a man – and a very attractive one. And she had felt that he was equally aware of her as a woman, until Liza told her about Mr Docherty.

A tear traced its way down Ilse's cheek. She should have known better than to believe a man like that could be interested in her. She should definitely have known better by now. Only old men seemed to like her.

Liza decided in the end that Dermott was less likely to attack her family if she was away, so she asked the governess to tell Mr Correntin as soon as she had left. Ilse could think of no reason for refusing, though she would have infinitely preferred not to see him alone.

Benedict was to drive his wife and daughter up to Fremantle where they would take the coaster down to Albany. Josie was wild with excitement and hardly slept a wink the night before. Harry was surly because he was not going with them.

With tears streaming down her face, Liza kissed each of her sons, for she considered Lucas just as much hers as the others. 'Be good and look after your father,' she said in a choked voice.

'Give Cathie our best love,' said Lucas, always the spokesman for the others. 'And don't worry, Mum. Seth and I are not children now.' He lowered his voice. 'We won't let anyone hurt him. And we'll look after Harry.'

So she had to give him another hug and wonder yet again what was driving her to go so far away.

Was this worry about Cathie and Francis just a foolish fancy, or was it as real as Dinny believed?

Seth grinned at her, holding back his emotions with banter, as usual. 'I'm tempted to hide in your trunks,' he teased. 'Are you sure you don't want me to come and look after you on the journey?'

'I want you here, looking after your father.' And when she got back she intended to tell Seth that Benedict was his real father, even if that reflected badly on her. Cathie had run away to find her real father. It was important that Seth know the truth.

She turned to Harry, who was scowling at her, bottom lip pushed out. Not allowing him time to protest, she folded him in her arms. 'I'm relying on you to keep your father from getting sad,' she whispered. 'No one can make him laugh like you can. That's why I'm leaving you here.' And also because an energetic child would find the long voyage very frustrating.

He was only partly appeased. That bottom lip still stuck out.

'Oh, darling, I do love you!' Liza gave him a quick kiss and turned to the two women, standing together behind the children. 'Agnes, this wouldn't be possible without you. How can I ever thank you for postponing your return to Perth?'

'You don't need to thank me,' Agnes said. 'If I'd looked after your daughter properly, you wouldn't need to go.'

But Liza knew differently. There would still have been Francis. It was more than time she met him.

And then they were in the cart rumbling down the track. She turned for a last look at her home, then blinked away her tears and looked straight ahead.

The following day Ilse turned up at Baileys' Farm accompanied by Harry. Matthieu invited her in, but she declined. 'I need to speak to you – privately. Harry, will you wait for me here?' She began walking towards the orchard.

Matthieu thought she seemed embarrassed, so let her take her own time to speak.

When the child was out of earshot, she stopped and said, 'I came at Mrs Caine's request to tell you that she's left for England and to ask that you pass this information on to her brother.'

He whistled softly. 'She's left already?'

'Do you think – will he still try to harm her family now that she's not here?'

He looked at her and shrugged. 'I think not, but if I see anything happening, I shall try to prevent it.'

She stared at him in surprise. 'You will?'

'Of course. What sort of man do you take me for?'

'I don't know.' She turned to leave.

He caught hold of her arm and swung her round to face him, but resisted the temptation to kiss her smooth skin because that might frighten her off. 'When I come back from Perth, may I visit you?' She flushed and did not seem to know what to say, so he smiled and amended it to, 'I *shall* be coming back and I *shall* definitely call on you, Ilse.' He saw a pulse beating in the white skin of her elegant throat. He would kiss it one day and make it beat even faster.

This time he let her return to the child and stood watching as they walked away. He was not surprised when she did not look back.

He found a perverse and slightly malicious satisfaction in contemplating his partner's rage when Dermott found out that his sister had left for England. Well, serve him right! It was stupid to cling to a desire for revenge. He had spoken about it several times. And this Niall, whom his partner had clearly idolised, must have been a very unsavoury character. A woman was entitled to defend herself against rape.

He ought to go back to Perth and tell Dermott that his sister had gone to England but he wanted to stay here, and for the stupidest of reasons – a woman.

Matthieu stared round the large room. It was a good house and an attractive piece of land, though his partner probably hadn't even noticed how pretty the bush was round here or how beautiful the lake could be made with a little effort. But the place had no prospect of growth in value as far as Matthieu could see, not unless someone put a lot of hard work in. It was not a good investment unless you liked the countryside and wanted to live there.

The thought came to him suddenly: he could

farm it, plant some vines. They made wine over in New South Wales, so why not here?

Was Ilse the sort to live quietly in the country and raise a family? Did he want to find out? *Bon dieu*, he was a fool for even thinking of buying the place! How Dermott would laugh at him!

In Pendleworth Jim and Bob Marshall were enjoying a glass of beer together. 'Have you heard?' Jim asked.

'Heard what?' Bob stared at the froth on the top of his glass, wondering how long he could spin this one out. He did not allow himself to spend lavishly on beer, not with a family to feed, but he enjoyed the company at the pub, the warmth and the bright flaring gas lights.

'About Mr High and Mighty Hamilton. He's only got a lass living in his house now.' Jim sniggered. 'Says she's his cousin, but Ma Midner won't work for him any more so folk don't believe him.'

'He should stick that mother of his in the Ben. That's what it's for. I wish we could stick our Dad there, by heck I do. He's broken them spectacles again, the old devil. I shall take the cost of the new ones out of his wages, though. He'll be sorry when he can't buy himself a glass of beer.'

'Never mind our dad, what do you think of Hamilton taking a girl in? She's from Australia, they say, and—'

'*What did you say?*' They stared at one another, then Bob said slowly, 'There can't be two lasses from Australia come to Pendleworth in one month, Jim lad. Maybe she's the one we're keeping an eye open for?'

'Nay, I thought of that, but this one's called Caitlin, not Cathie. She's looking after the loony, callin' her Auntie Janey, but folk are laughing behind their hands, thinking it's just a tale to make it look more respectable like, her warming Hamilton's bed.'

'Caitlin's not that much different from Cathie as a name. What's her surname?'

'They didn't say.'

'Then bloody well find out! We need to know.'

Cathie had now settled into a simple routine and her memory was gradually returning, though still not complete. She had, after some consideration, told Magnus what she thought her surname was and asked him about the Ludlams.

He frowned at her revelation. 'I heard Mr Matthew had a brother who was sent out to Australia in disgrace. Josiah Ludlam died out there, apparently.' He didn't intend to tell her what else they'd said about Josiah or how one or two of the older men still sniggered about him in unguarded moments. 'Do you think he could have been your father?'

'Josiah? Yes, that was the name of my mother's first husband. I grew up thinking he was my father, but one night I overheard my parents talking about my "real father" so now I'm not sure of anything.'

'That must be hard for you, lassie.'

She could only shrug. Everything had been hard since her arrival in England. And perhaps, if what she had remembered was correct, she deserved that, deserved even the penance of looking after an old lady who could offer her no companionship.

Magnus studied Caitlin's features as they ate their meal. He could not see any resemblance to the Ludlams in her face. Yes, she was dark-haired, but her hair was thick and bouncy while theirs was very straight. He thought of Mr Reuben and shook his head. No, they couldn't be related. She had broad features with an open, sunny expression most of the time, not a long, narrow Ludlam head like those on the medieval tombs in the parish church. The older Ludlams always had dour expressions, too, as if life had not been pleasant for them. Only Mr Reuben had an open look to him, and Magnus was glad he worked with *him*, not his father, Mr Matthew.

He was teased by some obscure resemblance in her face, however, something that did remind him of someone . . . but he could not pin it down so he said nothing. Maybe it would come to him.

Mairi had written to say she and her husband would be coming the following Sunday to meet the woman who was looking after their mother. It was a brief note, without the usual anecdotes of her daily life, and he realised how suspicious she was about their new 'cousin'. Well, he was sure once she'd met Caitlin, Mairi would feel better about the situation and realise he had not brought a mistress into his home but a decent, hard-working lass.

That conjured up a vision of Caitlin in his bed that brought a flush to his cheeks. He was a man, with a man's needs long unsatisfied, and could not help reacting to her, but he could not do anything about it. The way his mother was he had nothing to offer any woman but drudgery.

Though Caitlin seemed not to mind: singing about her work, chatting cheerfully in the evenings about what she had seen on her walks. Life had seemed so much brighter since her arrival. How would he ever manage without her now?

Before his sister arrived he suggested Caitlin take advantage of the fine day to go out for a brisk walk on her own. 'Please don't be offended, but my sister will not be satisfied until she has all the details of why you're living here and it'll be best if she and I have a talk in private first.'

'Will she pretend I'm her cousin, do you think?'

'Aye, I think so. Once she's met you and seen how well you're caring for Mum.'

'I hate people thinking I'm – you know—' Cathie broke off, her cheeks scarlet.

He nodded. 'Aye. So do I. I didn't mean that to happen.'

'It wasn't your fault. Who knows whether I'd even be alive if you hadn't intervened that day?'

He blurted out, 'Och, that doesna' bear

thinking of!' which embarrassed them both greatly. So he went off to fill the coal scuttle while she dusted the front room, determined to have everything perfect for Mairi.

Cathie left soon afterwards. It felt strange to be out on her own and when her feet automatically took her in the direction of Rawley Manor she didn't question the wisdom of this. She wanted to see Francis Rawley again because she felt she knew the name. She sighed. It was another of the missing pieces of her memory. How long was it going to take to recover fully, to be certain of who she was and exactly why she was here in England? Surely she hadn't just come here on a whim?

She walked briskly, intending to go further out into the countryside than had been possible with Auntie Janey shuffling along beside her, but when she got to the Rawley estate, she slowed down and studied the distant house thoughtfully. Again it was almost as if she could recognise it, but she couldn't think why. Today being a Sunday there was no one to be seen working in the grounds and even the horses were standing quietly in the shade at one corner of a meadow to the right, tails flicking occasionally to dislodge a fly.

As she continued along the narrow road the hedges gave way to a wall, and then to a neat gate-house. This time she didn't walk past, but stopped to study the view down the gravelled drive through the big wrought-iron gates.

A man came out. 'Are you lost, miss?'

'No. I was just admiring the house.'

'Begging your pardon, but Mr Stephenson doesn't like folk loitering round here.'

She was puzzled. 'Is this not a public road?'

'Well, it is, but if you'll take my advice, miss, and no offence intended, you'd best be on your way. Mr Stephenson has a way of making people sorry if they don't do as he wishes.' And had been even more unreasonable of late, so that everyone on the estate was afraid of angering him.

Cathie folded her arms and gave the man back stare for stare. 'If this were private land, I would move away at once, but as it's a public road I'll decide for myself. I'm told England is still a free country.'

He stepped back, shaking his head. 'I'll have to report you, then.' Mr Stephenson always wanted to know if anyone had been 'hanging around'.

From behind some trees, Francis heard the exchange and grinned. She was a lively one. Then his smile faded. If she was living in a Rawley or Ludlam house in Pendleworth, she'd soon find out how easy it was for his uncle to get her evicted. Perhaps he'd better warn her?

When she moved on, he hurried along the inside of the wall until it gave way to hedges again. Only last year his uncle had suggested building a stone wall all the way round the park. For once, Francis had dredged up the courage to say he didn't want a wall round his home and if his uncle erected one, he would pull it down again the minute he attained his majority. That had cost him a few furious scoldings about ingratitude and young people thinking they knew better than their elders, but the question of the wall had not been raised again. If his uncle had really wanted to build one, however, they both knew he would have done so.

Francis was waiting for the young woman as she strolled around a bend in the road. 'Hello again! I heard you talking to our gatekeeper.'

She scowled at him. 'And are you also going to warn me not to walk along this road?'

'No. Well, not exactly. It's just that my uncle can make things pretty unpleasant for people who annoy him so you should take care.'

She set her hands on her hips, angry at having her lovely walk spoiled. 'Well! Who does your uncle think he is? Lord of all creation?'

Francis grinned. 'Pretty much. He seems to think we're still in medieval times and the rest of the world is divided into serfs and gentry.' Then the grin faded and he sighed. 'When I come into my inheritance I shan't behave like that, I promise you.'

'My stepfather always said the gentry in England had too much power, but I didn't realise what he meant until now.'

He could see her studying him as if he were a curiosity, and didn't like it. 'I'm not real gentry, you know. My father married a woman from the lower classes and my uncle has never forgiven him for it. He hates even to hear her name mentioned.'

Cathie's head started to thump. *Rawley*. She had been wondering where she had heard that name before. Suddenly another set of memories tumbled into place, each one triggering the next. She groaned and put one hand to her temple as pain stabbed through it.

'I say, are you all right?'

He stepped forward to put an arm round her and she leaned against him, unable to answer until the roaring inside her head stopped. Then she moved away, shaking her head to clear it. He was still standing close to her, looking anxious, and was the same height as she was for all he seemed younger. She stared at him and knew in a blinding flash who he resembled. Her mother! He had exactly her mother's eyes and that same way of holding his head.

'Was your father's name Nicholas?' she asked, her voice coming out haltingly as she struggled to take in all the new information that was echoing round her skull.

'Yes, it was.'

She could think of no way to soften the shock. 'Then you're my half-brother. My real name's Cathie. Cathie Ludlam.'

There was dead silence for several moments. If birds were still singing, Cathie didn't hear them, and even though a bee paused to study her dress before deciding it was not a flower and flying on, she heard no sound from it, because she was watching Francis, hoping desperately that he would not reject her.

'Are you sure of that?' he asked hoarsely.

'Very sure. And – and now I can remember you as a baby, too. When my mother married your father, we all lived there.' She gestured in the direction of the house. 'That's why I kept wanting to look at it, why it seemed so familiar.' She sighed. 'Other things in Pendleworth have seemed familiar, too, but I was only a small child when we left so they don't look the same now. I remember a big wall and now that I've grown so tall, I look at it again and it seems quite a small one. So I'm never quite sure if I'm really remembering something or not. And when memories do come back, as they did just now, they're all vague and jumbled at first. I feel so impatient to understand everything properly. My mother always says I—'

'I don't want to hear anything about *her*, thank you very much. She abandoned me when I was a baby. They paid her to leave me with them and *she took the money. Sold me!*'

He turned as if to leave and Cathie grabbed his arm. 'That's not true. Really it isn't!'

He let out a snort of disbelief. 'She didn't tell you the truth because she knew it wouldn't reflect well on her to have abandoned her own son.'

Cathie was about to inform him that her mother didn't lie to her, but suddenly remembered that both Liza and Benedict had lied about her real father, so instead she seized on another piece of information which had fallen into place in her mind. 'It'd be very easy to prove it one way or the other.'

'You think so?' He tried to tug his arm away.

She grasped it with both her hands and shook him to make him pay attention. 'I *know* so! Please don't run away, Francis. Can't you see – if we are brother and sister, we should get to know one another.'

He stopped pulling, but his expression was sullen. 'I won't believe anything unless it's proven beyond doubt.'

'You can do that. Mum and Dad have been paying a lawyer from Pendleworth to report on you once a year. His letter usually arrives a month or two after your birthday.'

'Oh? And when is my birthday?'

'You were born in 1861, on the eleventh of August. At the Manor.' She gestured towards the house.

He swallowed, looking suddenly younger and less certain of himself. 'How did you find that out?'

Another memory slotted into place. 'We children could never forget we had another brother, because every year on your birthday Mother used to get sad and go off for walks by herself. And – is there someone called Sophia Ludlam living nearby? She writes to Mother, too, and tells her how you are.'

He shook his head helplessly. Who to believe? His uncle or this girl with her fresh, open face who didn't look like a liar to him. The idea that he was not an only child pleased him, but he tried to conceal that as he asked, 'How many half-brothers and sisters do I have – if you're telling the truth?'

'Four, including me. Seth is sixteen this year, Josie ten, and Harry seven.' She could hear how uncertain his voice was and laid her hand on his arm, offering comfort by her touch.

'What's the lawyer's name?' he managed at last.

'Lorrimer.'

He stared at her. 'There *is* a lawyer called that in Pendleworth. He doesn't handle our affairs, Patenby does, but Bernard Lorrimer is well thought of in the town.' He backed away from her. 'I'm – I'm not discussing it any further until I've seen him, found out if . . .' He let the words trail away, then turned before he could ask her to tell him about the others, for questions were teeming in his brain. Two half-sisters and two half-brothers. What were they like? Were they all as tall and fresh-faced as she was?

No! He mustn't accept what she had told him. Not yet! It would be too hard if his hopes were dashed.

She didn't try to hold him back, but stood with her arms wrapped round herself, watching him stride towards the hedge. As he reached it he stopped and turned round.

'Can you come here next week at the same time?' There was a long pause, then he said her name, 'Cathie? Will you?'

She nodded.

He pushed his way through the hedge then broke into a run. When he was quite sure he was out of sight he stopped to wipe the tears from his eyes, only to find more welling in their place. Not until he had full control of his emotions did he return to the house. This was something he intended to inquire into for himself. If his uncle got one whisper of it, he'd send Cathie away – as he might have sent Francis's mother.

Once her half-brother had disappeared from sight, Cathie walked on for a while, her thoughts in turmoil, then realised that she was hungry and the sun was high in the sky, so began to tramp back. Not knowing another route, she had to go past the front gates of the Manor, but she marched past without pausing. This was no time to be causing trouble or getting herself noticed.

Mairi and Elwyn arrived at noon bringing a basket loaded with home-cooked food. It warmed Magnus's heart to see how happy they both looked and how fond of one another they were, exchanging glances and smiles without even realising what they were doing.

Magnus showed them round, proud of how well the house was looking, then they sat with their mother, who was also looking well cared for.

'She knows how to keep house, at least,' Mairi admitted. 'But I still can't see why you brought in a stranger. You might have known it'd cause talk.

And now you want me to lie about her, say she's our cousin—'

'Second cousin.'

'It's the same thing.'

Elwyn patted her arm. 'We should meet her before we decide anything, love.'

She scowled at him. 'I still don't like telling lies.'

When Cathie returned, she found the table set for a meal and Mairi rather stiff for a few minutes. She studied his sister with great interest. Mairi was tall, about the same height as Cathie, but she was not particularly good-looking, being very thin with hair closer to ginger than Magnus's red-blond, and a skin covered in freckles. Her husband Elwyn was plump and genial, with thinning hair and the kindest expression in his eyes that Cathie had ever seen. Magnus had said several times how glad he was to see Mairi married to a man like this and Cathie could see why.

As the two of them discussed Janey's progress, Magnus's sister became rather more friendly, and in the end they found themselves in complete agreement on how best to look after her.

Mairi was equally relieved to find Cathie a decent young woman. She looked up once, catching Magnus staring at the lass with a fond smile. He called her Caitlin and there was a warmth in his voice as he said the name. If that had been any other man, she'd have said he was taken with the girl. She glanced quickly towards Elwyn and he grinned in a conspiratorial way.

After that she could not feel as suspicious of the girl's motives. If Caitlin had managed to break through Magnus's reserve, bring that happier look to his face, then she could not be bad. More than anything else Mairi longed for her eldest brother to find the happiness and love she had discovered in her dearest Elwyn.

'So?' her husband said softly as they strolled through the town towards the station.

'What do you mean by that?' Mairi demanded.

'Eh, my love, don't pretend you didn't notice how Magnus looked at her.'

She was silent until they turned the next corner, then said slowly, 'If she makes him happy, I don't care what her past is. He deserves something for himself.' And had to stop to wipe her eyes and let Elwyn give her a quick hug. 'Though he'll never be as happy as I am,' she said quickly, still feeling tearful.

When the visitors had gone, Cathie poured out the story of her encounter with Francis to Magnus.

He sat frowning in thought for so long that she asked impatiently, 'Well? What do you think of that?'

'I find it hard to believe – that you can be related to the Rawleys,' he said at last.

She chuckled. 'So does my brother.' Then her smile faded. 'But what upsets me is that they've poisoned his mind against my mother, told him she took money from them to leave him behind.

And she didn't. She wouldn't! They forced her to leave. I can remember now how she always grew sad when she mentioned him. It didn't really matter much to the rest of us. We knew we had a brother, but we never thought we'd meet him. Only now I have done and I like him. Isn't that wonderful?'

Magnus loved to see her excitement, and was beginning to think that this was her real personality, bubbling with enthusiasm for life. It was so contagious he was feeling happier by the day, in spite of his worries about his mother. 'Did you mebbe come to England to see him?' he wondered aloud.

She shook her head. 'No. Definitely not. I think – though I'm not perfectly sure of it yet – that I came to get away. And to find my real father. Only I still haven't remembered his name.'

'It'll come to you. Give it time, Caitlin lassie.'

She giggled, looking younger tonight. 'I like it when you call me "lassie". I love the way you talk.'

'Do ye now?'

'Aye, laddie,' she teased, trying and failing to imitate his Scottish lilt.

He watched her covertly as she got his mother ready for bed. At one stage she suddenly stopped and smiled at Caitlin, hugging her. Then the smile faded and she lapsed into the blank apathy that hurt him so much to see.

When Caitlin came down to join him for a quiet half hour in front of the fire, she said, 'Did you see how your mother smiled and hugged me?'

'Aye. I think in her own way she's grown fond of you. You look after her well. I'm grateful. So is Mairi.'

'I like to look after people. I just wish I could make your mother better, but I can't, can I?'

He sighed and shook his head.

Gradually the silence soothed him again. And Caitlin's company. Just to be with her in a room, not to be on his own . . . He cut those thoughts off short. He had no right to indulge in them. He leaned forward and lifted the coals to get the fire glowing more brightly. They didn't really need it, because it had been quite a warm day, but without it they'd not be able to heat the water for a last cup of cocoa, a ritual he looked forward to every night.

But once his mother died, what then?

Maybe – he hardly dared allow himself to hope – maybe then he could think of his own future.

CHAPTER 12

JUNE

The following day Francis saw his uncle staring at him in a jaundiced manner from across the breakfast table and tensed, waiting for criticism.

'You should go out walking again today,' Alexander said at last, after letting the silence drag on. 'It's giving you a better colour, making you look fitter. Your teachers were right.'

Relief filtered through Francis, but he shrugged and tried to look sulky. He glanced surreptitiously towards the head of the table. Was there something different about the old man today? Yes. His uncle's mouth looked pulled down at the left and his colour was bad, skin papery and dry. But no one would ever dare ask Alexander Stephenson how he was feeling because he seemed to deny the needs of his own body. There were days when he looked really ill but still he held himself upright, never giving in for a moment to bodily weakness.

Francis finished the meal quickly, then had to sit hiding his eagerness to escape until his uncle finally laid down his knife and fork, wiped his mouth with the table napkin and nodded dismissal.

The lad left the room as quickly as he could in case his uncle changed his mind.

He had decided to investigate his mother's actions today, though he felt afraid of what he might find. What if his uncle and his grandmother had lied to him? What if they really had sent his mother away from him? And – he hardly dared contemplate this – what if Cathie was right and their mother did care for him? Somehow he had no doubt that the young woman had been telling the truth when she had declared herself to be his half-sister.

If his uncle had really sent his mother away, he would never forgive him for it. Never.

There was a knock on the bedroom door. Hilda said, 'If you please, Master Francis, the master says you're to go out for your walk now.'

He scowled. There was no need to send the maids to chivvy him. 'Hilda, do you think there's something wrong with my uncle? His face looks different today.'

She glanced quickly over her shoulder. The servants had all noticed the same thing, but Mr Gower, the butler, had said they were to ignore it and Clifford, Mr Stephenson's manservant, said his master had refused to discuss it this morning and had acted as if everything was normal – though he'd moved more slowly, favouring his right side. 'When my granda had a seizure he looked like that, only he was much worse,' she told Francis in a low voice. 'There's nothing you can do about it. It made Granda right bad-tempered, though.'

She hoped it wouldn't make Mr Stephenson's temper worse because he had been really chancy lately, shouting at you for nothing then turning and walking off in the middle of saying something. Cook said it was old age. Hilda reckoned her master had been born bad-tempered. She was wondering about giving notice come quarter day. She didn't enjoy working here any more, even if they did pay well. Horace, the head groom, was trying to take liberties and getting above himself because the master favoured him. But where else could you get such work in Pendleworth? There were only the Ludlams and they were known to be stingy with their staff. Nor did she want to work in another town because her parents were getting on a bit and she liked to keep an eye on them. With a sigh she went back to her duties.

Francis left the house by the rear door. A brisk walk brought him to the edge of Rawley land. He pushed through one of the hedges on to a narrow lane that was not much used, then as he reached the town itself, kept to the back streets with their rows of smoke-blackened houses. He walked quickly, eager to reach his destination and a bit nervous of being seen. He could be sure his uncle would never drive along these streets, but could only pray that no one else would see him and mention it.

The worst moment was when he had to cross

Market Square to get to Lorrimer & Sons, whose offices were in one of the tall, grey-stone houses on the north side of the square. He slipped inside the front door quickly, panting from his haste and half-expecting to hear that thin dry voice behind him demanding what he was doing here and ordering him to come out at once.

'I'd like to see Mr Lorrimer,' he told the clerk. 'It's extremely urgent.'

'And your name, young sir?'

Francis hesitated then gave it, asking the clerk not to mention his visit to anyone else. He saw the surprise on the man's face because everyone knew that Patenby was the Rawleys' lawyer.

Within minutes Francis was shown into a large office which had an excellent view of the square, nearly empty now, but always crowded with people and animals on Thursday when it was market day.

Bernard Lorrimer shook hands then gestured to a chair. 'How can I help you, Mr Rawley?'

Francis looked into the kindly face and all his carefully prepared speeches vanished from his head. 'Is it true that you report to my mother every year on how I am?'

'Yes. We've been doing it ever since she left Pendleworth.'

'Did she – leave of her own accord?'

Bernard studied the anguished young face and decided the lad was old enough now to be told the truth. 'No. She ran foul of both Mr Stephenson and Mr Saul Ludlam, and they forced her to leave.

271

They wouldn't even let her say goodbye to you, from what my father told me. Your great-uncle's generation had a lot more power than yours will have. That sort of attitude is changing now.' And a good thing, too, he thought as he looked sympathetically at the young man who was clearly very distressed.

Francis found himself fighting a great wave of emotion that threatened to break and overwhelm him, so moved hastily to stand looking out of the window with his back to the lawyer. 'Did she take money from them for leaving?'

'No. Definitely not.' Bernard hesitated, then said gently, 'Mr Ludlam threatened to put her into an asylum for the mentally deranged, a dreadful place – the Ben hadn't been built then – and also threatened to accuse Mr Caine of theft. Your uncle prevented that injustice, at least, but he still sent your mother and Benedict Caine away to Australia without you.'

She had not wanted to leave him! The wave of anguish broke over Francis and nothing would hold it back.

Bernard got up and moved quickly to put an arm round the shoulders of the young man sobbing helplessly against his velvet curtains. He held the lad against him, patting his back and making soothing noises. Since he had sons of his own, he knew that lads of this age were not nearly as tough as they pretended.

It was some time before the storm of weeping

abated. Bernard proffered a handkerchief and gave Francis time to pull himself together. 'I think a cup of tea might help, don't you?' he asked gently when the damp handkerchief was offered back to him.

Francis nodded and watched Mr Lorrimer go to the door and speak to his clerk in a quiet voice. He was wondering what to do next, but was feeling so emotionally drained he could not think straight. The lawyer said nothing until the clerk brought in a tea-tray, which allowed Francis time to pull himself together.

'How did you find out about this?' Bernard asked as he filled a cup and passed it over.

'I met my half-sister. She told me. I didn't believe her at first, so she sent me to see you, said you could prove everything.'

'Your half-sister?'

'Cathie. She says her surname is Ludlam.'

Bernard frowned. The sister's arrival could really upset people and revive old scandals. 'I'd have thought your mother would have informed me of your sister's visit. Where is she staying? There might be difficulties with your uncle if he finds out she's here.'

Francis stared at him open-mouthed. 'Surely not?'

'He is still an influential man in this town and would be very averse to your meeting any of your mother's family. Since he'll be managing your affairs until you're of age, he has considerable power over your life. You'll need to take great care if you intend to go on meeting your sister, for her sake as well as your own.'

'Surely my uncle won't – he wouldn't *hurt* Cathie?'

Bernard shrugged. Who could tell? It was well known in Pendleworth that Alexander Stephenson still had a feudal attitude to life and to the estate he managed for his nephew. People employed there had to do what they were told or risk being thrown out. It was also known that he was getting grumpier and more unreasonable as he grew older. As he watched young Rawley sit up straighter, he had a sudden fancy that the lad had just grown up a little and this time when he spoke, Francis's tone was firmer.

'If my uncle tries to do anything to Cathie, he'll have me to answer to.' He frowned at Mr Lorrimer as something else occurred to him. 'Will *you* be in trouble if he finds out about the reports you've been sending?'

'None of my business is with the Rawley estate and I think I can look after myself legally.' Bernard hesitated, then said quietly, 'I shall deny saying this, but you might wish to check matters out very carefully once you take over as owner.'

Francis stared at him in shock. 'Is my uncle dishonest?' This was the last thing he had expected to hear.

'No, definitely not. But he's very harsh in his dealings with people of the lower classes. He doesn't hesitate to throw those he considers troublemakers out of their jobs and houses. I hope someone of your generation will be more generous to those less fortunate than himself. And you may perhaps wish to remedy past injustices.'

Francis gave him a very direct look. 'My uncle won't allow me to play any part in business matters at the moment, but I'll remember what you've said when I come of age, I promise you.'

Bernard glanced at the clock. 'I'm afraid I have a client coming to see me shortly, but will you ask your sister to come and see me? And Francis – if you need anyone to talk to, not as a lawyer but as an older friend – please don't hesitate to turn to me. I have sons of your age and I know you've never had a father to guide you.' Had he gone too far? No, the lad didn't seem to resent this offer.

'Thank you. I'll remember that. I've seen your sons and I wish I could meet them. You live quite near to us, don't you?' Bitterness rang in Francis's voice. 'I'm not allowed to make friends with anyone who isn't my "social equal" – as my uncle judges it.'

'That's a great pity. You must be very lonely.'

Francis looked at him, head on one side, and asked hesitantly, 'If I called at your house, would you introduce me to your sons? Would they want to meet me?'

'How will you get permission to do that?'

The young face was grim. 'My uncle is about to find out that he will either have to lock me in my room until I'm twenty-one or give me more leeway.'

'Be a little careful how you confront him,' Bernard warned. 'He can be a dangerous enemy.'

'He's pushed me too far. It's not just my sister's arrival. Things have been getting on top of me lately for other reasons.' The constant nagging to go hunting, to 'act the man' – as if he'd want to kill little animals. He couldn't even bear the thought of it.

Bernard wondered what one boy could do against a man accustomed to wielding power. He had in the past helped more than one person Alexander Stephenson had decided to destroy and was not himself well thought of by the man, he knew. But since the Lorrimers had a few useful family connections, Stephenson had not dared to try to hurt them – so far. Would offering friendship to this lonely lad change that? Bernard couldn't even begin to guess but he intended to risk it, for his conscience would not allow him to draw back now from such an acute need for help.

'Come round to the house any Sunday afternoon and I'll introduce you to my lads. We often have young folk visiting us then.' He would explain the situation to his eldest son, who was about the same age as this young man but did not have that grim, unhappy look to his face, thank goodness.

Francis gave him a singularly sweet smile, then it was replaced by a determined expression as he stood up. 'Thank you for everything, sir. I won't forget what you've said.'

He walked home very slowly, lost in thought.

As she waited near the little wood the following Sunday afternoon, Cathie began to think that Francis was not coming. Just as she was thinking she ought to start back, she heard a sound and turned to see him running through the woods. She beamed at him as he came to a breathless halt beside her, gulping in air and trying to speak.

'I thought – I'd missed you. My uncle wanted me – to stay at home. I had to escape.' He glanced over his shoulder. 'We'd better get out of sight in case he sends the grooms out to look for me.' He led her further into the woods to a clearing where there was a fallen tree and flourished a bow, hiding the emotion he was feeling at seeing her again under a jesting tone. 'Your throne awaits you, my lady sister!'

She chuckled, dropped him a curtsy and sat down on it.

He took a place beside her and studied his clasped hands. 'I went to see Mr Lorrimer and you're right – about our mother, I mean. She does pay him to report on how I'm going every year and he told me why she left. She didn't take money to leave, she was driven away by threats.'

'They never told us children the details.'

He explained then said bleakly, 'I'm nearly fifteen, Cathie. I've missed *years* of knowing my mother. Can you imagine how that feels?' He'd lain awake every night of that long week filled with bitterness. He'd almost burst out with the accusation several times, but had held back because in spite of his brave words to Mr Lorrimer he didn't really know how to deal with his uncle – just that from now on he would no longer allow himself to be browbeaten without fighting back.

Cathie laid one hand on his and glanced at him compassionately. 'That's terrible. And you've missed knowing your brothers and sisters, too.'

He met her eyes, which were filled with tears like his own. 'At least I've met *you* now, Cathie. And will you please tell me where you live before we go any further? I was thinking as I ran through the woods that if I didn't get here on time, I'd not know how to contact you.'

She told him her address, then he passed on Mr Lorrimer's message, which seemed to surprise her.

'Shall you go and see him?'

'No. Not yet.'

He decided that he would write to tell Mr Lorrimer her address, just in case anything went wrong or his uncle tried to harm her.

They were silent for a few moments, sitting companionably together, then she grimaced and confessed, 'I've, um, got some more of my memory back.'

'And?'

She looked at him, her face full of sorrow, and

the words burst out in a torrent. 'I'm so ashamed of myself. I ran away from home, let my uncle pay my fare to England – didn't even say goodbye to Mum and Dad. How could I have been so *stupid*? So cruel? And – and I knew Mum didn't get on with her brother, so it was even worse to let *him* persuade me to run away. I don't think he should have done it, so perhaps he isn't as kind as he seemed.'

It was the last thing Francis had expected to hear. 'Why did you run away? You said you loved your family. Did they ill-treat you?

'No, of course not! Never think that! It's just – I do love them only, well, I hated living in the bush. It's very lonely and you hardly ever meet new people. I felt I was going mad, wasting my life doing the same thing every day. And also I ran away because,' she hesitated then told him the rest, 'I overheard them talking one night. I'd always thought Josiah Ludlam was my father, but it seems he wasn't and I wanted to find the real one. My uncle told me who he thinks my father is because I look like the man, but it's not absolutely certain he's the right one, even then. Only I can't remember the man's name. Why can't I remember something so important?'

Tentatively, because he wasn't used to touching anyone, let alone a girl, Francis put one arm round her and gave her a hug. 'You will remember it one day, I'm sure.'

'I hope so. I don't mind helping Magnus look

after his mother – he's a lovely man, you must come and meet him – but the life I'm leading here is almost as limited as my life back home was.' She gave a wry smile as she looked down at her reddened hands and added, 'And there's just as much washing, which is harder to dry here. I don't call this summer!' She glanced up at the sky which was alternately clouding over and giving them brief glimpses of a cool sun.

When she explained more fully about her situation and Francis realised she was living with a man she had not previously known, he could not hide his shock. 'Look, you don't have to do that sort of thing! I'll give you some money and—'

'I don't need any money. I'm earning my own way.'

'Well, I'll *lend* you some money, then, and your – our – mother can pay me back.'

'My parents don't have much spare money because they lost so much in the bush fire.' Her lips set in an obstinate line. 'I'm not going to ask them for anything. I got myself into this and I'm going to prove that I can look after myself.'

'But you're living with a man. It looks so bad.'

She pulled away from him. 'I'm not doing anything wrong.'

There was silence while Francis thought about what she had said, then he muttered, 'I've never met anyone like you.'

'You've probably only met spoiled rich brats.'

'Yes.' Suddenly he understood why his father

280

must have fallen for his mother, if she was at all like Cathie. 'I think you're marvellous.'

She chuckled. 'I'm not, you know. I'm very ordinary.'

He couldn't agree with her. After a few moments had passed, he said thoughtfully, 'But you'd still better go and see Mr Lorrimer in case my uncle finds out about you and tries to hurt you or the Hamiltons. I don't think you're living in one of our houses, but if the place belongs to the Ludlams, well, they'll throw you out without hesitation if my uncle asks them to.'

She stared at him in dismay. 'I didn't think of that! Oh, I'd never forgive myself if anything happened to Magnus.'

He hesitated, then blurted out, 'Perhaps you could move out and just go in daily to look after his mother. It's not at all respectable – your living with him, I mean.' He hated the idea of people thinking ill of her.

She realised suddenly that she didn't want to move out, that the main reason for staying was to be with Magnus and have those golden evenings chatting quietly together in front of the fire. 'It's very respectable, I promise you,' she said lightly. 'I have my own bedroom and we've told everyone I'm his second cousin Caitlin. Now don't forget that – I'm called Caitlin Rutherford here. His sister comes to visit us, so that helps stop the gossip. Mairi is very well thought of and is a regular churchgoer. People know she wouldn't associate with me if there was – well, any wrongdoing between me and Magnus.'

'I still don't like it.'

She changed the subject. 'Let me tell you more about our family . . .'

When she left him, he stood beneath some trees watching her stride out along the road, admiring her upright posture and air of sturdy health.

He looked down at himself and grimaced. She must think him a mere boy. He'd grown so much in the past year he was all spindly. He was glad he was six foot tall and Cook had once told him he'd fill out in a year or two and be a fine-looking man, but he wished he looked more manly now. Why, he hadn't even started shaving yet. And the cough and lassitude from his influenza were still lingering. Some days it was an effort to do anything.

It felt important not to go home again without making some sort of stand, so Francis strolled past his own driveway, conscious of Roskin the gate-keeper staring after him. When he got to the gate of the Lorrimers' house, he hesitated for a moment then went to knock on the front door.

The maid who opened it said placidly, 'The young folk are all out in the back garden, sir, if you'd like to go round.' She pointed to the left.

'Um – is Mr Lorrimer there?'

'No, of course not. The master's inside with the mistress.'

'Well, I think it best if I see him first. He's the one who asked me to call, really.'

She looked surprised but held the front door open. 'Come in then, sir, and I'll let him know you're here.' She moved away, then giggled and turned back. 'Oops, I nearly forgot to ask your name.'

When he told her she goggled at him, gulped audibly and rushed away at top speed.

He liked the idea of a maid not being afraid to giggle. The ones at the Manor were terrified of doing anything to offend his uncle, and when Hilda slipped food to him she only did so because she was also terrified of upsetting Cook. His nursemaid had been dismissed the day he was put into short coats. His uncle had simply told him one day that Jenny had left and that he was to act like a big boy from then on for a tutor who would be teaching him to read and write. He'd cried himself to sleep for many nights after that and been smacked by the tutor for it. His grandmother had, he was sure, loved him in her own way, but that had never included embraces which might disturb her clothes or hair.

In this house Bernard Lorrimer came out into the hall in person to greet him, clasped his hand and looked at his anxious face. 'First act of defiance?' he asked, understanding immediately what was happening.

Francis nodded.

'You're welcome here, lad, always, but don't try to push all the barriers down at once with your uncle. No one can do that.'

Francis nodded again, feeling a lump in his

throat at the genuine caring shown for him by this man. He was taken round to the back to be introduced to 'the young people', which made him feel like a new boy at school again – terrified, alone against the world, as he had been when he was sent away at the age of eight.

Outside there were about a dozen youngsters. Four of them were playing croquet, two were sitting over a chess board, three were enjoying a lively discussion and three others were gathered around one of the new Ordinary bicycles, which a young fellow of about Francis's age was pushing to and fro with a proprietary air.

It was a moment before they noticed Mr Lorrimer's companion, then one by one they fell silent, staring.

When he had their attention, Bernard put an arm round his protégé's shoulders and said, 'Francis Rawley has come to visit us at my invitation. I doubt his uncle's going to approve, so I'd prefer you not to tell people yet about his coming here, but I'm truly delighted to see him.' He then drew Francis forward to the group round the bicycle. 'I don't know whether you're interested in cycling, but my son Johnny is a devotee – and I must confess he doesn't fall off the contraption all the time.'

Johnny grinned at his father and smiled tentatively at Francis. 'I've only had it for two weeks, but it's a wonderful improvement on my old boneshaker. Do you cycle?'

'I've never tried, but I wouldn't mind having a go – though I'm hopeless on horses, so I would probably fall off this as well.'

The three of them immediately assured him that the bicycle was really easy to ride, then began to explain the finer points of the Ordinary, with its huge front and small rear wheels, the sprung seat, the front and rear brakes, the superior bearings which made for a smooth ride, and above all its capacity to cope even with muddy conditions.

An hour later Francis reluctantly decided to return home and face the scolding he would no doubt receive for absenting himself without permission.

Johnny accompanied him to the gate. 'I'm glad you could come.' His tone was as friendly as his father's. 'We've seen you walking around the grounds of your house alone and felt a bit sorry for you.'

'My uncle is very old-fashioned and snobbish.'

'It must be hard for you not being allowed to make friends.'

Francis nodded, relieved when the other boy didn't press the point. Today had begun to show him what he'd been missing. These young people had all known one another for years and were comfortable together, and yet they'd welcomed him and tried to make him feel at ease. The lads at school were not nearly so kind.

'Come again any Sunday,' Johnny said as he opened the gate. 'We nearly always gather here because my parents don't mind the noise. If it's raining we go into the shed or conservatory.'

As Francis walked slowly home he felt deeply envious. If he couldn't have his family, he ought at least to have been allowed his friends. But his uncle had permitted him neither. He intended to change that, but it would mean making a stand and a lot of unpleasantness, too, he had no doubt.

Well, so be it.

As soon as he set foot indoors Francis was informed that his uncle was waiting for him in the library, the sort of message that usually sent a shiver of apprehension through him. Today he was glad the first confrontation had come at once so that he didn't have to sit and worry about it. Taking a deep breath, he made his way to the room which had been the scene of many scoldings.

As he hesitated outside the door, it suddenly occurred to him that this room, like the whole house, really belonged to him. It's mine, not my uncle's, he thought, looking round. That idea gave him a little more courage. He lifted his hand and knocked – loudly.

'Come.'

He went inside, looking round as if he had never seen it before. *His* room. *His* estate.

'Where have you been?' demanded Alexander in that carping snappish tone that meant his digestion was playing up again. 'I will not have you wandering off when you've been told to stay at home. I informed you that we were expecting guests. I was obliged to offer the Ludlams your apologies and say you were unwell.' The scolding continued for a long time, ending with, 'You will go to your room and . . .'

Somehow Francis could not stomach that after his golden afternoon. 'No.'

His uncle stared at him, open-mouthed. *'What did you say?'*

'I said no and I meant it. I'm not five years old, and I resent being treated as a child. I will not be sent to my room in that way again.'

'Oh, will you not?'

Francis stared at him. His uncle's lips had narrowed to a thin line and his face had gone white and chill. The old man's head was like a skull, set on top of its stringy neck. How yellow and unhealthy the whites of his eyes were and how frail he looked, yet how vicious! Francis forced himself to speak calmly because shouting never got you anywhere with his uncle. Only *he* was allowed to shout, and he had been doing a lot of that lately. 'I have no wish to be impolite or to quarrel with you, but I'm nearly a man now and expect to be treated accordingly.'

'A man? You'll never be half the man your father was! You can't even sit a horse like a gentleman, let alone behave like one.'

'My father was killed by his horse, for all his skill. I think I prefer my way.'

Alexander Stephenson's eyes bulged and he

moved across to the bell pull and gave it a sharp tug.

Francis turned on his heel before any servant could answer. At the door he paused to say, 'If you're thinking of sending the head groom to use force on me,' something which had happened once or twice when he was younger, though not recently, 'you might like to consider how that will look to the world, for I promise you I will fight every inch of the way to my bedroom and I shall not keep quiet about being treated so brutally.'

He walked out of the room and made his way to the conservatory his grandmother had loved, which he was the only person to visit nowadays. In its soothing warmth he paced slowly up and down until the shuddering feeling in his belly had settled, listening to see whether his uncle would send Horace and some of the outdoor men-servants to manhandle him to his room. The head groom seemed to do a lot of nasty business for his grandfather these days, terrorising the tenants for one thing. Francis intended to dismiss him the minute he turned twenty-one.

But although he stayed in the conservatory for over an hour no one came searching for him. In the end he heard the hall clock chime the quarter and went up to change for dinner, taking particular care with his clothes. He was downstairs again even before the clock chimed the hour.

His uncle entered the dining room by the other door and walked past him as if he didn't exist.

When the first course had been removed, Francis addressed the roast beef and potatoes that followed, doggedly but without any real appetite, determined not to betray his nervousness. It was another of his uncle's tricks to use silence to punish him, but in some ways that was easier to handle than conversation. It was always a strain trying to think of something to say or working out an answer that would not provoke a sarcastic comment.

After the meal was over, Francis looked questioningly towards the head of the table. *His* table, really, he reminded himself.

His uncle stared at him coldly. 'I shall decline to converse with you until I have received an apology for your insolence and a promise to obey me in future.'

'I did not intend to be insolent and am sorry if that's how you regard what I said. I merely wished to tell you that I am no longer a child and that it is inappropriate to treat me as one. And I cannot promise to obey unfair commands.'

'You dare speak to me like that!' his uncle began to shout, getting into such a passion that dribble trickled from the slack side of his lips.

It was a while before the tirade ceased, then Francis took a deep breath and said quietly, 'You're my uncle and I would not wish to be on bad terms, but I'm not a child any longer.' Before his uncle could start shouting at him again he pushed his chair back and walked out of the room.

The anger that followed him seemed almost tangible, but he didn't turn round. If he had done, he might have said more than he had planned, might have accused his uncle of sending his mother away. Francis would never forgive him for that, but as Mr Lorrimer had said, it would not be wise to try to change or challenge everything at once.

He knew exactly what was to come now because it had happened once or twice before – chill silences, servants forbidden to do things for him. But something had changed inside him today and that something was fuelled by both anger and anguish. He had a mother who cared about him and yet had been kept from him. He had brothers and sisters who were complete strangers to him, except for Cathie. He had had to endure long, empty years living with a man who had no warmth in his character, not a single iota. And he still had nearly six years to go until he would be free from his uncle. How was he to endure that?

He went to the billiards room and hit a few balls up and down the table with his usual indifferent success. He had never been good at sports, didn't seem to have an eye for a ball or much interest in the stupid things, either, though he might have a go at riding one of the new bicycles. What had Johnny called it? An Ordinary. It didn't seem at all ordinary to Francis. It seemed very modern and dashing. And unlike a horse, a bicycle could not bite or kick you.

When his usual bedtime of ten o'clock came, he debated staying up longer, but was tired and wished to mull over the events of the week. So he put the cues away and made his solitary way up the stairs.

He left the curtains open and as he lay staring at the patterns of moonlight on the bedroom floor, he acknowledged that life was going to be very unpleasant from now on. But then, it had never really been pleasant, so it was only a matter of degree.

What did his mother look like? He didn't even know. That thought brought tears to his eyes.

As soon as she got back Cathie poured out the tale of her encounter with her half-brother to Magnus and his sister, who had come on her own this week.

Afterwards Mairi asked hesitantly, 'What about old Mr Stephenson? He's going to be furious about this.'

Cathie shrugged. 'If he's angry, that's not my fault. He's kept my brother and mother apart all these years, and I won't let him keep *me* away from Francis. That poor boy looks like he's never had a good cuddle in his whole life. What can the old man do to me, after all? He's not my guardian.'

'He can have my brother thrown out of this house, though, and perhaps make him lose his job, too.' It had happened before and you couldn't hide things like that in a small town.

'But this has nothing to do with your brother!'

Magnus leaned forward, smiling reassuringly. 'Stephenson's a mean old devil, but I doubt it'll come to that, Mairi. It's the Ludlams who own this house and are my employers, and I think they value me as a worker.' Well, he knew they did.

She was not convinced. 'The gentry always help one another. Oh, Caitlin, please keep your meetings with your brother secret!'

'I'll do my best, for all our sakes.'

After Magnus had walked his sister to the railway station, he came back and helped Cathie put his mother to bed, then sat down at the kitchen table looking thoughtful.

She came to sit opposite him, clasping her hands together on the table and trying to read his expression. 'If he does try to throw you out because of me, then I promise you I'll leave at once.'

'I doubt he will. Mr Reuben is always very fair with us workers. He wouldn't allow it.' He looked at her and risked saying, 'I should be sorry to see you go, Caitlin lassie.'

'Should you?' She felt suddenly breathless.

'Aye.' He wondered whether to tell her that Jim Marshall had started asking questions about her, but decided against it.

Marshall was a good worker if you kept an eye on him, but he was a married man and not a womaniser so it couldn't be because she was such a pretty lass. Why then did he want to know?

CHAPTER 13

JUNE

One day Dermott turned up without warning in Brookley, riding a horse with his usual lack of care while his wife and sons rode behind in a cart driven by a man he'd hired to help about the place. They'd also brought along their young Irish maid to help Christina with the housework, but the governess had given notice when required to move to the bush.

By the end of a second long day of travelling with a wife alternating between a foul temper and floods of tears, Dermott was beginning to wonder why the hell he'd even considered living in the country. What would have been an easy day's journey in England or even in Victoria, and hadn't been too bad when he and Fiery Dan had ridden down here, had turned into an endurance feat with a cart and a wife who never stopped complaining about the insects, and the rain, and the lack of inns.

Matthieu had written to say that the farm was very close to the Caines' place. Dermott found that thought piquant. Thinking of Liza reminded him of his niece and he realised suddenly how much meeting Cathie had changed his attitude towards his sister. He wondered how the lass was doing in England. To his surprise he found himself hoping she was all right.

Which brought to mind the fact that his sister had several other children. For the first time he wondered if they were as pleasant to be with as Cathie. That thought was followed by a scowl. He was getting soft again and that wouldn't do at all. How Niall would have mocked him for that! Yet Matthieu, who was as mean a fighter as you'd hope to meet, didn't seem to mind acting soft sometimes. The man was a puzzle to Dermott. Oh, hell, life itself was a puzzle.

As they pulled up outside the inn in Brookley he edged his mount closer to where his wife was sitting in the cart, amused by the expression of disgust on her face. 'We're here, then,' he announced unnecessarily.

Christina stared at the inn in which she had lived as a young woman, then glared at the small settlement which now surrounded it. 'It hasn't changed much,' she declared, adding in a voice shaking with anger, 'How could you do this to me, Dermott Docherty? There's no *need* for us to come and live in a place like this!'

'Ah, shut your trap, woman! I'm sick and tired of your moaning.' He jerked his head towards the inn. 'Aren't you going in to say hello to your mother?'

She didn't move. 'I've told you and told you: I didn't want to meet *anyone* from my past.'

He leaned across to grasp her shoulder. 'Well, I do want to meet my ma-in-law. Either you get off that cart of your own accord or I'll drag you off it.'

Their eyes met for a moment, then she sniffed, gathered up her skirts and began to clamber down.

Dermott sat admiring her shapely legs till she was down, dismounted himself and went across to where she was standing. 'Come on, then.'

But as she straightened her skirts, he saw the apprehension in her face. 'You're nervous!' he said in surprise.

'Well, of course I am. My mother might refuse to speak to me.'

He took her arm and threaded it in his, patting her hand. 'Then we'll do this together.' As Christina threw him a grateful smile, he wished suddenly that she would smile like that more often. She almost looked pretty when she did. His steps faltered for a moment and he gave his head a little shake. Another moment of softness. It didn't do to be too kind to Christina or she took advantage and tried to rule the roost. Only – her eyes were red with weeping, she was desperately unhappy about coming to live here, and he didn't like to see that. She'd been a good wife to him in her own way.

When they walked into the inn Dorothy looked up, then gasped and turned bone white, clutching the counter as if about to faint.

With a muttered oath Dermott let go of his wife

and hurried across the room to support the older woman. 'Are you all right, missus?' His ma-in-law was light enough in weight, but was sagging against him as if she had lost the power of her limbs and had not uttered a single word.

As she moved across to join them Christina decided her mother had aged better than she had expected, but now looked like a working woman not a lady, which did not please her at all. 'I'm sorry to give you such a shock, Mother. Come and sit down for a minute.'

There was a shout and a small man came rushing to Dorothy's aid, standing with one arm round her shoulders and demanding furiously, 'What have you done to her?'

Dorothy raised her head. 'It's all right, Jack. I'm just – being silly.' She stared at her daughter. 'Is it you, Kitty? Is it really you?'

'Well, of course it's me.' She leaned over to plant a kiss in the air just above her mother's cheek. 'Though I'm called Christina now. I much prefer it. I don't know why you ever wanted to shorten my name in the first place.' She gestured to the burly man standing beside her. 'This is my husband, Dermott Docherty. He's Liza's brother.'

He nodded and held out a huge hand.

Dorothy stared at him in open-mouthed shock but pulled herself together enough to shake the hand quickly then let it drop.

'And I have two sons, so you're a grandmother. James and Charlie are waiting outside.' Christina forced a smile. 'I wasn't sure if you'd forgiven me, you see.'

'Oh, Kitty darling!' Dorothy held out her arms and after a moment's hesitation Christina allowed herself to be embraced, but pulled away as soon as she could.

Dorothy remembered of old that her daughter didn't like to be cuddled. 'Perhaps we could bring the boys in? I'd love to meet them.'

Dermott ambled over to the door. 'I'll fetch 'em.'

His face expressionless, Jack watched him go then turned to his wife, who was looking flushed and tearful. 'You sit down, love, and I'll make us all a nice cup of tea.'

'Thank you.' But Dorothy's eyes were on the door and when the two boys came in, she clapped one hand across her mouth and blinked her eyes furiously, not wanting to embarrass them by weeping. 'They look so like your father,' she whispered to her daughter. 'They have his hair and mouth.'

Christina turned to stare at them. 'I suppose they do. James, Charlie, this is your grandmother. I said we'd meet her, didn't I?'

The two boys came across the room, taking care to keep out of reach of their grandmother's outstretched arms.

'We're a bit big for kisses and stuff now,' James explained.

Dorothy let her arms drop and, as Jack cleared his throat, turned and smiled at him. 'Sorry, dear.

Kit— Christina, this is my husband, Jack Bennett. We – um – run the inn together. Brookley is quite a thriving little community now.'

Christine gave Jack, who was clearly of plebeian origin, a cool nod and made no attempt to take his outstretched hand. 'What happened to my father?'

'He died. The day you left, actually.'

'Oh! Oh, no!' Christina clapped both hands to her mouth. 'And I didn't know.'

Dermott put his arm round his wife and gave her a bracing hug. 'If only we'd known, we could have stayed to help you, but we were so taken with one another, we weren't thinking straight.' He dug his elbow into his wife's well-corseted side. 'Weren't we, love?'

'No.' She suddenly remembered that night: how he'd forced himself on her, then persuaded her to ride off with him through the moonlight, and how she'd been desperate enough to escape to do just that. Looking round, she wondered what would have happened if she hadn't met Dermott. Heavens, she might still be here! On a sudden impulse she put her arm through his and gave it a squeeze.

Dorothy was looking very tearful. 'Oh, Kitty, why *did* you run away? Why could you not have told me you'd met someone?'

'*Please* call me Christina. After all, you gave me the name in the first place.' She shrugged. 'I ran away because I was afraid Father would try to stop me marrying Dermott since he wasn't a gentleman. You know how rigid he could be about some things.'

'Yes, I do.' Dorothy smiled at her through a mist of tears. 'I never gave up hoping you'd come back, though, and now you have. Oh, I'm so glad, my darling, so very glad. You must tell me everything and then—'

'We've plenty of time for that, Ma,' Dermott interrupted. 'We'll be staying round here for a while because we've bought Baileys' Farm. Thought it'd be good for the boys – a healthy life in the country, getting to know their grandmother.' He looked through the kitchen door at the puny man busying himself making tea and wondered why his mother-in-law had not found someone better than this little snirp, who barely reached Dermott's shoulder.

Both his in-laws stared at them. '*You've* bought the Bailey place?' Jack exclaimed. 'Then what's Mr Correntin doing there?'

'Matthieu and I are business partners. He's keeping an eye on it for me.'

'Are you interested in farming?' Jack asked.

'No, I'm bloody not! I've brought a man to do the outdoor work, though I can turn my hand to most things if I have to. I'm not short of a bob or two, but I've been a bit busy over the past few years and I feel like taking things more easily for a while.'

'You're Matthieu Correntin's partner?' Dorothy

299

said, still trying to understand what Dermott was doing here. 'Why did he not say anything to me?'

'He didn't know Christina was your daughter. Seen much of him, have you?'

'He's eaten here a few times. He's always very pleasant.'

Dermott chuckled. 'That's a Frenchie for you, charming all the ladies.' Fraid you'll find me a bit blunt after him, Ma.'

She was frowning now. 'And you're Liza's brother?'

'Aye. I know she doesn't think much of me – well, I was a bit of a rough lad – but I'm hoping to mend things between us now.'

His smile was like that of a wolf about to pounce on a particularly choice morsel.

Dorothy, who knew the full story of how Liza had killed her brother by accident, and why, was still wondering what had persuaded her finicky daughter to marry a man like this. She decided to send a messenger to Lizabrook as soon as they had left for their farm. She needed to warn Benedict, who had just got back from putting his wife and daughter on the coaster in Fremantle – just in case Dermott meant to cause more trouble. Heavens, he was a large man and she'd guess he'd been in a few fights from the battered look to his face and fists!

And she definitely didn't want to be the one to tell Dermott that his sister had left for England, so she threw a quick warning glance at her husband, shaking her head. As usual, he nodded agreement. He could read her thoughts in a way Andrew had never been able to or wanted to. Some might say her Jack was beneath her, but she was happy with him and had never regretted marrying him.

She looked back at her daughter, who had a sulky expression on her face and looked as if she'd been crying. That hadn't changed. Poor Kitty – Christina rather – didn't seem to have it in her to be happy. Dorothy bustled about getting them a meal, proud of the table she set and pleased when her grandsons and son-in-law expressed their appreciation of the food. Her daughter hardly ate a thing and when she wasn't talking, simply sat staring round glumly. Dermott ate plenty and made up for his wife's silence, talking easily of this and that, mostly of how he had made his fortune. He seemed a pushy sort of fellow and reminded Dorothy very much of his father, Con, whom she still remembered clearly from the days he'd come to collect Liza's wages, when she was working as a maid for her and her first husband in Lancashire.

When they left, Dorothy stood waving goodbye until the cart had trundled out of sight then turned to Jack and said abruptly, 'We'd better warn Benedict that he's here. Would you go and ask young Pete from next door if he'll take a message to Lizabrook for me?' While Jack was undertaking this errand, she got out her inkpot and scratched a hasty note explaining what had happened.

For all his affability towards her she had not taken to Dermott Docherty. How could her pretty, finicky Kitty have fallen in love with a man like that? And at first sight, too? It didn't make sense. No, her daughter could only have married him for money – and to escape from Brookley.

But even that hadn't made her happy.

Then Dorothy thought of her two grandsons and smiled. Well, some good had come out of it all, anyway. She hoped the boys would come and visit often. She had always longed for grandchildren. Perhaps it wasn't too late for her to play a part in their lives.

When the lad turned up at Lizabrook and proffered the note, panting from hurrying along the rough track, saying Mrs Bennett had told him to bring it over as fast as he could and to wait for an answer, Benedict took it listlessly. Already the place seemed empty without Liza's cheerful voice and presence. She and Josie would be out on the ocean now, getting further away from him by the day. He had hoped she'd change her mind, right until the last minute, but although she'd wept as she said goodbye, she'd still boarded the ship.

He stiffened as he read what their friend had written. So Dermott Docherty was here in Brookley! If the fellow had had enough money to buy Baileys' Farm, then he must have done well for himself financially. Which was all the more galling because Benedict and Liza had been struggling since the fire and he'd had to sell another piece of Josiah's first wife's jewellery to pay for this trip to England.

If Dermott really had set the bush fire – and who else could it be? – well, Benedict was forewarned this time. The farm and furniture workshops were now protected by huge fire breaks and Dinny had asked her people to keep watch on the comings and goings nearby, promising them food in return for this service. And although Brendan was very friendly with Correntin, Benedict was sure Dinny's son would not allow any harm to come to his mother or the other folk on the homestead.

After a few minutes' thought he sent a message back to Dorothy and went to warn Dinny and Fergal to be even more on their guard. The three of them went to sit on the Riordans' new veranda, which looked out over the small stretch of water they had cleared so painfully from the swamp. Maybe while Liza was away he'd make a real effort and dig out some more.

'I never thought I'd be glad that Liza was away,' Benedict said grimly, 'but I am.'

'I am, too,' Dinny said quietly. She had never forgotten the day Niall Docherty had tried to rape her and the other one had just smiled. It was Liza who had saved Dinny, killing her own brother accidentally as she did so. Then Liza had driven the other brother away. 'Why has that man come back here? This land means nothing to him. Surely he doesn't intend to get his revenge on me after all this time?'

Fergal put his arm round her shoulders. 'You're not alone now, though, darlin'. I'll not let him touch you.' He looked at them, his brow wrinkled in puzzlement. 'There's no proof *he* set the fires. Isn't it possible that he has indeed come for a reconciliation as he told Dorothy?'

Benedict gave Fergal a fond glance. His friend had a very tender heart and an idealistic nature, always believing the best of everyone – which had led to a betrayal back in Ireland that had landed him in trouble with the English law for his polit- ical activities, and had brought him out here as a convict. Since he'd received his freedom Fergal had hardly left the homestead and now lived only for his family.

'I'd better go and tell Ilse and Agnes of our fears,' Benedict decided. 'They need to be on their guard as well. Ilse has met that Correntin fellow a few times now and Agnes thinks she's rather taken with him.' He nodded to them both and left.

Ilse looked hard at her employer as he spoke to them. He sounded crisper, more like the old Benedict Caine, the man she had met when she first came to work here. He had been so energetic and decisive then – and cheerful, too. But since the fires he had become short-tempered, snapping at people, often looking grim as well as weary. When he had returned from taking Liza to

Fremantle he had looked so sad she had felt sorry for him. Now, suddenly, she watched the energy within him flicker into a blaze and could see what he must have been like as a young man who had sailed across the world to carve himself out a piece of land in the colonies.

Later that evening Benedict went to stand on his own by the water, filled with determination not to let Dermott Docherty take away what they had gained from all their years of hard work. In the darkness he heard someone approaching and turned to see his older sons walking towards him. They came to stand beside him, one on either side, nearly as tall as him now.

'Lucas, Seth,' he acknowledged.

'We're old enough to help, Dad,' Lucas said. 'If Mother's brother has come to cause trouble, you're not facing him alone.'

Benedict put an arm round each lad's shoulders, standing between them feeling proud of his sturdy sons. They stayed there together in silence for a while and the slight pain in his chest eased. With sons like this a man could do anything. And Liza would be back within the year. He'd use that time to make things better for her here.

When Matthieu heard the sound of wheels and horses' hooves and saw who it was, he cursed softly under his breath. Dermott was going to be furious when he found out that his sister had already left for England, and Matthieu still had not come to a decision about what he wanted to do with himself.

He had been fighting the urge to go and see Ilse for the past day or two, because with a respectable woman regular meetings could only lead to one thing and he did not want to get married. Well, he thought he didn't. He wasn't sure of anything lately.

Taking a deep breath, he went forward to greet the Docherty family. 'So you've decided to inspect your property at last, have you?'

Christina didn't even look at him after an initial glance. She glanced round her in disgust then turned to her husband. 'This is even worse than Brookley, Dermott Docherty. I'll never forgive you for bringing me here!' Clambering down without his help, she stormed into the house, totally ignoring Matthieu.

Dermott grinned at him and rolled his eyes heavenwards. 'Women!'

The two boys slipped down from the cart and began exploring outside the house, calling to one another. The maid had stayed in the vehicle, staring round her with an expression almost as dismayed as that of her mistress.

'I was not expecting you to come down so soon, *mon ami*.' Matthieu folded his arms and leaned against a veranda post.

Dermott swung off the horse. 'Well, I had nowt better to do.'

As they unloaded the cart, Christina bombarded her husband with a series of demands: for wood and rope to build more bed frames, for benches inside and out, for another table. 'There must be someone round here who can cobble furniture together, for I know you've no skill at carpentry.'

'Benedict Caine makes fine furniture,' Matthieu said softly.

Dermott grinned. 'There you are, then. And we'll invite your mother to tea soon.'

'Not till I have things straight here, we won't. The boys will have to sleep on the floor for a day or two.'

'Before you decide anything,' Matthieu said quietly, 'there's something you need to know, *mon ami.* Your sister left for England a few days ago.'

Dermott froze. 'Are you sure of that?'

'Very sure.'

'Why didn't Christina's mother tell us?'

'She was probably more concerned with seeing her daughter again.'

Without a word, Dermott turned and stormed into the house. He fumbled through the baskets of provisions piled here and there on the floor and pulled out a bottle of rum, opening it and taking a swig. Then he turned to Matthieu. 'Show me around, will you?'

Christina opened her mouth to protest that she needed his help, then shut it again, looking at him thoughtfully. Might this news make him change his mind about living here?

Dermott was gone for over an hour, by which time Christina was nearly at screaming point and had retreated to the bedroom to lie on the bed weeping.

When he came to join her, her husband looked thoughtful. 'What am I going to do with you, woman?'

Her reply was muffled by the pillows.

He touched her shoulder and when she tried to shrug his hand off, turned her over by force and studied her swollen eyes. 'That bad, is it?'

She nodded. 'It's brought back to me how unhappy I was here.'

'Eh, you daft bitch. We were never going to stay for long, were we?'

'I don't want to stay at all.'

So he took another of his impulsive decisions. 'Then we won't. We'll go back to Perth tomorrow.'

She gulped and stared at him. 'Do you really mean that?'

He nodded. 'After which we'll go to England.'

She stared at him as if she didn't believe what she'd heard, then flung her arms round him and burst into tears again. 'Oh, Dermott, thank you, thank you!'

'What the hell are you crying for now?'

'Because I'm so happy.'

So he rocked her for a bit and patted her shoulder, thinking over his decision. She had been unhappy for a while now, and although he liked to be the master in his own home, which was not always easy with Christina, it didn't please him to see her so deeply upset. He looked round at the so-called farm, which looked more like a bloody cabin in the wilderness to him. The house was roughly built. Gum trees had set seedlings in the pastures which would need clearing again; the gardens were a tangle of dead plants except for a new patch Matthieu had cleared. It was all a big disappointment to him, nothing like he'd imagined, though of course he'd got it dirt cheap and would probably not lose when he sold it. He'd seen proper farms over in Victoria, country estates you could be proud of, but here in the west, they'd hardly begun to tame the countryside.

And finally, his sister wasn't around to torment. That took all the savour out of coming here.

He patted Christina's heaving shoulders. Yes, this was the right thing to do. It wouldn't hurt to see the old country again before he worked out what he was going to do with the rest of his life. He had spent nearly twenty years concentrating on making his fortune and since he'd achieved it, his heart wasn't really in trading any more. He'd have to find some other way to occupy his time, and Perth wasn't at all the sort of place he wanted to settle in. Too small by far. Call it a capital city? He called it a town, and a small one at that.

He looked down, enjoying the glow of happiness on Christina's face as she nestled against him. 'You'd better sort out what you want to take and what you want to leave here. I'm not hanging about.

We'll set off at dawn, so you'll need to get things ready tonight. And while we're in England, we'll go and visit that bloody aunt of yours you're always going on about.' He put her firmly away from him. 'Now, I need to discuss a few things with Matthieu. You get started on packing up again.'

His partner was standing by a ramshackle fence that any fool could have knocked down just by leaning on it. Dermott scowled round. Of all his impulsive acts, this was the worst. 'I want you to sell this place for me while I'm away. It's no use to me. We're following my bitch of a sister to England.'

Matthew gave him a long, level look. 'I might be interested in buying the farm myself. I'll give you ten per cent on what you paid, no more. If I don't buy it – and I haven't made up my mind yet – I'll sell it for you for ten per cent commission.' To his surprise it had upset him to see Dermott stalking around the place with such a propri- etorial air.

'Done!' his partner said promptly.

Matthieu didn't allow his thoughts to take him any further than that for the moment. One step at a time. First he would get to know Ilse better, and persuade her employer that he wanted to be friends.

Only as he sank towards sleep that night did he acknowledge to himself what a decision to stay would really mean – marrying Ilse, if she would have him.

He dreamed of warming up her cool skin, of running his fingers through her soft blonde hair and smiling into her blue eyes.

And woke at dawn to the bustle of the Dochertys' departure, glad to see them go.

Christina was so full of joy at the thought of returning to England that she spent what was left of the day happily sorting out the things on the wagon. But as she studied the boys' clothes and possessions she grew thoughtful. She was not looking forward to looking after them on a long voyage because they were a lively pair and always into mischief. Dermott usually treated this as a great joke but other people did not find their antics so amusing.

As the sun sank low in the sky, she stood watching the boys pushing one another and shrieking, running round, getting in everyone's way. When Matthieu came into the big living area, however, she saw him deal easily with James and Charlie, getting them to sit down quietly to eat some bread and cold kangaroo meat.

Hearing Dermott's voice outside, Christina went to join him. 'I've got an idea I want to discuss with you.'

'I'm hungry.'

'This is important and it won't take long. Come on!' She tugged at his arm, only stopping when they were out of earshot of the house. 'I've been thinking about the boys. They'll drive us mad on the voyage to England. Why don't we ask my mother to look after them for a year or so? She'd love it and you can see how short of money she is. Those dreadful clothes she wears!' Christina shuddered. 'And there's Matthieu down here as well. He'll keep an eye on them for us. He's very fond of them and they of him. It would save us a lot of trouble.'

When Dermott didn't say anything, she waited a minute before continuing persuasively, 'If we want to win over my aunt and make sure she leaves her money to me, we'll do better without the boys banging around. She's a real fusspot about her house and garden and you know what a mess and noise they always make.'

Dermott chewed the inside of his cheek thoughtfully as he considered this, not even aware that he had stopped walking or that Christina was waiting with unwonted patience for his response. 'We'd have to go and see your ma before we said anything to them.' It didn't occur to him to ask the boys if they wanted to stay here, any more than it had to his wife.

Christina hugged him. 'That's wonderful! Oh, Dermott, I can't believe this is happening at last.' She twirled him round, laughing up at him.

He grinned down at her. 'Eh, you daft lump! Life in England won't be perfect.'

'It'll be better than this.' The boys could join them later, when they were a little older. Matthieu would find someone to escort them to England. It was done all the time.

She felt deep satisfaction well in her. Now was not the time to tell Dermott that she was utterly determined to stay in England and was sure her Aunt Nora would help her do so, since she was now a wealthy widow with no children of her own. The two of them wrote to one another regularly and there had been several offers to pay for them to visit England.

If it hadn't been for Christina's stupid, bull-headed father, she could have gone to live with her aunt all those years ago instead of going to Australia and married a gentleman of education not Dermott Docherty – though he did have his good points and she'd grown fond of him. But no, her father had insisted all the Pringles go out to the colonies together. And look where it had led? Her mother was now running an inn and was married to a common fellow.

Brendan was worried. If these newcomers were staying on at Baileys' Farm, would Matthieu have time for him? He decided to go and see him, forgetting to tell Benedict that he wasn't working that day. Because he had slept badly he rose before dawn, knowing Matthieu often rose early, too.

He heard the unaccustomed noise before he got to the farm, so slipped into the woods and stayed hidden, watching in fascination.

The newcomers were loading the cart as if they were leaving. And they'd only arrived yesterday! The wife was shouting and shrieking, there were bags and boxes everywhere, but the two boys were nowhere to be seen. Where had they gone? After a few minutes it became clear that Matthieu was getting all the work done and that the big fellow, Liza's brother, was deliberately leaving it to him. Was Matthieu leaving as well? Worried, Brendan found a place from which to watch.

When they had reloaded the cart, the maid climbed up on it, sitting in the back with the boxes, and the man who'd come down with the Dochertys to work on the farm got up into the driver's seat.

From what they shouted to one another, it was plain that the man was driving them up to Perth, but Matthieu was staying! Brendan breathed a sigh of relief as the cart drove away.

When the dust had settled and quietness returned to the woods he walked out of the bush towards the farm, catching his friend making a cup of coffee in the kitchen.

'Come and join me!' Matthieu said, gesturing to a chair. Then he saw Brendan's expression. 'Is something wrong?'

'I want to know if you and that man intend to harm my family and friends?' Brendan stood very straight, feeling more like Beedit today, for some reason.

'I mean no harm to anyone at Brookley.'

'But your friend does. Only – why did he leave so quickly?'

'Because he found his sister wasn't here and took

314

a dislike to this place. He's going back to England to see his wife's aunt, so you don't need to worry about him any more. His sons are staying here, though, with their grandmother at the inn.'

Brendan sighed in relief and went to join his friend at the table.

Matthieu smiled at him. 'Will you come and work with me for a while, help me set this place to rights? I'll pay you.'

'I'm supposed to work for Mr Caine.'

'But if you work with me I can teach you to speak French. You won't find what you're looking for here or in England, but you may just find it in France.'

'What is it I'm looking for?' Brendan asked, not sure that he knew himself.

'Acceptance. A chance to prove yourself as a man. I'll send you to my family, if you like. They'll find you a job.'

Brendan could make no sense of this. 'Why would you do that? You owe me nothing.'

Matthieu stared down at his steaming cup. 'Because I was once a restless lad like you and would have got myself into trouble if it hadn't been for a stranger helping me. It sounds stupid, but all the payment he wanted was for me to help someone in the same way one day. And that's the payment I'd ask from you.'

Brendan considered this, studying his companion's face, then nodded. There were no lies written there. In fact, his friend looked happier than he had for a while. 'You'll need to talk to my family if you want me to work here and I'll tell them what I'm thinking of doing. Cathie ran away without telling anyone. It hurt her family greatly. It'll hurt mine when I leave, but I'm going to do things openly at least and say goodbye properly.' Because if he found a place where people accepted him, he would probably not come back. He suspected his mother already knew he would leave one day.

Matthieu nodded. 'All right. Now, help yourself to coffee and sit down. I'm enjoying the peace.'

Brendan smiled wryly. 'I must learn to drink coffee now, must I not?'

The dark liquid was as bitter as the thought of leaving his family. But he drank it all.

CHAPTER 14

JUNE–JULY

At Fremantle Dermott found a small ship which was taking a miscellaneous range of goods and a few passengers to Cape Town. This was a scruffy vessel which plied whatever routes would earn its owners the best money, and its passenger accommodation was not very comfortable. It was sailing the next afternoon, however, so after booking passages for himself and Christina, he retrieved the horse and rode back to Perth as fast as he could persuade the stupid creature to move. She was right not to bring the boys and they'd seemed happy to stay with their grandmother.

He'd half expected his wife to fall into hysterics at the thought of leaving the next day, and on such a small ship, but she stood still for a moment then started ordering him around. Fetch this, find that! For once he didn't complain. This was Christina at her best, as he'd seen her when they were first making their fortune – efficient and capable, not fussing, just getting on with things.

An hour later the maid was sent into town with a big shopping list and Dermott followed her a short time later to buy some more luggage and crates for their household goods, as well as hay for packing their best crockery which they'd send down to the farm.

At six o'clock they ate a scratch meal then the work continued, with the maid promised a bonus and a good reference for working through the night if necessary.

At eleven, blinking tiredly, Dermott began a letter to Matthieu giving him instructions about closing down the Perth house and taking the rest of their possessions to the farm. He did not write easily and it took a few swigs of rum to get the information down.

Not feeling in the least bit tired because at last she was going back to the country she had never stopped considering her home, Christina sat down at midnight to write a more elegant note, describing to Matthieu exactly what she wished stored and what was to be sold.

It was past one o'clock by the time they got to bed and as they had to be up again by four in the morning they did not bother to undress. Dermott grinned as he pulled up the blankets and closed his eyes. He was looking forward to seeing the shock on his sister's face when she saw him in England.

On the first day out the weather blew up a storm and both Dermott and Christina retired to their bunks, feeling unwell. It was three days before they came on deck again, by which time he was in a foul mood. Stinking seasickness! He'd forgotten how bad it made a man feel.

The weather continued brisk, but they made good time and gradually the worst of the seasickness passed. The captain, it seemed, had a bonus promised from the owners if he made a quick trip. Food was plentiful but not fancy, and the worst problem was boredom. Dermott had forgotten what it was like on a long voyage. If he never made another one in his life it'd be too soon, he decided gloomily, and began to wonder if he should stay in England after all. It would have been better on a proper passenger ship, with more folk to keep you company and things arranged to amuse you, especially now he could afford to go cabin class. But there would still be the seasickness when the weather grew rough.

At Cape Town they had to disembark and wait for another ship going to England, but were lucky to find one about to sail to France and took that instead. Full of bloody foreigners, but beggars could not be choosers.

Christina remained in excellent spirits. He had never seen her so happy or enjoyed her company like this. The fact that most of the other passengers did not speak the same language threw them together.

'Did you hate Australia so much?' he asked one day, as they were strolling round the deck.

She considered this, head on one side. 'It was

all right, I suppose, especially Melbourne, but I'm English, and I'll never stop being English.' She turned to give him a very level look. 'You'll have to drag me screaming on to a ship to get me back to Australia again, Dermott Docherty. I mean it.'

'Ah, we'll think about that when we see what England's like these days.'

'You mean – you'll consider staying there?'

'Aye. Eh, stop crying, you dafthead.' He pulled her into his arms and let her weep on his shoulder. She said she was crying because she was happy. Who could fathom women? But when she continued cheerful and unlike herself, he began to think very seriously about where their future lay.

'We need to get a better look at this lass as is living with Hamilton,' Bob Marshall told his brother. 'Have you seen her at all? Do you think she could be our sister?'

'When would I get a chance to gawp at her? I'm working too bloody hard and when I get home there's allus something needs doing. I never get time to feel the sun and wind on my face, shut up all day in that workshop. I'm fed up of it, I am that!'

'You still find time to come out for a sup of ale!'

'Ah, well, a man's throat gets dry after a day's hard work, doesn't it?'

Bob frowned. 'I suppose I'll have to go and take a look at the lass myself, then. As if I don't have enough on my plate with Dad.'

'You do that.' Jim counted up the change in his pocket and went to get another half-pint.

Bob went along Whalley Street the very next day, pushing his handcart and staring at the houses as if searching for a certain street number. He fell lucky. Just as he got near number twenty-two the door opened and out came a lass leading an old lady by the hand as if she were a small child. Pretending to shake a bit of grit out of his boot, he got a good look at her and what he saw made him whistle through his teeth. This had to be his half-sister! She had a look of the Marshalls to her, no doubt about that. She was tall, sturdy, and though her hair was much darker than his, she had that twisty bit at the right of the forehead that would never lie smooth, as they all did.

'Bloody hell!' he muttered under his breath. 'Who'd ha' thought it?'

She most resembled his younger brother Pat, though, with that same soft expression on her face. Just asking for folk to take advantage of you, it was, that expression. And they did take advantage of Pat, who was forever being asked to help some lazy sod for nothing.

Bob frowned as he wondered yet again why Docherty had written to tell them about this Cathie, who was, after all, Docherty's own niece. Did the bugger want her hurt? Bob wasn't having that, not if she really was a Marshall. He frowned as he took another long, slow look while she calmed the old lady down. She looked respectable, not much different from his own wife, really. But why was she dressed so plainly and living in Whalley Street working for Hamilton if her family was well-to-do? It didn't make sense.

He let her and the old lady walk past him, then strolled slowly home, marvelling at this unexpected outcome to his dad's randiness. The old sod! Good thing his father was past that sort of thing now – at least according to Sal – or they'd have a whole house full of bastards to look after. Bob didn't intend to tell his father anything yet about the lass because this needed thinking through properly. If there was any advantage to be gained from her presence, he intended to be the one to benefit because unlike his father he had a bit of sense in his noddle.

On his way to the pub that night he met Pat, who asked him if he'd had any luck in his search. He must have hesitated a bit too long because his younger brother beamed at him and exclaimed loudly, 'You did find our sister, then?'

Bob grabbed his arm and shook him. 'Shut up, you fool! Do you want everyone to know?'

'But what does it matter? Aren't we going to go and see her?'

'No, we're bleedin' well not. We're not going to do anything until I see my way straight.'

'What does Dad say?'

Bob scowled. 'Nothing, because I haven't told him.'

'He has a right to know you've found her.'

'Not in my book, he doesn't. Any road, he hasn't mentioned it again. It's us who'll have to think what to do – see if there's any money to be had from her family, mebbe.'

Pat gaped at him. 'Why should they give us money?'

'Have you forgot that our dear half-sister, bastard though she may be, is also half-sister to Master Francis Rawley? Because I haven't.' Bob snickered. 'Fancy *us* being related to them nobs. They'll hate that and they definitely won't want other folk to know about the connection, so if we play it right, they might give us a bit of money to keep our mouths shut.'

Pat stepped backwards, a disgusted expression on his face. 'I should have known you lot would mess things up. I were looking forward to having a sister an' I'm not threatening her with owt like that. Where is she?'

'Wouldn't you like to know?'

'I'll find out.' Pat turned on his heel and strode off.

Bob let out a scornful bray of laughter and called after him, 'By the time you've found out, me an' Jim will have getten oursen some money. Only we'll not share it with you, nor with the old man neither.' He marched off in the other direction, muttering 'Stupid sod!' under his breath two or three times, his mind already busy with schemes to get money out of the Rawleys. Only he'd have to do it carefully, because he didn't want to anger old Stephenson.

On the following Friday Magnus came home with a frown on his face.

'Is something wrong?' Cathie asked at once.

He hesitated, then said slowly, 'Young Mr Reuben was asking me about you today, what you were doing in Pendleworth.'

'Oh.'

'I told him you were my cousin and had come to look after my mother.' Another hesitation then he added, 'I'm not sure he believed me, though. He gave me a lecture about fornication.' Magnus had had great difficulty in restraining himself while he stood and listened. He'd thought Mr Reuben knew better than to believe him slack in morals, and suspected that Mr Matthew had insisted on the lecture, because Mr Reuben had seemed embarrassed by it and had finished abruptly.

Cathie's face turned scarlet and she said, 'Oh!' in a small voice. 'I thought if we said we were cousins people wouldn't think . . .'

'Eh, lassie, they're bound to talk. I've definitely harmed your reputation and I'm sorry for that.'

'You've never laid a finger on me, never been anything but respectful towards me,' she said hotly.

'What does that matter? Folk hereabouts enjoy a bit of gossip. Don't they in Australia?'

She stared down at her feet, still too embarrassed

to look him in the eyes. 'There were very few other people living nearby. From what I remember of our homestead, the nearest neighbour was about half a mile away. We often didn't see anyone outside the family from one week to the next. I'm not sorry I left, but I still can't remember my real father's name, however hard I try.' She looked at him in despair. 'What if I've wasted my time, hurt everyone – for nothing?'

'Eh, lassie, don't take on.'

Somehow his arms were round her and she was leaning against him, enjoying the rare sensation of feeling small and cherished against a man's hard body. When she looked up, Magnus was gazing down at her and she was sure that was fondness in his gaze. She smiled at him tentatively.

He brushed the back of his index finger up her cheek and said huskily, 'Och, we musna do this, lassie, not while you're living under my roof. Not even after you leave. With my mother how she is I have nothing to offer any woman but thankless hard work.' He glanced across the room towards the silently rocking figure as he said that, his expression sad.

'You have yourself to offer and most people work hard in one way or another,' Cathie corrected softly.

'It's not enough. I'm thirty with nothing saved.' He laid his hands on her shoulders and pushed her away from him, though a sigh escaped him as he did so. When his mother made a noise and stood up suddenly, he went across to make sure she didn't try to play with the fire again, but she did not respond to him, nor did she want to sit down, and in the end he had to push her gently into a sitting position.

Cathie didn't know what to say to him after that comment. Did it mean he was thinking seriously of her? She didn't know. But Magnus was wonderful, so patient and intelligent, and fun when he relaxed. Good-looking too in his own way, especially with that fierce expression on his face and that haughty way of holding himself as he strode about the town. A man of pride and integrity.

In fact, she admitted to herself, she liked him too much for her own good, thought about him during the day and dreamed of him sometimes at night.

She looked across the room to where he was trying to elicit some response from his mother. He loved his family very much and it was clear how upset he was about his brothers leaving. Oh, why was life never straightforward? Why were there always problems standing between you and happiness?

At Rawley Manor icy silence prevailed for several weeks. If Francis hadn't had the pleasure of his Sunday outings to look forward to, hadn't known he had a half-sister and was no longer alone in the world except for the great-uncle he'd grown to hate, he didn't know how he'd have borne it. Going over to visit the Lorrimers helped too, though he tried not to let his uncle know about that. It was reassuring to see a happy family who loved one another and welcomed visitors. Francis wanted a family and home like that himself some day, when he grew up.

Then one day he noticed his uncle looking at him differently, in a speculative way which made him suspect the old man was planning something. Silent scorn hadn't worked, but Francis was sure Alexander Stephenson would not let himself be easily beaten.

Worry about what the old man might do next, together with the thought that it was August and the date was fast approaching for him to go back to school, gave Francis some bleak moments. There was a perfectly good grammar school in Pendleworth, to which the Lorrimers' sons went, but he could see no prospect of persuading his uncle to allow him to go there.

'Can you not simply put up with the school for another two years?' Mr Lorrimer had asked the previous Sunday.

Francis didn't see why he should have to put up with it. He didn't fit in there and hated the rough discipline and poor food, not to mention the brutal teasing. Only he hated life at home too, so much that he was even wondering about running away to Australia to try to find his mother. Cathie was sure he'd be welcome at Lizabrook, but she insisted that running away caused more problems than it solved. And anyway, Francis was quite sure his uncle would send someone after him if he did try to escape – and would have the law on his side for years yet.

When Sunday morning came it was wet and very chilly, and although there were a couple of breaks the sky remained overcast and it rained heavily.

There was a knock on the bedroom door and Francis opened it to see Hilda standing there.

'If you please, Master Francis, your uncle says you're not to go out for a walk today. He doesn't want you catching your death of cold and the Ludlams are calling this afternoon.'

'He can't stop me,' Francis muttered.

She glanced over her shoulder. 'Oh, please, Master Francis, don't be setting his back up again. He's been that bad-tempered lately we're all afraid to open our mouths.'

'Thank you for delivering the message.'

He endured another silent luncheon, then returned to his room to change into his outdoor clothes. He thought he heard a sound outside and when he tried to open the bedroom door found it locked. Francis kicked it in fury. He could guess what had happened. He bent to stare under the door and thought he could make out a shadow. Was someone standing there?

Anger flared inside him and he pounded on the door. 'Let me out!'

'I have decided that your insolence must be

checked. You will stay in your room today until our guests arrive, then you will join us,' Alexander said, the first time he had spoken to Francis in more than monosyllables for weeks. 'And from now on I shall take steps to ensure your complete obedience.'

Francis did not reply. After a few moments he saw the shadow move and heard footsteps moving away. Ever since the seizure, his uncle walked with a sort of shuffle, as if one leg wasn't as strong as the other.

Francis waited five agonisingly slow minutes by the clock on his mantelpiece, then got out the spare key to his bedroom that he'd filched from the board in the butler's pantry, just in case he ever needed it. Slipping it into the lock, he turned it gently. The click sounded very loud and he held his breath for a moment, but nothing happened, so he risked opening the door.

He breathed a sigh of relief as he saw that the corridor was empty. Turning quickly, he locked the door again, then crept along to the servants' stairs.

At the bottom he met Cook, who gasped and clapped one hand to her bosom, then shot a quick glance around before she whispered, 'It's not wise, Master Francis. The master's in a foul mood today.'

'I've had enough of being treated like a child. I told him that a while ago and I meant it.'

She shook her head and gestured to him to pass. 'I didn't see you,' she muttered.

Daringly he kissed her plump cheek.

'Get on with you!' she said under her breath, but he had already gone.

Tears welled in her eyes. Master Francis was heading for bigger trouble than he had ever met in his whole life. She had seen how ruthless the old master could be with tenants if he was crossed, and was surprised he'd held off so long from retaliating to his nephew's disobedience. She went back into the kitchen feeling really worried. There was only so much she could do to help Francis or she'd lose her place. And if she left, who would care for that poor lad?

Outside it was raining again and Francis realised that in his haste to escape he had forgotten his outdoor coat. He hesitated but did not dare go back for it. Detouring to visit the stables, he picked up a horse blanket, which he wrapped round himself, keeping a careful watch for Horace.

He did not allow himself to think what things would be like when he returned. Today he wanted desperately to see his sister, needing the comfort of an hour or two with her.

Cathie was waiting for him on the edge of the woods, her face hidden under a large black umbrella with one spoke broken. When she heard him coming, she raised the umbrella and beamed at him.

They hugged one another, then he led the way into the woods.

Neither of them saw the stable lad watching them from behind some bushes. They had been spotted here the previous week. All the outdoor staff knew Master Francis was for it, but no one knew who the girl was and even today her face was hidden by the umbrella.

The woods were dripping with rain and Cathie was shivering. 'I'm not used to this cold,' she admitted when she saw Francis looking at her in concern.

'It gets a lot colder in winter, but dampness always makes it feel worse.'

'Is wearing a blanket the latest fashion for young gentlemen?' she teased.

He chuckled. 'I forgot my coat and didn't want to go back.' He didn't like admitting it but she had to know. 'My uncle locked me in my room. I escaped.'

Her smile faded. 'Francis, are you sure that was wise?'

'I'm not sure of anything lately. I just know that I've had enough of his bullying ways. I'm still thinking of running away to Australia to meet our mother. No one here really cares about me.'

'Oh, Francis, surely there's *someone*?'

He shook his head, gazing blindly across the clearing. 'The only one who'd really care if I ran away is Cook. I'm certain my uncle has no love for anyone these days. I'm not surprised he never got married, he's such a cold fish. My grandmother is probably the only person he's ever cared about in his life. Since she died, he's grown harsher with everyone, especially me. I hate him, Cathie, really hate him.'

'Oh, Francis, that's dreadful!' She gave him a quick hug. 'Well, there is another person who cares about you now – me.'

His eyes filled with tears so she held him close as she would have one of her other brothers, not saying anything, letting him recover in his own time. How dreadful it must be not to have any family who loved you!

And how badly she'd treated her own family, who definitely loved her!

When the Ludlam carriage drew up in front of Rawley Manor only Matthew Ludlam got out, his son Reuben having pleaded a prior engagement. As head of the household, he considered it his duty to keep on good terms with the other big landowners in the district, so visited Stephenson regularly. This time, however, Matthew had been asked to call.

Inside the house he joined his host in the library and there, in a dry voice that rasped with restrained anger, the old man confided his problems with his nephew.

Matthew frowned as the tale unfolded, shocked at the way the boy had behaved. 'Have you decided what to do about it?'

'Yes. That school hasn't toughened him up as I expected, so I've arranged to hire a private tutor.

However, I also need a strong man to help the tutor keep Francis in order, by force if necessary, and to share the duties of supervising him every hour of the day. I've engaged the tutor myself and he'll be arriving shortly, but I wanted to ask if you knew anyone suitable to help – maybe someone from your mill?'

'Who is the tutor?' Matthew asked.

'A military man fallen on hard times.'

'Do you intend to keep the boy a prisoner, then?' he queried in some surprise.

'If necessary.'

'Don't you think that's a bit – extreme?'

'No, I do not!' Surreptitiously Alexander wiped a trickle of moisture from the sagging corner of his mouth and tried to control his anger. 'I cannot subscribe to this modern idea of pampering the young. My sister treated Francis far too leniently and look where it's led. I intend to pull him into line over the next few years. I must do, for the sake of our family's heritage.' If he had a few years left. The matter was growing urgent because this numbness was not getting any better, and in fact he was not feeling at all well lately.

Matthew did not like the way the old man's body trembled with anger. Stephenson's colour had gone from an angry flush to a bone-white bleached look, as if he hadn't got enough blood in his body, and there was a viciousness in his tone that Matthew did not approve of. 'I suppose I could find you a strong man,' he said slowly, knitting his brow in thought. 'There are any number of those at the mill. I'll ask Reuben what he thinks. He's in charge of the workshop and knows our operatives better than I do.'

'Good. And now I wonder if you'd accompany me upstairs to Francis's room? It's time he found out what I have planned. I would be most obliged if you would have a word with him, too, to show him that I am not being unreasonable.'

Matthew hesitated, but the look of fragility beneath the anger, and that slightly twisted lip, convinced him it was better to humour the old man.

But Francis was not in his room and as Matthew definitely did not approve of such blatant disobedience, he promised again to find a strong man to work with the tutor.

When Stephenson broached another matter, which he had found out about from his head groom, Matthew was surprised at the scope of the old man's virulence. He agreed to investigate Magnus Hamilton's home arrangements, however, because he did not condone immorality among his employees any more than Stephenson did among his tenants. It was a Christian employer's responsibility to keep an eye on his dependants' morals.

Within days the voyage to England had started to restore Liza's health and spirits. Things had improved greatly since her first voyage to Australia in a sailing ship without even an auxiliary steam engine. Best of all for her this time was watching Josie's pleasure and the improvement in her health.

Her younger daughter had always been frail, prone to wheezing and a little pale. On the ship the wheezing vanished entirely and Josie became a gleeful and sometimes naughty child, making friends for the first time in her life and confiding in her mother that she wished the voyage would go on for ever.

'It's so much more fun on the ship than it was at home,' she said sleepily one night from the top bunk. 'I can understand now why Cathie ran away, but I still miss her, don't you? I do hope we find her in England.'

'I'm sure we shall,' Liza promised.

What her younger daughter had said gave her much food for thought when she went to bed later after a pleasant evening spent talking to the other cabin passengers. You could not immure your children in the bush for ever, and though it hurt to let them go, she would do it in future with better grace and make sure Benedict did, too.

And why Josie should feel so well now that she was away from the farm needed further consideration too. Liza had talked to the ship's doctor about that and he had said that such wheeziness could be affected by the climate and where the sufferer lived.

She fell asleep, feeling a little guilty that she too

was enjoying the change of routine. When she got back she would make sure Benedict left the farm more often. They could leave their sons in charge and travel to Melbourne or Sydney once they were on their feet financially again. Why not? And she'd definitely sell the rest of the Ludlam jewellery when she got back, except for the cameo ring for which she had a particular fondness. It was silly to keep something she never wore just because of Benedict's pride.

The ship made good time and soon there were only a couple of weeks left before their arrival in England. Much as she missed her husband and sons, Liza remained sure that she was doing the right thing coming to look for her lost children.

It made the young Lorrimers and their friends laugh to see Francis turn up wrapped in a horse blanket. He joined in because their merriment was not malicious. It was not unpleasant to be teased, he found, by people like this.

Mr Lorrimer walked outside with him when he left and gestured to the blanket. 'What happened?'

'They locked me in my room. I had a spare key so I escaped. But I forgot my overcoat.'

'Be careful not to push them too far.'

Francis blinked furiously. He hated to leave this happy house. 'They've pushed *me* too far, sir.'

Mr Lorrimer's only response was to pat him on the back.

Back at the Manor Francis returned the horse

blanket then stood outside the stables for several minutes, his stomach churning with nervousness about facing his uncle.

He went into the house via the kitchen. Cook deliberately avoided his questioning glance, so he knew something had happened while he was away. He didn't ask, just nodded to her and the kitchen maid and walked up the back stairs, hoping to postpone the confrontation for a while longer.

His bedroom door was now unlocked, which showed someone had been in. He hid the key with even greater care than before, hanging it outside the window on a thread attached to the ivy so that it lay beneath the lush green leaves. Spit and dirt disguised the thread, so that even if anyone did look, they'd have trouble finding the key.

No one came to summon him to the library so he waited until dinner time, getting dressed with care. He had never felt less hungry in his life, but was not going to lurk in his room like a coward.

His uncle was already seated and looked up as he entered the dining room to ask in that rasping voice he had developed recently, 'How did you get out?'

'Through the door.'

'Kindly return the key.'

'I've already put it back in the butler's pantry.'

Francis noted that his uncle was eating with more appetite than usual, in fact cramming food into his mouth, which puzzled him from a normally fastidious eater. The triumphant expression on the old man's face made his heart sink even further.

But nothing else was said over the meal – nothing at all.

Francis went up to his room afterwards with apprehension churning in his belly and vomited up what he had eaten. He didn't sleep well, either.

CHAPTER 15

JULY

'Is Hamilton living in sin?' Matthew Ludlam asked his son over breakfast the following day.

'Not to my knowledge.'

'He's renting one of our houses, isn't he? Stephenson told me about it, hinted we should turn him out.'

Reuben looked at his father in amazement. 'What's it got to do with him?'

'He was just being neighbourly, passing on a piece of information.'

'A piece of gossip! Anyway, I've already questioned Hamilton about the situation and he says the girl is his cousin, there to look after his mother who has softening of the brain and is getting worse by the month, poor soul. I've seen the woman myself – a very sad decline. And since Hamilton's sister has married and gone to live in Bury, he needs help.'

'Well, if you're sure . . .'

'I am sure they're not in an immoral relationship, Father.' Magnus Hamilton would have scorned to lie. Reuben wasn't sure whether the

339

girl really was a cousin, however, but had not pressed that point. 'And either I'm in charge of the workshop and those who work there or Mr Stephenson is – in which case I'll leave today.'

'Don't be stupid. I just don't want to have a foreman setting a bad example.'

Reuben gave his father a very level look. 'I mean what I say. Grandfather kept you without power right until his death. I'll not put up with the same treatment. I can earn my living in other places and I'm not greedy for Ludlam wealth.'

'Oh, don't be so touchy. You know you're in charge of the workshop. Anyway, Stephenson has another problem and I promised we'd help him . . .' He began to explain.

By the time he got to the mill, Reuben had walked his anger off. As he moved round the workshop, he studied the men, deeply resenting the fact that his father had given his word to find someone suitable to discipline Francis Rawley. Men of Stephenson's generation thought they could ride roughshod over anyone in their power, and for all his father's protestations, he was still too influenced by the way his own father had done things. Reuben would not carry on those traditions when his time came. He could still remember being afraid of his grandfather; had seen his grandmother weep several times after Saul Ludlam had treated her scornfully. She was well rid of him, they all were, and now they lived a happier life at the Hall, or would do if his father would stop trying to copy Saul by acting the tyrant.

Reuben knew, because she often confided in him, that his grandmother had supported some of his grandfather's many bastards during their childhood, those born to the maidservants upon whom his grandfather had forced himself. He often visited her because her cosy little house with its cheerful atmosphere was a relief after the formality of the big house. He wished he could have such a place for himself, only his father had made such a fuss when he'd suggested moving out of the Hall that he'd let the matter drop. For the time being.

Nor was he going to marry one of the suitable girls his mother and father were pressing him to consider. He'd choose his own wife – and did not want to marry anyone yet.

He beckoned his capable foreman to join him.

A few minutes later Magnus went over to Jim Marshall and said. 'Mr Reuben wants to see you in his office.'

Jim cast him a resentful glance as he put his hammer down. 'What for? I've done nowt wrong.'

'You're not in trouble.' Magnus watched him leave, frowning. Mr Reuben had not looked in the best of humours this morning. Which usually meant his father had been interfering in workshop matters again.

In the office Reuben waved Jim to a seat and he sat down uneasily, never having been asked to sit in here before.

'I don't want this to go any further, Jim. In fact, I want your solemn promise on that before I start. What's more, if I find you *have* been talking, you'll be out on your ear.'

'Nay, sir, you can trust me. What you say will go no further.'

'Mr Stephenson at Rawley Manor is having trouble controlling his nephew Francis —'

Jim sat up a bit straighter, all attention now.

'— and wants a strong fellow to help the new tutor keep the lad in order.' Reuben made an exasperated sound in his throat. 'I may as well tell you that I don't like us getting involved in this. I feel sorry for that lad. He's not had a happy life and it looks as if things are about to get worse for him. However, my father has promised to find someone to help Mr Stephenson and I thought you might fancy a bit of a change. You don't always seem best pleased with what you're doing here and the job at the Manor will pay a bit more.'

'What exactly do they want me to do there?'

Reuben spread his hands wide in a gesture of puzzlement. 'Who can tell? If it involves beating the lad then' – he hesitated before adding – 'I'd like you to let me know about it.' He would rather have sent Hamilton to do a job like this, if he had to send anyone, but he needed his foreman's skills here and Magnus had his mother to care for. 'Well, what do you think?'

'How much extra money if I do it, sir? It's a long walk out to the Manor.'

'They want someone to stay there – though you'll get a day a week off to visit your family.'

'Stay there?' Jim goggled at him for a minute then grinned. 'Fancy me living at the Manor! That's a queer one, isn't it?'

'You'll be staying in the servants' quarters. You'll get the same money as now, part of it paid to your wife, plus your keep and an extra guinea a month.'

Jim didn't hesitate. 'I'll do it, sir.'

'Right then. You're to report there at eight o'clock tomorrow morning. Clear your things here. You can have the rest of the day off. Oh, and send Hamilton in to see me, if you please.'

Jim closed the office door behind him then grinned round the noisy workshop. Fate was being kind to him and Bob. They'd wanted to meet the lad and now here was Master Francis being handed over to them like a gift.

When he left he headed towards Underby Street to tell his brother about it.

Reuben summoned Magnus to his office, gesturing to the chair. 'Marshall accepted.'

'I thought he would.'

'I've asked Jim to let me know if they're ill-treating the lad. I don't like this at all. If *you* hear anything . . .'

'I'll let you know at once, sir.' Magnus knew Caitlin would be upset when he told her about this. She was getting very fond of her half-brother.

Reuben then turned the discussion to some

modifications Magnus had suggested for some of the machinery. If things turned out as well as he expected, he would insist on the foreman being given a bonus for this and later a more important position in the mill. Almost as an afterthought he added, 'How's your mother, Magnus?'

'Worse, I'm afraid, sir. Caitlin couldn't even persuade her out for a walk yesterday. She just lay abed all day. I've asked the doctor to call in on his rounds tonight.'

'It's a hard time for you.'

'Aye, sir. I don't know what I'd do without Caitlin. She's marvellous with my mother. A born nurse, the doctor says.'

Later the same morning one of the Rawley carriages was sent to the station to fetch the new tutor who had been Sergeant Baxter until an injury left him with a pronounced limp and forced him to leave his regiment. The limp didn't stop him being a strong man still and he was well read for someone of his station, but his brief as 'tutor' was to make a man of Francis, not to mollycoddle him or worry too much about book learning.

Francis happened to be strolling in the gardens when the carriage returned from the station, for the weather had cleared today. He watched a stranger get out, surprised by what he saw. No gentleman, this, so what was he doing calling on Alexander Stephenson via the front door? Then the driver unloaded several items of luggage and it was clear that the man had come to stay. Apprehension shivered through Francis. What was his uncle planning now? He did not normally invite people to stay.

On a sudden impulse the lad hurried round the side of the house and concealed himself in some bushes near the library. One of the French windows was open because his uncle was a firm believer in the benefits of fresh air and since the old man was becoming increasingly deaf, the conversation was clearly audible from outside.

'Eli Baxter reporting for duty, sir!'

'Sit down, man.' There was a short silence, then, 'They explained to you what was required?'

'Yessir. But I'd like to hear it explained by you, if you don't mind. Can't beat first-hand information.'

'Yes, I suppose you're right.' Alexander took a deep breath and said the words aloud, distasteful though they might be. 'I want you to knock my great-nephew into shape. Literally if need be. He's a namby-pamby creature. Refuses to join the hunt or go shooting, wants to waste his time sketching, fools around at school. Lately he's been openly defiant of my orders and has been seen in the woods with a young woman of plebeian origin.'

Silence, then, 'What do you mean by "knock into shape"?'

'I mean that if necessary you will beat him until he learns to obey – not in a way that will mark him or injure him badly, of course. But I am not a young man and do not wish this estate to fall into the hands of a weakling, so the matter is urgent. You will spare no effort, do anything that is necessary to bring Francis up to scratch and as quickly as possible – as if he were a new recruit in your regiment.'

'If I treated him like that, it could be painful for him, sir.'

'It will be painful for the estate if the last of the Rawleys fails in his duty to care for it.'

Eli didn't comment on that. This was a rum situation if ever he'd seen one, but the old man was going to pay him handsomely and the extra money would help him buy himself a little inn he'd got his eye on. He'd give himself a year here, no more, and deal with this spoiled rich lad exactly as he'd dealt with unsuitable recruits in the regiment, not one of whom had ever got the better of him when he'd set his mind to it. Eli prided himself on that.

'My neighbour, Matthew Ludlam, is finding a man to help since you cannot be on duty twenty-four hours a day. The lad is cunning so will bear watching. We don't want him running off again.'

Francis closed his eyes and a sick feeling of dismay and fear shuddered through him. If he had ever needed confirmation of how much his uncle despised him, here it was. Only he hadn't needed it, for he had already known. He had not, however, expected Uncle Alexander to be prepared to have him beaten into submission. Anger flooded through him. Well, he would not do what they wanted! He hated horses and always would. He hated blood sports, too, and refused to kill animals for pleasure. But most of all he hated his uncle and would not cave in to his bullying.

He swallowed hard. At least, he hoped he wouldn't. Could he manage to stand firm against them all? He'd have to find the courage somehow. He thought suddenly of the mother he had not been allowed to know. Yes, he would cling to that painful thought as he faced them.

How best should he do this? He would have to think about that. And quickly.

His uncle was speaking again. 'You will be given a room in the west wing next to my nephew, Mr Baxter, so that you can keep an eye on Francis at all times. The other man will be here tomorrow and will act as general servant to you both, but his main purpose is to act as guard and see the boy doesn't escape.'

'Yes, sir.'

There was the sound of a bell ringing and the library door opening. Francis stumbled to his feet and made for the woods. Perhaps he should run away now, while he could? But once under the trees he slowed down and acknowledged that it was impossible. He had no money with him and did not dare go back for any. And he had no one close enough to run to – only his half-sister, and he did not intend to bring trouble to Cathie who would be powerless if his uncle turned the full force of his anger on her.

After some thought Francis made his way across the fields to the Lorrimers' house, knocked on the door and asked to speak to Mrs Lorrimer. The maid recognised him and ushered him straight into the hall, then her mistress came out and took him into her sitting room.

'Is something wrong, Francis?'

His voice cracking with pain, he told her what he had overheard and asked her to pass the information on to her husband. 'I don't think there's anything he can do to help me, but I feel someone should at least know what's happening.'

'You poor boy.' Her voice was soft and warm and made him want to weep in her arms, so he stood up hastily and said, 'I'd better get back now. They'll be looking for me.'

'What exactly are you going to do?'

'Resist them. Any way I can.' He looked at her, his eyes very blue and over-bright, his soft blond hair gleaming in the sun. 'They may knock me about, but I doubt they'll kill me. And whatever they do, I won't let them turn me into a person like my uncle.'

As they walked towards the front door he stopped at a sudden thought. 'I wonder if I could write a note to my half-sister and ask you to send it to her? I've been meeting her on Sundays in the woods and she'll wonder what's happening if I don't turn up next week. I don't want her going to the house and asking for me, and I don't want them knowing who she is, though they do know I've been meeting a young woman.'

When Francis got back to the Manor he went in by the kitchen door. Cook looked at him pityingly, but said only, 'Your uncle wants to see you at once. He's sent the grooms out to look for you.'

'Where is he?'

'In the library.'

How he hated that room, Francis thought as he knocked on the door. When his uncle's reedy voice told him to enter, he found them waiting for him, his uncle and the new tutor, a burly man with a somewhat battered face.

'So they found you!' Uncle Alexander snapped.

'No one found me. I came home from a walk in the woods and received a message you wanted to see me, so I came at once.'

'You're not to go out on your own again.' With a triumphant, sneering smile, his uncle explained what had been arranged.

'So I'm not to go back to school in the autumn then?' Francis asked, trying to act as if this was all news to him, as if he didn't know what to expect from this 'tutor'.

'Did I not say so?'

'Well, I'm glad of that at least.'

Alexander was suddenly unable to bear the sight of his nephew. That the Rawleys, a fine old county family, had degenerated to the point where this milksop was the heir galled him more each day.

'Take him away, Baxter, and find out what he can and cannot do. You're in charge, now.' Anger beat so strongly within him that he felt dizzy, but a few deep breaths and he started to calm down. He had to conserve his strength. The second seizure had frightened him and now he was concentrating all his energy on the main thing he needed to do before he went to meet his Maker. He had to live long enough to make a man of his nephew.

He began to walk up and down the room, gesticulating and muttering, so that when Ethel peeped in, she backed out again hastily. The master was in one of his moods again. Gave her the shivers, it did, seeing him like that.

Upstairs Francis showed the tutor to the west wing, trying to keep his manner calm and polite even though his stomach was churning with nerves.

'Your uncle says we're to use the old schoolroom,' Eli prompted after he had nodded approval of the comfortable bedroom he'd been assigned next to the lad's.

'Did he? Very well.' Francis led the way up another flight of stairs, staring round yet another room where he had been unhappy.

Eli studied him assessingly. Weak physically, still a boy not a man, for all his height. He'd seen new recruits who looked like this before and had found out the hard way that you couldn't force muscles on to young bodies until they'd grown into their adult strength, whatever you did.

'I've a lot of experience with lads your age,' he warned. 'Your uncle wants me to teach you to ride properly, use a gun, hunt – all the usual gentlemanly pursuits.'

As quietly and politely as before Francis told him, 'I won't hunt. I'm a bad enough rider without risking myself over fences and hedges. And I won't shoot birds and animals, either, when I don't need them for food.'

'It's your duty to do as your uncle wishes.' He was surprised at how steadily the lad gazed back at him, even though Eli had stared down generals in his time. Had the old man underestimated this boy?

'Only if it does not go against what I believe to be right, Mr Baxter.'

A firm believer in starting as you meant to go on, Eli lashed out and caught Francis on the side of the head, sending him staggering across the room. 'I have your uncle's permission to use force to persuade you into better behaviour and shall not hesitate to do so. It's not for you to make conditions, only to obey orders.'

'I can't stop you beating me, Mr Baxter,' Francis said. 'You're much bigger than I am. But I must tell you that you won't change my mind.'

Eli watched the lad steady himself against the table, realised his tone was that of one reasonable adult speaking to another, and again wondered what was going on here. The old man downstairs had not been reasonable, not at all, but sadly he held the purse strings. 'You'll have no chance of holding out against the three of us. If you think about it, you'll see that your wisest course is to do as you're told,' he warned.

Francis braced himself for another blow, but it didn't come.

'How about we start with target shooting? Your uncle says you've refused even to handle a gun.'

'Yes, I hate the things. So I'm sorry but I won't learn to shoot.' Another hefty thump was his answer and it hurt. His head ringing with pain, it took Francis a moment to stand up straight again. He moved to the other side of the table. No use making it easy for this brute to thump him.

'Who's the lass you've been meeting?' Eli watched the lad become very still and pale.

'Just a friend.'

'You young men will sow your wild oats!' his tutor jeered. 'Well, that's going to stop, too.'

Anger brought hot colour rushing into Francis's face. 'I've not been sowing any wild oats and I'm not lying! She's a friend and that's all! Who's been maligning her?'

'Your uncle simply informed me that you'd been meeting a lass in the woods and that it was to stop. Who is she?'

'None of your business.'

'You'll tell me. And you'll learn to answer smartly when I ask a question.'

'I'll not tell you.'

Eli thought he'd rarely seen a lad look so

despairing and yet so steadfast. He wondered what had driven the old man to treat a youngster with such a steady, honest face in this cruel way. Well, that was enough violence for now. Give the lad something to think about then give him time to do that thinking, that was the trick of it.

'We'll go out for a walk, then, and you can show me these woods of yours. Walking is surely not against your principles?' As Francis moved reluctantly towards the door, Eli added sharply, 'And hold yourself upright as you walk. Slouching is bad for the spine and a sign of slovenliness.'

The lad stood and thought about the order – that was going to change very soon, Eli decided – then shrugged and squared his shoulders as if it didn't matter.

As they went outside the sunlight revealed a handsome young fellow with a clear, innocent face, not at all like the brutal youths Eli had mostly dealt with up to now. This was the sort of lad any father would be proud of. Eli had had a son once, but he'd died of cholera in India and so had Eli's wife.

He suddenly wished he had not taken this job. But having done so, he wasn't going to admit failure. And besides, a few beatings never hurt anyone. He was living proof of that and so were the many men he'd turned into good soldiers.

When Bernard Lorrimer came home that night, he listened in silence to his wife's tale. 'Unfortunately we have no right to interfere.'

353

'But surely we can do *something*?' she begged, still upset. No lad should have to face such callous treatment. No lad should ever have such a bleak look in his eyes.

'There's nothing we can do, not even if we can prove they've been beating him. The law gives them that right.'

'You mean we can't do anything officially,' she corrected, knowing him better than to think he'd turn his back on poor Francis.

They stared at one another then he said carefully, 'The situation would have to be very desperate indeed for me to intervene unofficially.'

'I know, dear. But Francis does have a mother in Australia who cares about him. Could we not send him to her?'

'If it becomes desperate I may consider that,' Bernard promised. He would also go and see Cathie Ludlam the very next day and deliver Francis's note in person. He was relieved to have found exactly where she was living and meant to discover whether she was in need of help of any sort.

As he walked slowly up the stairs to bed he thought yet again how glad he was that he had an independent income and useful connections so did not have to kow-tow to arrogant bullies like Alexander Stephenson. He was, however, surprised at the Ludlams' involvement in something like this.

That reminded him that Cathie still carried the

Ludlam name and made him wonder whether to inform Sophia Ludlam that her son Josiah's adopted daughter was in Pendleworth. The old lady had apparently been very fond of her grand-daughter as a child and might be glad to see her again and help, if necessary. No. Not yet. Best to wait and see what happened. You did not take action on mere suppositions.

But he would definitely go and see Cathie the following day.

His wife was equally wakeful and making her own plans. Her cook knew the cook at the Manor. She would ask Mrs Sark, who was the soul of discretion, to find out from her friend Barbara how things were going over there.

That evening Dr Barnes called at Magnus's house on his evening rounds, examined Janey, commented on how well cared for she was nowadays and shook his head over her lack of response to his questions. 'She is entering the final stage of the illness, I'm afraid, Mr Hamilton. They decline very rapidly when they get like this and often simply starve to death. Are you managing to feed her still?'

Magnus had to force the words through a throat suddenly constricted with tears. 'Not always. Caitlin is very good with her.'

'I can see that.' The doctor turned to the young woman and noted how clean she was in her own person. 'And how have you found your charge lately?'

'She wouldn't eat at all yesterday,' Cathie told him. 'Though she's been a bit better today.'

'You can only do your best with her. Afterwards, if you ever want a job as a home nurse, Miss Rutherford, I can find you work.'

She looked at him in surprise, then beamed at him. 'I never thought of that.' Her smile faded as she added, 'I shall have to earn my own living if anything happens to Aunt Janey. It wouldn't be proper for me to stay here on my own with Magnus.'

Clifford Barnes, who had also heard the gossip about her and Magnus Hamilton, decided yet again that gossip was usually a liar and he would continue to trust his own judgement about such matters. These were obviously two decent people doing their duty by an ageing relative, and so he'd tell the next person who hinted at anything else.

In the middle of the morning there was a knock on the front door and when Cathie went to answer it she found a stranger standing there, a gentleman by his appearance.

'Miss Ludlam?'

She wondered how he knew that when they'd told everyone she was called Rutherford. 'Yes.'

'My name is Bernard Lorrimer. May I have a word with you?'

She gaped at him. 'You're my mother's lawyer!'

'Yes.'

She held the door open. 'Come in.'

In the back room Janey Hamilton was slumped in a chair, not needing any bonds to restrain her because today she would only move when someone made her. 'I'm looking after Mrs Hamilton for Magnus and his sister,' Cathie said softly. 'She doesn't know what she's doing.'

'Poor thing. It can't be easy for you.'

'She wasn't too bad until the last few days. Now she lies or sits wherever I leave her. It's upsetting my cousin Magnus greatly.'

Bernard held up one hand. 'We both know he isn't your cousin.'

She looked at him nervously. 'Sorry. I've got into the habit of calling him that. You won't tell anyone, will you? Oh, please don't! We only say it to stop people saying such terrible things about us.' She stared him straight in the eye as she added, 'Things that are quite untrue.'

'I believe you, Cathie. Do you want to tell me what happened to bring you here?'

So yet again she had to explain what she had remembered about her flight and voyage to England. When she had finished, he sat looking thoughtful and she ventured to ask, 'Do you know who my real father is, sir?'

He shook his head. 'Your mother never told me anything except that you were not Josiah Ludlam's child. I gather someone forced himself upon her when she was quite young.'

Cathie gasped in shock: 'No!'

Her voice rang with such anguish that Bernard

immediately regretted his tactless remark. 'You didn't know that?'

'No. At least, I don't think I did.' She shook her head, trying in vain to penetrate the veils which she suspected still concealed some of her memories. 'I can't believe I'd have come here looking for him if I'd known that. But now that I am here, I intend to find him and learn something about that side of my family – however he became my father.'

'Well, let's see. Your mother lived in Underby Street for many years, that I do know, and some of her old neighbours may still be there. You could ask them what they remember.' Bernard walked along that street sometimes as a short cut to vary his path home on fine days when he spurned using the carriage. 'I think the clogger's shop has been there for a good many years and in the same family, so the people there are most likely to have known your mother.'

Her expression brightened. 'I'll go and ask them.'

Bernard cleared his throat, seeking a tactful way to ask but not finding one, so just saying bluntly, 'Are you all right for money, my dear? If not, I could let you have some.'

She raised her head proudly. 'I'm earning my keep here, thank you.'

He frowned. 'Not very suitable employment for a girl like you.'

'Magnus needs me, and since he saved my life

at Liverpool docks I'm happy to repay him by looking after his mother.' She looked sadly at the old woman. 'The doctor says Aunt Janey is probably nearing the end now and will soon refuse to eat at all. He's known patients like her choke if you try to force food on them, so has advised me not to do that. But I intend to look after her 'til she – 'til Magnus doesn't need me any more, then I'll decide what to do next.' With a hint of a smile, she added, 'The doctor has already offered me other nursing work.'

Lorrimer was surprised at that. 'Dr Barnes has?'

'Yes.'

'That's a great compliment coming from him. He and his nurses are well respected in Pendleworth.'

'I've always enjoyed that sort of thing. If I'd been a man, I'd have become a doctor.' She spread her hands wide in a helpless gesture. 'I read somewhere that a woman did become a doctor in America some years ago – Elizabeth Blackwell she was called. I've never forgotten her name.'

'There's a woman doctor in England, too. Another Elizabeth – Elizabeth Garrett Anderson. I remember reading about it – oh, it must be ten years ago now. She had a lot of trouble getting permission to study and take the exams, though. I don't think there's been another one brave enough since.'

Cathie sighed. 'I envy her. But I have no money and no family here, so I can't hope to follow in her footsteps.' She looked at him with determination in every line of her body. 'But I can earn a living nursing. That's something, at least. And it'll mean I can stay in England. I'm not going back to living in the bush.'

He wasn't sure what he thought of women becoming doctors and would definitely have forbidden his own daughters to try. Changing the subject, he produced the letter Francis had written. 'I'm afraid I have some bad news for you about your half-brother. He's written you this note. Perhaps you had better read it, then if you have anything to ask me about, you can.'

She read it quickly, murmuring in dismay, then exploding into angry words as she finished it. 'How can they treat him like this? Is there nothing *you* can do to help him? I'm sure my mother would pay whatever it cost.'

'Unfortunately the law is on Mr Stephenson's side. He is your half-brother's legal guardian and has a right to chastise him.'

Cathie closed her eyes and when she opened them again they filled with tears. 'Francis is such a lonely, unhappy boy! He doesn't deserve this. My other brothers and my sister and I have been so very lucky in our parents' love. I never realised how lucky till I met Francis. Oh, I do wish I had not hurt my parents so!' Then she began sobbing and Bernard was so upset by her distress he took her in his arms as he would have his own daughters.

Cathie didn't weep for long, but pulled away and wiped her eyes. 'I'm sorry.'

'My dear, you have good reason to be upset.'

She gave him a determined look. 'If I hear they're hurting Francis, I shall have to try to rescue him.'

Bernard did not try to hide his shock. 'My dear girl, you must do no such thing!'

'I can't leave him to endure such cruel treatment. He's my brother and I've grown very fond of him.'

Bernard produced one of his business cards. 'Please don't do anything rash. If you ever have reason to believe that Francis needs rescuing, come and see me at my chambers or at home – any time of day or night. Promise!' He took out his little silver propelling pencil and scribbled his home address on the back of the card, explaining where his house was.

She took the card from him. 'Thank you, sir. I promise to let you know. But you'll not stop me if I see a need to act.'

He saw her looking at the pencil, which was a novelty to most people, and showed her how it worked, glad to introduce a lighter note into their conversation. He had been the first person in Pendleworth to have a propelling pencil, the first to ride on the underground railway in London a few years previously, the first to send his wife one of the new picture postcards purchased on one of his trips to London.

Talk of such novelties distracted her for a while,

then he took his leave with the warning, 'Please don't try to do anything to help Francis without consulting me.'

'I'm not going to let them hurt him.'

Bernard was so worried by her stubborn expression that when he went home he discussed it with his wife. 'I had to admire her spirit,' he admitted. 'She's a fine young woman.'

'Is she – decent?'

'I believe so. It's not right, her living with a strange man, but I'm convinced there's nothing untoward going on between her and Magnus Hamilton.'

'Perhaps you should tell the Ludlams who she is?'

He pursed his lips. 'Perhaps. But Matthew Ludlam is a friend of Stephenson's and might tell him, which could only cause more trouble for Francis. Matthew is a weak reed under that pompous exterior, so terrified of jeopardising his damned dignity he never does anything out of the ordinary. His father destroyed his spirit when he was young – as Stephenson is trying to do to young Francis now. I pray he won't succeed.'

But if the need ever arose, he would go and see Matthew's mother Sophia, who was both kind and wise, he decided. He handled all her legal affairs now, because when her husband Saul died she had immediately moved out of the Hall and insisted on being independent from her sons. She not only enjoyed helping those worse off than herself, but had known and loved Cathie as a child. And best of all, she was not afraid of Alexander Stephenson, for whom she did not attempt to hide her dislike.

CHAPTER 16

JULY

When Magnus got home from the workshop that evening, he found Cathie looking very downcast and his mother slumped in her chair, not even rocking to and fro. He tried in vain to coax a glance or a touch from Janey, then gave up.

'You must have had a bad day with her, Caitlin?'

'She hasn't misbehaved, but she hasn't eaten a thing.' Cathie hesitated then said, 'And I had some bad news of my own today as well.'

He could see she was holding back tears only with difficulty so said at once, 'Tell me. You can serve the meal afterwards. You need to talk to someone after a hard day with my mother.' Only – Janey did not seem like his mother any more. There had been no glimpses of her old self for several days and he longed for her to be released from her failing body – longed for it and yet felt guilty about those feelings.

'Oh, Magnus . . .'

He jerked out of his sombre thoughts to see Cathie's lips quivering and tears on her cheeks. In spite of his resolution not to touch her, he took her in his arms and drew her against him. 'Tell me, lassie,' he murmured against the soft dark hair.

So she poured out the news of Mr Lorrimer's visit and how Francis was to be imprisoned and ill-treated. Magnus found himself stroking her hair and making soothing noises as the tale faltered to a close.

She didn't tell him about the suggestion that she call and see the clogger because by the time she had told him that she was probably the result of a man forcing himself on her mother she was sobbing uncontrollably.

He let her weep, his heart twisting with anguish for her.

'I'm sorry,' she gulped as she began to calm down. She tried to pull away from him. 'You have enough troubles of your own – and bad ones, too. You don't need mine as well.'

'You're sharing my troubles. Why can I not share yours?' he said simply.

'Oh, Magnus.' She lifted her face and stared at him as she held back the words 'Magnus, my love', which she would have liked to add. The feeling had crept up on her as she watched him care so tenderly for his mother, saw his joy at his sister's visits and experienced his kindness towards a stranger like herself. And she loved his tall, strong body, too. The mere touch of his hand was enough to set her tingling with longing. Why had it taken her so long to realise what all this meant?

'Caitlin, lass, this is not . . . we mustn't . . .' He let the words trail away and stepped backwards.

She could only assume that he did not care about her as she cared for him, so took a deep breath and said with false brightness, 'Well, now that I've wept all over you, I suppose I'd better get you your tea.'

He told himself it was better to keep his distance for the moment because he was a man, with all a man's desires, and she was a very bonny lass. So he sat down by the table and watched her bustle about the kitchen, neat and careful in her work as always. He could at least enjoy watching her.

'I'm afraid they're sending another man to help guard your brother,' he said as she finished cooking his food. 'Mr Ludlam is helping his friend, Mr Stephenson, so they've sent Jim from the work-shop. He's a rough fellow though not cruel, I think. But Mr Reuben was in a bad mood all day about it and your poor brother will be so carefully watched I don't see how you *can* do anything to help him.'

'Well, I'm not going to leave Francis to be ill-treated!'

'We'll keep an eye on the situation and if we find out that things are bad, the best thing is for us to go and see your Mr Lorrimer.'

She gave him a glowing look. 'You'll help – come with me, if necessary?'

'Aye, of course I will, Caitlin. But we'll keep our eyes and ears open first. A lad doesn't die of a strict upbringing.'

She thought of Francis, so soft-hearted he wouldn't even go shooting, of the way his eyes lit up when he saw her, the way he held on to her hand as if he needed the human contact. 'Perhaps his body won't die, but something inside him will wither, I'm sure, if he doesn't have anyone to care for him and only meets with ill-treatment.' She set a plate of fried ham and potatoes in front of Magnus and cut a thick slice of bread for him as well. He had a hearty appetite, which was not surprising in such a big man, and she loved to watch him enjoying his food.

She found her own appetite returning as they shared the meal.

As Cathie was lying in bed later she suddenly remembered her own mother saying once that it didn't matter where you lived as long as you were with the man you loved. She knew she could be happy with Magnus, was happy with him, even in the present difficult circumstances.

Oh, if only he loved her as she loved him. But how could he? He was older, far more sensible, must think her stupid – but he *had* held her in his arms today . . . and it had felt wonderful . . . and . . . on that thought she fell asleep.

The following day Janey was a little better, allowing herself to be dressed and moving willingly enough down the stairs and around the house. Cathie decided to take her out for a short walk, but was a bit worried when they started off at the way Janey's eyes did not focus on anything at all. She decided only to go to Underby Street, to ask about her mother at the clogger's shop, because it wasn't far.

The narrow street had small shops in it as well as terraced dwellings. She stopped for a minute to stare around. Had her mother really been born here? It could not have been more different from Lizabrook homestead. The clogger's shop was on the right, halfway along the street, with CLOGS painted in big red letters above the window. That same window was grimy and had a few clogs scattered about in a kind of display, with a panel of wood behind them so that she couldn't see inside.

She remembered suddenly looking at a picture in a book of Dutch people wearing clogs and wondering aloud how people could wear such stupid footwear. Her mother had laughed and told her that clogs were very comfortable and weather-proof, then had fallen silent and stared into the distance. Cathie could now guess that this was because she had once lived near a clogger's shop. She wished she knew which house had been her mother's.

She decided to go inside the clogger's, but had to pull Janey quite hard to make her move forward again and noticed with dismay that the older woman was standing limply, as if she might fall down at any moment. A bell rang as she opened the door and Cathie looked up to see it bouncing about on a spring above her, giving off a tinny tinkle. The interior was very dim because the panel at the back of the window blocked out the light. The shop was empty, but from the back room came the sound of hammering.

No one came out, so after a few moments Cathie picked up the handbell from the counter and rang it.

'I'll get it!' a man's voice called and a fresh-faced young fellow came out of the rear door. He greeted her with a friendly smile, saying, 'My brother will be with you in a minute. He's just finishing summat.'

'Oh. Right.' She stared at him, deciding he had a kind face and wondering if he'd know anything. Time seemed to pass very slowly and when no one came out from the back she risked saying, 'I didn't come for clogs, but to ask if anyone used to know my mother. She lived round here once. Her father had a second-hand clothing shop. Liza Docherty she was then.'

He gaped at her as if he couldn't believe what he was hearing, then beamed and came round the counter. 'You're Liza Docherty's daughter?'

'Yes.'

'Eh, lass, I'm that glad to see you!' he said, seizing her hand and shaking it vigorously.

'You are?'

'Aye. You see, I think you might be our half-sister.'

In the rear doorway Bob opened his mouth to tell Pat to shut up, but it was too late. The stupid sod had to let it all out, didn't he? Bob closed his eyes and breathed deeply. Bloody pity Pat hadn't been working that day. His brother worked in a variety of casual labouring jobs, which came and went in a chancy way that Bob would have hated. He liked to be sure that money would be coming in every single week, but the clogger's could only support one of them as well as their father, so his four brothers had had to find other ways of earning their living.

He studied the lass again before he spoke, liking what he saw. She didn't seem to have noticed him and was still staring at Pat in shock. Well, he didn't blame her. Fancy blurting it out like that! *I think you might be our half-sister.*

'You know about me?' she asked.

'Aye. Dad got a letter from Australia, saying you were coming to England,' Pat volunteered.

Bob closed his eyes in anguish. It was getting worse! Pat'd be telling her how short of money they were next.

'But no one knew . . .' Her voice trailed away. Two men had known: her Uncle Dermott and – she groped in her mind for a name and found Matthieu Correntin, which brought up an image of a small, neat man seeing her off on the ship. But only her uncle had known the people in Pendleworth, so he must have made it his business to warn them that she was coming, though why he should do that she could not think.

There was the sound of someone clearing his

throat and she turned to see a man wearing a leather apron step forward from the back of the room, wearing clogs that made a thumping noise on the bare wooden floor.

He came across and held out his hand. 'I'm Bob Marshall and this is my brother Pat. You must be Cathie?'

She was beyond words as she took the hand, shook it briefly and studied the two men. She was suddenly quite sure they were her half-brothers. It was like looking in a warped mirror – faces, bodies, everything spoke of a connection between them and her. They were very alike, big men with broad shoulders and dusty brown hair. But Bob had a more closed sort of expression as if he never gave anything away without good reason, while Pat's expression was warm and friendly. Indeed, he was still beaming at her and she could not help returning his smile.

He reached out to touch her hairline. 'You've even got the twisty bit that won't lie flat. Aye, you're a Marshall all right.'

Bob decided they were both a right pair of soft ha'porths, so took charge. 'Dad's nipped out but he'll be back soon. Why don't you come through to the back, Cathie?' He looked at Janey as if not sure what to do about her.

'This is Mrs Hamilton,' Cathie said. 'She's not well. I'm being paid to look after her.'

'Eh, she's changed so much I hardly recognised her. Used to see her around the town. Our other

371

brother works with Magnus Hamilton so we knew his mother was poorly, but not how bad.' He indicated the rear door.

Cathie moved towards it, tugging Janey, but it was a minute before the older woman started moving, as if she'd forgotten how. 'I'll have to bring her with me,' Cathie said apologetically. 'She wanders off sometimes if I don't keep an eye on her.'

He shrugged. 'I don't suppose she'll do much harm.'

The small kitchen clearly doubled as a workshop and would have been better for having its stone-flagged floor swept and scrubbed. Janey would not sit down on the chair Bob pulled out from the table and made faint distressed sounds when Cathie tried to make her.

'Poor owd thing,' said Pat.

'Ah, leave her standing where she is,' said Bob, who didn't care two hoots about the old loony, but wanted to make a good impression on his half-sister.

'What's my father's name?' Cathie asked hesitantly. 'I was attacked and hit over the head in Liverpool and I still can't remember some things clearly, though they're coming back to me bit by bit.'

'Teddy Marshall. Edward, really, but no one ever calls him that.'

Cathie closed her eyes as the name fell into place and other things with it. She remembered her parents discussing her 'real father' one night in bed and worrying that meeting him might upset her. The main thing she wanted to know was out before she could prevent it. 'Why did he not marry my mother?'

'He offered, but she didn't want to marry him from what he's let drop,' Bob told her, for he was old enough to remember all the fuss when Liza Docherty ran off. 'You can ask him yoursen when he gets back, if you don't believe me.'

Pat pulled a chair towards her. 'I allus wanted a sister,' he said with another of his warm smiles.

Before she could sit down there was a noise outside the back door and an old man came in. He must have been big once but he was stooped now and looked as if he was wearing a larger man's skin. He had a shiny pate, with a tangle of grey hairs scattered to either side of a rather square-shaped head. And he was distinctly dirty, smelling sour even from across the room.

Cathie looked at him in shocked dismay. This couldn't be her father, surely? She turned to see Bob watching her.

'He isn't very lovely, is he?' he said with a sneer. 'But he's the only father we've got.' He pronounced it 'feyther'.

Teddy scowled at them all impartially. 'What are you lot doing lazing around while I have to go out an' deliver the bloody clogs?' He cast an unfriendly glance in Cathie's direction as he added, 'And Sal won't want you bringing your women friends in here. She'll go hairless when she finds out and then you'll be for it.'

'Did you get the money?' Bob demanded, cutting him short and holding out one hand.

'A' course I did.'

'Give it here, then.'

Teddy wriggled his shoulders uncomfortably and held out a few coins.

Bob counted them. 'Where's the rest?'

Teddy's voice took on a whining tone. 'I had a real thirst on me and me back was aching. It was just the one drink. You can't grudge your old father one little drink.'

Cathie shuddered and wondered how quickly she could get away.

'It'll come out of your wages,' Bob said implacably, then recalled that his half-sister was watching and turned to see the horror on her face. He gave a bitter laugh. 'Not much cop, is he? But he used to be a good clogger once – and at least he had enough about him to get us lot. I don't think us lads are owt to be ashamed of, and you look healthy enough.'

Teddy turned to stare at her. 'What're you talking about, our Bob? I'm used to daft talk from Pat here – soft as butter *he* is – but you usually talk sense. Not but what she's not a pretty lass. Reminds me of someone.' He frowned at Cathie and took a step in her direction, head on one side as he studied her.

She recoiled and bumped into Pat.

'Dad won't hurt you,' he said easily, steadying her. 'And he's not a bad father, really. He used to belt us when we were young, but he allus provided well for us and we never went hungry.'

She looked up at Pat. A bit taller than she was and his father was right – he did have a soft expression on his face. Turning, she looked across at Bob who was chewing one corner of his lip as if puzzled over what to do next. Well, she was puzzled, too.

Janey solved the problem by collapsing to the ground like a rag doll.

'Isn't she Magnus Hamilton's mother, the one as has gone crazy?' Teddy demanded. 'What's *she* doing here? She should be locked away in the Ben, that one should.'

Cathie ignored him and knelt by her charge. 'Come on, Aunt Janey,' she urged, tugging at the older woman's shoulders. 'Stand up and I'll take you home.'

But there was no light of comprehension in those dull eyes and Janey made no attempt whatsoever to move, just curled into a ball.

Pat knelt beside her. 'What can I do to help?'

Cathie sat back on her heels. 'I don't think there's anything much we can do. I shouldn't have brought her out today. I just wanted to see if you were . . .' Her voice faded and she blinked away tears of guilt at doing this to the poor creature on the floor next to her. After Janey's behaviour of the past few days, she definitely should have kept her at home.

Pat laid one hand on hers. 'Well, I'm right glad you've come, but you'll need help getting her back. I'll carry her for you, if you like.'

'Better we put her in the handcart,' Bob said abruptly from right behind them. 'And I think we need to talk before we say owt else, don't you?' His eyes slid for a moment towards their father.

Cathie nodded in relief. She did not want to tell the old man who she was and shuddered at the mere thought of him touching her.

'What's going on here?' demanded Teddy from across the room. 'Who is that lass?'

'She's the one as looks after the old lady, isn't she?'

'Well, what's she doing in our kitchen?'

'Come to look at some clogs.' Bob turned back to his brother. 'You carry the old lady out to the front, Pat lad, and I'll bring the handcart round.' He frowned at his father. 'And you can get on with shaping the next batch, Dad. Where are your glasses?'

His expression surly, Teddy went over to get them from a shelf and perch them on his nose.

'If you do some good work today, I'll maybe forget about the drink money,' Bob said.

'Ah, y're a good lad.' Teddy went to open a door, revealing a small room with a workbench along one wall. It was even untidier than the kitchen. He seemed to have completely forgotten Cathie's presence.

Bob went out of the back door without another

word and Pat bent to pick up Janey, settling her carefully in his arms. 'Eh, she's light as a child. It's sad when they get like this, isn't it? But I'm right glad we've found you, Cathie lass.' At the door he hesitated, then added in a low voice, 'Our Bob can be a bit sharp sometimes and cares too much about money, but he's had a lot to put up with from Dad. We thought you'd be rich.'

'I don't have much money, just what I earn.'

Pat smiled again, still blocking the doorway. 'So you're living at Magnus Hamilton's house, are you?'

She nodded. 'Yes, and we're telling folk I'm his cousin, so they won't think we're . . . we're . . .' She flushed hotly.

Pat nodded and tactfully didn't pursue that point. 'I know where he lives. I'd like to bring my wife round to meet you, if that's all right? And we've got two little children, lasses they are – Gilly and Nan. You'll be their auntie. Eh, they'll like that.'

He was so blessedly normal it brought tears to Cathie's eyes as she followed him out. At the door she paused to glance over her shoulder at the old man. He threw her a suspicious look, then bent over his work again.

With a shudder she hurried after Pat, wishing desperately that she'd never started looking for her father. He was horrible! Absolutely horrible! No wonder her mother hadn't wanted to tell her about him.

What had she got herself into now?

★   ★   ★

Francis woke up to sunlight dancing on the walls of his room and a figure looming by the window. He jerked upright and felt sick at the sight of his so-called tutor standing there.

'Time to get up, lad!'

Francis blinked. 'What time is it?'

'Six o'clock.'

'But breakfast isn't till eight.'

'There will be no breakfast, no food at all, until you've fired a gun.'

'Do you intend to starve me, then?' Francis asked in amazement.

'It's your choice. There's plenty of food if you do as expected.' The old man had come up with this suggestion the evening before, though Eli wasn't sure he liked the idea.

'I'm not firing any guns.'

'You wait till you've hungered for a while and see how you feel about it then. Now up and get yourself washed. I've told them to bring cold water. We're not having you namby-pambying yourself.'

Francis got up, trying to keep his face expressionless.

When they got back another man was waiting in the passageway next to the kitchen, wanting to see Baxter.

'Jim Marshall?' Eli asked. 'Good. You'd better come upstairs. Bring your bag.' When they got to Francis's room, he explained, 'Jim's come here to help me, and will be keeping an eye on you when

I'm not around. He'll be sleeping in here with you from now on, and you'll both be locked in at night. We don't want you going wandering through the woods again, do we? Or running off anywhere, either?'

And so began one of the longest days Francis could ever remember. He found the hunger difficult, but less difficult than being beaten. When his stomach growled, his new tutor smiled. The other man said nothing, doing as he was told and staring at Francis from time to time with a look of faint puzzlement on his face.

The hardest thing was that they required Francis to attend meals with his uncle when he had to watch them serving all his favourite foods to the old man, who ate with loud appreciation. All they allowed Francis was water. Marshall ate in the kitchen.

The maids avoided Francis's eyes as they served the others. Eli Baxter answered the occasional question from Alexander Stephenson about his experiences in India and attended to his own meal when not required to speak.

When they came out of the dining room, Jim was waiting for them in the hall.

'Master Francis has had his dinner now,' Alexander jeered. 'Take him up to his room. I want a private word with Baxter.'

As he slowly climbed the stairs, followed by his new keeper, Francis wondered what had made his uncle suddenly begin to treat him like this.

When Baxter came up to join them later, he said curtly, 'You two might as well go to bed now.' He closed the door on them and there was the sound of a key turning in the lock.

There was an awkward silence, then Jim said, 'I suppose he's right, lad.' He did not know how to address a young man like this, who would be rich one day, especially when he was here to guard and help bully him. He scowled at that thought. He hadn't realised what they were going to be doing. It seemed a bloody funny business to him, starving a rich lad, it did that! Weren't there enough folk in the world going short without this?

Francis walked slowly across to the bed, sitting down on it for a minute, eyes closed, feeling slightly disoriented.

'You all right?'

Francis looked up to find the man standing beside him. 'No, not really. I feel dizzy.'

'You might as well do as they ask. Never seen folk so determined t'get their own way.'

Another silence, then Francis said, 'Well, I'm not going to. And if they want to starve me to death, it seems I can't stop them.' He began to undress, ignoring the other man as he had ignored his schoolmates in the big dormitories.

He put his nightshirt on and got into bed, but found it hard to sleep. Had Cathie got his note? Was she thinking of him? A tear trickled down his cheek, but now that the lamp was out, the man lying down across the room would never know he was weeping.

On his own narrow bed Jim lay awake for a while, puzzling over what he should do. If they were going to kill the lad, he'd leave before it happened and tell Mr Reuben, he decided in the end. He wasn't going to get involved in something like that. That damned Baxter fellow might even try to blame him. As for the old sod, he was barmy. You only had to look at his eyes to see that. It happened like that sometimes when folk had a seizure as the old fellow clearly had. It affected their brains as well as their bodies. He should be locked up in the Ben.

Which led to another thought. If they killed this lad, how would he and Bob get any money out of Cathie's family? He wished he could ask his brother's advice. They'd said he could have Saturdays off, but that was three days away. And he had to keep an eye on the lad on Mondays on his own while Baxter took a break. They were going to send a groom to help him on those days. That damned sergeant had threatened to pound him senseless if he let the lad escape.

It was daft, all this was! And he'd been stupid to accept the job without finding out exactly what he'd have to do. He kept thinking how angry Bob would be if anything happened to Cathie's other half-brother.

Just as he was falling asleep, he suddenly realised what he could do – till he could ask Bob's advice.

He could smuggle in some bread to the lad to keep him going, like. It'd be easy enough to filch a piece or two from the kitchen. And from what he'd overheard, that fat old woman they all called Cook wouldn't mind, even if she knew what he was doing. She was fond of Master Francis, one of the maids had said. Which no one else in this damned place seemed to be.

With a relieved sigh Jim let himself slide into sleep.

With Janey in this new and distressing phase, Cathie waited a day or two to tell Magnus about her family. Then one evening she could hold her news back no longer.

He stared at her in surprise. 'You're Jim Marshall's sister!'

'Half-sister. And I've not met Jim yet, only Bob and Pat.'

'I can't believe it!'

'Don't you like Jim?' she asked.

He shrugged. 'It's not so much a question of disliking him as of – well, understanding what he's like.'

'Tell me. And be honest, please.'

'Well, he's a bit of a rogue. A good worker when he sets his mind to it, but he'd rather find ways of avoiding too much work. The other men like him, though. And he's always pleasant enough. But you have to keep him up to the mark.'

'And the other brothers – have you had much to do with them?'

'No. I've seen Bob around the town, of course, and I've employed Pat a few times for labouring jobs. He's a good worker, but has no feel for the machinery or I'd have given him a steady job. And your father? What about him?' He couldn't remember what the clogger was like, because his mother had always insisted on them wearing proper shoes, however worn and scuffed.

'Horrible. I don't want to tell him who I am, though I suppose it'll come out one day.' She hesitated, then said, 'I'm not sorry I came to England, and I think I could get very fond of Pat, but I wish I'd never met my father. Mr Lorrimer says he forced himself on my mother and Bob says he did it so she'd have to marry him, but—'

She could not hold back the tears and Magnus could not prevent himself from again taking her in his arms and comforting her. But he didn't kiss her. It was hard not to, but if they were to live together decently he did not dare start kissing that soft, generous mouth, or he might not be able to stop.

When she pulled away, she gave a half-ashamed laugh. 'I feel better for telling you, but I'm sorry to weep all over you again. Um – would you mind if my brothers visited me here? Pat said he'd bring my nieces round to meet me.'

'Of course not, lassie. They're your family.'

She smiled at him and the words were out before

she could prevent them. 'You feel like family, too, Magnus. I've been calling you cousin for so long you seem like one.'

He could not say the same to her. She did not affect him as a cousin would, not at all. And she affected him so strongly it was getting harder by the day to hide his true feelings.

CHAPTER 17

AUGUST

'Mummy?' Josie said one night as they were lying in their bunks.

'Yes, love.'

'I'm glad we're going to England. Is that wicked of me?'

'Why should it be wicked, darling?' Liza asked, puzzled.

'Because we wouldn't have come if Cathie hadn't run away and then the poor little baby died.'

In the darkness Liza smiled, though her reaction was bittersweet. 'No, it's not at all wicked of you, Josie. And I'll tell you a secret: I'm glad we're going too. I'm missing Daddy and the others dreadfully, but I'm really looking forward to seeing England again. And most of all to seeing Cathie.' She hadn't told Josie about Francis, not wanting to have her purpose inadvertently revealed by the child.

'Won't she be surprised to see us?' Josie giggled at the thought. Soon she was asleep, her breathing soft and even with none of the gasping that had sometimes worried them all during the dry, dusty summers in Australia.

Liza lay awake for a long time, however, her thoughts turning as they often did to her two missing children. She prayed every night that she would find Cathie safe and happy in England. Only – if the poor girl had found her father, it must have upset her dreadfully. A man like Teddy Marshall could not possibly have grown pleasanter over the years and those boys of his had been bullies, full of suppressed energy and violence. What would they have said to a half-sister who suddenly turned up in Pendleworth?

And then there was Francis. Liza was not sure how she was going to manage to see him, but she would do it even if she had to camp on the doorstep of the big house where she had been so unhappy with her second husband.

Matthieu read Dermott's scrawled note, whistling softly in amazement.

Brendan, who had been working with him on clearing the vegetable garden, looked up and asked, 'Not bad news?'

'No, but Dermott and Christina have left for England already and want me to close up their house, so I'll have to go up to Perth. I wasn't really sure they'd go, you know.' He hesitated, then asked, 'Do you want to come with me?'

Brendan looked down, avoiding his eyes and shaking his head. 'People treat me like an animal up there.'

'Only if you let them. We'll dress you so smartly

they won't dare do that. I think my clothes will fit you pretty well. And we might take the boys with us as well, to see if they want to keep anything from the house.' Trust Christina not to think of her sons' needs and wishes.

He smiled. Even though it had only been a few days, James and Charlie had already settled in happily with their grandmother, who was talking of building an extra bedroom on the back for them and who didn't seem to mind the little dog's presence in her inn yard at all, but who did insist on good manners and discouraged cruel practical jokes.

After some persuasion Brendan had a chat with his parents about Matthieu's suggestion. Dinny didn't know what to say, for she too avoided leaving the homestead, but Fergal encouraged him to go and face the demons that were keeping him imprisoned at Brookley, saying sadly, 'You haven't committed a crime as I did, son. There's no need for you to hide away from the world.'

The small cavalcade set off early one morning, taking their time about travelling to Perth. The boys were well behaved most of the time, and when they weren't Matthieu corrected them swiftly and firmly. He corrected Brendan, too, who grew nervous whenever they encountered other travellers, trying to teach the young man to behave with pride in everything he did, as Matthieu's old grandfather had taught him during his own years of youthful uncertainty and rebelliousness.

The house in Perth showed signs of a hasty departure, but three days' hard work soon sorted out its remaining contents. Matthieu then decided to buy a small all-purpose vehicle and found Brendan surprisingly knowledgeable about this, and even more so when it came to choosing some horses. 'You are good with animals, *mon ami*,' he commented.

'I like them.'

'It's a useful skill. I have a cousin who breeds horses in France. Maybe I should send you to him once your French is good enough.' They were talking regularly in that language now, and Matthieu made the two boys join in the lessons. They were very ignorant for a rich man's children, but touchingly responsive to praise and encouragement.

Matthieu had not realised how much he would enjoy guiding these young people and decided ruefully that he had a gift for it. The desire to have children of his own had taken him firmly by the throat now, as well as the desire to see more of Ilse.

When they'd taken the boys back to Brookley, they went on towards the farm. It felt like coming home and the shock of that made Matthieu fall silent.

'Is something wrong?' Brendan asked.

'*Je ne sais pas. J'ai* . . .' Matthieu hesitated, then admitted, 'It feels like coming home. It's a long time since anywhere gave me that feeling.'

'My mother would say the land is welcoming you.'

Matthieu shrugged, then brightened as they saw Ilse and Harry on the track ahead of them. The sight of her made him realise suddenly how he could arrange matters so that he would see more of her. He shoved the reins into his companion's capable hands. 'I'll see you at the farm.'

Brendan watched him stride towards Ilse and drew his own conclusions.

'Frau Hebel,' Matthieu raised his hat and the two of them stood looking at one another.

Ilse tried in vain to stay cold and correct with him, but things had been quiet since Josie and Liza had left, and Harry was more interested in tagging after his father than in his schoolbooks. Even Agnes seemed abstracted lately.

'You look well,' Matthieu said softly. 'How do you manage to remain so elegant in such surroundings?' He offered her his arm. 'I wonder, may I walk with you for a while? I need to ask you something privately.'

She did not answer directly, but looked down at Harry and said, 'Why don't you run home and help your father in the workshop?' He was off almost before she had finished speaking. Then she looked at Matthieu, flushed slightly and took the arm he was offering.

He used his free hand to clasp her hand as it lay on his arm, smiling when that brought a little extra colour into her cheeks. 'As you know, I'm now partly responsible for Mr Docherty's two sons, who are staying with their grandmother and are cousins of Harry's. I wondered – if Mr Caine approves, of course – whether you would consent to give them lessons as well? It would be good for Harry to have company of his own age, and of course Mr Docherty would be happy to pay you extra.'

She had hoped for something more personal because, heaven help her, she'd been thinking of him and wondering if he was thinking of her. But still, this would surely bring her into more contact with him? Was he doing it on purpose? 'I would be happy to do that, but only if Mr Caine agrees.'

'Then perhaps I could come back to Lizabrook with you now and ask him?'

They strolled along, with Matthieu telling her of his trip to Perth. He had been feeling tired, but now felt full of energy and made a humorous tale of it, pleased to make her chuckle.

She thought she had never walked with a man whose steps matched hers so well, or who took so much trouble to entertain her.

Forewarned by Harry of a visitor approaching, Benedict had stopped work and had a quick wash. He was not sure of how to greet Docherty's partner, but was glad of any company at the moment because the evenings dragged without Liza's company, pleasant as Agnes and Ilse were.

When Matthieu had explained his request, Benedict readily gave permission and after much discussion it was decided that Charlie and James should come across to Lizabrook in the mornings, since there was a schoolroom of sorts and equipment there already.

After all the arrangements had been settled Benedict hesitated, then asked Matthieu if he would like to share their evening meal.

'I'd love to, but Brendan will be waiting for me at the farm.'

'Oh, we'll send his brother to let him know there's a meal here.'

The two men sat down on the veranda and began to chat over a pot of tea. Matthieu feigned enjoyment, though at this time of day he would have preferred a glass of wine. He'd brought a few dozen bottles back with him from Perth and was seriously considering starting a vineyard here, since the rear part of his land lay on a gentle slope. He asked Benedict's opinion and that led to an enthusiastic discussion of viticulture, a topic in which Benedict had no experience but about which he was happy to learn.

'We have some grape vines planted,' he said, 'but the fruit is for eating, not wine making, and we dry some to make raisins. The fire missed them, fortunately, though it ruined our orchard. I can let you have some cuttings if you want.'

'Thank you. And we still have more apples than we can possibly use. Neighbours should help one another, do you not think?'

'I didn't realise you intended to settle here

permanently, Mr Correntin,' Benedict was saying just as Ilse came to summon them to the big communal table.

She looked at Matthieu in surprise when she heard Benedict's words and saw him nod, then look across at her and smile.

When the meal was over, Matthieu asked Ilse to walk with him to the gate.

As they reached it, he stopped and took both her hands in his. 'My dear Ilse, I would very much like to court you. I wonder – would you give me a chance to show that I can make you happy?'

She stared at him in shock. 'You are very direct.'

He shrugged. 'I see no need to procrastinate. We are both free to make our own decisions.'

She bent her head, not moving, her thoughts in turmoil. At last she looked up at him and said painfully, 'I was not happy in my first marriage. I could not rush into anything, even though I am – not averse to the idea.'

'So we shall take the time to know one another better.' He watched one hand go up to her throat, saw the fear in her eyes and could not help asking, 'Was it very bad, your marriage?'

She nodded, her eyes suddenly bleak.

'I am not a hard man to live with, nor am I violent. And I am prepared to court you properly, give you as much time as you need.' He took her hand and raised it to his lips. 'Give me a chance, *chérie.*'

She nodded, then said softly, '*Ja. Warum nicht?*'

He smiled wryly. 'You do not sound – *enthousiaste*.'

'I'm sorry. It's just you've taken me by surprise. I had thought you were using me to gain information about the Caines.'

'*Chérie*, I would never do that.' He smiled gently at her, finding to his surprise that he too liked the idea of a gentle courtship. 'I shall come and take you for a stroll tomorrow evening. We shall talk and start getting to know one another.'

She could only nod, then stand and watch as he sauntered away. When he turned at the bend in the road to wave, she raised her own hand in response and made her way slowly back to the house. She would tell Agnes, ask her advice.

But she rather thought that Matthieu Correntin would make a charming husband.

At Rawley Manor Jim Marshall sat eating his tea, amazed at the plentiful feasts served to the servants, but also sickened that the poor lad who owned this house was now into his third day without food. And Eli had let slip that the old sod was happy about that. Eli wasn't, Jim could tell that. For all his shouting and blustering, he did not seem at all comfortable with what he was doing.

When no one was looking Jim slipped a piece of bread into his pocket, cursing himself for putting this easy job at risk by this act, but driven by a feeling that it was just not right to starve someone on purpose.

When the meal was over he got up with the rest, reluctant to return to his charge, wondering if Baxter and the old sod had again forced the lad to watch them eat in the big dining room in the main part of the house.

'A moment, if you please, Mr Marshall,' Cook said, leading the way into the small office to one side of the kitchen where she made up her menus and did her accounts.

Jim followed her and waited. What now?

'You put a piece of bread into your pocket, Mr Marshall.'

He stared at her, feeling resentful. What did it matter to her whether he took a piece of bread or not? There was more than enough for everyone. 'I get hungry sometimes between meals,' he muttered by way of an excuse.

She hesitated then said slowly, 'Or maybe you feel sorry for Master Francis?'

Oh, hell, she'd guessed! 'What if I do? I suppose you're going to tell the old man and get me into trouble? Lose me my job?' He pulled the bread out and flung it on the table, turning to leave. 'Well, go ahead then. Don't worry about my poor family and . . .'

She rushed to catch hold of his arm and bang the door shut again. 'I wouldn't say anything if I thought that bread was for Master Francis.' For a long moment they stared at one another then she asked quietly, 'Was it?'

Jim nodded, watching her warily, trying to read

her expression. To his surprise he saw tears in her eyes.

'Oh, thank goodness!' She plonked a kiss on his cheek. 'Thank you!' The kiss was followed by a rib-cracking hug, for she was a buxom woman. 'Now you wait here, Mr Marshall, and I'll find you something better than a piece of dry bread for that poor lad.'

'Well, make sure it isn't big enough to be noticed. That sod Baxter can see a fly thinking!' Jim rubbed at his cheek. What did she want to go a-kissing him for? She must have a soft spot for Master Francis. Bit of luck, that. He listened at the door and heard her outside sending the two maids on errands, then moving quickly to and fro in the kitchen.

After a short time she came back with something flat wrapped in a cloth and held it out to him. 'I don't want any of the maids involved in this. If I lose my place for it, I don't care. I'd have gone long since if it hadn't been for Francis. Here!' When Jim was slow to take it, she slapped it into his hand. 'It's bread and a slice of roast beef. I've squashed it flat so it won't show under your clothes, though if they find it, you can always say it's for you. And don't leave the cloth lying around. Bring it back to me tomorrow.'

Jim tucked the little parcel into his jacket pocket and nodded to her. 'All right, missus. Cook, I mean.'

She gave him a tearful smile. 'I don't know how

to thank you, Mr Marshall. I've helped bring that lad up and I can't bear to see him tortured like this. He's a gentle soul, is my Francis, and what's wrong with that?' She blinked her eyes furiously. 'I'll have something else waiting for you tomorrow.'

When he had left, Cook wrote a note to her friend Hatty, who was the cook at Mr Lorrimer's house and who had said her employers wanted to be informed of what was going on with Francis Rawley.

The following day she sent the kitchen maid across to deliver the note, something she did occasionally when things were quiet. Lasses that age worked better for the occasional brisk walk or other treat, to her mind.

Oh, she did hope the Lorrimers would be able to help poor Master Francis! She couldn't sleep for worrying about her lad. She stood frowning for a moment as she wondered again why Jim Marshall was helping him? He seemed the most unlikely person to have a soft heart.

Jim hid the sandwich under his pillow and waited until he and the boy were locked in the bedroom for the night. Francis lay down on his bed, not undressed yet, looking limp and totally exhausted.

Jim took the parcel across to the bed. 'I've got something for you,' he muttered, holding it out.

Francis didn't even open his eyes.

Jim laid a hand on the boy's shoulder and was

upset when he flinched away, upset too at how wan he was looking. That Baxter was a master at hitting folk so it didn't show and strong with it, too, though Jim thought *he* might be able to hold his own if Baxter ever turned on him. The Marshall boys knew how to defend themselves, by hell they did! Lowering his voice he whispered, 'It's food.'

Francis jerked upright and stared at him. When he opened his mouth to speak, Jim clamped his hand across it and hissed, 'Howd your clack, you fool! Do you want *him* to hear us?' He pulled his hand away and was relieved when the boy swallowed and sat staring at him.

'Is this more torture?' he asked at last, his voice low enough not to be heard.

Jim breathed a sigh of relief before growling in an equally low voice, 'No, it bloody isn't! I don't go around starving folk or torturing them. If I'd known what I was getting into I'd not have taken this job. Here!' Again he held out the parcel.

When Francis unwrapped it and saw the food inside, tears began to pour down his cheeks.

Jim stayed where he was, ready to quieten the lad if necessary, but after a few moments the tears dried up and Francis picked up the flattened sandwich. 'Better eat it slowly, lad,' Jim advised. 'Or you'll just bring it straight back up. Best of all if you just ate half of it tonight and kept half for the morning.'

Francis nodded and took a small bite, chewing

it carefully and closing his eyes in sheer bliss. When the sandwich was half-finished he stared down at it, reluctant to put it away.

Realising what he was thinking, Jim took the bread out of his hand, wrapping it in the cloth again and taking it over to his own bed. 'I'll keep it till morning for you. Baxter won't search my things, but he might search yours.'

Francis nodded and went across to get a drink of water. They allowed him a full carafe morning and evening, but yesterday Jim had filled the carafe a third time without Baxter realising it. 'How did you get the food?'

Jim shrugged, a bit embarrassed about his own softheartedness. 'That cook of yours saw me putting a piece of bread in my pocket and guessed what I was up to, so she give me a proper sandwich for you.'

'Why should you help me? You've been hired to watch me.'

'I can't abide to see folk go without food. Not when they don't need to. Never could.' Jim had made sure his own kids never clemmed, had always brought in a regular wage and slipped the odd jam buttie to Pat's kids when his younger brother was short of work. Not that he wanted folk knowing that, or they'd think him a soft touch.

Francis looked at him, the gaze of someone much older than a mere fifteen years. 'I'm grateful to you. I can't do anything to show my gratitude now, but when I come into my inheritance in six years' time, I'll see you're rewarded, I promise you.' In a tone of surprise, he added, 'It's my birthday soon. I'd forgotten that.'

Jim perked up. 'Well, I'd appreciate any help you can give. I do have a family to look after.'

Francis was trying to think, trying to ignore the hunger that the half-sandwich had done little to assuage. 'Can you get me some more food?'

'Cook says she'll have something ready for me tomorrow. But we'll have to be careful.'

'They didn't tell me your other name. Only Jim.'

Jim looked at him uneasily. 'They said I shouldn't tell you, that it'd be better for me if you didn't know.'

'I can't find you again to reward you if I don't know your full name, can I?'

Jim shrugged. 'Well, it's Marshall, Jim Marshall. And I work at Ludlam's normally, so I'm easy enough to find.'

Francis stared at him in the flickering light from the candle. 'What did you say?' he whispered.

'Marshall. And—'

'Do you know a girl called Cathie?' Francis asked in a low, urgent voice.

Jim stiffened. Now what? 'Might do,' he admitted, glancing instinctively over his shoulder towards the door. 'Why?'

'She's my half-sister.'

Jim grinned. 'Oh, that. I know. She's our half-sister, too.'

Silence, then, 'She found her real father?'

'Aye. Just walked into the shop one day, Bob said, to ask if anyone in the street had known her mother.'

'My uncle doesn't know she's here in Pendleworth and he mustn't,' Francis said urgently. 'If he did, he might try to harm her.'

'He'd have us lot to deal with if he tried to hurt her,' Jim said, his hands bunching into fists at the mere thought. 'We look after our own, us Marshalls do.' Even that daft Pat could be relied on to stand by you in times of trouble.

Francis gave him a beaming smile. 'Look after her carefully, then. She's a wonderful person.' His gaze grew thoughtful. 'That makes us sort of step-brothers, doesn't it?'

'Eh, I dunno about that. What I do know is, if we go on talking they might hear us. An' any road, I'm tired if you aren't.' It was exhausting working for that sod Baxter, who kept you on the hop all day long. Magnus bloody Hamilton was nothing compared to the ex-sergeant and it'd be a relief to go back to Ludlam's, though Jim would miss the fresh air. He went across to his bed, embarrassed by all this show of emotion.

Francis nodded and began to get undressed, feeling better than he had for days – though he was still ravenous and light-headed. One sandwich a day wasn't nearly enough.

When his companion started snoring, gentle bubbles of sound that covered any other noises, Francis allowed himself to weep again. But these were tears of hope because he'd found a friend just when he'd given up hope. He smiled through the tears at that thought. No, not a friend. He had spent enough time with Jim Marshall to know that he would do nothing without hope of reward. An ally. That was a better word for it.

Francis frowned in the dark and wriggled into a better position to ease the strain on his bruised arm, which Baxter had twisted behind his back this morning till he'd thought it was going to break. Strange how the pain only made him feel more determined about resisting them. He had never thought of himself as a particularly brave person, still didn't, really. Maybe Jim would carry messages for him? Not written ones, though, which could fall into other people's hands, only verbal messages. He was sure Mr Lorrimer would reward Jim for that.

He slept badly and woke with a start at dawn as Baxter erupted into the room and shook him awake to get dressed. He didn't say anything in response to the petty bullying and slapping around. His uncle was not the only one to use silence as a weapon. And when he had washed and changed, he went down and watched them eat breakfast, sorry he had not been able to eat the half-sandwich. It was not until he was washing his hands before luncheon that he managed to eat it and later Jim slipped him some bread and cheese. Your courage held up even better when you had food in your belly. And an ally living beside you.

The following morning Hatty passed the note to her mistress, Edith Lorrimer, saying indignantly, 'I've heard from my friend Barbara at the Manor, ma'am. It seems they're trying to starve that nice young lad into obeying them.'

Edith read it through quickly, her heart sinking. 'Oh, heavens! May I keep this to show to Mr Lorrimer?'

'Certainly, ma'am.'

'Hatty, you're a treasure.'

Bernard read the note twice then closed his eyes for a moment, shaking his head in disbelief.

'Can't we do something to help him now?' Edith asked.

'I'm afraid not. It's only been a few days, and anyway, how can we prove anything?' After some thought he said slowly, 'I'd like to speak to this Jim Marshall in person, though. Who is he? Why is he helping Francis?'

They called Hatty in to ask what she knew about Jim Marshall.

'I'm afraid I don't know anything, sir.'

'Can you try to find out, Hatty?'

'I'll be seeing Barbara on Sunday, sir. We usually go to church together. I can't do anything till then. They don't like me visiting her at the Manor.' She went back to her kitchen, feeling disgusted by the cruel ways of some folk who ought to know better, 'deed they ought.

'I'll ask around, see if anyone knows who Marshall is,' Bernard said.

Edith looked at her husband, her eyes filled with tears. 'That old man is *wicked*.'

'I agree absolutely. But he is still Francis's lawfully appointed guardian.'

Jim found his brother Bob waiting for him at his home when he had his first Saturday off. He was a bit annoyed about that because he had wanted to spend time with his wife and kids. He was surprised at how much he'd missed them. But Bob insisted they go for a walk so that they could talk privately and wouldn't take no for an answer.

'Well?' he demanded as soon as they were clear of the house.

Jim scowled at him. 'Well, what?'

'Tell me about it.'

Feeling superior for once, Jim described his first few days at the Manor.

By the time he had finished, Bob was frowning. 'I think you're a fool to risk helping him.'

'Easy for you to say. You don't have to sit and watch a poor lad starving, do you?'

'Are they trying to kill him, do you think?'

Jim shrugged. 'I don't reckon so, just force him to do what they want. I don't know why he won't go hunting or shooting. Seems daft to me to argue about that sort of thing.'

'What's the lad like?'

'Soft, but all right. A bit like our Pat, really.'

Bob rolled his eyes. 'Just what we need. Another daft ha'porth to keep an eye on. But Francis did promise you a reward one day?'

'I told you he did.'

'Right then. You'd better keep feeding him. But you watch your step. Don't let them catch you.'

'He wants me to get word to his sister about what's going on.' Jim grinned. '*Our* sister. Funny to be related to the nobs, isn't it?'

'I'll go and see her for you and let her know what's happening.'

'Right then. I'm going home now.' His wife, not usually demonstrative and often sharp-tongued, had flung her arms round him and burst into tears when he returned this morning. It was a funny sodding world, it was that.

Francis realised one day that his fifteenth birthday had passed. He hadn't even noticed it himself, because the days seemed to run together, each one as unhappy as the last. He felt distant most of the time and very weak physically. In his bleakest moments he wondered how long it would be before he died.

His meetings with Cathie seemed like a distant dream now, a wonderful taste of what it meant to have a family. If it hadn't been for Jim, he did not know what he would have done. Killed himself, perhaps. The thought that there was someone who cared enough to help him, when the outside world seemed to be ignoring him, made a big difference. As did the food Jim smuggled in to him.

But Francis did not for one moment consider giving in to his uncle. He would not, could not, be like him. And if that meant betraying his class, well, so be it. He would not betray himself.

CHAPTER 18

AUGUST–SEPTEMBER

It took Janey Hamilton several weeks to die. Her body clung tenaciously to life, though it grew so frail and thin she hardly caused a bump under the covers. Her mind seemed completely dead now, and she never walked again or ate of her own accord after they returned from the clogger's shop.

The house was so quiet now that Cathie sometimes sang to keep herself cheerful, but the songs faded of their own accord and she spent a lot of time lost in her own thoughts – and regrets. She found time hanging very heavily on her hands and joined a penny library, devouring books as she sat with the old lady. It was ironic that she had come to England to avoid an isolated life, and found herself in a similar situation. But Magnus needed her and she would not let him down. Besides – she smiled – she had the evenings with him. That compensated a lot for the quiet days.

Bob Marshall had called one afternoon to tell her about the situation at the Manor, but with Janey dying inch by inch Cathie had to set aside her worries about Francis and concentrate on her charge. At least Jim was slipping her brother some food; looking after Janey was all she could do for Magnus now. His deep sadness had dimmed the bright energy he had always radiated before and he, too, often seemed lost in thought.

Knowing they would soon lose their mother, Mairi came over from Bury every single Sunday, sometimes with her husband, sometimes on her own. On one visit she thanked Cathie for what she was doing. 'I don't know what Magnus would have done without you, and it's relieved my mind knowing you're here. I felt guilty about leaving him with her, but Elwyn needed me, too, and I thought Magnus would have to put Mum in the Ben when I'd gone.' She sighed and changed the subject. 'You've remembered everything about your past now?'

'I think so.' Cathie reached out to poke the fire, avoiding her companion's eyes. 'It's a sorry tale of a wilful girl, I'm afraid. I ran away from home to find my real father – and to escape from life in the bush, which is very lonely. I'm not sorry I left and I'm never going back, but I'm very ashamed of the way I did things.'

'You've written to your family, though?'

'Several times. But it's not the same as saying goodbye properly, is it? At least your brothers said goodbye. And I haven't heard from home yet, because there hasn't been time for a reply to get here from Australia.'

Mairi let the silence lengthen for a few moments

then asked hesitantly, 'What will you do after Mother dies?'

Cathie shrugged. That thought was worrying her as well. 'I don't know. Dr Barnes said once that he could find me a job nursing. I do have to earn a living and obviously I won't be able to stay here.'

'If you're stuck for somewhere to live, you could come and stay with Elwyn and me for a time. That'll help allay the rumours, make people think you really are our cousin.'

'Thanks, but I want to be near my brothers, especially Francis.'

'Well, if you're ever in need, the offer is still open.'

When Mairi left to catch her train, several neighbours were standing on their doorsteps gossiping. She gave Cathie a hug, winked at her and whispered, 'That'll make them think twice.'

She watched Mairi and Magnus walk along the street, then went inside again to wash up the tea things.

It was funny, she thought, how many half-brothers she had here now. Francis and three Marshalls. She really liked Pat, though she deplored his lack of ambition and easy-going ways. There were times when his family went hungry, she guessed, but he was making little attempt to find himself a more permanent job. She was sure Bob's family didn't go hungry and had already discovered how hard he worked and how deter-mined he was to better himself. But he wasn't nearly as nice as Pat. Too determined. Too sharp with everyone. And then there was Jim, who seemed to care for no one but himself, but who was sneaking food to Francis. He was a puzzle to her still.

Best not to think of her other half-brother, she told herself, plunging her hands into the hot water. Best just to get on with her work here till she was needed no more. Then she'd see if she could help Francis, whatever Mr Lorrimer said.

The day after Mairi's visit, Dr Barnes came to visit Janey just as Cathie was trying yet again to give her charge a drink of milk. He suggested gently that she was only prolonging the painful decline by doing this.

'But I can't just let her starve to death!' Cathie protested, horrified.

'My dear,' he put his big hand over hers and looked at her very solemnly, 'it'll be a merciful release. Let her go.'

'It's hard to do that to anyone.'

'Yes. But you're a good nurse and will have nothing to blame yourself for.'

She plucked up her courage. 'Afterwards, you did say you'd find me other nursing jobs?'

'I'll be happy to do that. There's always a call for good nurses. Have you ever assisted with childbirth?'

'No. It's mostly been accidents I've had to deal with, or nursing my younger brothers and sister

409

when they were sick.' She pulled a wry face. 'I've done a lot of that. I'd like to learn more about childbearing, though. In fact, if I were a man I'd like to be a doctor.'

He laughed indulgently. 'Each to his own sphere, my dear. Or *her* own sphere, I should say. I find women better at nursing the sick than men, and we men are better at learning the complexities of doctoring. Don't let these foolish, strident "new women" turn your head. Elizabeth Garrett Anderson may *call* herself a doctor, but no one of sense is going to take her seriously. No wonder she treats mainly women and children. No man would let himself be examined by her or have faith in her capabilities. Women like her are going against nature by becoming doctors. It is a fad which will soon fade away.'

Cathie could see he felt strongly on this point so bit back a sharp response. She had better not contradict him if she wanted his help. Later that evening she complained about his attitude to Magnus.

'I'd not like to see you trying to become a doctor either, lassie,' he said. 'It's not that you couldn't learn what to do, never that – I know how intelligent you are – but I wouldn't want you to have to see the dreadful sights doctors face.'

'I think about *helping* people, not about whether they look nice or not when they're in pain,' she said quietly.

'Well, you're helping me more than I can say

with what you're doing for my mother. She hasn't been easy to look after. I don't know how to thank you.' He hesitated, then added, 'You must get very bored here on your own now, so I brought you this.' He went across to where his jacket was hanging on the door and pulled a little parcel wrapped in brown paper out of it.

She opened it in delight, finding it a volume of poetry. 'Oh, I shall love this!' When she turned to the flyleaf she asked, 'Would you inscribe it for me?'

'Aye.' He went into the front room to fetch the ink and fitted a new nib into the holder with its mother-of-pearl handle. He held it out to show her. 'This was the last present Mam ever bought me and I shall always treasure it.' Then he dipped the nib carefully into the ink pot and wrote in her book in his fine copperplate script.

When he handed it to her, she read: *To Cathie, to whom I owe a great deal for her help with my mother. Fondest regards, Magnus.* 'I shall always treasure this.' She ran her fingers over the fine leather binding, wondering if the word 'fondest' meant anything special, then telling herself not to be so foolish.

'It's getting late now, but maybe we can read some of the poems together in the evenings. I can show you my favourites.'

'I shall look forward to that.' She clasped the book to her bosom.

He looked at her glowing expression and love

surged up in him, so that he nearly spoke his feelings aloud. But he had vowed to do nothing about it while she was still under his roof. It would not feel right, somehow, as if he were taking advantage of her.

Bob had come to the house several times now with messages from Francis. They had stopped starving the lad, it seemed, but only because he'd grown very thin and weak. They didn't want to kill him, Jim reckoned. Well, Baxter had said as much one day, when frustration had made him confide that he'd never expected this one to be so hard to crack.

'Oh, I wish I could do something to help him!' Cathie exclaimed. 'But at least they're feeding him again.'

'Only bread and water.'

She clicked her tongue in distress. 'That's not fit food for a growing lad. Why, you should have seen what my brothers Seth and Lucas ate! Mother always said they had hollow legs.'

'Our Jim's took a real liking to your Francis,' Bob told her another day as he ate a piece of the cake Cathie had baked. He waved it at her. 'Good, this! I wish my wife could make 'em, but she says bread and jam come to the same thing.' After another appreciative bite, he returned to his topic. 'Never seen owt like it, our Jim getting upset. That sod don't usually care for anyone but hissen and his family.'

'I'm glad of it.' She sighed and confided, 'When Mrs Hamilton dies, I'm going to try to rescue Francis. Will you help me? Will Jim, do you think?'

Bob goggled at her. 'You can't be serious, lass!' He did not intend to risk prison by breaking into the Manor, or being thrown out of his home and shop, which would be almost as bad.

Her lips set in a mutinous line. 'I am serious. Very serious. What they're doing isn't right. Francis could go to our mother in Australia. I know she'd be delighted to have him.'

'Nay, they'd guess and have the ships searched for runaways.'

'Maybe. But if we rescued him just before a ship was leaving, they might not have time to do that. Magnus is going to find out about sailing dates for me.'

'Sweet on him, aren't you?'

She flushed. 'There's nothing going on between us.'

'The more fool him, then. If I had a bonny lass under my roof, I'd not let her sleep alone.' In contradiction of that he added, 'Mind you, I'm not having anyone messing around with my sister, so you let me know if he tries owt on.'

She smiled at him. She was getting to know the Marshalls now. Truculent, but loyal. Doing whatever it took to make a living for themselves and their families in a hard world.

Changing the subject, Bob asked suddenly, 'Do you still want to keep who you are secret from my father? Only he's asking why I keep coming to see you. How the old sod knows about it, I don't know, because I haven't said a word. It's a good thing my Min knows the real reason because he went and told her about it. He'll not go running off with tales to her again, though, not if he wants the money for his ale.'

She spoke slowly, choosing her words with care. 'I don't see how any good can come from telling him, given the sort of man he is. At present the fewer people who know who I am the better. As far as everyone is concerned, I'm Caitlin Rutherford, Magnus's cousin.'

'Ah, but do they believe you?' There was still gossip about her and Magnus.

'They pretend they do because his sister is very respectable and she tells them I'm her cousin, too. The important thing is that no one should find out who I really am.'

'Aye, you're right. That old sod at the Manor might try to harm you, an' maybe us as well.'

That week the Lorrimers invited Reuben Ludlam to dine with them. When he arrived he found he was to be the only guest and could not hide his puzzlement because he did not know them nearly well enough for an intimate family evening like this, since they did not visit at the Hall and he'd only met them at his grandmother's.

'I need to talk to you privately about something,' Bernard said. 'This seemed the best way to do it.

Come into my study for a few minutes, would you?'

Edith was already walking away, so Reuben followed him into the cosy, book-lined room just off the hall. 'What do we need to talk about?' he asked in puzzlement.

'Jim Marshall.'

Reuben stared at him. '*Jim Marshall!* What has he to do with anything?'

'He's guarding Francis Rawley.'

'Yes. Though not by my wish.' His father was still very vague about when Marshall would be returning to the workshop and what exactly he was doing at the Manor, which was annoying because for all his grumbling ways, Jim was a skilled and experienced workman who was sorely missed.

Bernard took the plunge and asked, 'Do you know that they're trying to starve young Francis into submission?'

'*Starve him!*'

'Yes. He's apparently grown very thin. At first they gave him only water, but now they've got him on bread and water.'

'That sounds a bit drastic, but my father says the lad's been seriously misbehaving.'

'Only to the extent of refusing to hunt or shoot. You must judge for yourself whether those are heinous crimes.'

Reuben frowned. 'I heard he'd been sent down from school for misbehaving as well.'

'No. He was sent home because he'd been ill. Stephenson has hired a private tutor to toughen him up.'

'But my father said —'

'— what Stephenson told him. I've written to a chap I know and he's been to see the headmaster. It appears Francis is a gentle lad who can't stand to kill things. He used to be teased by the other lads for that and he didn't work particularly hard, but that's all. No question of him misbehaving. Rather the reverse, in fact.'

There was a silence while Reuben took this in. 'I feel sorry for him, then,' he said eventually. 'Stephenson can be vicious when his pride is injured. In the past my father has kicked one or two families out of our houses to oblige him, though I've put a stop to that now. How do you know all this?'

'Their cook's been sending me messages and I arranged to meet Jim on his day off last weekend to question him in detail. He isn't happy about the situation, so with Cook's help he's been slipping extra food to Francis, but he has to be careful and can only smuggle so much in. The so-called tutor is an old military man and keeps a very firm hand on things. I'd – um – appreciate it if you didn't tell anyone else about that, though, or Jim too will be in trouble.'

'No, of course not. But I don't see what we can do about it. Stephenson *is* his guardian, after all.'

'Jim thinks Stephenson is behaving irrationally.

He's apparently had a seizure of some sort and his behaviour has changed. All the women servants are terrified of upsetting him these days.' Jim's actual words were, 'The old sod's crazy. There are more sensible folk locked up in the Ben, there are that!'

Reuben let out a long, low whistle.

'This treatment could permanently damage Francis's health if it goes on. Growing lads need good food and he wasn't in the best of health anyway. So what I wondered was whether you could get your father to talk to the old man and see whether *he* thinks Stephenson is – well, completely rational.'

Reuben pursed his lips. 'I'll *ask* Father, though I'm not sure whether he'll agree to it. He believes people of our class should support one another. But I'll definitely ask him.'

'I'd be grateful.' Bernard could see that he'd given Reuben a lot to think of so said in a lighter tone, 'And now that is decided, let's go in to dinner.'

But although the food was excellent, none of them ate heartily or were very good company. It was hard to do justice to a plate full of good food when you knew a lad was being half-starved only a few hundred yards away.

As he took his leave, Reuben said, 'If you think of any other way for me to help, don't hesitate to ask. I take it you're prepared to do something yourself if things go on for too long?'

Bernard nodded his hand. 'Yes, I am. After all,

he has a mother in Australia who'd give him a home and be thrilled to do so.'

'Bit drastic, sending him to Australia.'

'Very. And definitely against the law. I shall only do that in an emergency, to save his life.'

Janey Hamilton died during a stormy night in early September. She had been gasping for breath all day, faint pitiful sounds. Cathie had never kept watch over a deathbed before but she did that night, sitting quietly beside Magnus while the space between his mother's breaths seemed to grow longer and longer. Then suddenly the breathing stopped with a faint rattling sound.

Silence enfolded them and for a moment or two neither of them moved. Then Magnus murmured, 'Lord keep her safe!' and reached out to close his mother's eyes.

When Cathie laid her hand on his shoulder, he turned to her and raised his hand to cover hers. 'I'm glad she's gone. Is that wrong? She would have hated to be like this.'

Thunder shook the house and lightning slashed across the sky.

'I don't think it's wrong.' Cathie had once helped Dinny lay out an old man who had been brought to her when he fell ill and died while passing through Brookley, so she knew what to do. And the human body was not something she feared. 'I can lay her out if you'll bring me some warm water.'

'Is there no end to your kindness, lassie?' he said in a wondering tone.

She did not dare say it, but she thought: Not where you're concerned, Magnus, as she waved him away.

When she had finished her task, she realised with surprise that it had grown light and that the storm had passed, leaving a freshness and sparkle to the air, with droplets of water on the window panes catching the early rays of the sun. She opened the window wide and stayed for a moment beside it, breathing in the fresh scents.

When she went downstairs she found Magnus sitting at the kitchen table with his head propped on his hands. He looked up as she came in and she saw that his cheeks were wet.

Going across to push the kettle on to the hot centre of the range top she said quietly, 'I must move out of here now.' She had already found a place which offered lodgings to 'young women of decent character' and could only hope they would not heed the gossip about her.

'I suppose so. What shall you do? Do you need any money?' Not the time to speak of their future with his mother still unburied.

'I have a little money saved and Dr Barnes said he could find me a nursing job.'

'You're not leaving Pendleworth?' Magnus hesitated then added, 'I don't want you to go away, Caitlin. This isn't the time, but – well, there are things I want to say to you, lassie.'

She stared at him. Did this mean what it sounded like?

He looked back at her gravely. 'We'll talk about it later.'

Her heart lifted at the warmth in his eyes, but she remembered her brother and knew she must help him before she thought of herself and Magnus. 'I can't go away while they're ill-treating Francis – but I wouldn't want to anyway. My mother sometimes teased me, said I was her little legacy from Lancashire. And the strange thing is I feel at home here as I never felt at home on the farm, though my parents love it in Australia and so do my brothers.'

She liked the lively people of Pendleworth who faced hard lives with determination and good humour; even liked the sound of their rather raucous voices as they called to one another across the streets. She stopped sometimes to watch children play. If she ever had any children, she would not shut them away on a bush homestead. Her walks had shown her a different Lancashire as well, with its green rolling moors beckoning her to go striding across them. She would do one day.

Magnus's voice came out harsher than he had intended. 'Caitlin, ye canna go against a man in Alexander Stephenson's position.' He knew before she spoke that he was wasting his breath, for her face took on that determined expression he had come to know so well. She was unlike other young women of his acquaintance, more self-reliant and outgoing, and he didn't know whether this was because she had grown up in Australia or whether it was just her own nature.

'I can go against him if I have to,' she insisted. 'I've waited until your mother didn't need me any more, but I can't wait any longer. I'm going to ask Bob and Pat to help me, and if necessary we'll break in one night and rescue Francis.'

'Look – wait until we've buried my mother and I'll . . .' Magnus broke off to say, 'We can't discuss it now.' He'd have to think good and hard about this. He wasn't having her getting in trouble with the law. 'I need to tell my sister that Mother's dead and arrange a funeral. Caitlin, would you go over to Bury for me today and tell Mairi? There are plenty of trains and I'm sure she'll want to come back with you.'

'Of course.' That would also solve her problem about staying in the house without the nominal chaperonage of Janey.

Mairi might be able to talk sense to Caitlin about rescuing Francis, Magnus decided as he wrote a quick note to his sister, telling her of their mother's death and explaining Caitlin's situation. If they couldn't dissuade his lassie, well, he'd have to find a way to help her rescue her brother. He had never broken the law in his life before – never had the time to get into trouble, for he had been busy helping raise his brothers and sister ever since he could remember – but for Caitlin he would do even that, he suddenly realised. 'And since Mairi will be here, you can stay another night or two, eh? Maybe she can help find you somewhere to stay among her old friends at church.'

And there they left it. Cathie went to get ready and he sat down to make a list of all he had to do. Once the funeral was over he would also have a quiet word with Bob Marshall and beg him to refuse if Caitlin asked him to do anything stupid. Stephenson employed gamekeepers and outdoor staff. They might even shoot at her. Magnus couldn't bear to think of her being hurt.

CHAPTER 19

SEPTEMBER

At Rawley Manor Jim woke up just before dawn and heard a sound he couldn't place for a minute or two. He lay there frowning as he tried to work out what it was, then suddenly realised it was coming from the other bed, so got up and padded across to see what was wrong. He found Francis tossing and turning, his breath rasping in his throat, his face flushed.

'You all right, lad?' Jim asked.

Francis rolled his head to stare at him, then muttered, 'Feel awful. Bit sniffly yesterday, dreadful s'morning.' He raised his head but let it drop almost immediately. 'Dizzy. Chest hurts.'

Jim got dressed rapidly and began to pound on the wall that adjoined Baxter's room. Trust the sod not to come early today. He heard signs of someone stirring next door, but Baxter didn't open the door for what seemed a very long time. Jim hadn't minded being locked in before because it meant they got a warning if someone was coming, but he minded it now. Very much. What if the lad went and died on him?

Suddenly that locked door seemed a stupid thing

to accept, but when he'd come here he'd thought these nobs knew everything. Only they didn't. And the old man was definitely barmy. Being rich didn't save you from that. Jim sighed in relief at the sound of boots clumping towards the door.

A key turned in the lock and Baxter erupted into the room with his usual noise and scowls. 'Why were you banging? And why is he still lying there?'

Before he could go across and yank Francis out of the bed, as he had done once or twice before, Jim grabbed his arm. 'The lad's ill.'

'He's pretending.'

'See for yourself.'

Baxter went over to the bed. Francis was muttering and tossing, seeming unaware of them now, his face flushed, his breathing stertorous. 'Stupid sod. Can't even stay healthy.' Baxter stared sourly down at the lad whose spirit he hadn't been able to break and whom he had grown to dislike intensely.

'It was getting wet two days ago what done it, I reckon,' Jim told him with relish. 'You should've let him change his clothes after that walk, like *you* did. He's caught his death o' cold an' it's all your fault.' He went to stand on the other side of Francis, looking down at him. 'I reckon he needs a doctor. Unless Mr Stephenson *wants* him to die.'

'Of course he doesn't.' Baxter breathed in deeply, still studying Francis and listening to his laboured breathing. 'You wait here. Don't let him get out.'

'Does he look like he can go anywhere?' Jim folded his arms and stayed where he was as Baxter went tramping off down the corridor again. Why did the stupid twit allus make so much noise when he walked?

It was a full half hour later before anyone came to see them, by which time Jim had bathed Francis's forehead and tried in vain to get him to drink some water. When he risked a peep out of the door, puzzled by the slowness of the approaching footsteps, he saw old Stephenson shuffling towards him. Darting back inside, he took up his position on the far side of the bed again, arms folded. If the old man didn't send for the doctor, he was leaving here and telling that Mr Lorrimer what was going on. And even if they did send for the doctor, once Francis was better Jim was still going to leave. He'd had enough of this, more than enough. Give him a good honest job in the mill any day, even with Magnus bloody Hamilton breathing down your neck.

Without saying a word Alexander Stephenson stood by the side of the bed and observed his great-nephew: thin and flushed with fever, definitely not faking. 'Damnation! Can the lad do nothing right?' he demanded.

Francis opened his eyes and stared at him. As he recognised who it was, hatred blazed in those eyes along with the fever. But he didn't say anything and nor did the old man. After a minute Francis sighed and closed his eyes again.

'Send for the doctor, then!' Stephenson ordered. 'And send a message to Cook to prepare some beef tea.' He went away feeling furious with his stupid great-nephew, muttering to himself in a way that made Hilda stare at him in astonishment as she passed him in the corridor. And when he insisted on going down to breakfast in his night-shirt, his manservant stared too.

Jim stayed by the bed, sponging the lad's body as the fever rose because he had seen his wife do this when one of his own kids was ill. He was more relieved than he'd have admitted when the doctor finally arrived towards the middle of the morning. Since Baxter was suffering from the belly gripes – and serve the bastard right for eating so much! – and had had to rush out a minute ago, Jim was on his own.

Dr Barnes looked down at the boy and frowned. 'Has he always been so thin?'

After a quick glance over his shoulder, Jim whispered, 'They've been starving him to force him to do what they want. No food at all for the first few days I were here, then only bread and water since, an' that's four or five weeks now. It's no wonder he's took ill.'

Footsteps came hurrying back.

'Don't say I told you or they'll turn me off an' then he'll have no one to look out for him.' Jim took a hasty step backwards.

Clifford Barnes closed his eyes for a moment in sheer horror. He could not believe that a lad who

426

was the owner of all this should have been brought so low by deliberate ill-treatment.

'Why is the boy so thin?' he asked the tutor.

Baxter glanced sideways at Jim, but found him gazing at the floor. 'Outgrown his strength,' he offered.

Clifford bit back a sharp response. 'Well, whatever the cause, he needs feeding up. Beef tea, for a start. Some lightly poached fish. Stewed fruit. Custard. And get a fire lit in here. We don't want it too hot, mind you, just steady warmth and a little fresh air from the window.'

'The master doesn't believe in pampering young men,' Baxter said, as if a request for a fire on a chilly autumn day were unreasonable.

'It's a case of either pamper him or lose him!' the doctor snapped. 'I'll speak to Mr Stephenson myself before I go.'

When Clifford Barnes went downstairs, no one came into the hall so he went into the library which he knew to be Stephenson's usual refuge. Here there was a blazing fire in contrast to the icy temperature in the bedroom and the rest of the house. The old man was sitting in front of it with a tray full of food on a small table before him. Clifford Barnes's gorge rose at the contrast.

Alexander turned round. 'Who asked you to come in here?'

'I'm the doctor. You sent for me.'

'I don't need a doctor. Go away!' He flapped one hand irritably.

Clifford Barnes stared at him, seeing the signs of recent degeneration and a seizure of some sort, and wondering why he had not been called in when this happened. 'I need to speak to you. Your nephew is in a bad way.'

The old man stuffed another forkful of ham into his mouth and said indistinctly as he chewed it, 'He deserves it. Don't be misled by that angelic face of his. Francis is wicked and disobedient, should have been beaten into shape years ago. *Would* have been if it hadn't been for my sister's foolish fondness for him.' He cackled with sudden laughter. 'But he's learning to toe the line now. Oh, yes, he's learning what is expected of him.'

Clifford stared in shock as the old man started a rambling monologue about his nephew being the son of an ill-bred and coarse woman, and how shameful it was to see a good family brought down to this. From that the old man went on to decry modern manners then fell on his food again, muttering to himself as he picked among the plates with greasy fingers.

When he looked up a moment later to see the doctor still standing there, he rang a little hand-bell and laughed again, a high-pitched sound which sent a chill running down Clifford Barnes's spine. He knew seizures could cause changes in personality, but he had never seen a more marked case of it.

'Are you well?' he asked. 'Pardon me, but you seem to have—'

'I'm perfectly sound. Don't need your help.'

A maid came hurrying into the room and bobbed a curtsy.

'Show the doctor out!' Stephenson snapped.

'But what about your nephew?' Clifford demanded.

'Do what it takes to get him better, but don't spoil him. Deal with Baxter. And don't come near *me* again. Just send the bill. Doctors always send bills, don't they? Damned leeches.'

Clifford turned and left the room, pausing in the hall to say, 'I need to speak to your cook.'

The maid nodded and led the way to the rear of the hall.

'Wait!' He caught hold of her arm before she could push open a baize-covered door. 'Has Mr Stephenson been acting strangely lately?'

Fear settled on her face for a moment and she glanced round to check no one was near before nodding. Then, as if afraid of even that small action, she pushed the door open, hurrying ahead of him to prevent further speech.

'I'd like a word with you in private,' he told Cook.

'I'll join you if I may?' Baxter, who had been standing warming himself near the fire, moved forward.

'I have nothing further to say to you, sir,' said Clifford crisply.

'But I'm the boy's tutor.'

'Then I say shame on you for treating him like that.'

Baxter glared at him. 'What do you mean? Who's been saying things?'

'No one needs to say anything. If you think I'm blind to the bruises on his arms and legs, or to the way he has grown over-thin, then you're taking me for a fool – which I'm not. I have no confidence that you will heed my instructions, so prefer to give them to Cook.' He spoke loudly enough that the two maids in the kitchen could hear every word and by their expressions they were relishing what they were hearing.

Before Baxter could reply, Cook led the doctor into her own room and closed the door firmly on the tutor.

'I'm that glad to see you, sir,' she said, pulling out a large white handkerchief and mopping her eyes. Then, after a glance towards the door, she beckoned him across to the window and whispered, 'How is he, really?'

'Francis is very ill indeed,' Clifford admitted. 'He's got a raging fever.'

'That's because they wouldn't let him change his wet clothes the other day.'

'I have orders from Mr Stephenson to do what is necessary to ensure that the lad recovers, though I'm afraid I can't promise anything. His constitution has been weakened by this ill-treatment.' Clifford saw her shocked expression and said slowly, 'I think it will be best if I send a nurse to look after Francis. Your part will be to provide light, nourishing food. And you are to let me know personally if anyone tries to prevent that.'

'Mr Lorrimer is taking an interest in Mr Francis, too,' she whispered, with another glance towards the door. 'Me and his cook are friends and I let them know how things are.'

'Is he now?'

'Yes. Mr Francis got friendly with his sons, you see, though he was forbidden to talk to any of the young folk round here. Eh, they've treated that lad shamefully, they have that, even before Mr Baxter came to be his tutor – though he's like no tutor I've ever seen, 'deed he isn't, the brute.'

Clifford patted her shoulder. 'Pull yourself together, my good woman. And be sure you let your friend know how things stand.'

She blew her nose loudly and muttered, 'No use weeping. There's cooking to be done. Egg custard. Easily swallowed. Compôte of stewed fruit. Goes down without them noticing it.'

When Dr Barnes went back into the kitchen he approached the tutor who was still standing by the fire and didn't look too well himself. 'I'm sending a nurse to look after Francis.'

'I don't think that's necessary, sir. Jim can do what's needed.' Baxter gave a huge sneeze.

'I'll judge what is and isn't necessary. Mr Stephenson has given me express orders to ensure the lad's recovery – though that I cannot guarantee. Moreover, if you have a cold, you should stay away from him.'

Baxter stared at him in amazement. 'He *can't* be that ill!'

'He is. And his poor physical condition makes me seriously worried about his ability to recover – some blame for which lies at your door, sir!'

'I've done nothing I wasn't ordered to,' he protested.

'Then shame on you for accepting such unreasonable orders from a man who is clearly in his dotage!' snapped the doctor.

As soon as he got home, Clifford sent a message round to Magnus Hamilton's house, for with Janey Hamilton dead he hoped the young cousin would be willing to take on another nursing job. Most of his regular nurses were out on jobs, there being a spate of babies among the town's more affluent families, but he had great confidence in Miss Rutherford. Some women had an instinct for caring for others and she was one of them.

The messenger was lucky enough to find Cathie packing her bags after Mairi's departure. The funeral had taken place the previous day and now she had to move out. One of Mairi's friends from chapel had agreed to take her as a lodger, but Cathie wished she did not have to leave Magnus on his own.

Within minutes of receiving the message she was round at the doctor's house.

'Miss Rutherford, are you free to nurse Francis Rawley?' he asked, tapping his pencil on the desk and scowling out of the window. 'The lad has been ill-treated at his uncle's orders. He's thin and covered in bruises, and sadly he has contracted a severe inflammation of the lungs.' Her face turned so white he stared at her in shock. 'Is something wrong?'

Cathie pulled herself together. If she betrayed her connection to Francis she was sure she would not be allowed to look after him. 'I've just been rushing around rather a lot and I haven't eaten yet today, but I'm well, really I am.'

'How soon can you be ready to go to the Manor?'

'Within the hour.'

'I'll arrange for a cab to pick you up, then. You will live in there till the patient recovers.' He paused, as if waiting for something, then prompted, 'You haven't asked about payment?'

How stupid of her! 'I – um – trust you to see that I receive a suitable wage. And I am relieved to get any job. I feel it proper to move out of my cousin's house now that my aunt has passed away.'

'Very well, then. You'd better go and get ready. I shall be calling to see Francis morning and evening, but these are my instructions . . .'

On the way back to the house, Cathie called to inform Mairi's friend that she would not now need the lodgings, then hurried home. She packed her bags at lightning speed and scribbled a note to Magnus, explaining what had happened and assuring him that she would find a way to send him a message once she was settled in.

She was delighted at this unexpected opportunity to see Francis, but her delight faded to terror when she saw how ill he was. He was stick-thin and looked dreadful, wheezing and struggling for breath. She could not bear to lose him now, not when she had just found him!

Standing opposite her by the sickbed Jim said quietly, 'Just tell me what to do, lass. I'm not used to nursing folk, but who else is there to help him save you and me? I don't trust that Baxter an inch! That sod would do owt for money.' He lowered his voice still further as he added, 'And old Stephenson is as barmy as they come, though he pulls hisself together when posh folk come to the house. You should see him the rest of the time, though. Eh, he should be locked away, he should that.'

As the ship neared France the weather calmed down again and Dermott staggered up on deck desperate for some fresh air. Christina had been an absolute shrew for the past two days, acting as if she was the only one feeling unwell.

Some children were playing near the rail and he stood watching them, wondering suddenly what his own sons were doing. He wished he hadn't left them in Australia. He was proud of his sturdy lads and their high spirits. Still, Matthieu wasn't a fool and he'd keep an eye on them.

Things had, Dermott decided gloomily, gone downhill rapidly since he'd left Melbourne. He was losing his grip and it was more than time he pulled himself together. He must have been mad to buy that sodding farm, even at such a low price.

His sister and her husband were fools. Who else but fools would settle in the middle of bloody nowhere and work themselves into an early grave clearing and farming a patch of sandy scrub? Let her rot there from now on, for all he cared! He hoped she found Cathie quickly and went right back to Australia and he never saw her again. Except he still needed to find out where she had buried their brother Niall. He couldn't feel easy till he knew that.

When he went back to the cabin, he pulled out his last bottle of rum and took a good big swig.

'Do you have to drink it like that?' Christina demanded. 'We do have glasses.'

'You should try a bit yourself. It helps in rough weather.'

'Nothing helps. I feel awful!' She moaned and pressed a hand to her forehead.

'Ah, pull yourself together, woman!' he told her. 'We need to plan what we're going to do when we get there.'

She raised her head. 'Go to see my aunt, of course. What else?'

Just to show he was still master and not getting soft, he said, 'Not till we've been to Pendleworth and visited my mother's grave, we aren't.'

That made her screech at him like a fishwife. But having made the decision, he wasn't backing off. He was still master in his own household and intended to remain so. Besides, he knew what Christina would be like when she got together with that aunt of hers. They'd both be looking down their nose at him. He was going to have a very serious talk with her before he let her anywhere near the old lady.

And, he realised, he did have a fancy to visit some of his childhood haunts again. He wanted to show the folk from Underby Street how well he'd done for himself. He wondered if Teddy Marshall was still alive, which reminded him again of his niece. Not a bad lass, Cathie. He didn't wish *her* any harm. Maybe he'd see her again, too.

Only desperation would make him undertake such a long journey again. England it was going to be from now on. And respectability. Dermott grinned at the thought.

Liza watched the buildings of Liverpool grow more distinct as the ship approached the docks. The sky was grey and the wind icy, but although she was warmly wrapped she kept shivering and her head was aching. She turned to Josie, standing beside her wide-eyed. 'Are you cold, love? Would you like to go below?'

'No. I want to see everything. Isn't it big?'

So Liza stayed on deck with her daughter until her teeth were chattering, then had to go and rest in her cabin until they were allowed to disembark.

What a time to feel poorly! She told herself not to give in to it and tried to remain cheerful.

When they disembarked, Josie laughed at how awkward it was to walk steadily on land, and remained bright-eyed and interested in everything she saw.

Feeling distinctly wobbly, Liza signalled to a porter, who took their luggage and found them a cab. Since the afternoon was drawing on, she asked him to recommend somewhere respectable to stay and he drove them to a small but comfortable lodging house.

While Josie was investigating every detail of their bedroom, Liza consulted the landlady about train timetables for the following day, determined to go straight to Pendleworth. Surely Cathie would be there?

'Never fear, we'll get you to the station on time,' the landlady said genially. 'Excuse me for asking, but you don't look well.'

'I think I must be starting a cold. I feel very shivery.'

'I'll bring you up some tea and we'll give you a fine supper tonight too. That'll make you feel better. You'll be sick of ship food. It's got no nourishment in it by the time you've been at sea for a few weeks. My late husband was a sailor and you wouldn't believe the tales he had to tell.'

But in spite of the landlady's cosseting, Liza could not eat much of the evening meal and decided to go to bed early. It was wonderful to have so much space and not to be surrounded by the noises of other people, but if only her head would stop aching.

'Are you sure we'll be able to find Cathie?' Josie asked as they got ready for bed. She had asked the same question a dozen times already.

'We'll ask Mr Lorrimer to help us,' Liza said, not giving her a goodnight kiss because she didn't want to pass the cold on.

The following morning Liza felt so bad she could hardly lift her head. Josie flung on some clothes and went to fetch the landlady, who tutted and sent for the doctor.

He diagnosed influenza and insisted Mrs Caine spend the week in bed. She felt too ill to argue.

Josie proved as devoted a nurse as her big sister and the landlady was a cheerful soul who took everything in her stride, keeping an eye on Josie, taking her to market and sending her out on a sightseeing trip with a young neighbour on the Saturday, because Mrs Caine was looking a bit brighter.

But Liza could not help fretting. To come so far, then to be held up like this! And although she was recovering she was still so weak and wobbly she could not think of travelling yet.

Cathie began to sponge Francis down again as his fever rose. Jim helped her turn him and it didn't occur to either of them to worry that he was naked. This was no time for false modesty. For the past two days, they'd taken it in turns to sleep and had hardly left his side. He was holding his own, but barely.

Baxter did little to help them, coming to stand in the doorway occasionally and watching them. He was now suffering from a streaming cold and the doctor insisted he was not to go near the sick lad.

They thought nothing of it when they heard footsteps in the corridor, then a rasping voice asked, 'Who's the young woman?'

'Cathie turned to look at the man she guessed was Alexander Stephenson, shocked when she saw the wild look in his eyes. 'I'm Caitlin Rutherford, the nurse Dr Barnes sent to look after your nephew.'

'He didn't say you were young and pretty.' Alexander came to stand on the other side of the bed from her. She had a vague memory of an old gentleman who had come to the station and made her mother leave Pendleworth, but would not have recognised him in this wild-eyed person whose clothing was liberally stained with food.

She said nothing, just continued to sponge down her half-brother.

'Like it, do you?' he asked. 'Like tending men's bodies?'

'My job is to look after sick people, sir. It doesn't matter to me whether they're men or women. My last patient was an old woman.'

'Make sure nursing him is all you do. He doesn't deserve any of the extra comforts you women can offer a man.'

She became suddenly aware that Francis had come out of his delirium and was staring up at his uncle. 'Lie still,' she said quietly. 'Let us cool you down.'

He turned to stare at her and his mouth opened in shock as he recognised her.

Fortunately, Alexander Stephenson was already turning away. 'Get him better,' he threw over his shoulder, 'then we'll make a gentleman of him.'

When he had gone Francis said, 'Are you real?'

Cathie leaned closer to whisper, 'Yes. Very real. I've come to nurse you. But I'm called Caitlin now. Can you remember that?'

But he had fallen into another doze.

'It's to be hoped he don't give you away,' Jim said gloomily. 'The fat would be in the fire, then.'

His hopes were not realised. The very next morning, Francis said wonderingly, 'Cathie. You *are* real. I'll be all right now you're here.'

From the doorway Baxter said sharply, 'Why is he calling you Cathie?'

She shrugged. 'I don't know. Perhaps he's confusing me with someone. His mind is still wandering.'

He stared at her thoughtfully, but did not press the point. There was something going on here. She and Marshall were altogether too comfortable together. It was as if they were both working against him, and a good general didn't allow the troops to band together against him.

That evening he found Marshall talking to the cook in a corner of the kitchen and lingered behind the door, listening to them. What he saw made him swell with fury. The sod had been slipping the lad food all along. He went storming along to see the old man.

Alexander looked up in annoyance as Baxter came into the library. 'What do you want?'

'I want to fire Marshall. I'm not satisfied with him.'

The old man shrugged. 'Up to you. You can bring in one of the stable lads instead to help that nurse.'

Baxter hesitated. 'There's something else. Francis called that nurse Cathie. Does he know anyone called Cathie?'

'What did you say?'

'He called her Cathie.'

'I thought she was called Caitlin!'

'So did I.'

Stephenson scowled at him. 'Well, you just get rid of Marshall. I'll deal with the nurse if I have to.' He didn't like having a woman tending the lad. They were too soft, women were.

CHAPTER 20

SEPTEMBER

Dermott handed Christina out of the train at Pendleworth station and paused to look around the platform. 'This place hasn't changed much, any road.'

She was more concerned with their baggage, counting the trunks and cases off the train then tugging at her husband's arm because he was still staring round. 'Where are we going to stay?'

'Where's the best hotel?' he asked the porter, tossing him a coin.

'The new one, sir. Just opposite the station. I could wheel your luggage across easy.'

'You do that, lad.' He swept Christina a mocking bow and offered her his arm, ignoring the sour look she cast at Market Square.

When they were installed in the hotel's only suite, Dermott went to gaze out of the window. 'It's not raining for once. Come on, let's go and have a proper look around.'

'You go. Visit your mother's grave, or whatever it is you want to do, then we can leave this horrid town tomorrow.' She went to huddle by the fire which was just starting to blaze up in the grate of the large draughty sitting room.

'I'll go and see Mam's grave tomorrow. Today I want to go back to the street I was born. Don't you want to see your old house? We could get a cab out to Ashleigh.'

'I don't want to go anywhere, let alone our old house. I'm tired of travelling.' She flung herself down on a sofa. 'When you go down, ask them where that tea is. I ordered it ages ago.'

He grinned and left her to her misery. She'd been sulking ever since he refused to take her to Paris or let her go shopping in London. Tomorrow he'd drag her out for a stroll whether she wanted it or not. Today he was quite pleased at the thought of some time to himself.

It felt strange to be back. As he strolled along, he noted the civic improvements in the town centre with a snort of amusement. Library, floral gardens, new Town Hall. You might doll up the main street, but behind it on one side was the ugly mass of the gasworks and on the other the big chimney of Ludlam's mill. That damned thing stood where it always had, belching out black smoke as if to set its mark on the huddle of terraced streets that clustered around it.

Only, he thought in deep satisfaction, nowadays he'd not need to kow-tow to a Ludlam – or to a Rawley, either.

Underby Street looked different. What had been his da's secondhand clothing shop was now a

443

haberdasher's, with a window crammed full of the bits and pieces women seemed to need. But opposite it, the clogger's shop was still there. New sign, same pile of clogs in the window. He sauntered across just as a fellow came barrelling along the street, bumping into him with a muttered apology and slamming open the door of the clogger's without looking behind him. Intrigued, Dermott followed and listened to the conversation.

The man started talking as soon as the back door of the shop was open. 'That sod Baxter's just sacked me. Didn't even give me time to pack. Said they'd send my luggage home before the end of the day.'

The other man put down his chisel. 'What have you been getting up to now, our Jim?'

'That's the whole point. I've done nowt but look after that lad.'

Jim took three steps one way, met the wall and retraced his steps till he hit the sagging sofa. 'Stephenson's up to summat. An' our sister's out there still. I don't like this, Bob, I don't like it at all. What if they're intending to hurt her?'

'Ah, you're imagining things. An' if they've sacked you, you'd better get over to the workshop, hadn't you? Make sure Ludlam's still have a job there for you.'

Dermott left the shop quietly. What had happened to old Teddy? Was he still alive? He grinned. The Marshall lads were still getting themselves into trouble and Cathie had obviously found her family. The sons seemed to accept her well enough and Dermott discovered with mild surprise that he was glad the lass was all right. Then he frowned and stopped walking for a moment. But was Stephenson really intending to harm her? Why should he do that? She was related to the old man through marriage.

A few paces later he stopped again, even more surprised to discover that he'd feel responsible if anything happened to Cathie. He'd sent her over here – but not for anyone to harm. He definitely wasn't having that.

As he moved on he decided to look into things. And when he met one of his old cronies walking along the street, the sort of fellow who was good at finding things out, it seemed meant to be.

Not till he was re-entering the hotel did Dermott realise this meant staying on a bit longer in Pendleworth. Christina would go mad about that. He grinned. Well, let her.

They would only go and see that aunt of hers when he was good and ready.

Grumbling all the way, Jim headed towards the mill, standing in the small gateway the workers used and gazing across the yard with a jaundiced eye. He hated being shut up inside this damned place. Ah, to hell with it! He'd give himself an hour or two at home first, then come back later. No one would know what time he'd been fired, would they?

But as luck would have it – this was definitely not his day – his foreman came into the yard just as Jim was turning to leave.

Magnus greeted him with, 'I thought you were working at the Manor.'

'I were. Only they don't want me no more.'

'Oh? Lost your place, did you? What have you been doing?'

Jim hunched one shoulder. 'Not helping 'em kill that young lad. I'm better out of that business. But our Cathie's still there, an' how they'll treat her without me to keep an eye on things, I don't know. Anyone as treats their own kin like that old sod's been treating his nephew wouldn't think twice about harming the lad's nurse.'

Magnus pulled him quickly round a corner. 'What do you mean? Who's trying to kill Francis Rawley? Is Caitlin all right?'

'If you ask me, nothing's right up there. That old fellow's lost his wits and gone nasty with it. He's got 'em starving and beating that poor lad.'

Magnus stared at him in horror. 'You're not making this up?'

Jim stuck his chin out. 'Cathie's my sister. Us Marshalls look after one another. An' young Francis is *her* half-brother, so he's a connection, too. He seems a nice lad to me, but that tutor is a nasty bit of work, does just what the old lunatic says. An' who's to stop 'em now I'm gone? Tell me that, eh!'

'I've got to go and bring her home again.'

446

Jim cocked one eye at him. 'Got an interest in our Cathie, haven't you? I thought as much. I hope your intentions are honest, then. We won't stand for you messing her around.' He loved saying that to Magnus Bloody Hamilton.

Realising he'd betrayed himself, Magnus shrugged. 'Yes, they are honest. And if I'd been at home when she got that offer, she'd never have gone to work for Stephenson in the first place. She doesn't realise the power rich folk have.' There had been tales of strange happenings out at the Manor for a while. Everyone in town knew it wasn't a good place to work.

'Ah, you're right there. They've got too much bloody power.' Jim kicked idly at a stone and watched it bounce off the mill wall. 'Talking of rescuing the lad, she was. Not afraid of anyone, that lass isn't. Only we couldn't rescue him till he got better because he was like to die.'

Reuben Ludlam walked past just then, then realised whom he had seen and turned back. 'What are you doing here, Marshall? I thought you were working up at the Manor.'

Jim shrugged. 'They don't want me no more.'

Reuben hesitated, then realised it wouldn't be wise to talk openly out here so said abruptly, 'Come into my office.'

Magnus began to follow them.

'I'll send him back to the workshop when I'm done, Hamilton.'

But Magnus could not bear to be left out, not

when Caitlin might be in danger. 'Begging your pardon, sir, but my cousin's involved and I'm worried about her.'

'Cousin?'

'She's the one nursing Francis Rawley.'

'You'd better join us, then.' Reuben led the way into his office.

Jim was offered a chair and if he hadn't been so worried about what was happening at the Manor, would have enjoyed himself, sitting there like a bloody nob.

'Tell us what's going on!' Reuben ordered. When Jim had finished his tale, he began tapping his right index finger against his left in a way he had when thinking hard about something. 'Mr Lorrimer is worried about the lad, too. I think it's time for us to intervene. I'll send someone to – no, will *you* go to his rooms for me, Hamilton? Insist on seeing Mr Lorrimer straight away and tell him what's been going on. Ask him to come round here. I'm not helping harm someone.'

But before anyone could decide what to do, Cathie found herself in serious trouble. Alexander Stephenson had been puzzling over where he'd heard the name 'Cathie' and suddenly realised that it was the name of Francis's half-sister, the one who had borne Ludlam's name. Only she wasn't a Ludlam, it had turned out, but a bastard brat foisted on to Josiah by *that woman*.

Fury sizzled through him. *Her* daughter had

wormed her way into the Manor and that could not be allowed.

When a maid knocked on the door and would have come in with a tray, he shouted to her to go away. 'Tell the servants to get their own food. I don't want mine yet.'

Once she had left, he began to pace up and down again, laughing as he suddenly thought of a solution.

He walked across to the door. Seeing no servants lurking in the hall he crept up the stairs, grinning at what he was going to do. Luck was with him. Even his own bedroom was unoccupied.

Taking a worn leather purse from his drawer, Alexander filled it with sovereigns and slipped it into his pocket. Then he tiptoed up the next flight of stairs to the nurse's bedroom and looked for somewhere to hide the purse. He found an empty travelling bag under the bed, hid the purse in it and pushed the bag back into place. There'd be no reason for her to look inside it – not till it was too late.

He went downstairs again and rang for his own food, eating it with a hearty appetite.

Afterwards he went up to his room to change his clothes, but no sooner had he got there than he rang for his manservant and made a big fuss about his missing purse, insisting it had been stolen. 'Send for the police!'

'But, sir—'

Stephenson raised his voice. 'Do as I say or you'll

lose your job. What do I pay you for? I give the orders here and don't you forget it.'

Cathie heard the noise of the old man shouting in the distance, but ignored it. She was finding it hard to manage without Jim's help and was tired after several disturbed nights. But she had her reward when Francis woke up and looked at her, really looked at her for the first time with his eyes clear of fever brightness.

His eyes lit up. 'Cathie?' Then he looked round in terror. 'What are you doing here? You're in danger.'

'I'm nursing you. And it's all right, they don't know who I am. I go by the name of Caitlin Rutherford. Can you remember that? Caitlin. Besides, there's nothing your uncle can do but dismiss me.' She smoothed the sweaty tangle of fair hair from his forehead. 'How are you feeling, love?'

He closed his eyes. 'Dreadful.'

'Can you drink a little beef tea, do you think? I have some keeping warm by the fire.' She'd been spooning tiny amounts into his mouth as well as lukewarm water and milk. Every spoonful seemed a step forward in the battle to save his life.

'Not hungry.'

'Just have a sip or two.'

But although he struggled to do as she asked, after a few mouthfuls he pushed the spoon away. 'So tired.' Closing his eyes, he fell asleep again almost immediately.

Two hours later Baxter opened the door. 'You're wanted downstairs, Miss Rutherford.'

'Is something wrong?'

'Not my place to say.'

Her thoughts were more on her patient than herself. 'If Francis wakes, will you give him something to drink? Even a spoonful helps, I'm sure.'

'Yes.' Eli watched her go. Stephenson was up to something. There were two policemen downstairs with him and he had a triumphant look on his face. What was the old sod plotting now? Eli looked down at Francis, who was sleeping uneasily. He hoped the lad would not wake up. What did he know about sickrooms and invalids?

The head groom was waiting for Cathie at the top of the stairs. 'I'm to take you down, miss.'

She looked at Horace in puzzlement. She knew her own way down.

In the library were two policemen and Mr Stephenson, the latter sitting by the fire with a blanket over his knees. Cathie hesitated by the door.

'She's the one!' Alexander declared at once, pointing one bony finger. 'She's the only one who could have taken it. All the other servants were having their dinner. Besides, she's a stranger and they're not. I should have known better than to employ someone like her. The sort of women who go nursing are no better than they ought to be.'

The policemen, who had heard all this before as they waited, shifted uneasily. The young woman

451

at the door not only looked fresh-faced and respectable but bewildered – though you couldn't always tell, of course. They exchanged glances that told each they were not sure of this situation.

Cathie stepped forward, her heart thudding. She was determined not to be cowed by anyone, so she addressed Mr Stephenson directly. 'What are you accusing me of? I haven't taken anything.'

'Then you won't object to us searching your room, miss?'

Cathie stilled as Mr Stephenson smiled. She had taken nothing, but she hadn't been near her room for hours. 'I haven't taken anything,' she repeated. 'I haven't even been near my bedroom since early this morning. I've been looking after Francis who is still very ill.'

Alexander Stephenson leaned forward and nearly spat the words at her, 'Don't you dare call him Francis in that familiar way! A slut like you . . . I shouldn't have taken you into my house.'

'I'm not a slut!' she exclaimed indignantly.

He ignored her and began to rant on again, going over the same ground as he had already covered several times. The droop to his mouth was even more marked this morning and as he wiped moisture from it impatiently with a crumpled handkerchief, his hand shook.

The two policemen exchanged another glance. The sergeant had told them to obey Mr Stephenson, who was rich and influential, but the old man was talking so strangely that if he hadn't been who he was, they'd have dismissed everything he said as rubbish.

When the flood of words eased, one of them said quietly, 'Could you show us your room, miss?'

'What am I accused of taking?' Cathie asked on the way up, but they didn't answer.

They searched her bed, lifting the feather mattress, then the more solid mattress beneath it, while she stood there with her arms folded, getting angrier and angrier. They then began to investigate her drawers, pulling all her underwear out, to her great embarrassment, and leaving it scattered on the untidy bed. Finally, one of them looked beneath her bed and pulled out her travelling bag.

He opened it and said, 'Aaaah!' then looked sternly across at her. 'Is this yours, miss?' He held up a shabby leather purse.

'No. Definitely not. I've never seen it before.'

'Then how did it get here?'

'I should think,' she said bitterly, 'someone put it there to incriminate me while I was looking after Francis.'

They gave her disbelieving glances.

'We'll have to take you down to the police station,' one of them said. 'If you'd just put your coat and hat on, miss?'

'To the police station?' She could not believe this was happening to her.

'If you please, miss.' They were waiting for her in the doorway.

She looked from one to the other. 'But let alone I didn't take that purse, what's going to happen to Francis? He's ill and Mr Stephenson dismissed Jim Marshall this morning. There'll be no one to look after him. He could *die!*'

But they would not listen to her and she found herself being escorted outside and helped into a shabby cab, which then drove them into town.

Dermott's informant Bert came to find him at the hotel, but he was still out. The proprietor suggested the visitor see Mrs Docherty if the matter was so important. After some hesitation he agreed.

Christina swept down the stairs dressed in all her finery, took one look at the scruffy creature waiting in a small room at the rear of the entrance hall and nearly went back to her suite. Then she decided to find out what her husband was up to and controlled her annoyance. 'Well? What do you want?'

'I need to see Dermott. Urgent, it is.'

'*Mr Docherty* to you.'

He grinned. 'It weren't *Mr Docherty* this morning when him an' me had a chat an' he asked me to keep me eyes open.'

Ignoring his impudence, she said loftily, 'I'm his wife. Tell me and I'll see he's informed.'

Bert shook his head. Dermott had mentioned money and women never paid you as much. Mean buggers, women. 'It's for his ears only.'

'How much?' She had a little purse hanging under her skirt and pulled it through the side slit.

Bert pursed his lips, then breathed a sigh of relief as Dermott walked in.

'You're soon back, lad.'

'Ah. Heard summat, didn't I, *Dermott*?' The last was spoken with a mocking glance towards Christina.

'Tell me.'

'That nurse you was interested in has been arrested. Down at the police station, she is. Stole a purse, they say.'

'Who's she supposed to have stolen it from?'

'Stephenson.' Bert scowled as he said the name. His brother had worked in the gardens up at the Manor till Stephenson took a dislike to him, and the head groom had beaten Tom up before they sacked him, saying he'd better keep his mouth shut about what was going on up there. Here was a chance to get even with the sods.

Dermott stood chewing his lip, thinking. 'Is she down at the police station now?'

'Yes. I come over here straight off soon as I heard.'

'Good lad.' He handed over a coin, the value of which made Christina suck in her breath angrily. 'And if you find out anything else, either about the young lady or the folk at the Manor, let me know at once.' He glanced sideways at his wife. 'No one else. Me.'

'Ye're a good lad, Dermott,' Bert said with a grin.

'Aye, but I'll be an angry lad if you go boozing before I've sorted this lot out.'

Bert's smile faded. 'Aw, just the one.'

'Up to you. But if you come to me with ale on your breath, I'm paying nowt more.'

Bert fingered the coin and decided he could wait to celebrate. He'd go and find his brother, who still knew folk up at the Manor.

When the man had gone, Christina turned to her husband. 'You're not going to get involved in this, surely?'

Dermott had been wondering why he was bothering, but this annoyed him. 'I'm going to find out what's happening before I do owt. She *is* my niece, after all.'

'The daughter of a woman you hate.'

'I don't hate Cathie, though.'

Cathie was feeling terrified. They'd questioned her again on arrival at the police station, then locked her in a cell while the sergeant 'considered the situation'. She didn't know what to do. Her first thought was to ask for Magnus, then her cheeks burned at the thought of him seeing her in this situation. She'd written to him from the Manor a few days ago, but had not received a reply.

After a few moments she remembered Mr Lorrimer with a sob of relief. She knocked on the door of the cell and called, 'Excuse me!' But no one came.

She went back to sit on the narrow bench, feeling

quite sick with worry now. What was going to happen to her? She could be tried and put in prison. She shivered at the thought. Even being locked in this chilly cell was horrible. It made you feel as if you were suffocating. And it was so cold that in the end she wrapped the folded blanket round her shoulders, glad of its rough warmth.

When she heard the sound of a key in the door, she stood up, relieved. Surely they'd come to tell her it was a mistake?

But it was a woman with a tray on which was a piece of bread and butter and a thick cup of strong tea. A policeman stood just outside the door.

'Constable, could you ask the sergeant if I can speak to him, *please*?' Cathie pleaded.

He shook his head. 'Sergeant's having his dinner. He'll see you later.'

'But this is urgent. I need to—' He shut the door in her face and all she heard were footsteps tramping down the passage, then silence.

She couldn't hold back the tears as she picked up the cup of tea in fingers that trembled. What was she going to do? What if no one believed her?

CHAPTER 21

SEPTEMBER

Thinking about matters carefully over his midday meal Sergeant Horly decided he needed more information about this alleged theft at Rawley Manor. He had had considerable experience of criminals and prided himself on his ability to spot a liar at ten paces. He did not think Miss Caitlin Rutherford was either a criminal or a liar, unless she was the best actress he had ever met – which was just vaguely possible, but not probable. He chewed his lamb and mashed potatoes slowly as he turned things over in his mind, for he did his best thinking while eating. When he had pushed that plate away, he went on to eat his apple pie and custard with equal deliberation and enjoyment.

Mr Stephenson's message had referred to the young woman as a 'slut of a nurse'. Having met her, Sergeant Horly could not agree with this description and wondered at its use. What's more, his men said Mr Stephenson had spoken wildly and if he hadn't been a rich man they would not have believed a word he'd said. Only – Alexander Stephenson *was* a very rich man and therefore

Sergeant Horly intended to treat this case with particular caution and care. He did not want to lose his job.

The first thing to do, he decided as he licked the last traces of the custard thoughtfully from his spoon, was to find out more about the situation. He swallowed a final mouthful of tea and heaved himself up from the table to send one of his men out to the Manor again to question the servants.

Constable Dimmott went to the back door of Rawley Manor, having no desire whatsoever to meet Mr Stephenson again. When a young maid opened it, she squeaked in shock, did not invite him in and called for Cook to, 'Come quick! There's a policeman at the door.'

Cook came to stand before him with arms folded and asked brusquely, 'Can I help you, constable?'

Cecil Dimmott seized the moment by giving her a winning smile. 'The sergeant needs a little more information about Miss Rutherford and I'm sure what you say is bound to be reliable.'

She glanced over her shoulder and lowered her voice. 'We've orders to let no one into the house, I'm afraid, but I'm happy to talk to you here if you're quick. More than happy, because you'll never persuade me that Caitlin Rutherford is a thief.' She swelled with indignation at the mere idea and repeated firmly, 'Never!'

'You wouldn't know anything about the nurse's whereabouts during the earlier part of the morning when the theft occurred, would you?'

'Indeed I would. I've asked the maids who were cleaning upstairs within hearing of the master's room and neither of them saw or heard a sign of her round there. Not a sign! And every time they passed Mr Francis's door, she was right there, looking after him. Though one of them did see the master go upstairs just after she'd taken his lunch tray away.'

'It was very sensible of you to make inquiries, ma'am, if you don't mind my saying so, because who can understand what's going on inside the house better than those who work here?' He waited and sure enough further information was forthcoming.

'Caitlin Rutherford is a devoted nurse and she's saved Master Francis's life, whatever *a certain person* says. You wouldn't find anyone more caring than her, not if you searched all of Lancashire, you wouldn't.' Cook hesitated, then added, 'And to tell you the truth, Mr Stephenson has been behaving very strangely of late. If it weren't for Master Francis I'd have left months ago.'

In her indignation her voice had risen on the last words and suddenly the man the constable thought of as 'that mad old bugger' erupted from behind an inner door, looking furiously angry.

Cecil Dimmott nearly dropped his helmet in shock and Cook let out a loud screech before clasping one hand to her bosom and muttering, 'Giving a body palpitations like that!'

'I'll give you palpitations,' Stephenson shouted

in a piercing voice that could have been heard a hundred yards away. 'You're dismissed, you fat, stupid female! And make sure you get out of my house within the hour! You're as much a slut as *she* was. That's why you're defending her.'

Cook drew herself up with great dignity. 'I shall be glad to leave.'

'No references. And I'll make sure you don't find another job in Pendleworth.'

She did not answer, but turned and marched away with stately tread. When Stephenson darted forward and gave her a shove which sent her staggering into a wall, she righted herself quickly and glared at him. 'That is *not* the behaviour of a gentleman.'

He laughed wildly, then turned back to the constable. 'As for you . . .'

Cecil Dimmott, who had been observing this behaviour in utter amazement, took a step backwards, but the old man followed him, jabbing one finger into the constable's chest to emphasise his words.

'I shall be complaining to the Chief Constable. Daring to come here and question my servants without my permission.' Spittle dribbled unheeded out of one corner of his mouth and his words were slightly slurred. 'There was no need for it. *No need at all!* I've told the police what they need to know. It's their duty now to lock that slut up. Are they daring to challenge my word? Are you, fellow?'

Cecil retreated another step, but the old man followed, bony finger still jabbing.

'She's as bad as her mother before her, that one is. She stole my nephew out there in Australia, destroyed our good name. Women like her should be locked away. Blood and breeding will out. But I'll not let any more women near that boy till he grows up. Not one! He's to be made into a man, do you hear me, not a namby-pamby fool!'

Prudently Constable Dimmott continued to back away, unable to make head or tail of all this. After a few paces, the old bugger stopped following him, but the shrill voice followed him all the way to the edge of the kitchen gardens and when he looked back he could see Stephenson glaring at him.

As he hurried down the drive, Cecil shook his head and settled his helmet more firmly in place. There was something very strange happening here, no doubt about it, and he wouldn't be in his sergeant's boots for anything.

When the constable got to the end of the drive, he slowed down as the gatekeeper came out of his cottage, clearly wanting to speak. After a quick look behind him to make sure he couldn't be spotted from the house, Cecil stopped. 'Did you want to speak to me, sir?'

'Is summat else wrong at the big house, then?' Roskin the gatekeeper asked.

'Just pursuing inquiries.'

'There was a right old fussation up there this

morning. They sacked Jim Marshall, then that tutor left as well. Baxter, he's called. Treated poor Master Francis something shocking, my wife tells me. She helps with the washing up there.' Roskin drew breath and rushed on, 'Just packed his bags, that Baxter did, and brought 'em down here hissen in a wheelbarrow. When I asked what were up, he told me he knew when to beat the retreat. Said he'd had enough of working for a madman. Then he left his bags near my back door and walked into town. Came back in a cab to collect 'em half an hour later and off he went. What do you think of that, eh?'

'Very strange. Do you know where this Baxter has gone?'

'No. But I envy him, I do that. I wish I could leave here, too, only I'm tied to this house, aren't I? Wife came home proper upset today.' Roskin shook his head and sucked in air loudly through a gap in his teeth before continuing, 'Says she's never seen the likes of it. They've accused the nurse of stealing – as nice a lass as you'd ever hope to meet, my wife says – and that poor lad still at death's door, hardly able to draw breath. And who'll be next, tell me that, eh? At this rate we'll none of us have jobs here no more. We'll be turned out to starve in the streets – or he'll accuse *us* of theft next.'

A pause, then he added in a low voice, though there was no chance of anyone overhearing him, 'None of the maids don't think she did it, you know. They think the master must have put the purse in her room hissen.'

Which gave Cecil Dimmott a great deal to mull over on his way back into town, and set deep frown lines in his sergeant's brow when the constable passed the information on.

In Liverpool Liza's influenza lingered and it was lucky she had both a caring landlady and a daughter who, like her older sister, seemed to delight in looking after sick people. Josie bustled to and fro, full of importance, bringing drinks and helping her mother wash or change her night-gown. In the afternoons, when children got home from the new elementary school just down the road, Josie sometimes went out and played with the landlady's nieces if her mother didn't need her. The improvement in her health which had begun on the voyage had continued on land, and she was as loud and full of energy as any of them, without any of that dreadful wheezing.

After two long weeks, during which Liza fretted at her incarceration first in her bedroom, then in the landlady's front parlour, she declared herself fit to travel again. Josie and the landlady both protested that it was too soon, but she overrode them, even though she still did not feel her usual self.

By the time she got to the station, she was regretting her rashness but decided she could rest again when she got to Pendleworth. While a porter helped them on to the train and dealt with their large pile of luggage, she got into the carriage on legs that trembled and sank gratefully down on the seat, leaning her head back against the upholstery, infuriated that she was still so weak.

By the time they arrived Josie had told her mother several times that she was very pale, and indeed Liza was feeling so dizzy and weak that she found it difficult to think clearly.

A fatherly porter retrieved their luggage with Josie's help while Liza sat on a bench, then he escorted them across the square to a hotel which was new since she had lived here. They went into a very modern-looking reception hall, where small square tables and wooden settles were arranged along the walls with great precision and where the wallpaper pattern was so strong that it hurt Liza's eyes, especially when taken in conjunction with the equally strong pattern on the carpet that ran down the centre of the floor. The walls were also embellished by several pictures of Scotland grouped tastefully around a picture of Her Majesty, looking heavy and elderly and sombre.

As they were waiting for a fussy old lady in a virulently purple and green outfit to be attended to, Liza put a hand up to her aching forehead and rubbed it. She felt very wobbly and distant and was longing to lie down. Then she heard a loud voice she recognised and gasped in shock. Stiffening her spine, she turned to face the owner of that voice, hoping she had been mistaken.

But she had not.

At the other end of the hall Dermott broke off in mid-sentence and stopped moving so abruptly that his wife bumped into him. He continued to stand there, looking equally shocked.

Before either of them could say a word, everything began to whirl round Liza and the last thing she heard was her daughter's scream.

When she awoke she was lying on a sofa with Josie kneeling beside her sobbing and Dermott standing by a fireplace scowling. For a moment she could not speak, only meet his gaze and hope her fear of him did not show. She was amazed at how like Da he looked now, only he had a much healthier colour in his cheeks than Da had ever had and was far better dressed. She had not expected that resemblance and it threw her into confusion. Dermott was the one to break the silence and his deep voice also reminded her of Da's, even though it did not have the same lilting Irish accent.

'You look older,' he said abruptly. 'Nor I didn't expect you to faint at the sight of me.'

Josie bounced to her feet, hands on hips, to declare, 'She's been really ill with the influenza, that's why she fainted. And you're a very rude man, whoever you are. Go away and let me look after my mother.'

He stared at the diminutive defender in surprise, then chuckled. 'Eh, you're as feisty as your sister Cathie, you are. You'll be Josie, I suppose.'

'How do you know my name?'

Liza tugged at her daughter's skirt to pull her closer. She forgot her differences with her brother, for her main worry would not be held back. 'How long have you been in England, Dermott? Have you seen Cathie? Is she all right?'

'My wife and I only arrived in Pendleworth this morning, and no, I haven't seen her.' He gestured towards the woman standing beside him. 'I believe you two already know one another.'

As he hesitated, wondering whether to tell her that her daughter was in trouble, Christina stepped forward with a toss of her head and a shrill scrape of laughter. 'Your Cathie's in jail, actually.'

'I don't believe you!' Liza recognised Kitty Pringle with a further feeling of shock. How could *she* be Dermott's wife? She tried to sit up, but her head was still spinning and with a low groan she let it fall back on the cushions, raising her arm to shield herself from the light streaming through a window opposite.

Dermott could not stop staring at his sister. She hadn't looked like Mam when he'd seen her in Australia, because he didn't remember his mother as a young woman, let alone a vibrantly beautiful one like his sister had been then. But now Liza looked pale and drawn, as their mother often had, and there was a touch of grey in the hair at her temples. The resemblance shook him to the core and he regretted, as he had many times, not having

467

written to his mother. It would have been grand to have seen Mam just once before she died, even better to tell her that her 'bad lad', as she had often called him, had done well for himself. The thought made a lump come into his throat.

'Cathie *is* in jail,' he said quietly, taking hold of his wife's arm and giving it a little shake as he muttered, 'Shut up, you!' Raising his voice again, he told his sister, 'I was just going out to see what it was all about when you turned up.'

Liza was so chalky white he let go of Christina and moved across the room to crouch beside her and say abruptly, '*You* aren't in any state to do owt about it, that's for sure. Let them show you to a room and leave me to see if I can help your lass.'

'*You?* After what you did to us?'

He ignored her accusation. 'Who else is there? You're in no fit state to do anything. And as it happens, I like my niece, in spite of her being *your* daughter. I wouldn't want owt bad to happen to Cathie.' He turned to his wife. 'An' while I'm gone, you mind that sharp tongue of yours, Christina Docherty, and help our Liza settle in. I'll be back when I can.'

Christina shrugged. 'Oh, very well. But why you want to help her after swearing you'd get your revenge all these years, I can't think.'

Still standing protectively beside her mother Josie looked at her uncle and said loudly, 'I won't let anyone hurt my mother.'

Dermott smiled, a genuine smile this time. 'Eh, lass, I'm frit at the mere thought of upsetting you.'

Josie stamped her foot. 'I mean it!'

Eh, he thought, what a nice little lass! He looked at his sister and said in a gentler voice, 'I'll see that Cathie's all right. I got quite fond of her in Perth.' Then he scowled at Liza again in a way that said he still had not completely forgotten what lay between them.

She could not hold back a sob at that look. 'It was an accident, Dermott, one I've rued every day since then.'

'What did you do with his body?'

'Buried it next to Josiah's. His grave's been carefully tended, believe me.'

The silence was so charged with anger and emotion that Josie looked from one to the other in apprehension and even Christina held her tongue.

Then Dermott turned away, saying with a harsh edge to his voice, 'I'm getting soft in my old age. I find I like my nieces so I'm not going to hurt their mother. I'll go and see what's up with Cathie.'

Christina watched him go, then turned to stare at Liza. 'Well, you *do* look a mess!' She patted her own elaborate hair-do, cast a complacent glance at herself in the mirror over the mantelpiece, then went to ring the bell. 'I suppose we'd better get you to a room now before you faint again.'

Some people never change, Liza thought as a sturdy maid helped her to another bedchamber and Christina followed, issuing sharp instructions but doing little to help.

Liza had a sudden desperate longing for Benedict. Dermott sounded as if he meant it about liking Cathie, but she still found it hard to trust her brother and would never forgive him for setting that fire and destroying all Benedict had worked so hard for. But the most important thing at the moment was to help Cathie.

Magnus pounded along the streets from the mill to Market Square and burst into the offices of Lorrimer & Sons. 'I need to see – Mr Bernard Lorrimer – right away,' he told the clerk, panting from his mad rush.

The clerk eyed his height uneasily and said in a nervous voice, 'I'm afraid he's with a client at the moment, but—'

'Then you'll have to disturb him, won't you?'

'I can't do that.'

Magnus came right up to the counter and gripped the edge of it. 'Look, I've got an urgent message from Mr Reuben Ludlam. Very urgent. If you tell Mr Lorrimer I'm here and why, he'll definitely see me.'

'If you give the message to me, I'll—'

Frustrated and desperately worried about Caitlin, Magnus pounded on the desk and roared, 'Show me where Mr Bernard Lorrimer is this minute or I'll open every door in the place till I find him myself!'

A door opened at the side and a gentleman Magnus recognised by sight came out. 'Is something wrong?'

'Very wrong,' Magnus said before the clerk could do more than open his mouth. 'Are you Mr Lorrimer?'

'Yes.'

'Mr Reuben sent me. It's urgent, about' – he didn't want to name Francis in public, so amended what he had been going to say to '– the lad who's ill.'

Bernard gave him a quick, assessing glance then said, 'Wait a moment, please.' He stuck his head round the door of the room he had just left and said, 'My deepest apologies, Mrs Grey. I'm called away urgently. But I will attend to that matter, I promise you.' He then led the way to another room. 'I presume you're talking about Francis Rawley?'

'Aye. Jim Marshall's just been dismissed – for no real reason – so Caitlin's up there on her own with young Francis. Mr Reuben and I are worried that Stephenson is planning something nasty. He's been acting very strangely of late, by all accounts. So not only may that poor lad's life be in danger, but Caitlin's too if she gets in the way. Mr Reuben suggests you come over to the mill and speak to Jim yourself, then mebbe we can plan what to do.'

Bernard looked at him in surprise. 'Who are you? And what is your connection with this, if I may ask?'

'I'm Magnus Hamilton and Caitlin's my cousin.'

'I beg to differ – I have discussed this already with Miss Ludlam.'

'Sorry. I've got used to calling her that in public.' Magnus flushed as he added, 'I want to marry her. Only she took this job at the Manor before I could stop her. I was at work so I couldna even say goodbye, and although I've written to her I've not had a reply, which isna like her. So I'm more than a bit worried. I was going to walk out there on Sunday and see if I could catch sight of her, mebbe even speak to her – or at least ask one of the other maids how she is.'

Bernard was touched by the love glowing in the other man's eyes as he spoke of Cathie and warmed to him immediately. 'We'd better go and see Reuben at once, then. He and I have been worried about Francis for some time.'

The two men strode through the streets, coats flapping, with Bernard clutching his top hat to stop it blowing away while Magnus carried his cap in his hand, for he hated to wear anything on his head.

As they walked Bernard said, 'It was dangerous, her going to nurse her brother. If they find out who she is, she could be in real trouble and Stephenson is still a powerful man in these parts.'

'If he touches her, I'll make him sorry for it, powerful or not,' Magnus said curtly.

Again Bernard gave him a close scrutiny. 'Yes, I believe you would. But that might land you both in more trouble if the law is on Stephenson's side. We must take great care how we approach this.'

Magnus didn't bother to argue. What did laws matter if Caitlin was in danger? He should have spoken sooner of his feelings and to hell with convention. He *would* speak as soon as he found her. He couldn't believe how bleak life was without her.

At the mill Jim was watching Mr Reuben pace up and down his office while he enjoyed a cup of tea and some shortbread biscuits that a lad had brought in all fancied up on a tray with a lace-trimmed cloth on it. What it was to be one of the nobs and get waited on like this! When Mr Lorrimer and Magnus came in, however, he set the cup down and jumped to his feet, knowing it was not his place to sit in the company of his betters.

After Jim had told his story again and filled in more details about what had been happening at the Manor, it was decided that Bernard would go there and ask to speak to Cathie, pretending a legal reason to do with her family, while Reuben urged his father to call on Mr Stephenson and ask to see Francis.

Magnus and Jim could do nothing but go back to the workshop, though neither of them could settle to anything.

Matthew Ludlam flatly declined to intervene in the affairs at the Manor, and he and his son had a short, sharp argument after which Reuben returned to his own office near the workshop, waiting for his friend to return.

Bernard was back within the hour, jumping out of the cab before it had drawn up properly outside the mill and yelling at the driver to wait.

Magnus, who had been keeping an eye on the yard through the window of the workshop, shouted to his assistant to, 'Take over, Sam!' and raced along to the office, closely followed by Jim, who was determined not to be left out. They arrived in time to hear Bernard say, 'Cathie was arrested for theft this morning and is in custody at the police station.'

'That lassie would never steal anything!' Magnus said indignantly.

'What's she supposed to have took?' Jim asked, frowning.

'I don't know. Stephenson refused to speak to me except to say that I could find the slut in jail, where she belonged. And the gatekeeper told me that not only has the tutor packed his bags and left, but the cook also has been dismissed. The whole house is in an uproar, it seems.'

'Who's looking after Francis, then?' Jim asked. 'Eh, I were counting on Cook to do that. She's right fond of the lad.'

'I don't know who's caring for him.' Bernard moved towards the door. 'I'm going to the police station to see what I can do for Cathie before I worry about Francis.'

'I'm coming with you,' said Magnus at once.

'Shall I go and see what I can sniff out at the Manor?' Jim offered. 'Though I'd better take my brother with me. They've got a rough fellow running the stables and outdoor staff there.' And if that Horace wasn't benefiting from his master's strange behaviour, Jim would eat his hat.

'Good idea. Take a cab and tell it to wait for you while you're there. I'll pay.' Reuben tossed a coin towards him.

Jim raced through the streets and burst into the cobbler's shop. 'Hey up, lad. I need you to come out to the Manor with me. Mr Reuben's paying for a cab. I reckon if we can get hold of one of them maids, she'll tell us what's going on.'

'What the hell are you talking about?'

'They've arrested our Cathie for theft an' Mr Reuben wants to know what's happening to Francis. The poor sod's not out of danger yet an' if there's no one to nurse him anything could happen to him.'

Bob put down his tools and the unfinished clog and began untying his apron. 'Sod this Francis, I want to know how our sister is. That lass'd not steal a farthing.'

Jim glared at him. 'Cathie's got a fancy lawyer going to look after her, but there's no one to look after Francis.' He didn't know why he felt so responsible for the poor lad, but he did. 'Let alone I reckon he's our ticket to better things when he turns twenty-one, I like him an' he's our step-brother or summat like that. But them chaps in the stables would beat up anyone who looked sideways at 'em, and I don't want to go out there on my own.'

Bob shrugged. 'All right. But best be prepared, eh? No bugger's going to attack me without regretting it.' He went to a corner of the room and tossed Jim a walking stick his father used sometimes which had a hard knobbly handle, taking an old axe handle for himself and slotting it through his belt.

They hailed a cab at the station and set off for the Manor, burly men fairly radiating determination and a willingness to settle the hash of anyone who got in their way.

Dermott arrived at the police station just behind two men who seemed to be together. One was well-dressed, clearly a gentleman, the other a working man in oil-stained clothing. Dermott eyed the latter sideways, not used to meeting anyone so much taller than himself and wondering idly what this one would be like in a fight. He stood impatiently, waiting for the gentleman to finish his business first because he'd get nowhere by causing an upset.

'I believe you have a Miss Rutherford here,' Bernard said. 'She was working as a nurse out at the Manor.'

Dermott took a step closer. Was this fellow talking about Cathie? Why had she changed her name?

The policeman nodded and said 'Yes, sir' in an obsequious voice.

'I'm Miss Rutherford's lawyer. I'd like to see Sergeant Horly, if you please.'

The policeman looked surprised, but said politely, 'I'll go and fetch him, sir.'

While he was away, Dermott cleared his throat to attract attention. 'Excuse me, sir, but I think I'd better introduce myself. Dermott Docherty. If you were talking about a young lady whose real name is Cathie, I'm her uncle.'

'I wasn't aware she had an uncle still resident in Pendleworth.'

'I'm not resident here. I've just arrived from Australia – and so has her mother.'

'Mrs Caine is here?'

'Aye, but she's been ill, so she sent me to find out what's going on.'

The sergeant came in at that moment, annoyed at being disturbed while he was taking his afternoon tea. When he recognised one of the three men waiting at the counter, he straightened up. This one, at least, was well known to him and was respected in the town. 'Can I help you, Mr Lorrimer?'

'I'm representing Miss Rutherford. Has she been arrested?'

Sergeant Horly felt even more puzzled. 'Well, not exactly arrested, sir. More like – um – detained for questioning. We're still investigating the case.'

Dermott edged forward. 'I'm the lass's uncle. I don't believe she'd take anything.'

'The purse in question was found in her travelling bag, under her bed.' After some hesitation, the sergeant added, 'Sir.'

Magnus stepped forward, for he had no intention of being left out of this. 'Caitlin is innocent.'

Sergeant Horly drew himself up. 'And you are, sir?'

Magnus hesitated, then said rashly, 'The man who's going to marry her.'

This caused another dead silence as everyone stared at him.

Dermott grinned and gave him a quick nudge with one elbow. 'Well, if that's so, you'd better come and see her mother. Ask permission, like.'

'Aye, I will. Once we've got her out of here.'

Sergeant Horly decided that no harm could come from releasing the young woman into a lawyer's charge. In fact, it was a good way out, given his present doubts. 'If you'll come this way, Mr Lorrimer, I'll take you in to see Miss Rutherford. You other gentlemen will have to wait here, I'm afraid.'

Dermott considered this for a moment, then shrugged and took a step backwards, waving Bernard through the gate in the counter, which the constable was lifting to let him through. 'Give her my love and tell her her mother's here.'

He turned to study Magnus. 'What's this about marrying my niece, then? Isn't this a bit quick? She can't have been in England more than four months.'

★　★　★

478

Cathie looked up as heavy footsteps came along the stone-flagged corridor. She felt as if she had been here for an eternity, but it could only have been a few hours. What would happen next? What did they do with people they'd arrested? She wished she could send a message to Magnus, but they hadn't even brought the sergeant to see her when she asked, just left her sitting here.

'I didn't do it,' she declared as soon as the door opened. She'd decided to say that loudly at every opportunity.

'There's someone to see you.' Sergeant Horly's expression betrayed nothing.

'Who?'

'This way, if you please, miss.'

He gestured to her to follow him, so she did, wondering who would know she was here. What if it were Magnus? She felt hot with embarrassment at the thought of him seeing her in this shameful dilemma, but pride stiffened her bearing. She knew she hadn't taken anything, whatever they said or did to her. She must hold on to that.

When the sergeant opened a door and waved her inside, she found herself in a small room which contained a table and two chairs only. Mr Lorrimer was waiting there for her and she blushed with shame that he should find her in this predicament.

'When I heard what had happened, I assumed you'd want me to represent you, Miss Ludlam.'

'I didn't do it.'

'I'm quite sure you didn't.' He pulled out one of the chairs and when she had taken it, he sat down opposite her, smiling reassuringly.

'Begging your pardon,' the sergeant asked, taking up position against the wall to one side, arms folded, 'but is the young lady's name not Rutherford?'

'No, it's Ludlam. She's a relative by marriage of the local family.'

The sergeant swallowed hard. This changed the situation considerably.

Bernard's tone was confident and easy. 'Miss Ludlam thought it wiser to use another name while in Pendleworth, Sergeant, because of Mr Stephenson's hostility towards her mother and family – though she kept me aware of what was happening, of course.'

'His hostility?'

'Yes, Sergeant. Miss Ludlam is Francis Rawley's half-sister and Mr Stephenson has been refusing to let her mother see or communicate with Francis since he was a baby.'

'I see.' Now here was a motive for harming the young woman. Sergeant Horly frowned as he considered it.

'Was the purse found on Miss Ludlam's person?' Bernard asked.

'Well, no, it wasn't, sir. It was found in her travelling bag, under her bed.'

'And when did the purse go missing?'

'Early this morning.'

'I was with Francis,' Cathie interrupted. 'I hadn't been near my room since the early hours of the morning, when Jim called me to take my turn with Francis.'

'Jim?' queried the Sergeant.

'Jim Marshall. He's been employed to help look after Francis.'

'Sent to the Manor by Mr Reuben Ludlam,' Bernard intervened. 'Jim is a trusted employee at the mill.'

The sergeant thought it over. 'Why was *he* not there this morning, then?'

'Mr Stephenson dismissed him, which is why Mr Reuben Ludlam and I are particularly worried about Francis. The lad could die if he's not properly cared for at this delicate stage in his recovery. And Mr Baxter left suddenly today as well.'

Sergeant Horly decided it was more than a bit suspicious for Marshall to be dismissed at the same time as the girl was accused of theft. And the tutor had slipped away without waiting for his wages from the sound of it. It took a lot to make a man do that.

Cathie turned to the stern, grey-haired policeman. 'Can't *you* insist that someone go and look after Francis? He's been so ill.'

'I'm afraid we can't go into the house unless invited, Miss, any more than Mr Lorrimer can, and we certainly can't question what Mr Stephenson is doing in his own home.'

She looked back at the lawyer, tears welling in her eyes. 'I'm so afraid for Francis.'

'Let's deal with your problems first,' Bernard said quietly. 'Your Uncle Dermott is waiting for you outside, and there's also a tall, fierce young man with a Scottish accent.'

Her face softened at once. 'Magnus.'

'He says he's your intended.'

Rosy colour stained her face and for a moment her eyes glowed with happiness, then she slumped in dejection. 'I didn't want him to see me like this.'

Bernard turned to the sergeant. 'Could you release Miss Ludlam on my security? I'll see she doesn't leave Pendleworth, though I don't think she'll even want to, with a mother and fiancé here.'

Sergeant Horly nodded. 'That would be a useful solution' – his eyes met Bernard's as he added – 'for the time being.'

'Mother's here!' Cathie exclaimed. '*My mother's here in England?*'

Bernard smiled at her. 'So I'm told. I haven't seen her myself. She's been ill and is waiting for us at the hotel.'

With that the two men went off to attend to the formalities, leaving Cathie locked in the little room which was only marginally better than being shut in a cell. If her mother had come all this way, it could only be to see her. What had happened about the baby? Had her mother brought it with her? Guilt flooded through Cathie once again for all the trouble she had caused, then her thoughts turned back to Magnus. Had he really said he was her intended? Did he mean it? She was lost for a few moments in a happy dream of being his wife, but then reality pressed down on her again and she got up to pace the room.

It seemed a long time before those heavy footsteps came clumping towards her again and the sergeant led her outside into the public room of the police station.

She stopped in the doorway with eyes for no one but Magnus.

He could wait no longer but pushed past the constable and went behind the counter to gather his beloved into his arms. 'Ah, lassie, my bonny lassie! Why did you leave me?' And heedless of the audience, he kissed her soundly.

When he drew away, they both became suddenly aware of where they were and flushed scarlet, but she still clung to him.

'Why did you no' answer my letter, Caitlin?' he asked softly as they moved back to the other side of the counter. 'I've been frettin' to hear from you. We didn't even manage to say goodbye properly.'

She looked up at his dear face. 'What letter? I've received none.'

Bernard exchanged amused glances with Dermott, then intervened. 'Shall we leave? I don't think any of us wants to linger here.'

'And have you no word of greeting for your uncle, lass?' Dermott asked as Magnus and Cathie turned towards the door, both still with dreamy expressions on their faces.

She gave him a very direct look. 'I don't think you deserve a kind word. You must have known sending me here would hurt my mother and that was cruel.'

'Ah, well, you wouldn't have accepted my offer if you hadn't wanted to come. And anyway, if she and I can let bygones be bygones, surely we can do that, too?'

She gave him a suspicious look. 'I need to see her first and say I'm sorry. And you should apologise, too.'

He chuckled. For the second time that day a niece had put him in his place.

'Are you all right, Miss Ludlam?' Bernard asked.

She stared round her as if she'd never seen Pendleworth before. 'I will be all right once I've seen my mother. And then we have to decide what to do about Francis.'

He blinked in surprise at the determined tone of her voice, but she was already striding ahead with Magnus, her arm threaded through his, his head bent over her and the two of them talking in low voices.

Liza was lying on a chaise longue in the bedroom, with Josie beside her begging her to eat a piece of fruit cake and drink some more tea, when there was a knock on the bedroom door.

'Come in!'

The door opened to show Cathie standing there uncertainly. Liza burst into tears and held out her arms. Josie shrieked with delight and the small table with the tray on it went flying as she rushed across to her sister.

As the three of them hugged one another, Magnus smiled and closed the door. This was not the time for him to introduce himself to the mother.

He went to join Cathie's uncle and the lawyer in the Dochertys' sitting room. 'What are we going to do for the lad?' he asked. 'Caitlin's right. We canna leave him in that man's hands.'

CHAPTER 22

SEPTEMBER

When Francis awoke his head felt much clearer, but to his surprise no one was sitting with him and his room had not been tidied. The clock on the mantelpiece said four and he realised he had slept away the day. He stretched and decided he was hungry. Where was Cathie? And Jim?

With a huge effort because he still felt weak he managed to reach the bell pull and tug it. It seemed a very long time before steps came up the stairs and to his disappointment they didn't sound like Cathie's. Hilda peeped into his room but didn't come any closer.

'Where's C— Miss Rutherford?' he asked.

'She's left.'

Francis stared at her in horror. No! He needed his sister. 'Jim, then. I need help.'

'He's left as well, and so has Mr Baxter.'

'But why?' How would he manage without them? What was his uncle planning now?

'I'll send someone to help you, sir. Do you want something to eat or drink?'

Suddenly a cup of tea seemed the most desirable

486

thing on earth. 'Tea. And one of Cook's scones. Thank you, Hilda.'

Tears filled her eyes and she whispered quickly, 'Your uncle dismissed Cook this morning as well.'

At the sound of footsteps coming up the stairs, she put one finger to her lips and hurried away.

What on earth had happened? Before Francis could even begin to work it out, his uncle peered into the bedroom.

'So you're awake at last!'

'Yes.'

'She's gone, that slut has. Anyway, you're better now, I can see that. You don't need a nurse mollycoddling you.'

Francis felt too weak to do more than lie there. He made no attempt to contradict his uncle because this man seemed like a caricature of the upright and impeccably dressed man who had dominated his childhood, and a frightening caricature at that to someone who could barely lift his arm. His uncle's hair had not been brushed and his eyes were wild. Even his speech sounded different, slurred and rambling.

'No more women for you, boy! I'm going to take charge of you myself, make a man of you.' As he heard footsteps Alexander turned and left the room, but his voice echoed down the corridor as he began to berate the maid and order her to take the tray back and send it up with one of the male servants. 'None of you women is to go anywhere near him.' His voice faded away.

A few minutes later Mr Stephenson's valet came up with a tray and helped Francis to relieve himself then drink a cup of tea. He didn't feel hungry but forced down most of a piece of bread and butter because he knew he needed to build up his strength. Something was wrong here and he felt terrifyingly helpless at the moment.

After the valet had gone it seemed very quiet and Francis lay there worrying, before slipping gradually into another long, healing sleep.

Jim and Bob took a cab out to the Manor, but left it in a nearby lane. Reuben Ludlam's name had worked wonders with the driver and he didn't even ask for payment in advance, just nodded and went to put a nosebag on his horse.

'Nice out here, isn't it?' Jim said as they walked through the woods. 'No neighbours to pester you. That Lorrimer fellow lives just over there in that big house. Eh, these nobs have a nice time of it – well, all except poor Francis. Can't understand why his father left him in the care of that old fellow. Stephenson's as nasty a piece of work as I've ever met.'

'Shut up, you fool. Someone will hear us.' Bob did not share his brother's liking for the country-side. It gave him the creeps to have no one around.

When they got near the house Jim led the way through the gardens. A maid was taking in some washing from the long clothes lines hanging in a place like a barn without walls. It had amazed Jim that they'd build a place especially to dry clothes.

'Hey, Ethel!' he called in a low voice.

She jumped visibly then grabbed a clothes prop, holding it in front of herself in self-defence.

Jim showed himself. 'It's only me. I came to find out how the lad is.'

She cast a terrified glance around. 'Keep back near the wall, then. If they see you here, they'll dismiss me and come after you. Horace is in a nasty mood today and the master don't want no strangers near the house.'

'Where's Cook gone?' He trusted her more than anyone else.

'To Mr Lorrimer's.'

'Do *you* know how the lad is?'

'Hilda saw him last time she went upstairs. She said Master Francis looked a bit better. Only the men are allowed near him, though, and if they start ill-treating him again, me and her are leaving. Near drove him to his death last time, they did.' She clutched a pillow case to herself, looking near to tears, then shook her head and continued to unpeg the clothes and fold them.

'I was hoping to get a message to him,' Jim said.

'Well, you've no hope of that.'

'Is he still in his old bedroom?'

'Yes.' She didn't look at him but continued to work and speak in a low voice. 'What do you want to know all this for?'

489

'It's not me as wants to know, it's the lawyer, Mr Lorrimer.' Jim had a sudden idea. 'And if you have to leave here sudden-like, I think you should go to his house first. He'd probably pay you for information and help you if there were any problems.'

A man came out of the rear of the house and stood watching her, so Jim kept back in the lengthening shadows near the wall. Taking down the last few items, she picked up the heavy basket and returned to the house. The man continued to scan the grounds for another minute or two, then followed her inside.

'I don't reckon we'll discover owt else,' Jim said to his brother. 'Let's go back.'

In town Bob went home and Jim went to tell Mr Reuben what the maid had said and what he'd suggested to her.

Reuben smiled approvingly. 'Good thinking, Marshall. I'll send a note to Lorrimer about it. Now you'd better go and tell Magnus Hamilton what you've told me. He's not long been back and he's fretting for fear his lass will do something rash to help her brother.'

Jim nodded. As he got to the workshop the siren went so he waited till the other men had left, then told Magnus what he'd found out.

'We'd better leave things for the moment,' Magnus said.

'I don't agree,' Jim said thoughtfully. 'I think tonight would be a good time to get the lad out.'

490

Magnus stared at him in surprise. 'I didn't think you cared about anyone else but yourself.'

Jim wriggled uncomfortably. 'Aw, well, I never could abide cruelty. An' starving that lad were cruel. It brought him near to death. That old sod is planning summat else now, or why would he get rid of everyone?'

'I think we should give Mr Lorrimer and Mr Reuben a chance to rescue Francis first.'

'But—'

Magnus's tone was exasperated. 'We can't just break into the house, can we? You said yourself they've got men on guard out there.'

Since Bob had also refused point-blank to help him break into Rawley Manor that night, Jim let matters drop. But he still thought they were missing a good opportunity.

The following morning Cathie woke up and lay for a few moments listening to Josie breathing softly and sweetly beside her. It was wonderful to see her mother and sister and to know herself forgiven, sad though she was that her mother had lost the baby. She had vowed never to let anyone down again as long as she lived, which meant she had to do something to help Francis escape.

She was relieved when Josie began to stir because she could not bear to stay still another minute. With much giggling and teasing, they both washed and dressed, then Cathie opened the door into her mother's room very gently.

'I'm awake, my darlings.'

'How are you feeling, Mum?'

'All right as long as I don't do anything. Oh, Cathie, I've been lying here worrying about Francis. I can't bear it if I lose him now, when I'm so close.' Her expression grew determined. 'I won't let them hurt him – or keep us apart – any longer.'

'We'll leave you to get dressed, then we'll have a council of war.'

By eight o'clock all three had had breakfast and had decided to seek help.

'Mr Lorrimer first,' said Cathie, 'then if he won't do anything, Uncle Dermott.' She hesitated and looked across at her mother. 'And there's Magnus, too.'

'Who is he?'

By the time Cathie had lost herself in a tangle of explanations, Liza had a very fair idea of what her daughter's feelings were about this young man. 'I'm looking forward to meeting him.'

'I think he – well, he said he'd be coming to see you to ask . . .' she blushed furiously, '. . . to ask if we can get married.'

Josie squealed and grabbed her sister's arm. 'You didn't tell me you had a sweetheart!'

'I had to tell Mum first.'

Liza smiled warmly. 'I'm so glad for you, darling, and I can't wait to meet your Magnus.' Trust Cathie to fall in love in the middle of a crisis. Nothing but love could have brought that glowing look to her daughter's face. Cathie looked older, more mature, and not once had she worn that sulky expression Liza had always hated to see marring her face.

Just before nine o'clock Cathie went round to Mr Lorrimer's office, determined to get things moving. She met him just as he was arriving for the day. 'We need to rescue Francis,' she said bluntly as soon as he had taken her inside.

'My dear, we can't just walk into someone else's house, however strong our suspicions that something is wrong. If we did that we'd be acting against the law.'

'If we don't do it, Francis may die, and law or no law, I won't let that happen.'

'I'm going out to the Manor again today and I shall insist on seeing Mr Stephenson. If he will not co-operate, then we'll work something out.'

So Cathie had to trail back to the hotel and wait around, fidgeting so much that Liza suggested the two girls go out for a walk.

In fact Bernard and Reuben only got as far as the front door of the Manor where they were greeted by the butler, looking embarrassed and unhappy as he told them he regretted that Mr Stephenson was not receiving guests today. Immediately he had finished speaking he attempted to close the door.

When Bernard put his hand out to prevent this,

493

a large man with a ruddy complexion materialised from one side. 'My master doesn't want no visitors. And if you try to get in, I've only to shout for help and it'll come running.'

The two men were left looking at the closed door.

'What now?' Reuben asked.

'We go and see your father. He's a magistrate and can issue a warrant for us to see Francis and check that he's all right. I'll be acting as the lad's mother's lawyer. Will you come with me?'

'Yes, of course. Father should be in his office by this time.'

But once again Matthew Ludlam refused point-blank to help them.

'If that lad dies, how will you live with yourself, Father?' Reuben pleaded.

'You're grossly exaggerating the situation, all on the word of a young woman who is, by all accounts, no better than she ought to be. If she really is Francis's half-sister, then she was telling lies about her relationship with Magnus Hamilton when she was living with him. Alexander was quite right about her lack of morals. I'd have dismissed her myself. And I'm not at all pleased with Hamilton's part in this, either. We need to be able to trust the men we place in positions of authority to set a good example to those beneath them.'

'Father, whether that's true or not, Mr Stephenson has still been behaving very irrationally and—'

'If people came to my house and tried to tell me how to manage my affairs, I'd be extremely angry, too. I don't blame him in the slightest for showing you the door. I don't know what the world is coming to when a gentleman cannot have his privacy and home respected. Your generation is altogether too hasty and reckless, Reuben, as I've told you many times before. And as a lawyer, Mr Lorrimer, you should know better than to get involved in what are essentially private matters. I'm only thankful I have no business dealings with you myself.'

'But Father—'

'No more! Get about your business.' He glared at his son, who glared right back but said nothing, then he turned to the other man and said frostily, 'Now, Mr Lorrimer, I'm busy and so is my son. We have a mill to run. Reuben, I believe you have an appointment at the foundry this morning.' He waved one hand in dismissal, picked up a pen, dipped it carefully into the silver and glass inkwell and began to write in a precise copper-plate script.

Outside the office Reuben ran one hand through his hair and looked unhappily at Bernard. 'I'd better go to the foundry. Once I've seen to that little matter, I've nothing else pressing so I'll come round to your office. And if my father complains about anything else, I'll give notice.'

'I didn't mean to put your livelihood at risk when I asked for your help.'

'I've been thinking of leaving for a while. He still treats me as a child, just as his father treated him. It's all right. I've had several other offers of employment and this episode has ended any sense of loyalty I might have felt towards my father and Ludlam's. I'll come and see you later. A few hours won't make much difference, surely?'

'All right. I'd better go and tell Mrs Caine about the impasse.' Bernard walked away feeling shaken by the depths of animosity Ludlam had shown, and deeply worried about Francis, as well as guilty about involving Reuben.

When his son had left the mill Matthew decided to act. He would be master in his own mill! He rang the little brass handbell that stood ready on his desk and told his senior clerk to send for Magnus Hamilton.

Magnus was shown into the owner's room but was not offered a seat.

'I hear that the young lady who was caring for your mother was not related to you in any way.'

How had he found that out? 'No.'

'I will not tolerate such moral lapses in my employees, especially those in positions of authority and trust. You're dismissed. Get your things and be out of this mill within the half-hour.'

Magnus gaped at him for a minute, then as it sank in what was happening and why, he went right up to the desk. 'I'll go nowhere until I've said my piece.'

'How dare you?' Matthew reached for the handbell.

Magnus took it out of his hand and sent it hurtling into the corner of the room. 'I merely wish to inform you, *sir*, that the young lady in question and I have never shared a bed, nor committed an immoral act. And if you say one word to harm her reputation, then I shall sue you for slander.'

Turning on his heel, head held high but colour flaring in his cheeks, he walked out past the clerk who had come running at the sound of the bell.

Matthew Ludlam gaped after him, then pulled himself together as he saw his clerk waiting for orders. 'I have just dismissed Hamilton. See that he leaves the premises within the half-hour. If necessary seek help and *throw* him out.'

Magnus stalked along the short corridor, slammed the door to the office back so that it crashed into the wall and left it swinging wide behind him. Hands clenched into fists, he strode across the yard and into the workshop without a word to anyone.

'Is something wrong?' his assistant asked, following him to the desk set in a corner.

'Aye, there is. I've just been dismissed.'

Sam's mouth dropped open. The men nearby, who had been shamelessly eavesdropping, stopped work to exchange glances of astonishment.

'But why?'

'Because Mr Ludlam chooses to believe a pack of lies about the young lady who was caring for my mother.' He scowled round and raised his voice. 'There has been nothing immoral between myself and my betrothed, Miss Rutherford, and if I hear of anyone saying there was, I'll take whatever action is necessary to shut that person's mouth. Whether it's a mill owner or a labourer.'

The clerk who'd entered the workshop behind him stood near the door with the air of one in fear for his life and everyone went reluctantly back to work.

Magnus slammed drawers open and shut, taking out his personal possessions.

Jim watched what was happening from the side of the workshop. Them bloody nobs allus stuck together. Stephenson must have put Matthew Ludlam up to this. Anyone who sacked a fellow as hard-working as Magnus Hamilton was a fool. He wondered if Mr Reuben knew about this. No, he couldn't. He wouldn't have let this happen. He thought the world of Magnus, Mr Reuben did. Jim forgot all his former animosity towards his foreman. To his mind, they were all in trouble. If old Ludlam got a taste for dismissing folk for nowt, who would it be next?

When Magnus had his possessions sorted out, he hesitated, then called Sam across again. He had to make sure they could not accuse him of something else that was untrue. 'I'd like you to check what I'm taking, Sam. Jim, you come over here for a minute as well and bear witness.'

In silence the two men looked over the small pile of personal possessions and nodded.

Magnus took off his working apron and piled his things into it. Then, without a word, his features stony, he put on his overcoat and cap, picked up his bundle and walked towards the door.

With a squeak of fright, the clerk moved out of the way then followed a few paces behind.

Magnus did not so much as glance at his companion but marched back across the yard, heedless of the rain, to fling open the door to the office and go into the senior clerk's room. 'I've come for my wages,' he declared.

The senior clerk goggled at him.

'I've worked this whole week except for today and I expect to be paid for that.'

'B-but you were dismissed.'

Magnus raised his voice. 'I wasna dismissed for anything to do with my work here, only because our employer chose to believe slander and calumny, so I canna see why I should forgo my rightful wages. And if I'm *not* paid, then I shall seek legal advice about the matter.'

'I'll – um – have to ask Mr Ludlam.'

'Aye, you do that. But I'll no' move from here until I've had what's due to me. And you can tell him that, too.'

After a hurried discussion Matthew authorised the payment of the wages, furious that someone he had dismissed would dare to demand things of him but wanting Hamilton out of the mill before his son returned.

When the money had been counted out of the cashbox, the clerk took out an envelope.

'A minute, if you please,' said Magnus, very haughtily. 'I'd be obliged if you'd fetch in another witness and get out the wages receipt book so that I can sign for this. And I'd like a copy receipt for myself as well. We don't want any confusion about this money, do we? There's already been enough confusion about my morals.' When Reuben came back to the mill and discovered that Magnus had been dismissed out of hand, he went storming into his father's office where the two men had another furious argument. Reuben seriously considered walking out of the mill there and then, returning home and packing all his belongings. He could go to his grandmother's because he was pretty sure she would support him and give him a bed till he could decide what to do. He knew he was her favourite, for she was a lively old lady and had sighed over her son's increasing intransigence and resemblance to his father several times recently.

However, after some thought he decided he was better off staying where he was at least until the matter of Francis Rawley was resolved. If he needed help, there were several strong fellows in the workshop and Jim Marshall to hand.

'You're wrong to dismiss Hamilton,' he told his

father, 'and you'll regret it.' Then he walked out of the office before he said too much.

His father's sarcastic tone followed him out. 'Why don't you get back to your own work? I'm not paying you to race round town interfering in other people's business.'

Reuben had to contain his frustration until later in the afternoon. When he met Bernard they agreed that it was a bit late to do anything until the next day, but both were determined to help Francis.

Cathie and Josie were walking along Market Street when they saw a tall figure in the distance. Cathie caught hold of her sister's hand. 'There's Magnus. Come and meet him.'

But when they ran across the street, she stopped in dismay as he covered the last few yards that separated them. She had never seen Magnus look like this, so furiously angry. 'What's wrong?'

'I'll come into your hotel and tell you. It's no' something to be spoken of in the street.'

'My mother wants to meet you, anyway.'

'Aye, well, this may change her mind.' Then he realised how harshly he was speaking and looked down at her. 'Eh, lass, I'm sorry if I sound so curt.' For a moment they looked at one another, his expression softening and hers warm with affection. Then he realised she was not alone. 'And would this be your little sister, then?'

'Yes. Josie, this is Magnus.'

He offered his hand. 'Pleased to meet you, Josie. I'm sorry we couldna have met on a happier day.'

In silence they walked back to the hotel, where Cathie left him in the hall and hurried up to her mother's room.

'We met Magnus in town. Something else must have happened because he's absolutely furious. He wants to tell us about it in private.'

'We must go and find a sitting room downstairs.' Liza stood up and led the way down. When she was introduced to Magnus, she could not help thinking what a fine upright fellow he was and approved heartily of the fondness he and Cathie betrayed for one another in every glance, every gesture.

Just as she was about to ask a maid where they could talk in private, Dermott came running down the stairs whistling.

He stopped and looked at the group, noting Magnus's tight-lipped expression. 'What's happened now?'

'We're about to find out when we can find somewhere private to talk,' Liza told him.

'Come up to our sitting room.'

She hesitated, but he was looking at her in such a roguish, challenging way that she put up her chin defiantly and followed him. She would not spurn help, even from him.

When they were all settled, Magnus explained what had happened. 'I don't think Mr Reuben knows about this and I wish to assure you now,

Mrs Caine, that nothing untoward has ever happened between your daughter and myself.' He paused to subdue another surge of anger. 'I was going to ask you for her hand in marriage today, but until I find other employment that's not possible. I think Mr Reuben will give me a reference so I should be able to get employment, but I canna be sure of it.'

'The Ludlams and Stephensons allus did stick together,' Dermott said cheerfully. 'And if this Mr Reuben won't write you a reference, I will.'

Magnus looked at him in puzzlement. 'But you don't know anything about me.'

'No one will know that. All they'll care about is that I'm a man of substance. We'll address it care of my wife's aunt, who's as respectable as they get.' He went to slap Magnus on the back. 'If you're smart, though, you'll work for yourself from now on. A clever fellow can earn a hell of a lot more that way.' He grinned. 'Even if he insists on absolute honesty.'

Cathie stood up and went to thread her arm through Magnus's. 'I don't care whether you have a job or not. It makes no difference to our engagement.'

'Well, I care. I care very much.'

Liza looked from one to the other. 'There is plenty of employment in Australia, Mr Hamilton. A hard-working man can make a decent life for himself and his family out there. And I'm sure my husband would help you.'

'I thank you for saying that but I don't want to leave England. Do you, love?'

Cathie's throat tightened and she looked at her mother, pleading for her understanding. 'No. I can't go back.'

Magnus turned back to her mother. 'I'll find something, Mrs Caine, don't worry.' He looked at her uncle. 'And you may be right, sir, about working for myself. I have had a bellyful of old fools who interfere in things they don't understand.'

'So,' said Dermott, 'now that's all settled, we'd better plan how to rescue Francis.'

Cathie forgave him a lot for that speech. 'Yes. That's the most important thing at the moment.'

'Mr Lorrimer and Mr Reuben went out to the Manor this morning but were denied entry,' Magnus said, for Reuben had come and told him what had happened before leaving for the foundry. 'It sounds as if the old man has brought some of the outdoor staff in to make sure no one gets near Francis.'

'Even grooms and gardeners have to sleep,' said Dermott, smiling a hungry tiger's smile.

'But we can't take the law into our own hands,' Liza protested. 'Cathie's already in trouble with the police. That matter still has to be settled.'

'Then we'll keep her out of it,' said Dermott.

'We certainly will,' Magnus agreed.

'Just you try!' she snapped. 'I know the inside of the house. You don't.'

'Jim knows it, too,' said Magnus. 'He'll show us

the way.' He went to take her hands and gaze earnestly into her eyes. 'Stay out of this, love. Please. I don't want you getting hurt.'

'He's right, lass,' Dermott agreed. 'This is men's business.'

Christina, who had been listening on the other side of the door leading into the bedroom while she finished dressing, swept in just then with a rustle of silk shirts and a waft of perfume, demanding and getting everyone's attention.

Cathie was spared the necessity either of refusing point-blank or telling a lie. She hadn't changed her mind. She intended to help rescue her brother before it was too late, and no one, not even Magnus, was going to stop her.

CHAPTER 23

SEPTEMBER

Late that afternoon Dermott left the hotel, telling Christina he was off for a stroll but actually intending to call on Bob Marshall and enlist his help. 'Fancy a bit of fun out at Rawley Manor tonight, lad?' he said as he walked into the shop.

'If you mean breaking in to rescue that lad, no, I bloody don't. It's all right for rich folk like you. If things go wrong, you can find yourself a lawyer and get away with it, but chaps like me are allus left holding the baby.'

Teddy peered out of the little workshop. 'What's up?' He blinked at Dermott and edged into the room, smiling. 'Eh, if it's not Dermott Docherty. You look just like your da! Poor old Con. He didn't make old bones, did he? How are you going, lad? Put on a bit o' weight, haven't you? Must be eating well.'

'Aye, I've done all right for mysen.'

Teddy had a sly expression on his face. 'We must drink to that sometime – when Bob gives me a copper or two. Mean, he is. Sits on the money like he's hatched it hissen. You got sons, Dermott?

506

Well, don't let 'em take over when they grow up or you'll never be able to call your soul your own.'

Bob rolled his eyes, but said nothing. They'd had this argument too many times before.

Pulling five bob out of his pocket, Dermott pressed the coins into Teddy's hand. 'You go and buy yourself a drink on me, old fellow. I'll join you another time. I've got a bit of business with your Bob tonight.'

As Teddy thanked him profusely, Sal walked out of the scullery. 'You can buy a glass or two for your wife for once, Teddy Marshall, 'stead of spending it all on your useless friends.'

The pair were out of the house within a couple of minutes, already arguing about her demand for him to give her half the money.

'That'll keep them out of the road.' Dermott studied Bob, eyes narrowed. 'How about I slip you a bit of money to help us? Will that make you change your mind?'

'How much?'

'A pound.'

'Might be interested. Paid in advance. An' you'll have to promise to pay for a lawyer, too, if owt goes wrong.'

'It's a bargain.' Dermott shook hands then passed over some more money. 'Right then, you send someone to fetch your brothers an' I'll be back in a few minutes.'

'They'll want payin', too, mind.'

Dermott knew very well that Jim would help

break into the Manor for nothing, but he enjoyed showing off his money and these small amounts meant nothing to him, so he nodded and went on to his next piece of business. 'Where does that Magnus Hamilton chap live? Whalley Street? Right, I know where that is. I'll go and fetch him.'

'He'll not get mixed up in summat like this.'

'Care to bet on that?'

'No, I bloody don't.' Bob was going to nip home and give his money into his wife's safe-keeping before he went anywhere. He and Min didn't intend to wind up like his father when they were old, not if hard work and frugality would prevent it.

Cathie could not settle. Josie was sitting with their mother. Funny how her little sister liked looking after sick people too, and it was lovely to see her looking so well.

Her mother was looking a lot better today and they'd had a lovely long talk together, so now it was time to do something about Francis. The more she thought about it, the more determined Cathie became to go and see him. If she went to the kitchen door at the Manor, she reckoned she might be able to slip into the house without anyone noticing or even get one of the maids to let her in. It was a pity Cook was no longer there. She'd have been the best ally of all.

Even if Francis was still too ill to leave, Cathie felt she would feel better just to know that he was recovering – and so would her mother, who had spoken so wistfully of him as a baby and asked innumerable questions about what he was like now. She didn't want to worry her mother, who was still not herself, so decided to slip out before anyone could stop her. She smiled, remembering how Magnus had said he'd tie her up, if necessary, to prevent her running into danger, and her uncle had agreed with him. Men never admitted that women could do things too.

She put on her darkest clothes and was just about to creep out of her room when Josie came in.

'Are you going out, Cathie?'

'Shhh!'

Josie lowered her voice only marginally. 'Can I come, too? Mum's fallen asleep and there's nothing to do here. I'm not at all tired.'

'Not this time, love.' Cathie glanced out of the window, hoping the rain would hold off. It was getting dark and the gas lamps were shining on the occasional puddle and showing the huddled shapes of people making their way home.

'Where are you going?'

Cathie hesitated, then looked at Josie very seriously. 'If I tell you, you must promise not to let anyone else know.'

The child nodded, eyes wide in her thin, freckled face.

'I'm going out to the Manor. I'm sure I can slip in by the servants' entrance without anyone noticing me. I have to see Francis and make sure he's all right.'

Josie's mouth fell open. 'Ooh, Cathie, they said you hadn't to. They said it was too dangerous.'

'I'll be very careful, I promise you.' She moved towards the door. 'I trust you to keep quiet about this, mind.' She didn't wait, but slipped out and went quickly downstairs.

Josie went to sit on the bed, kicking her heels against the side of it. She was bored. Had nothing to do. It wasn't fair. And they *had* told Cathie to stay away from the Manor. Tears welled in her eyes. What if something bad happened to her sister? She should tell her mother, only she'd promised not to.

The tears overflowed. She didn't like this. She didn't know why, but it didn't *feel* safe. Cathie always rushed into things and told people she'd be all right, but that wasn't true. Look what had happened to her sister in Liverpool. What if Cathie hadn't eventually remembered who she was? They might never have seen her again.

What if someone at the Manor killed their Cathie tonight? Josie whimpered and bit her hand to prevent herself from crying out.

Cathie made her way out towards the Manor, walking briskly to warm herself up. She slipped through the grounds as quietly as she could, her breath clouding the air in front of her, for there was a real nip in the air tonight. Avoiding the

510

stables, where the head groom kept a particularly nasty dog, she stopped near the rear of the big house. The windows of the kitchen and servants' quarters were lit up so she crept forward till she could see inside.

The two maids were cooking dinner, both looking unhappy, and a man was sitting in a chair watching them. Surely that was one of the gardeners?

She fidgeted around, willing him to go away so that she could speak to the maids. It seemed a long time until he did and then, just as she was moving forward to make herself known, the butler came in, looking upset, so she stepped hastily back into the shadows. Gower was an old man, almost as old as his master, and his feet always hurt him. He sat down looking exhausted and said something to the maids, one of whom tossed her shoulder at him as if irritated by his remark.

A bell rang and Gower heaved himself to his feet and left.

Cathie didn't waste time but hurried across and tried the latch. The door wasn't locked so she simply walked in. As one of the maids looked up and saw her, she let out a screech. The other gaped for a moment, then as footsteps came towards the kitchen, gestured frantically towards the pantry.

Sighing with relief that Hilda had not given her away, Cathie slipped inside the pantry and stood very quietly, listening.

'What were you screeching about?' a man's voice asked.

'I nicked my finger,' Hilda said, sticking her forefinger into her mouth and sucking it as proof.

'Stupid bitch. You take care with your cooking.
You burnt the meat last night.'

'I'm not employed as a cook.'

'You are now.'

As the footsteps went away again Hilda opened
the pantry door. 'Eh, it's dangerous for you to
come back here, Caitlin lass. The master can't
speak your name without he curses you. What do
you want?'

'To see Francis. Is he all right?'

'We aren't allowed near him any more. One of
the men takes his food up and sees to him – well,
they're *supposed* to see to him, but that lot spend
more time lolling around than they do working.'
And she was beginning to suspect that the grooms
were taking things from the house, things the
master might not notice – not in his present state –
but which the maids who dusted every day had
definitely missed. She and Ethel hadn't said
anything. Well, they were afraid to, if truth be
known. She'd never thought much of the outdoor
staff, but they hadn't troubled her when they
stayed outside. Now, things were changing by the
hour and she didn't like it one bit.

'When's the best time to go upstairs?' Cathie
asked.

'Eh, you'll never!'

'I have to see Francis.'

'When they're eating their meal, I suppose – but

you'll need the key.' Hilda jerked her head in the direction of the butler's pantry. 'You could get it now while Gower's with the master. There's allus a spare key or two, and *he* won't notice if one's missing. Number six, top row, it is.'

'Thanks, Hilda.' Cathie hesitated. 'Look, if anything goes wrong tonight, you should fetch Mr Lorrimer. He'll help me.'

'You ought to get out while you can,' Ethel said sourly. 'If things don't get no better I'm leaving, even if I don't get my quarter's wages. One of them grooms tried to shove his hand down my dress this morning and I'm not having *that*! The cheek of it!'

Hilda shook her head. 'You hide in the broom cupboard for now, Cathie. I'll come and tap twice on the door when it's safe. But I shan't admit I've seen you, mind.'

'Thanks.' She went along to the butler's pantry, her nerves on edge, trying to make no sound as she walked. She took the key to Francis's room, then went and hid in the broom cupboard where time seemed to pass very slowly. She jumped at every noise of someone passing and was relieved when there were two knocks on the door.

Francis had been left on his own for most of the day. He made sure he got up and walked around the bed several times, even though he still felt weak and dizzy. When they brought him food he ate as much as he could, determined to build up

513

his strength. But it would take a few days, he knew, before he was fit enough to escape, so he tried to look weak and helpless when anyone was with him.

His uncle was acting so irrationally and looking at him with such hatred that Francis had begun to fear for his life.

The key turned in the lock and the door opened. When he saw Cathie walk in he thought for a moment he was feverish again and seeing things. Then he realised she was not an illusion, but was there in the flesh.

She flew across the room to hug him. 'You look a bit better,' she said, holding him at arm's length to study his face.

'I am. But I'm still so damnably weak. Oh, Cathie, what are you doing here? Has my uncle let you come back?'

'No. I sneaked into the house. I had to see you to make sure you were all right. I need to think first where I can hide, in case they come back.'

He stared frantically round the room. 'Under the bed is the only place. There isn't room in the wardrobe.'

She lifted the edge of the counterpane and bent to look under the bed, nodding, then locked the door again. Sitting next to him, she put her arm round his shoulders, which seemed all bone and no flesh. 'Francis, what is your uncle up to now?'

'He says he's going to make a man of me without the help of any women, and I'm to start on

Monday by learning to ride properly.' He gave a bitter laugh and looked down at himself. 'As if I'll be well enough to go riding by then.'

She shivered. She could imagine the scene when Francis failed to do as ordered. 'Keep your voice low, love.'

'He won't let the maids near me any more,' Francis whispered, 'and when he comes, he rants on and on about you and your mother. Cathie, it's too dangerous for you here. Get out while you can. *Please!* He's lost his mind and – and I think he might really harm you.'

Even as he spoke, they heard someone approaching.

Cathie wriggled quickly under the bed while Francis lay down, trying to look as if he had just woken up. The door crashed back on its hinges and his uncle walked in.

Alexander Stephenson peered round the room. 'They shouldn't have left you on your own, boy. Won't have that.' He came right up to the bed to stare at Francis. 'All *her* fault you're such a weakling. Nicholas should have known better than to marry her, but then *he* was a great disappointment to us all as well.' He stretched out one bony hand and shook Francis's shoulder. 'Look at me when I'm talking to you. No manners, the young haven't.' He let go and walked out again.

Cathie poked her head out from under the bed, but Francis made a sign at her to get back and stayed where he was. He hadn't heard his uncle walk away. This happened sometimes. Sure enough, the door was flung open a minute later and Alexander rushed in again to stare round the room and then at his nephew. After a moment or two he walked out just as suddenly without a word of explanation.

Only when he had heard his uncle shuffle off along the corridor did Francis whisper, 'I think it's safe to come out now.'

'He looks dreadful,' Cathie said, shocked at how much her former employer had degenerated even in a few days. 'His face is all slack on one side and he's not walking properly. We have to get you away from here and let someone know about him. I'm going to stay till later and then we'll creep out together.'

'I don't think I have the strength.'

'You must!' She hesitated, then added, 'Our mother's arrived in Pendleworth and is longing to see you.'

He gaped at her as if he couldn't believe what he was hearing.

She went on gently to cover his confusion, 'She's been ill with the influenza, so she's not herself. Josie's with her. They're at the Railway Hotel.'

'Does she – want to see me?'

'Very much. It was one of the reasons she came to England.' When tears filled his eyes, she patted his hand and sat staring down at her lap, giving him time to recover.

He gave a shamefaced laugh. 'I'm not normally

so prone to tears.' He smeared the moisture from his cheeks with the back of his hand. 'So *stupid*!'

She gave him another hug. 'We'll soon build you up again once we get you out of here. I'll stuff you full of food till you burst out of your clothes. Now, you try to get some rest and we'll wait for everyone to settle for the night.'

Dermott was enjoying himself. He'd had enough of sitting on his arse playing the rich man and relished the idea of a bit of action. Christina might spend half the day fancying herself up, but he felt like a stuffed fish in some of the clothes she insisted on him wearing. He was a man, not a tailor's dummy.

Magnus stood beside Dermott as they waited for Pat to arrive at the clogger's shop. He was not enjoying himself, had never in his life before planned to break the law and had only come along because if someone didn't rescue Francis, he was quite sure Cathie would try to do so herself. His expression softened for a moment at the thought of her then the worries came tumbling back. He hadn't even a job now. How could he marry without a way of supporting his wife?

The shop door clanged and Pat came tramping in, smelling of fresh air and beaming at them like a schoolboy offered a treat. 'Eh, the streets are quiet. I reckon we're the only ones awake now.'

Dermott took charge. 'Right, then. We need to plan this properly.'

'We can get in through the back after they're all asleep,' Jim said at once, not intending to kow-tow to Magnus Bloody Hamilton tonight.

Magnus looked across at him. 'I don't like breaking into someone's house.'

'Can you think of owt better?' Jim demanded. 'They're not going to open the door and *invite* us in, are they?'

Dermott pressed his point home. 'If we don't do something – an' quickly – our Cathie will. That lass is as wilful as they come. You've got yourself a right handful there, lad.'

Jim let out a snort of amusement at the thought of being brother-in-law to Magnus as well as step-brother to Francis Rawley. He was going up in the world an' would have folk kissing his arse at this rate. He just hoped he could find a way to get himself some money to match his new position.

'Right then, we might as well go,' Dermott decided, moving towards the door.

Magnus followed him out, grim-faced.

The three brothers looked at one another.

'Buggered if I know what to think about that one being involved,' Jim said.

'I like Magnus,' said Pat, who had been mainly silent but who was determined to earn his pound. Why, it'd pay off all their debts and still leave a bit in his Tess's purse.

The five men made their way through the quiet streets.

'I'm glad that rain's held off,' Jim said. 'I fair hate water dripping down my neck.'

'Shut your trap!' Dermott growled.

'Ah, there's no one to hear us here. An' I still think we should have took a cab.' Jim caught Dermott's eye, muttered something to his brother and shut up.

Dermott found himself walking next to Magnus, with Jim and Bob behind him and Pat trailing behind on his own. Funny bugger, the Scot, he thought, glancing sideways, but he and Cathie seemed happy with one another. He shivered. Eh, he'd forgotten how cold it always felt in this damp climate.

When they got to the edge of the town Jim took over, leading them on to the Rawley estate by a roundabout route that avoided the gatekeeper's cottage and, more importantly, his dog.

There were lights showing in the Manor and they could hear the noise from a distance.

'What the hell's going on?' Dermott muttered.

When they got round the back they saw a group of men sitting in the brightly lit servants' quarters, drinking, laughing and smoking pipes. There were several empty wine bottles on the table.

Through another window they could see two weary-looking maids clearing up the kitchen.

'They're not usually up this late,' Jim worried.

One of the men ambled into the kitchen and said something at which the older maid picked up a rolling pin and threatened him with it.

Dermott grinned, then the amusement faded.

'Looks like we'll have to wait a bit,' he whispered to Jim, who was standing next to him.

'Aye. Look at that lot sitting lording it inside. They normally stay in the stables.'

He led them into the vegetable garden where there were benches to sit on and they sat in silence, shoulders hunched against the cold, every one of them tense and on edge.

When Liza woke she felt better than she had for a long time and lay smiling across at the dying fire. She had found one of her missing children and would soon see the other. Poor Francis! If only she could take him home with her. Not till she started to get up did she look at the clock, surprised to see that it was nearly morning. When she heard a sound from the next room, she tapped on the connecting door and went in.

Josie, usually so cheerful, was lying weeping on the bed, still dressed, and there was no sign of Cathie. Liza rushed across to cuddle her. 'What's wrong, love?'

'It's Cathie. She's gone to rescue Francis. She went hours ago and she's not come back. I promised not to tell, but I'm so worried about her.' Josie pressed one hand to her heart. 'I'm worried *here*, Mum!' She sobbed even harder.

'Tell me exactly what she said.' Liza sat on the bed to listen to the whole tale, then stood up, her expression determined. 'I'm going to ask your Uncle Dermott to go after her.'

The corridor was quiet with a gas wall lamp burning low at one end. A light was still showing under Dermott's door, so Liza knocked.

Christina opened it. 'It's about time . . . Oh, it's you.'

'Can I speak to Dermott?'

'He went out.' She glanced back at the clock. 'He said he'd be late, but I didn't think he'd be gone this long.'

Liza moved into the room, not wanting to disturb the people nearby. 'Where on earth did he go at this time of night?'

Christina hunched one shoulder. 'He didn't tell *me*. I'm only his wife. Men are all alike. Think they know everything. Why? What's wrong?'

'I think Cathie may be in danger.' Liza thought things over quickly then asked, 'Do you know where Magnus Hamilton lives?'

'Heavens, no! Why should I?'

'They keep a night porter on duty. I'll see if he knows.' Liza made her way downstairs and asked the porter, but he had never heard of Magnus Hamilton. 'Find me a cab, then!' she ordered.

'At this hour? They'll all be at home asleep. Surely it can wait until morning, ma'am?'

'No, it can't. Send someone to wake a cab driver up, if you please. This is an emergency.'

She went back to her room to put on her outdoor things, worried sick. Her daughter should have been back hours ago. Something must be wrong. And of course Josie insisted on going with her.

521

She would insist her younger daughter stay in the cab, though.

It was time to confront Alexander Stephenson.

About eleven o'clock, Cathie went to see what was happening in the rest of the house. She'd expected it to be fairly quiet, but it wasn't. Most of the noise was coming from the kitchen. It sounded like drunken men, which puzzled her. She tiptoed upstairs to the maids' rooms, but their bedroom was empty so she took the risk of going near Mr Stephenson's, but all was quiet there, too, with no sign of a light. Was he in bed or not?

She returned to Francis's room, taking the utmost care to move silently and to listen before she turned any corners. She found him leaning back against the pillows, fully dressed but looking exhausted, and her heart was wrung with pity.

'Is it time to leave now?' he asked, jerking upright. 'What's happening?'

'There are men in the servants' hall and they sound to be drinking heavily. I can't think where Hilda and Ethel are. They're not in their rooms. And your uncle's bedroom was dark, so he's either asleep or still sitting in the library.'

'He doesn't seem to sleep much lately and wanders round at all hours of the day and night,' Francis worried. 'What if we bump into him?'

'We're stronger than he is. We'll push him out of the way and run for it,' she said cheerfully. But she doubted Francis could run anywhere, so they'd just have to take the utmost care how they moved around the house.

Suddenly there was the sound of someone walking along the corridor.

Cathie dived for the bed and wriggled under it, banging her head on the chamber pot. She heard Francis getting under the covers.

The door opened and the head groom spoke, sounding slurred and full of scorn. 'So there you are, all tucked up safe and sound, Master Francis. The master were worried you might have flown away so he sent me up to check.' He belched loudly and sniggered. 'That old fool doesn't know what time of day it is any more, but why should we care about him? We're having a fine old party down there. Don't you wish you could join us?'

'All I wish is to sleep.'

A loud burp, then, 'Ah, you're a milksop, you are.' 'Tain't right you owning all this. He's right, you don't deserve it.' He went out, laughing derisively.

Cathie slid out from under the bed. 'Now's our chance. He won't come to check on you for a while.' Her voice grew gentler. 'You don't have to do anything but walk very quietly. Once we're out of the house, I'm going to take you to Mr Lorrimer's. That's not far.' She'd carry him if she had to, or push him in a wheelbarrow. She'd find a way to get him out of this dreadful place.

CHAPTER 24

SEPTEMBER

Cathie and Francis tiptoed along the corridor and down the main stairs, because they would have to go out of the front door to avoid the revellers at the rear. However, Gower usually left the key in the lock, so she thought it'd be all right. If he hadn't done so tonight, she would go to the butler's pantry for it.

She was worried by how wobbly Francis felt as he leaned on her arm and how bloodless his face looked, but knew his only hope was to get away from here so didn't suggest going back.

When they reached the landing, she gestured to a small sofa and he sagged down on to it while she went to check the stairs and hall. They were empty and quiet. Pray they stayed so!

When she returned, Francis had his eyes closed. 'Come on, love,' Cathie said softly.

He nodded and forced a smile that was hardly more than a softening of the strained expression on his face, then let her help him to his feet.

They got down the stairs without mishap and she put one finger on her lips. He nodded and they stood still to listen. There was the faint sound of someone moving about in the library, presumably his uncle, but they could not let that stop them.

'Not far now,' she murmured in his ear.

When they got to the front door, the key was there and she closed her eyes for a moment, thankful for this small mercy, before turning it. The click of the lock sounded loud in the quiet hall and they both froze for a moment. But no one came.

Cathie turned the big brass handle gently and started to pull the door open.

From the back of the hall a voice screeched, 'What are you doing?'

She turned to see her worst fears realised.

Alexander Stephenson rushed towards them from the library, brandishing a walking stick and yelling for help at the top of his voice.

'The whore of Babylon's returned! Don't let her escape! Horace, where are you? "Vengeance is mine, saith the Lord." Now she'll pay the price of her sins.' He tried to hit her.

Francis stepped in front of her, but Cathie pushed him aside and as the stick came down towards her head, dodged quickly. She grasped it in both hands, tugging and bringing a further torrent of abuse from Alexander as they struggled for possession.

Francis wanted desperately to help her, but his legs were shaking so much he could only cling to a small table.

Cathie managed to wrest the stick from the old man but he rushed across the hall and grasped the bell pull, continuing to abuse her verbally. She turned to draw Francis across to the door, but even as she flung it open, men poured out from the rear of the hall.

Horace roared, 'Stop her!' and with yells the men rushed towards them.

Alexander cackled gleefully. 'Now we've got her. Kill the whore! Kill her!'

Cathie pushed Francis outside, whispering, 'Hide!' and turned to bar the way, brandishing the walking stick. For a few moments she fought them off while Francis staggered down the steps, but it was no use. Though she got in a few blows, eventually numbers prevailed. One man tore the stick from her hands and another leaped upon her, pushing her to the ground. Still she fought fiercely, using her nails and feet as weapons. But there were too many of them.

Outside at the rear of the house Jim watched as the men in the brightly lit servants' hall suddenly stopped talking and turned their heads. Then Horace shoved his chair backwards so roughly it fell over and he yelled something. As he led the way out, he was followed by the rest of the men.

Before the watchers had time to do anything, the two maids crept after the men, then came running back and rushed out of the back door, clearly fleeing.

'Catch 'em! Find out what's happening,' Dermott ordered.

Jim stepped forward, arms outstretched to stop the two women, but at the sight of him, Hilda only shrieked and tried to go round him, so Magnus caught her while Jim stopped Ethel.

'Stop that bloody screaming, you two! No one's going to hurt you,' Dermott shouted when the hysterical women would not listen.

'It's all right, Hilda,' Jim said soothingly. 'These are friends of mine. We've come to rescue Francis.'

'What's happening in there?' Dermott demanded.

'They've caught Caitlin and Master Francis. There'll be murder done if you don't rescue them,' Hilda exclaimed.

'Caitlin's here?' Magnus asked in dismay.

'She came earlier, said she was here to rescue that poor lad.' Hilda cast a panic-filled look over her shoulder. 'We didn't hear anything, so we thought they must be biding their time, but the master suddenly started shouting for help and we saw them catch her, so me and Ethel decided to go over to Mr Lorrimer's for help, like Jim suggested.'

'I were going anyway, soon as I could slip out,' Ethel said indignantly. 'I reckon that lot were planning on having their way with us. They wouldn't let us go to bed, kept sniggering at one another and grabbing us when we were clearing up. It's not safe for a decent woman to work here any more and you wouldn't get me back, not if you paid me a hundred pounds, you wouldn't.'

'Good idea to go and fetch Lorrimer.' Dermott stepped back and waved them on. 'You tell him what's happening here and we'll see what we can do to save them two. Tell Lorrimer it's urgent, say we need a legal adviser.'

The two women ran off into the darkness.

Jim and Magnus were already running towards the house and the others followed.

The kitchen was still unoccupied, the outer door swinging open. Jim led the way towards the front of the house, looked back to check that the others were with him, then put one finger to his lips and opened the door to the main entrance hall. At first no one noticed them and they heard Cathie's voice, raised in anger.

'Can't you see he's run mad?' she begged. 'If we don't get help for Francis, that old man will kill him! Do you want to be involved in murder?'

'Kill her now!' Stephenson urged. 'She's a whore, like her mother.'

With a growl of anger, Magnus tried to push Dermott out of the way, but the other man held him back and hissed, 'Listen a minute. Let's find out what they're up to.'

Horace ignored his master and swaggered over to Cathie, who was held securely by two of his men. He raised her chin with his forefinger and laughed. 'We've got help for Francis now you're here, haven't we?' He eyed her in a suggestive way as he added, 'And you'll have other uses, too.'

'I'll be missed,' she threatened. 'They know where I am and they'll come looking for me.'

He snorted in amusement. 'Well, if they come, I'm sure you'll tell them you're working happily here again – for Francis's sake.'

As the implications of this sank in, she stared at him in shock.

Francis staggered across to her side. 'You'll not touch her. This is my house and—'

With a contemptuous laugh, Horace shoved him aside, sending him reeling into a statue that tottered on its plinth then crashed to the ground.

Cathie tried to get away from the men holding her, kicking and struggling, but they just laughed. Despair filled her. She had made things far worse by coming here tonight.

Then she heard a noise and turned to see Magnus stride forward from the rear of the hall, followed by her uncle and the three Marshall brothers. After staring for a moment in disbelief, she realised she was not seeing things and let out a sob of relief.

Magnus made straight for the two men holding his beloved and although they let go of her to face him, he punched one of them on the jaw so swiftly the man was knocked sideways before he could do anything. Once he fell, he did not move. The other one grabbed a bronze statuette from a side table and threatened Magnus with it. Before he could strike, Cathie grabbed the statuette from behind, allowing Magnus to get to him as well. Still holding it before her, she stepped hastily out of the way, pulling Francis with her. After a very short exchange of blows, the second man joined his companion on the floor, to lie dazed and groaning, not even trying to get up again.

In the centre of the hall the others were fighting, Dermott disposing of his opponent with ease and turning with a laugh to help Jim, who was fighting off two men.

As they made sure of their victory, a voice rang out from the door of the library. '*Stand still or I fire!*'

They all turned to see Stephenson standing there with a pistol in each hand. His eyes were glittering with malice and his hands were quite steady.

'If you don't get out of my house this minute, I shall be forced to shoot you. *Her* first!' He aimed one of the guns in Cathie's direction and said in a conversational tone, 'And believe me, I should be delighted to do that.'

Francis immediately stepped in front of his half-sister. 'Then you'll have to shoot me first, Uncle. Kill the last of the Rawleys. Are you prepared to do that?'

There was a moment's silence before Stephenson said, still in that chill controlled voice, 'Get out of the way or suffer the consequences.'

Francis did not move. As Cathie stirred behind him, he pushed her back.

Pat, who was slightly behind the others, seized the moment to hurl his cudgel at Stephenson. As it caught him on the shoulder one of the pistols went off and Dermott cursed loudly. The other pistol clattered to the ground. So fiercely did the old man fight, however, that it took all three Marshall brothers to subdue him and tie him to a chair.

Horace and three other men stayed where they were, standing at one side of the hall, nursing their injuries and scowling.

Magnus helped Francis to a chair then turned to Cathie, who flung herself into his arms.

Into this scene walked Bernard Lorrimer, to stand gaping near the front door at the sight of the destruction in the entrance hall and the two men lying on the ground.

Stephenson was quiet now, but he glared across the hall from the chair to which they'd tied him. 'You've come just in time to rescue me from these intruders. They were going to rob me.'

Bernard's eldest son hovered by the door, primed with instructions to run and fetch the police if it was too dangerous to intervene. He looked as shocked as his father by what he was seeing.

'What's happened?' demanded Bernard, looking at Magnus and ignoring Stephenson.

'These men have broken into my house,' Stephenson shouted. 'I want the police fetching at once. *At once!*'

'Someone shut the old fool up,' Dermott said, wincing.

Cathie realised that her uncle was holding his arm and blood was dripping from it on to the floor. She hurried across to look at it. 'You've been shot.'

'Aye. And the bugger wasn't even aiming at me,' he said.

'Jim, go and fetch a tea towel from the kitchen!' she ordered and, as he hurried off to do her bidding, began to ease Dermott's coat off.

Magnus explained to Bernard Lorrimer exactly what they were doing here, with interruptions from Stephenson who kept yelling, 'It's lies, all lies!'

Bernard thought quickly, knowing there was trouble ahead. 'I think we'd better go to my house and leave Mr Stephenson here in the care of his remaining servants.'

Magnus frowned. 'Is that wise? He'll only lie about what's happened here tonight.'

Bernard lowered his voice. 'He'll lie anyway, but we have the two maids and I'd rather take Francis to safety. I think I'll have enough credibility with the police for them to listen to me.' Even as he spoke, there was the sound of a carriage driving up to the house.

'Who the hell is that?' demanded Dermott, trying to twist out of Cathie's hands.

'My coachman, I hope,' Bernard said. 'I told him to follow me.'

'It's ours!' his son called from the doorway.

'Good, then this needn't take long. Francis and

Mr Docherty had better ride in the carriage. Cathie, you go with them. The rest of us can walk back to my house.'

Within minutes the hall was clear of everyone but the outdoor servants, the grooms and Stephenson, still tied to the chair.

Horace approached him and began to undo the knots in the curtain cord. 'Shall we get you to bed, Mr Stephenson?'

Stephenson batted his hand away. 'No, we shall *not*! Send for Matthew Ludlam. *At once*. As a magistrate, he has the authority to demand the return of my nephew.' He spoke more sensibly than he had for a day or two. 'Well? What are you waiting for?'

Only when Horace had left and the other men retreated to the kitchen to nurse their wounds did Stephenson start to mutter again, then, catching sight of himself in the mirror, he made his way up to his bedroom and rang for his man to set his clothing to rights.

'Not getting away from me,' he said several times as his valet helped him change. But his head felt strange and it was hard to stand up, so he sat down abruptly and forced himself to breathe slowly and carefully till the tingling sensation in his arm had gone.

The valet noticed, when his master resumed dressing, that he was moving awkwardly, but did not dare comment.

★   ★   ★

As soon as Bernard Lorrimer got home, he sent his coachman to fetch Sergeant Horly. The two cooks currently residing under his roof, helped by the maids from the Manor, got everyone hot drinks. While Cathie tended her uncle's arm, which the bullet had only grazed though it bled a lot, Edith Lorrimer persuaded Francis to lie down on the sofa.

The parlour was full of men with bruises, but there was an air of great relief and even jubilation about them all.

Bernard, less sanguine that the affair was over, questioned everyone about the part they had played that night and asked Francis a lot of questions about his treatment in recent weeks, the answers to which horrified everyone.

Jim was able to confirm what he said in a gruff voice, trying and failing to hide his sympathy for the lad.

When the carriage was heard on the drive, Bernard went out to greet Sergeant Horly who had dressed hastily and brought the constable on night duty with him, realising from the coachman's garbled tale that there was big trouble among the 'nobs' of his small kingdom.

'Let me explain the situation first,' Bernard said smoothly, 'then you can question the others. A cup of tea, perhaps, as we speak?'

What Alfred Horly heard made his blood run cold. He definitely did not relish being caught in the midst of such a quarrel. 'I think you'd better send for the Chief Constable,' he said gruffly. 'I'll start questioning everyone, but it's all too much for me, sir, it really is.'

So the coachman was sent out again, and one by one the people involved went in to see the sergeant in Bernard's study, while the constable stood duty in the parlour to make sure the ones who had not yet been questioned did not collude about their stories.

When the coachman returned he was alone. 'The Chief Constable's been called out to the Manor,' he announced.

The sergeant was not the only one to experience a sinking feeling on hearing that.

Some time later they heard a horse approaching the house. Bernard looked out of the window. 'It's one of the grooms from the Manor.'

'What the hell's happening?' Dermott growled. His arm was now throbbing and he was angry that he had so tamely allowed this lawyer fellow to take over. They should have locked up Stephenson and sent for a doctor to certify him insane.

The message was for Sergeant Horly, who was requested to attend the Chief Constable at the Manor.

'I'm coming with you,' Bernard said.

'Better not, sir.'

On the way to the Manor on the spare horse the groom had brought, the sergeant overtook a cab also making for the house. Since he could make out a woman's silhouette inside it, he reined in and bent to speak to the occupant. 'Excuse me, ma'am, but there's trouble at the Manor. You should leave your visit until another time.'

'My daughter Cathie's there, probably at the centre of the trouble,' Liza said. 'She may need me.'

'Ah. Well, Miss Ludlam has moved to Mr Lorrimer's house now, so perhaps you should go there instead.'

'Thank you.'

He gave instructions to the cab driver and carried on, not looking forward to the scene he was sure would greet him at the Manor.

When Cathie saw who was getting out of yet another cab, she let out an exclamation of surprise. 'It's my mother. Mr Lorrimer, she hasn't seen Francis since he was a baby. Is there somewhere private they could meet?'

He led her and Francis into his wife's little sitting room and then went out to bring his visitor in.

Francis gripped Cathie's arm. 'I'm afraid.'

'Don't be.'

Liza paused in the doorway, glancing quickly at Cathie with a half-smile of greeting, then looking at her son, her eyes devouring him. Behind her Bernard closed the door quietly.

'Francis?' Liza asked in a voice husky with emotion.

He stared at her for a moment, this small woman with a mass of dark hair only lightly streaked with grey. He had had no idea what she looked like, only Cathie's description, and she was much younger than he had expected. He hesitated, then saw the love in her face and said, 'Mother,' the word more like a sob. As he walked towards her, tears ran down his cheeks.

Liza was sobbing aloud, so was he, and Cathie went over to put her arms round both of them and hug them wordlessly.

After a few minutes, Liza pulled back. 'Look at us all! And you hardly steady on your feet, Francis love.' As she and Cathie helped him across to the sofa, she murmured, 'What has that wicked old man done to you?'

Cathie would have liked to let them chat, but she was worried about the sergeant being summoned to the Manor. 'Mum, I think we're still in trouble. Mr Stephenson is mad, but he has lucid moments and if he persuades the Chief Constable that we are in the wrong, they might take Francis back to that place again.'

He gulped, 'I can't face it. They'll kill me this time.'

Liza straightened up, thinking furiously. 'Then we must act quickly to get you away.'

'How?' Cathie demanded. 'They've left a constable on duty here. And anyway, where can we go?'

'I know one person who would help us, I'm sure,' Liza said thoughtfully. 'We should get Francis away now, before they do anything else.'

'But what if the constable won't let him go?'

'We won't ask his permission.'

Francis looked from one to the other and smiled. 'You're very alike, you know.'

They both looked at him in surprise, then assessingly at each other.

'No, we're not,' said Cathie.

'Not in appearance, but in nature. Are you always so impulsive, Mother?'

Liza smiled reluctantly. 'It has been known. Now, how are we to arrange this?'

Cathie pursed her lips, then said, 'Magnus and Uncle Dermott.'

'You trust my brother?'

'Yes.'

A few minutes later, Cathie went back into the parlour. 'Time to change your bandages, Uncle Dermott.' Before he could stand up, she went to put her arm on his shoulder and squeeze it warningly. 'Magnus, will you help my uncle up the stairs, please? He's lost a lot of blood and I don't want him fainting on us.'

Dermott stared at her, then lowered his eyes and said in a feebler voice than usual, 'It is hurting again. I think you've got these bandages too tight.'

Magnus stood up without a word, his face expressionless. What was his lassie up to now? He'd not let her run into more danger and was relieved that she was at least not acting on her own, but turning to him.

The constable looked from one to the other. 'You're not to leave the house.'

'No, no. I'm just taking my uncle upstairs. He should probably lie down for a while,' Cathie said soothingly. 'Will that be all right, Constable? I want to give my mother and my half-brother some time alone together. She hasn't seen him since he was a baby.'

'As long as no one leaves the house,' the constable repeated doggedly.

Three hours later, the sergeant returned, accompanied by two more constables. He had not been able to persuade the Chief Constable that Mr Stephenson might be lying because somehow the old fellow had managed to appear near-normal. What he now had to do in the line of duty stuck in his throat.

'I have orders to take Francis Rawley back to his uncle,' he said to Bernard.

'You can't mean that? Isn't there going to be some sort of hearing first?'

'Mr Stephenson has agreed to drop all charges if the lad is returned,' Sergeant Horly said woodenly.

'Then it's a good thing the lad is no longer here.'

In the parlour Jim grinned at the constable, who was listening to this with a horrified expression on his face. 'Don't worry, lad. You couldn't be expected to keep watch on everyone, could you? And Francis getting away has probably prevented that old lunatic from murdering him.'

While the sergeant and his men searched the house from attic to cellars, braving sarcastic comments from the two cooks and what seemed to them like a whole regiment of uppity house-maids in the kitchen, Bernard Lorrimer sat in the parlour, arms folded.

'I shall have to ask you to come down to the station, sir, and to bring these gentlemen with you,' Sergeant Horly informed him at last, stiff with dignity.

'Certainly. What time would suit you?'

'Now.'

'Are we not to be allowed breakfast first?'

The sergeant hesitated.

'If I might suggest,' Edith Lorrimer put in, 'after such a night, we could all do with a good break-fast, the sergeant and his men included. It won't take long to serve up a quick meal.'

Sergeant Horly hesitated and was lost.

As he ploughed his way through a plate piled high with delicious ham and perfectly cooked eggs, he said not a word. When Bernard would have spoken to him, one of his men cleared his throat and shook his head warningly.

The food worked its usual magic. As the meal ended, the sergeant looked at his host. 'A word with you in private, sir, if you please.'

In the study he asked bluntly, 'What's going on?'

Bernard raised one eyebrow. 'Just between you and me?' Receiving a nod, he went over Alexander Stephenson's unreasonable hatred of Francis's mother and how the lad had been kept from her for all these years. 'Do you have sons, Sergeant?'

'Four, sir. And fine lads they are, too.' Horly could not hide his pride.

'Then you will understand what an unhappy life poor Francis has led. And you've already heard from Jim Marshall about how he was beaten and starved.'

'The Chief Constable won't believe me, sir. I tried to tell him, truly I did, but he thinks the sun shines out of old Stephenson's arse, begging your pardon for my language. He – er – is a bit inclined to kow-tow to the gentry, the Chief Constable is.'

After a short silence, Bernard said, 'I would be obliged if you'd allow me to send a message to Mr Reuben Ludlam and to change my clothes before we leave.'

As well be hanged for a sheep as a lamb, the sergeant reflected. 'If you're quick, sir.'

CHAPTER 25

SEPTEMBER

Reuben Ludlam received a message that his friend Bernard Lorrimer was at the police station and needed his help urgently on a matter they had discussed before. Just as he was preparing to leave the house, a maid turned up to say that his grandmother would like to see him at once and he was not to delay an instant as it was a matter of life and death.

'Tell my grandmother I have another matter to deal with and shall be with her in an hour or two, Ruth,' he told the elderly maid, who had been with her mistress for over thirty years.

'Begging your pardon, Mr Reuben, but your grandmother said not to let you go anywhere else *no matter who sends for you* till you've seen her. Please, sir.'

He frowned, trying to understand what this could mean. 'Can you not tell me why?'

'She said not to.'

'Then I'm afraid she'll have to wait. There's someone else who—'

Ruth clutched his arm, looked round as if afraid of being overheard and whispered, 'Mr Reuben, she's got Francis Rawley there and the police are looking for him and I'm *that worried* she'll get herself into trouble. You know what she's been like since the old master died.'

She was wringing her hands and there were tears in her eyes, but it was the mention of Francis's name that did it. 'Very well. I'll send for the carriage and—'

'I have a cab waiting outside, Mr Reuben.'

Sophia Ludlam was waiting for her grandson in the parlour of her little house, eyes sparkling with mischief and belying her seventy years, stiff limbs and crown of silver hair.

'What are you up to now, Grandmother?' he asked, bending to kiss her wrinkled cheek and inhaling the scent of lavender that always hung around her.

'I'm seeing that justice is done.' For a moment she looked sad. 'At last I have a chance to make up for another of Saul's unkindnesses. The children he fathered are all grown up now and either married or in good employment. But this matter – well, it's been haunting me for years.'

'So what is it we need to do for Francis?' he asked gently. 'You are talking about him, aren't you?'

Sophia clicked her tongue in exasperation. 'I told Ruth not to mention the details until I'd checked that you would help me.'

'I'm glad she did. There are other people involved, and in trouble too, I think.'

'Tell me.' She listened intently.

★　　★　　★

Matthew Ludlam sat in the library of Rawley Manor, thinking how much Stephenson had aged lately and how rambling his speech was at times. But that was just the result of old age and some sort of minor seizure, nothing more sinister. Reuben was quite wrong about that. And since Stephenson was the legally appointed guardian of young Francis, no one had the right to try to take the boy away from him, and so Matthew would order as local magistrate.

There was a knock on the door and Gower came in. He bowed to his master. 'Excuse me, sir, but there's an urgent message for Mr Ludlam.'

Stephenson waved one hand and Gower handed over an envelope. 'The messenger said he'd been told to wait for a reply, sir.'

Matthew read the note impatiently, then gasped and read it again.

'Is something wrong?' Stephenson asked, fingers drumming on his chair arm.

'My mother wishes to see us both at her house at two o'clock this afternoon. She regrets her inability to come here, but she has difficulty walking these days.'

'I haven't got time to pay visits. Got to get the boy back.'

'It's about the boy that my mother wishes to see us.'

'What? Is he with her? If so, I'll send my men over at once to fetch him and—'

Matthew looked at the clock on the mantelpiece.

'It's only two hours to wait until the time she specifies. I think we should humour her in this.'

Stephenson glowered at him, then shut his mouth.

Matthew stood up. 'I'll send a carriage for you later, if you like.'

'I have my own carriage and Horace is perfectly capable of driving me there.'

When Matthew had left, he rang the bell and summoned his head groom, who was the only one who understood how he felt. They would take another couple of men in the carriage with them, strong ones, who could subdue the boy if necessary. They weren't coming back without his nephew.

'See how you like that!' he said aloud and began to pace up and down the library, talking of what he was going to do and why.

Horace left him to it. Funny how the old man could seem quite reasonable when he wanted to, then start rambling like this. However, Horace intended to ensure that the lad stood no chance of escaping again. He was looking forward to continuing this new and very enjoyable life, from which he intended to emerge with plenty of money after the old fool died.

After Francis had rested at Mrs Ludlam's house, he and his mother spent an hour chatting quietly of this and that while he picked at a tray of food and she persuaded him to eat 'just a little more, love'.

When he fell asleep suddenly Liza sat beside him, feasting her eyes on him, alternately marvelling at how much he resembled her second husband Nick Rawley and feeling bitterly angry about all the years she'd been kept away from her second son. She knew Cathie would understand her need to be with Francis and not resent it, and besides, Cathie had Magnus now, such a fine, reliable young man.

But, oh, Alexander Stephenson had a lot to answer for! And Liza did not intend to let him get his hands on her boy again. If Sophia Ludlam could not help her, then Liza would find someone who could and steal her son away, if necessary.

At half-past one she woke Francis gently and helped him to dress as smartly as possible in his newly laundered clothes. Afterwards she smoothed the collar of his shirt and reached up to pat his cheek, a motherly gesture that brought tears to his eyes.

'No one ever did such things for me before,' he said in a choked voice.

'Well, I'm going to drive you mad fussing over you from now on. But this is not the time to give way to our feelings,' she ordered, though she too felt like weeping. 'And besides, every minute we can spend together is so precious, my darling, that we mustn't waste time on regrets. Sadly I can't stay here for more than a few weeks. I have a home and husband in Australia.'

'I wish I could go there with you.'

'So do I. I'd love you to meet your brothers.' She brushed away a tear and scolded him gently. 'Look what you're doing to me.'

'Would your husband let me live with you, do you think?'

She smiled. 'Oh, yes. Benedict is a kind, generous man. If you were able to come, he'd welcome you with open arms and treat you as a son. Now let's go down and get you settled before they arrive, love.'

She'd called him 'love', Francis thought as they went slowly down the stairs. She said it easily and tenderly, and every single time she used that simple word it made him want to weep.

Downstairs they found Cathie and Magnus waiting for them, though a sulky Josie had been relegated to the kitchen to help prepare some refreshments. Magnus had been home and changed into his Sunday best, a dark, slightly old-fashioned suit which seemed to make the burnished red-gold of his hair shine even more brightly in the small room. He and Cathie were gazing at one another in a fond, besotted way. Liza nudged Francis and winked at him as they watched this.

A cab came clopping along the lane and they all stopped talking to listen. Impatient as ever, Cathie slipped across to the window to check who it was. 'Only Uncle Dermott.'

Liza felt amazed that she could wait so comfortably for the brother who had once terrified her.

She'd have said age had mellowed him, but she doubted it ever would, for he was still a rogue. You only had to look at his eyes to realise that. But he had never had the viciousness of Niall, so perhaps having money had softened him. He was talking now of bearding Christina's aunt in her den and making sure she named her niece as her heir. The poor woman would probably be putty in his hands, because he could be charming when he wanted, but Liza would never forgive him for burning them out – and she was quite sure he'd done that, whether he admitted it or not – even though she found it useful to form a temporary alliance with him.

Dermott entered the house with his arm in a sling and Christina beside him, magnificent in rustling fuchsia taffeta silk and an elaborately draped bustle. He introduced his wife to his hostess and nodded to everyone else.

'I think we'll need the chairs from the dining room,' Sophia said. 'Magnus, dear, could you fetch them in for us, please? I'm expecting quite a few people this afternoon.' She was already treating Magnus like a favourite nephew.

'I'll help you,' said Cathie at once, bouncing up.

Francis watched her with a half-smile. 'Isn't she *splendid*?' he said to his mother in a low voice. 'I've never seen a girl with so much life in her.'

'Yes.' But the thought was bitter-sweet to Liza. Cathie was far too full of life ever to settle down to the quiet of the bush. Well, it was clear to her now that her elder daughter's future lay here in Lancashire. That would always make her sad, but you could not hold your children prisoner.

Bernard Lorrimer was the next to arrive, bringing with him the three Marshall brothers, faces shiny with washing and hair carefully parted and slicked down. At first glance they looked like their father and that upset Liza, bringing back unhappy memories. Then she looked more closely and saw the difference in their expressions, the way they looked you straight in the eyes and stood close together for support in the face of all these rich people. They had a look of Cathie, too. No, they were definitely not like Teddy Marshall, who had once raped her so brutally.

Reuben Ludlam arrived next, accompanied by his father, both of them very stiff with one another.

And then came another man who was a stranger to most of the people there but whom Sophia greeted with a, 'Peter dear, I'm so grateful you could join us.'

The elderly gentleman smiled at her in a besotted way that made Matthew glare at him, then modify the glare as Peter Corton, a fellow magistrate, turned and offered his hand with a warm smile.

Finally, the Chief Constable turned up with Sergeant Horly beside him, quiet and very alert.

When they were all seated, Sophia cleared her throat. 'If you will all bear with me for a few more moments, we have one more person still to come – Mr Stephenson – and given the antipathy he feels towards Liza, I feel she should leave us to deal with him.'

There was a chorus of murmurs of agreement.

'Liza, dear,' Sophia went on, 'I wonder if you would oblige me by waiting in the dining room, as we discussed earlier?'

Francis stared down at his hands and could not prevent them from trembling. His mother took one of them in hers and squeezed it, whispering, 'Courage, love!' before standing up. He nodded, but he could not help thinking that if they took him back to the Manor, he might die of terror – even before he died of further ill-treatment.

As Liza left, Cathie took her place on the sofa beside Francis, and Magnus went to stand protectively behind them.

An awkward silence fell and when it was broken by the sound of a carriage drawing up in the lane, Sergeant Horly was not the only one to let out a sigh of relief.

Alexander Stephenson was shown in by Ruth. He made a tight little bow to Sophia and said, 'Ma'am,' then saw his nephew and said, 'Aaah! I see you have caught him.'

Cathie bristled with indignation, but held her tongue. Sophia had assured them that she knew just how to deal with Mr Stephenson and they had to trust her judgement now, because he still had the law on his side. But Cathie didn't intend to let anyone take Francis back to that place, law or no law. They'd have to tear him out of her arms literally – and so she'd told Magnus and her kind hostess. She took hold of her brother's hand and felt it quiver in hers.

'Please be seated, Mr Stephenson,' Sophia said quietly. 'We have a few matters to discuss.'

'I think not, ma'am. All I have come for is my nephew whose guardian I am. I wish to keep him out of the hands of his half-sister, a woman of dubious morals and—'

'I'll no' stand silent if you start insulting my Caitlin,' Magnus announced, stepping forward and glowering at the old man, who lifted his nose and stared back with a sneering expression on his face.

'Please, Mr Stephenson,' Sophia said. 'Let us do this graciously.'

'I'll stay for a few minutes. That's all I can spare.' He took the chair she offered and sat on the edge of it, resting his hands on his walking stick and glaring at his nephew.

'There are a few things we wish to tell these two magistrates as we try to resolve this unhappy situation,' Sophia began. 'Gentlemen, Mr Stephenson may be the legal guardian of this lad, but he has abused the trust placed in him. Jim, will you please tell these gentlemen how Francis was treated?'

When Alexander tried to get to his feet, Magnus stood up and put his hands on the old man's shoulders to press him down.

The Chief Constable said quietly, 'Please listen to this, sir. After all, if you're in the right, what have you to fear?'

'Of course I'm in the right. It's *she* who is in the wrong.' He cast a murderous glance in Cathie's direction.

Jim related how Francis had been beaten severely and starved for a long time until not only his health but indeed his life was threatened.

Matthew Ludlam, who had not heard the details before, listened with a look of distaste on his face, but when Jim stopped speaking, said coldly, 'Mr Stephenson is still the legal guardian, however. And since Francis has no other close relatives, we have no alternative but to . . .'

'But he does have other relatives,' Sophia said. 'He has a mother who has been prevented from seeing him since he was a baby, but who has paid for yearly reports on how he was growing and has written to me regularly all these years, so desperate was she for news of him. He most certainly does have other relatives.'

'That might be a better solution, you know,' Peter Corton proposed to Matthew. 'Sending him to join his mother for a few years.'

Alexander Stephenson started sputtering with rage.

'I cannot agree with that,' Matthew said. 'The woman is of common stock and not fit to raise a gentleman's son. She lived with us for a time, till it was discovered that she had foisted her bastard children on my brother Josiah. M'father told me all about it and I think . . .'

Sophia interrupted him. 'Your father didn't tell you the full truth, Matthew. Josiah was always aware that the children were not his but loved his adopted daughter so much that he gave his life to save hers. I've tried not to blacken your father's name to you, but Saul was a wicked man and I believe Mr Stephenson is cut from the same cloth.'

This time Sergeant Horly risked his superior's wrath by helping Magnus to hold Stephenson back.

'The two of them caused a great deal of un-happiness, not only to me,' Sophia went on, her voice faltering for a moment, 'but to Liza. And surely you can see that this poor maltreated boy needs a mother's care?'

Matthew's voice was cold. 'Not such a mother, I'm afraid.'

'You cannot judge that without meeting her.' Sophia sighed and raised her voice. 'Liza, I think you should join us now.' She had hoped to avoid this confrontation, but her son was a stubborn and bigoted man who saw everyone outside his class as inferior. Thank goodness her grandson did not take after him.

As the folding door opened, everyone turned round to watch Liza come into the room. She looked composed but pale as she paused for a moment to look round.

Stephenson shouted, 'This is a trick! That

woman is not worthy to raise a Rawley. She is a whore and she—'

'Please, Mr Stephenson,' Peter Corton said. 'This abuse can do no good. If you would sit down again, we could discuss the boy's situation quietly, sir, then—'

'Discuss it? I'll discuss nothing.' Stephenson took a quick step sideways, dodging Sergeant Horly. He darted across the room and struck Liza across the side of the head with his stick, yelling, 'You'll never have him, you low-bred gutter bitch!'

She pushed him away but he raised the stick again.

Francis was on his feet, shouting, 'I'll not go back to him. I'd rather die!'

Just as Magnus and the sergeant reached Stephenson, he stiffened and let the stick fall. When he opened his mouth only a gurgling noise came out and he staggered sideways.

Liza stepped back, holding one hand to her stinging cheek.

'Don't let him hurt her!' Francis called.

But Alexander Stephenson was beyond hurting anyone. He crumpled slowly to the ground, where he lay twitching.

Sophia's voice cut through the noise. 'Another seizure. Someone loosen his clothing.'

Francis pushed past Magnus, ignoring his uncle and rushing to put his arm protectively round his mother. 'Are you all right? Did he hurt you?' He raised one hand to the weal across her cheek, nearly weeping. 'He did.'

She summoned up a smile. 'It's nothing, love.'

'Come over to the sofa,' he said urgently, putting his arm round her. 'Let Cathie look at your cheek.'

'Aye, you go and sit down, our Liza,' Dermott bellowed. 'That old sod's not going to hurt anyone else. He doesn't look to me like he'll be fit to look after himself from now on, let alone your lad.'

Francis sat down beside his mother, his arm still round her shoulders, feeling shaky but relieved. The sight of that red mark filled him with rage and horror that anyone could strike a woman like that.

Jim knelt by Stephenson while Cathie was still looking at her mother. He loosened the old man's collar and tie and slipped a cushion under his head. 'He's unconscious,' he told her as she joined him, 'but still breathing.'

Sophia hobbled across to join them. 'I doubt there's much anyone can do to help him. I think Mr Stephenson should be taken home and looked after carefully. I'm sure the doctor will confirm that his mind is disturbed as well as his body.' She looked across at her son. 'What now?'

'Well,' Matthew said grudgingly, 'this does change matters. Even if Mr Stephenson recovers, I doubt he'll be in a fit state to act as guardian to anyone.'

'And seizures can twist the mind as well as the body,' Sophia said sombrely. 'My own husband had to be restrained in his final weeks after such a seizure, as you will remember, Matthew.'

He nodded. He remembered only too well his father's final days. It had been a trying time for them all.

Silence fell as the old man was carried out. Once he had left a weight seemed to lift from the group and they began to talk again.

With Francis and Cathie on either side of her Liza struggled to pull herself together. Her cheek and head were still hurting for it had been a violent blow. She could feel no sense of triumph at what had happened to her attacker, though, because it was sad to see anyone brought to that state.

Sophia cleared her throat. 'I think we should settle this matter now, and I wish to state, for both magistrates' benefit,' she fixed her son with a stern gaze, 'that Mrs Caine lived with us for several months when the children were small, and I never found her anything but a caring and competent mother. She is in no way immoral and never has been. Does not Francis deserve a mother's care now? He clearly needs nursing back to health and he has had a very lonely and unhappy childhood with that wicked old man.'

'That's all very well,' Matthew said peevishly, annoyed at the turn events had taken, 'but she lives in Australia and his home is here.'

Francis spoke up suddenly, with a bitter edge to his voice. 'Rawley Manor is no home to me, sir. I have nothing but unhappy memories of that place. What I want, if you don't mind, Mother, is to come and live with you in Australia until I turn twenty-one, at least.'

Liza's smile was so radiant that it brought tears to Sophia's eyes and even Matthew Ludlam could not doubt the woman's love for her son.

'Francis, darling, I can think of nothing I'd like better than to take you home with me,' Liza said. 'Nothing in the whole world.'

'I have no objections to that,' Peter Corton declared, frowning at his pompous fellow magistrate, 'and if you wish to bring an application for custody of your son before me, Mrs Caine, I'll make a ruling to that effect.'

'The case is in *my* jurisdiction,' Matthew snapped, bristling. 'It's all very well to talk of sending the lad off to Australia – and I'm not denying that a sea voyage might do him a world of good, for I am shocked at how ill he looks – but who's to look after the Manor while he's away, not to mention overseeing the care of Mr Stephenson if he survives?'

'I don't care if that place falls into ruins,' Francis muttered. 'And I never want to see my uncle again.'

When Liza poked him with her elbow and shook her head slightly, he said nothing more.

'Why not let his prospective brother-in-law look after the Manor?' Sophia asked. 'Magnus seems a very sensible and capable young man to me, and Reuben has always spoken well of him.'

Matthew scowled at the man he had dismissed only two days before. 'I don't think—'

'Good idea,' said Reuben. 'I cannot too highly recommend Magnus Hamilton. He's worked at the mill for over ten years and has risen to a position of responsibility there. Indeed, I have it in mind to go into partnership with him myself on another venture, so impressed am I by his capabilities.'

His father glared at him.

Cathie smiled to see her beloved flushing under this unstinted praise.

Bernard winked at Magnus from across the room.

'There is also the question of what to do with Mr Stephenson,' Matthew went on. 'He must be properly cared for, as befits his station.'

'I could do that, sir,' said Jim, seeing an opportunity. 'I don't want to go back to work in the mill. I like living in the fresh air. There are cottages on the estate. I dare say one could be found for my family – and perhaps for our Pat, too, because one man can't stay awake twenty-four hours a day and the old bug— er, fellow, hardly sleeps a wink these days. Me an' my brother will look after him right and proper.'

'Jim has taken excellent care of Francis,' Bernard Lorrimer put in.

'We can consider that, I suppose.' Matthew Ludlam pulled a sour face, but with his mother beaming and nodding at him, felt he could do no other than agree. 'But everything must be made comfortable for Mr Stephenson, as befits his station. And Francis must be raised properly and given an allowance of his own, as well as money being made available so that he can return to England when he reaches his majority – or sooner if he is unhappy in the Antipodes. Still, Patenby can see to all that, I suppose.'

'I'd rather Mr Lorrimer handled my affairs from now on,' said Francis. 'I trust him and I've never liked Mr Patenby.'

'Now, lad, you can't just . . .' Matthew began.

'I asked Patenby several times to help me,' Francis said, 'told him how bad things were with my uncle. But he refused to do anything.'

'I don't like the man, either,' Sophia agreed. Knowing how her son liked to be the one in charge when it came to details, and hoping this would assuage his wounded pride a little, she coaxed Matthew into supervising the handing over of all Rawley Estate business to Mr Lorrimer's practice.

'You will accept this responsibility and look after the Manor while Francis is away, Mr Hamilton, will you not?' she begged afterwards.

Magnus looked at her dubiously. 'I would enjoy trying, but I feel bound to admit that I have no experience of running an estate, ma'am.'

'You're used to handling men and organising work, though, and my grandson speaks very highly of you. We could perhaps give it a trial? What do you think, Matthew dear? Would that not be best for all concerned?'

559

He seized on that. 'Yes, a trial would be the best thing.' He cast a disapproving look at Magnus. 'I could ask our bailiff to work with Hamilton, and if he did not prove suitable . . .'

Magnus swallowed hard and looked at Cathie, his love for her showing clearly in his expression. 'Is that what you want, my love?'

'I'd like it very much.'

'You *are* getting married, I presume,' Matthew asked, with another of his disapproving looks.

Magnus gave him a glowing smile. 'Indeed we are, sir.'

'And the young woman will be staying with her mother until then?'

'Naturally! And I will repeat what I said before, sir. Nothing immoral has ever happened between the young lady and myself. I love her too much.'

Those words made Liza beam at him and then exchange smiles with her son.

Seeing that Francis was looking extremely weary, Sophia suggested he go and lie down for a while, and Matthew waved a hand at Liza. 'Yes, take him to lie down. He'll require careful nursing, mind.'

She managed to hold her tongue till they were out of the door, then laughed up at her tall, too-thin son and said, 'Let's get you tucked into bed, then, my lad. Magistrate's orders.'

She noticed Josie peering out of a door at the back of the hall. 'Come and help your new brother, darling,' she called and swept them both upstairs, giving Francis his first experience of how his mother could spread joy around her like a warm golden blanket.

When everyone had left, Magnus and Cathie walked back into town discussing their future.

'How soon can we be married, my little love?' he asked fondly.

'Only you could call me "little"! And we can be married as soon as you like. It takes three weeks to call the banns, doesn't it? Mum will be wanting to get back to Australia, but she'll stay for a few more weeks and by then Francis will be in a better condition to travel.'

'You're sure about staying here?' Magnus asked anxiously. 'You'll miss your family.'

'Very sure about staying. It's not just you' – she waved an arm around – 'but everything. I love it here in England. It's a sort of – don't laugh at me – but Lancashire is my inheritance, somehow.'

'You said once that your mother joked that you were her legacy from Lancashire.'

'Yes.' Cathie's expression grew sadder. 'It's going to hurt, though.'

'Losing your family?'

She nodded, looking up at him through tear-drenched eyes. 'I've heard people talk about it before in Australia, how they never stop missing the people and places they've left behind, even though they're happy with their new lives. I know Dad still misses the farm he grew up on, only his brother took that over, so there was no place for him here. I don't think Mum misses things as much as he does, though. And she has such a happy nature, she'd make herself at home anywhere. I just wish it didn't take so long to get there, so that I could go and visit them sometimes.'

'Maybe one day we'll manage a visit.'

'Maybe. But we're going to be busy for a while. Francis once told me the Manor was an unhappy place and said the tenants had been cowed and bullied. I'd like to make it feel happy again. And,' she blushed as she spoke, but said it nonetheless, 'I'm also hoping we have lots of children.'

'So am I.' They stopped walking to smile at one another and steal another kiss.

They went first to his house in Whalley Street, both reluctant to join the others. There they found two letters lying on the mat from the second post.

He picked them up, wondering who could have written to him, then gasped as he saw the handwriting.

Cathie, who had been moving towards the kitchen to make a cup of tea, turned round quickly. 'Is something wrong?'

He ripped open one of the envelopes and moved into the kitchen to read it in the light.

She stared in shock as tears began to roll down his cheeks. 'Magnus darling, what is it?' She went to put her arm round his waist. 'Tell me.'

He smiled at her through his tears and hugged her close with his left arm. 'This is from our

Hamish. He wrote from Cape Town to prove that he won't forget to write to me. He's enjoying the voyage. Oh, Caitlin, lassie, he really did write to me.'

She knew how much that meant to him. 'You must let Mairi know at once. And maybe one day you'll hear from your other brothers.'

'Mebbe.' But even to know that one brother was not lost to him helped.

He dropped Hamish's letter on the table and began to open the other. 'This one's from Mairi.' After a quick perusal, he beamed at her. 'She's expecting a child.'

'Oh, that's wonderful news! I'm going to be an aunt!' Cathie pulled his face down and kissed him very gently. 'And you're going to make the best uncle in the whole world. Now,' she forced herself to be brisk, 'you go and change out of your best things and I'll make us a cup of tea.'

A little later, refreshed by some quiet moments together, they set off for the hotel.

Liza saw them coming from her window. The two were arm in arm. Cathie was gesticulating energetically with her free hand as she talked and Magnus, head bent a little, was listening with a tender smile.

Liza had no doubt their future would be a happy one, whatever life brought. She liked Magnus and she had never seen Cathie looking as happy as she was now. After their wedding, she, Francis and Josie would have to start the long journey back.

In the meantime she was determined to enjoy every moment with her two lost children, whose futures seemed set for happiness.

She blinked away a tear and turned to Josie. 'Do you want to be bridesmaid?'

Josie beamed at her and nodded.

Liza turned to Francis. 'And since Benedict can't be with us, you'll have to give Cathie away.'

He exchanged delighted glances with Josie, then said, 'I'd love to.'

'Right. We'll have to set matters in train quickly. Oh, my loves, it's going to be such fun!'

EPILOGUE

JANUARY 1877

As the ship docked in Albany, in the south of Western Australia, Liza stared at the crowd gathered to welcome them. Her heart lifted as she picked out Benedict, with Harry sitting on his shoulders. So he had got her letter in time to come and meet them! She waved furiously and saw the moment when his face lit up and he waved back.

'There's Dad!' squealed Josie, jigging up and down.

Francis stood silently beside them, nervous now. How would Liza's husband feel about him?

It was a while before they were able to leave the ship, but then Liza went rushing across to throw herself into Benedict's arms, careless of her dignity, and he swung her round and round, laughing with her, heedless whether anyone stared at them or not.

Harry rolled his eyes in embarrassment at his parents' antics and looked at Josie resentfully. 'You've grown. You're taller than me now. Seth wanted to come but he and Lucas have to look after the farm. They send their love.'

'This is Francis,' she said, aware of how nervous he was.

Harry looked up at him. 'You're our lost brother, aren't you?'

Francis nodded, unable to think of anything to say.

Harry studied him, lips pursed. 'You're very tall. Dad says I'll be tall when I grow up.' Then his mother swooped down on him to hug him in spite of his wriggles and protests.

Benedict went to swing Josie round and kiss her soundly, then turned towards the young man.

'It's very kind of you to let me come and visit, sir,' Francis began nervously.

'Eh, I've always got room for my Liza's son,' Benedict said. He took the hand Francis offered and used it to pull the lad into his arms and give him a proper hug, upset by how frail Francis looked. 'We'll have to feed you up. We'll get Dinny to make up some of her potions. She'll know what to do.'

Francis had not dared hope for a greeting so warm. 'You don't mind? My coming, I mean?'

'Eh, of course not, lad. There's always plenty of love to spare in our house.' Benedict grinned. 'And any road, I'll be setting you to work. We can always do with another pair of hands around the farm. Don't think you're going to live an idle life here.'

'I'll enjoy that.' Francis felt the last of his worries begin to fade.

They set off the next day in the big cart, travelling slowly. Benedict told them the amazing news that Ilse had married Matthieu Correntin and described the wedding. Liza shared with him her amusement at the way Dermott had brought his wife's posh Aunt Nora to Cathie's wedding, and how he already had her wrapped round his little finger.

'You've forgiven him, then?' Benedict said, scowling.

'Sort of. He did help us rescue Francis after all. That makes up for quite a lot.'

'Hmm.'

Because Francis was still not strong and because Benedict was enjoying this rest from his hard labours of the last few months, they did not hurry, taking their time to introduce Francis to the Australian countryside and the custom of offering generous hospitality to travellers when there were no towns or inns to stay at.

By the time they arrived at Lizabrook, Francis was looking tanned from the long sunny days and had found how much he loved the heat of the Australian summer.

Benedict stopped the cart at the spot he had planned and gestured towards the water. 'There, love, it's a proper lake now. Me and Matthieu hired some men and got it done.'

The water was rippling in the sun and beyond it stood their new home, already beginning to weather in the fierce heat of summer. Liza flung her arms round him. 'Oh, it looks wonderful, Benedict.'

'I sold one of your brooches and it gave me enough money to do all this. We didn't realise how valuable those jewels were, love. I'm going to finish the house next, if you'll agree to sell another piece of jewellery.'

'I've never cared about such things, only about you and my family.' Then she turned to beam at the three children in the rear of the cart. 'And my children of course – *all* my children!'

Benedict clicked his tongue and the big horses started moving forward again. People were coming out of the two houses near the lake, waving and calling excitedly to one another.

As if she sensed his uncertainty, Liza reached behind her to take Francis's hand and Josie took his other one.

'It'll be all right,' Liza said softly.

Francis looked from his mother to his little sister and his heart swelled with love. He had never felt so happy in his whole life. Home, he thought wonderingly. I've got a real home and family now.